"I know best this time," he whispered...

His arms had gone round her, and it frightened her to feel their power. She couldn't escape, even if she wanted to, and he said he knew best. Maybe he did... He kissed her closed eyes and her cheeks and the place in her throat where her pulse was fluttering so. That was gentle and infinitely pleasing, but there was also the reality of those frightening, powerful arms.

You didn't struggle against such strength. You gave in to it. He kissed her until she was weak and clasped her hands in his thick hair to keep from falling, and now his hands—those wonderful hands she had always admired—were caressing the line of her back and flanks, almost as if she were a pony. It had a mesmerizing effect, and she leaned against him, surrendering...

The Senator's Daughter

MARY BRINGLE

Atlanta
2/15/87

To the nuptial
couple — some
steamy trash for
you!

Love,
Mary

CHARTER BOOKS, NEW YORK

THE SENATOR'S DAUGHTER

A Charter Book/published by arrangement with
the author

PRINTING HISTORY
Charter edition/November 1986

ISBN: 0-441-75883-5

Charter Books are published by The Berkley Publishing Group,
200 Madison Avenue, New York, New York 10016.
PRINTED IN THE UNITED STATES OF AMERICA

BECAUSE SHE HAD BEEN CURSED WITH A VERY GOOD MEMORY, Carlotta Madigan would always be able to remember—to the slightest detail—everything about the night of her father's murder. The restaurant where she and Nickie Croft had been having dinner she would be able to picture perfectly, years after it had closed, just as she would remember Nickie's gray jacket and amber eyes, even though she had never seen him after that night.

Later, when the coroner's report came out, she could almost gauge what she had been doing during the last half hour of her father's life. She thought she'd probably been finishing her *osso buco* at about the time the knife slashed into his chest for the first time. There had been a little pause between the first stab and the other two, probably giving her time to hunt out the last of the marrow. While he lay bleeding on the carpet of that room in Washington, Nickie had been trying to persuade her to go dancing at Arthur, the club Richard Burton's ex-wife owned, and Carlotta had been evasive, wondering if she really wanted to sleep with him after all. All the time her father lay helpless and bleeding, she had been weighing the pros and cons. Nickie had nice features and really beautiful eyes and hands, but he talked too much about trivial things. For example, he really seemed to want to go to Arthur, it was tremendously important to him, and this eagerness to be seen in the right place with the right girl was so obvious it made him appear rather juvenile. He was four years older than she was, and a man of twenty-seven had no right to seem juvenile. Her decision not to sleep with him came at about the time her father slipped into the unconsciousness which preceded death, and he must have died just about when the coffee came.

A smaller, less robust man than Tom Madigan would have died much more quickly with those lethal chest wounds. A lesser mortal would never have held out for thirty minutes before surrendering himself to eternity. Carlotta often repeated these comforting thoughts to herself. Awful as it was to know that Daddy had suffered pain and maybe even—for the first time in his life—known fear, it made her proud to realize that he had not gone away from her willingly. What kept tormenting her was the little split image that came to her over and over again. On one side, in Washington, her father, dying his long death. On the other, herself, in New York, following up the *osso buco* with an escarole salad and then telling Nickie that yes, she guessed she would have the raspberries, if they were fresh.

It wasn't fair. She should have been able to save him. She hated Nickie Croft ever after, simply because she had been with him on that night, and not with the person she had loved best in all the world.

ONE

SHE DIDN'T REALLY LIKE TELEVISION VERY MUCH. THERE wasn't anything on, as far as she could see, that was half so interesting as real life. Still, if you were from a family in politics, you grew used to the hum and buzz of news broadcasts, debates, interviews, hearings. No one in her family had ever watched TV for entertainment.

It was so quiet in the Fifth Avenue apartment after Nickie reluctantly dropped her off that she turned on the set in her room automatically. It was a big, gloomy apartment, and could seem eerie at night if you were alone. Her father only kept it for those occasions when his wife and daughter wanted to go to New York to shop, and consequently there was very little of Tom Madigan's spirit here. If the apartment reflected the taste of any Madigan, it was that of her mother, poor Mama, so quiet and shy and insignificant beside the giant of a man she had married. A portrait of Martha Carshaw Madigan hung in the dining room. While her mother was alive, Carlotta's only response to the portrait had been a sort of amazed admiration for what had once been her mother's real beauty. Now that Martha was dead, carried off by a stroke, it made Carlotta sad to see the painting. She looked away from it whenever she passed through the dining room.

The phone rang, but Carlotta decided not to answer it. She

was sure it would be Nickie, asking if her headache was better, if she wouldn't like to come out for a nightcap after all. He would never be brave enough to invite himself up for a drink and then overpower her, the way men did in novels and movies, by the sheer force of his manliness. He was just a boy, like so many of them. Not, of course, that she wanted any man to overpower her. The thought of it made her queasy and she gave a little shiver of disgust. No. What would be nice, however, was a man who was so powerful, so confident and courageous and good, that you wouldn't dream of denying him anything he wanted.

She decided she would have a long, hot bath and go to sleep early for once. The headache she had fabricated for Nickie had threatened to become real, but she knew it was only the wine she had drunk and the disappointment of discovering that amber-eyed Nicholas Croft just didn't measure up.

While the tub filled, she went into the room which had been Martha's. She could only recall five occasions in all her life when her father had slept here, and they had all been when she was much younger. Still, she thought that he must keep some clothing in the Fifth Avenue apartment—*some* sign of him would surely be present. Her mother's New York clothes had been packed up and given to charity a little over a year ago, and Martha's closet was sadly empty. Carlotta shut the door quickly and began to poke through the drawers of the large bureau. In the bottom drawer she struck pay dirt, for there, along with half a dozen shirts, she found a neatly folded dressing gown of pale blue winter cotton, unmistakably male and monogrammed with his initials: TJM. He had so many of them, the only bathrobe he would ever wear, and they all looked the same. It was possible this one had never even been worn, but Carlotta was delighted all the same. It was so familiar and sort of homey to find one of her father's trademark items that Carlotta smiled with real pleasure for the first time that evening. She took it with her back to her room.

She began to undress, taking no notice of the gangster movie playing itself out on the screen. Shots rang out and women screamed, and Carlotta placidly undressed. Although she could have paused, looked up, and seen herself naked in the gilded mirror opposite, it didn't occur to her to do so. Unlike most beautiful women, she spent little time in front of a mirror. She didn't need reassurance, and she wasn't at all narcissistic; she knew exactly what she would see if she glanced up: a tall, slender, creamy-skinned woman with long legs, high breasts, and auburn hair. Why bother? Her friend Rachel spent half her life peering into mirrors, but that was because Rachel's particular beauty was changeable, unpredictable. Rachel was always tampering with her physical self, striving for some new perfection, forever unsatisfied. Carlotta thought it a waste of time.

The soft material of the TJM bathrobe seemed deliciously comforting as it settled around her bare skin. Smiling again, she knotted the sash and went to turn the water off. Tall as she was, she was certainly no match for her father. The long robe hissed over the tiles and her arms were lost in the sleeves.

She's going to be tall, Tom, said a voice from the past. Mama. Carlotta had been about twelve at the time, dismounting from her horse back on the ranch in Montana. The Indian pony, it had been. She had felt leggy and gangling, overhearing her mother's words. Was there disapproval? Would it be a bad thing to be tall? She had looked anxiously at her own tall father, who had winked at her and said, *Of course she is, Martha. She's my daughter, isn't she?*

Carlotta turned the water off and began to brush her long, thick hair. If she had inherited her height and her eyes from her father, it was Martha who had given her the hair her various admirers were always trying to find poetic names for. Like sherry held to the light, they said, or the most subtle part of a flame. It made her laugh, because any serious attempt to wax poetic over the color of a person's hair struck her as comical. What would Nickie have said, for example, if Carlotta had leaned across the table and murmured that *his* hair was the exact shade of freshly baked whole-wheat bread?

From the next room she could hear the news begin. She walked through and flipped the channel, turning to what seemed to be a movie. She didn't want to hear the news, not even by accident. No more burning bodies from Vietnam, please, no napalmed villages or massacres. No more assassinations on the home front, either. Just last spring they had murdered Robert Kennedy and Martin Luther King, and it seemed to Carlotta as if this year, 1968, was the most violent she could remember. In spite of her father, she wasn't really political or even well-informed. He had tried to keep his wife and daughter away from the sorrier aspects of his profession, and in Carlotta's case he had succeeded. Martha had now and then become involved in a pet project, usually something to do with the Indians, and then he would indulge her and give as much of his valuable time as he could to the wife he adored. How lucky her mother had been, Carlotta thought, scooping her hair up and pinning it on top of her head. How lucky to have won the love of such a man, to have lived her life at his side. No matter how many little jokes were made about what a womanizer Tom Madigan had been before he married, no matter how easily and charmingly he continued to flirt with pretty women, Carlotta was sure of one thing: from the moment he met Martha Carshaw of Philadelphia, there had never been anyone else for him. He was like that. Wholehearted, nothing by halves.

She got into the hot water, gasping at first, and then, as her body accustomed itself, sighing with pleasure. It was so pleasant to lie here, rubbing perfumed soap over her smooth skin, hearing the reassuring drone of the voices from the television without bothering to listen to what they said. And what if she had let Nickie come up? It might be his hands gliding over her breasts now, rousing little ticklish sensations, pausing, gliding downward—but no. Although the thought had been mildly exciting at first, it would have turned out differently. He would be too eager, and it would all be over in a very short time, and then he would apologize and try to make it up to her in some fumbling, tired way that would embarrass her.

Rachel was always telling her that she just hadn't found the right man yet. "You'll know when you do—you'll just *know*," Rachel had solemnly assured her, a week before her marriage to Cotter Vere. Presumably Rachel had just *known* about Cotter, and yet what was she doing? Having an affair with a distinctly weird rock musician before she'd been married a year. Rachel and Cotter were in London now. Maybe even at this moment Rachel was in bed with her lover—who was English—while Carlotta wallowed around in a tub soaping herself and musing over her unexciting sex life. The thought annoyed her. Briskly, she pulled the plug and stood up, water streaming from her body. She had a sudden desire to see her only other really good friend. Lee had been as close as a sister to her when they were growing up, and it seemed a terrible shame that they had lost contact now. Lee had what Rachel lacked—wisdom—and Carlotta yearned for advice.

She was still thinking of her when she stepped back into her bedroom, wrapped in Tom Madigan's robe. Nothing could have been more astonishing to her than the sight of her father's face looking out from the screen. He seemed to be smiling right at her. She knew the photograph well—it had been taken on the ranch and was a great favorite with the media people. He was grinning, braced against a Montana wind, master of all he surveyed—a man larger than life. She stared at him, and then the picture faded and the movie resumed. For a moment she thought she had hallucinated, but then, in an instant, she felt a gathering terror.

She ran to the television set, kneeling in front of it as if in prayer, and frantically switched channels. A commercial for spaghetti sauce . . . an elk in a forest . . . two cops . . . *oh, please, oh, Daddy,* and then the serious face of a newscaster.

"We interrupt this program to announce that the death of Montana Senator Thomas J. Madigan has been confirmed. Madigan was discovered earlier this evening, at a Georgetown address the police are not disclosing, with stab wounds to the chest. He was pronounced dead on arrival at Georgetown University Hospital. The senator was fifty-nine years old. No other details are available at this time. We now return you to our regular programming."

The picture appeared again briefly.

Carlotta remained kneeling in front of the set. Her eyes were dry and she was perfectly still. She felt incapable of any movement, as if she had been turned to stone.

In a room on the top floor of a frame house in Berkeley, Lee Redwing was trying to study for the next day's exam on torts. It was her least favorite subject, one that made her wonder if she should be in law school at all. She wore jeans and a tie-dyed T-shirt, like all the other grad students in the rooming house, because it was an inexpensive kind of wardrobe and, unlike many of them, her means were limited. Her black hair hung straight down her back in approved flower-child style, but this was not because she was conforming to the prevalent fashion, but because she was a Cheyenne Indian and had always worn her hair in this manner.

There was a commotion outside, feet running up the stairs toward her room. Her privacy was about to be invaded. "Hey, Lee," came the voice of one of the bearded guys from the second floor. She turned and confronted him.

"Hey," he said, "I'm really sorry to bother you when you've got this heavy exam, but I thought you might want to know?"

"Know what, Joe?"

"Some senator from your state got murdered. It was just on the tube. Madigan, from Montana."

Nothing could have been further from her mind than Tom Madigan. She felt as if her entire past had just taken a flying leap and air-expressed itself from Montana to California. She was so surprised that she lost her normal composure and sprang to her feet with a little grunt that alarmed Joe. "Are you *sure?*" she whispered. "Sure it was Madigan?" He nodded.

She followed him down to the kitchen, a communal space where the television was kept. They were all gathered around, watching an announcer extoll the many virtues of the dead man.

"In some ways," the announcer told them, "Thomas Madigan, or Big Tom as he was affectionately called, was one of the last of the authentic American heroes. He was a nineteenth-century type surviving into the twentieth century, a figure who always seemed larger than life. He was a man of vast wealth, but not a man of the boardroom. He was a rancher, a Westerner from Marlboro Country, who also happened to be a member of the most exclusive club in America — the United States Senate."

"What's his record like?" a girl asked Lee.

"In the Senate? Not bad."

"Known as a ladies' man in his bachelor days, the handsome senator, who married the late Martha Carshaw of Philadelphia when he was thirty-four years of age, became a devoted husband and family man. He was mercurial and flamboyant, perhaps to a fault, but no one ever doubted his sincerity or commitment to the principles of—"

"Oh, shit," someone muttered. "Why do they always shoot the good guys?"

"He wasn't shot," someone else pointed out. "He was stabbed."

"A search has been mounted," the announcer told them, "for the person police believe to be responsible for the crime. The name has not been released in the interest of national security."

"What do you think, Lee?" Joe was addressing her with respect. She was the authority in this matter, since none of the others came from the state of Montana. "How about a candle-light vigil to express solidarity with the senator's values?"

Lee had circled her knees with her arms and was rocking back and forth rhythmically. "Don't bother," she said without lifting her head. "He was a bastard."

"Well excuse me, Lee," said Joe in a puzzled voice. "If he was such a bad guy, how come you look so upset?"

"I used to know his daughter," said Lee. "She was my friend."

Later, lying sleeplessly in her bed, she was visited by a kaleidoscope of images: the senator striding toward her across the sunlit field, hand in hand with Carlotta, who could hardly keep up; the senator's big, wide smile, which always made her feel cold inside when she was small; Carlotta looking at him with that adoring, puppylike rapture and wriggling with bliss when he hugged her; Mrs. Madigan's skittering eyes, which always seemed to be trying to ignore something and spoke worlds of pain to Lee.

She turned over onto her stomach and burrowed for a cool place in the pillow. The images were no less strong in this new position; it was as if a jangled home movie were being played out in her head. She even thought she could smell Montana. Here, in this old house that normally smelled of incense and pot and accumulated cooking odors, Lee fancied she could detect the scent of sagebrush and clean mountainy air blowing down from the Continental Divide.

Here was Carlotta, running toward her, her bright hair flying in the wind, like something from a shampoo commercial. "Lee!" cried Carlotta, "I have some thing to show you!" What had it been? A new foal, a seashell from a trip east with her mother . . . It didn't matter, and Lee could not remember, but the vivid image of the child Carlotta had been, running toward the child Lee had been, was almost more than she could bear.

Lee got up and went to sit at her desk. Sleep was out of the question. She sat in the dark, giving herself over to the memories.

She hadn't been born on Madigan Ranch, but she had come as a child of three. Too young, of course, to understand what a monumental change of fortune the move made to her parents. Her father had become the senator's ranch manager, a position he had held on another ranch Helena way, but what a difference! When she was old enough to understand such things, her mother often told her (as if she could scarcely believe her luck) that the neat frame house on Madigan Ranch was like a mansion compared to the shack-like affair Lee had been born in.

The house Mrs. Redwing so prized was comfortable, with four rooms up and four down, and a modern indoor bathroom. One of her older brothers told her how, in the house on the other ranch, you had to take a flashlight to the privy at night. Not, he would repeat dramatically, because of the dark so much, but to avoid sitting on a rattlesnake. "Once there was a big one, coiled up right on the seat," he would tell her, and then he would imitate the hissing, teakettle sound of a rattler, hoping to scare her. But she didn't scare easily, not even back then.

She couldn't remember how old she had been when she first saw Carlotta, but she remembered the circumstances perfectly. She had been sitting on the front steps of the house, playing jacks, when the senator's big Land Rover came roaring up. The senator got out and approached the house, his booted feet eating up the distance in no time at all. He was wearing jeans, just like all the other men did, and there was a Stetson on his head, but he looked different from all other men to Lee. It wasn't because he was a white man—she'd seen plenty of them—but she couldn't quite put her finger on what set him apart. Not then.

Later, she would be all too aware of what made Tom Madigan special. She would be able to feel the invisible shield of power that accompanied him everywhere, and even admit, grudgingly, that he was a man of great physical beauty, but on that afternoon she only knew that he made her feel uncomfortable. Even when he tipped his hat and grinned at her, or maybe especially then.

"Well, now, sweetheart—do you have any idea where your dad has gone?"

"Gone to White Sulphur Springs."

The senator had gone right up the steps, his long, booted legs passing close to her, and entered the house as if it were his own. She could hear him calling to her mother, and then their two voices in a conversation. Something about feed. She was deciding to return to her game of jacks when she became aware that the Land Rover was not empty. There was another passenger, a girl of about her own age, sitting quietly and looking at her with undisguised curiosity.

Lee scowled at the girl and executed a perfect round of double-knock eightsies. Even though she could not see the girl, her initial impression had been a powerful one. Red hair like fire, icy-blue eyes, and a hungry, devouring look. Lee flung the jacks out for ninesies and heard the door of the Rover open and the sound of boots on packed earth. When she looked up, the girl was standing before her, and Lee could scarcely believe her eyes. She was wearing the most peculiar pants Lee had ever seen—they were tight at the girl's slender waist, but there were big pouches over the hips, and they were tucked not into normal cowboy boots but into black, tight tubes of leather. She was also wearing a white blouse with some kind of tie at the neck and a fancy jacket. Lee tried not to stare. She was intensely aware of her own clothing—Levi's with a red cotton shirt that had a button missing. It was a hand-me-down from her brother.

The amazing apparition spoke. "I'm Carlotta," she said. "What's your name?"

"Lee. I'm Charlie Redwing's girl, Lee."

"What's that game you're playing, Lee?"

"You never heard of jacks?"

Carlotta shook her head, and Lee saw that her expression was, if anything, humble. "I'll show you," Lee said, throwing the ball up, rapping the porch twice, and plucking up a jack. She would do onesies, this being Carlotta's first experience with jacks. She could see that Carlotta was anxious to try for herself, but was worried about planting her oddly covered bottom on the dusty planks of the porch. There was something else, too. Carlotta's ears seemed to be attuned to the sound of her father's voice, as if being away from him made her nervous.

"Sit down, Carlotta, and I'll let you have a turn."

Carlotta stared yearningly at the jacks, and then, as if making a brave decision, sat beside Lee and took the ball in her hand. She was a quick learner, Lee had to give her that, and when the senator emerged from the house, the two of them had been giggling. He had squatted down, then, and done something extraordinary. He had run one of his hands over Carlotta's long, burnished hair, and the other over Lee's black hair. It had not been the casual, rumpling gesture adults sometimes affected with children, but a long, loving caress.

Lee could still remember, after all these years, the shivery feeling of dismay that seemed to begin in her backbone. At five, six, she had felt it, and she had looked covertly in Carlotta's direction to see if Carlotta was likewise disturbed. What she saw there was sheer bliss. Lee and the jacks had been forgotten, and the senator and Carlotta had walked off, hand in hand, to the Land Rover. Carlotta waved goodbye, though. She even called Lee by name. "Goodbye, Lee," she cried, shaking herself as if she had been in a trance. "Oh, Lee, goodbye."

"That's Miss Carlotta," her mother had told her a few minutes later. "She's the senator's only child, honey, and she's the apple of his eye. She's just your age, and already she's a princess."

"She wears funny pants. Is there something the matter with her legs?"

"I believe that's what people wear in the East when they go horseback riding. Miss Carlotta's mother, Mrs. Madigan, is from the East, Leana."

East or no East, the jacks had apparently not been altogether forgotten, because after that day Carlotta and Lee were allowed to play together. It had happened gradually, but after the first few awkward encounters, they discovered that they actually enjoyed each other's company. Carlotta, like Lee, was a fast runner and an excellent climber of trees. She had a good imagination and could weave amazing plots, setting up imaginary situations in which she and Lee were in great peril and had to use their wits to escape some dreadful death.

"Look, Lee," Carlotta would say, standing at the edge of the stream that meandered through the ranch. "Pretend bad people are after us, and we can only escape if we get across the river by the time I count to ten. Use the stepping-stones, and if you stumble and get wet, too bad for you."

Mysteriously, the horrible pants were retired, and Carlotta appeared in more normal garb, though never in Levi's like Lee's. They were made of some soft, pliable material, and they came in all sorts of colors, and Carlotta explained that her mother's dressmaker had made them for her. Cowboy boots made an appearance also, instead of those things that had looked like pipes, and Carlotta told Lee that she was now riding her pony with a Western saddle.

"It's much nicer," she said.

Lee had never known of the existence of any other saddle, and at the time she had attributed the change in Carlotta to her own superior influence.

"Oh, *sure*," she said aloud, speaking in the darkness of a room so far removed from the Madigan ranch she might now be dwelling on Mars. "Oh, right, Lee, it was all you."

She tried to reconstruct the bitter dialogue that must have gone on between Tom and Martha Madigan during that summer. "Carlotta needs a friend of her own age," she had the senator say in his soft, deep voice. "There's nothing wrong with the little Redwing girl."

She paused, trying to remember the exact sound of Martha Madigan's voice—a sonorous voice, clipped in a way that was foreign to Lee's ear. A patrician voice. Yes, she had it. "But Tom," said the ghostly Martha, "surely you must see that it is inappropriate for Carlotta to become too close to little Lee? She's a nice enough child, I'll grant you that, given her . . . well . . . origins. But don't you see how heartbroken Carlotta will be when the time comes when they must separate? And it will come, Tom. The lives of a United States senator's daughter and an Indian ranch hand's daughter? They hardly mix, do they?"

"No, *ma'am!*" whispered Lee, laughing. "Sure as shit, they don't." And yet she did not hate Carlotta's mother, that sad lady from the East who had never understood the stakes of the game she had bought into by marrying Tom Madigan. Martha was not to blame. She honestly believed that she would be able to bring her aristocratic values to Montana and raise her child in the manner she thought fit. The time the Madigans spent in Washington only built the delusion up; Martha had never understood that when she entered the state of Montana she surrendered any claims to autonomy. In Montana, she found herself dwelling in her husband's kingdom. It was a world where little girls did not wear hacking jackets and jodhpurs, and where they might elect, as their best friend, a child of Cheyenne blood whose father was a mere employee.

Martha Madigan might supervise the creation of a French Provincial boudoir, but directly beneath it there would be a room full of the stuffed heads of antlered beasts. She had been in alien territory, and Lee pitied her. She saw the long, slender, heavily bejewelled fingers shaking as they coaxed an imported English cigarette from the silver case, and she felt a terrible sadness. The bright and beautiful hair of Martha Madigan seemed especially sad, mirroring, as it did, the hair of her daughter.

And what of that daughter? What would happen to Carlotta now?

Lee pulled on her robe and left her room, going out onto the landing. In the stillness she heard muffled groans from a room further down the hall, someone making love or having a bad dream—it didn't matter. She went down the stairs and into the darkened kitchen, which smelled of fried onions. A street lamp cast enough light so she could see the big jug of red wine on the counter. She found a tumbler, rinsed it out, and poured herself a healthy share of wine, reminding herself to drop fifty cents into the communal jar in the morning. The wine tasted sour and vinegary, but after a little it produced the warm effect Lee needed, the illusion of well-being. Unlike the others in the boarding house, Lee was uninterested in drugs.

She and Carlotta had tried some grass—it would have been during the last summer they spent together, before Carlotta was sent to school in Switzerland—and waited for the miraculous high to begin. They had been sitting in a clump of cottonwood trees, well shielded from prying eyes, and it had been that wonderful time, at the end of a long, hot afternoon, when a hush stole over the land, preparing for night.

"Nothing," Lee had said. "I'm not getting anything. How about you?"

"Sort of a headache," Carlotta had replied, indicating her temples with a delicate gesture. "Here."

Carlotta's father was a heavy drinker, but it never seemed to harm him, or make him lose control. The tumbler of pale amber whiskey in his hand was simply a part of the senator, like his hand-tooled boots or his roaring Land Rover. Martha was another matter. Her drinking was much more secretive, a habit, Lee guessed, acquired after years in Montana, and carried with her to Washington and Europe and her visits back East.

The first time Lee had seen Martha was the first time she entered the Madigans' house, what her own mother called the "Big House," to distinguish it from the Redwing establishment and the barns and paddocks and outbuildings that made up the vast spread of the Madigan ranch.

They had entered the house from the back, passing over a veranda and into a huge, cool kitchen. The kitchen had red tiles on the floor, and black cooking ranges so large they seemed menacing. At a big oak table sat a blonde, stocky woman who was shelling peas. She smiled and said hello in a voice that seemed vaguely foreign. Lee studied her with fascination. She had a great quantity of fair hair which she had braided into a coronet, and she wore a plain white dress, as if she were a nurse. Lee could see no resemblance to Carlotta in the woman's face, still less in her body.

"Hello, Inga," Carlotta said. "This is Lee."

Lee sat down at the table, continuing to believe that the white-clad woman was Carlotta's mother. She had never heard the name "Inga" before and imagined it to be a kind of white folks' affectionate term for mother. Inga had fetched them glasses of milk and plates of blueberry muffins with fresh butter, and when they had finished, Carlotta thanked her mother and led Lee out of the kitchen and through rooms so large Lee found herself staring in wonder.

She followed Carlotta up stairs so broad and dark they seemed to belong to a courthouse, and then there was another long stretch beneath some gloomy portraits, and at last Carlotta flung open a door and said, "Here's my room. We can play in here."

Lee had never been interested in dollhouses, but she understood, standing in the radiance of her friend's room, just what perfection could be. Everything was in delicate shades of peach and apple green, and Carlotta's bed was a big four-poster with a canopy. Lee would have been afraid to sleep in it, and she was more intrigued by a little velvet couch with a headrest that was near one of the long casement windows. She asked Carlotta if she shared the room with someone, pointing to the couch, but Carlotta shook her head. In one corner of the room stood a life-size fawn, its spotted coat looking so real that you'd be fooled if not for the eyes, which were like the eyes of a Walt Disney creature. Carlotta said it came from a toy store in New York.

Lee had been trying out the velvet couch, slipping onto its luscious surface gingerly, when the door opened and a woman entered the peach-and-apple bower with a frown. She was tall and slender, like Carlotta, and her hair was the same fiery color, but the woman's hair was cut short and swept back from her face in two triumphant wings. She wore a plain gray dress that hissed as she walked, and a string of beads around her neck. Even at the age of six, Lee realized that the plainness of the woman's costume was deceptive: if Carlotta was a princess, this, then, must be the queen.

"You're Charlie's little girl, aren't you?" Carlotta's mother said. She smiled, her eyes darting anxiously from her daughter to the Indian girl on the chaise longue. Her anxiety had transmitted itself to Lee, who felt that she was trespassing. In some ways she had never ceased to feel it, not in all those years. Mrs. Madigan was never less than kind to her, but it was a kindness she had to force. If Tom Madigan was more open and natural with her, it was because of his different nature.

In a couple more years, when she was eight or nine, Lee came to see something important about the Madigans: never were two married people so fundamentally different. She was never at ease with either of them, yet with Carlotta she slipped into a deep and powerful friendship that was to last for ten years. They were as odd a couple, in their way, as Carlotta's parents, but the bond between them had been genuine and, each thought, unbreakable. Secretly, they had called themselves sisters.

"Here's to you, sister," Lee whispered, lifting her tumbler of sour wine.

Now, more than ever, she was glad she had never told Carlotta the secret she had carried with her for years. At first, she had been tempted to confide in Carlotta, because she didn't understand what she had seen. Later, it was out of the question. She had never spoken of it, of what she had glimpsed in the old, unused shack on the ranch. Nobody had used it for years, and Lee's father was always talking about pulling it down. She had peered in, that day, out of simple curiosity. She had been seven at the time, and used to seeing the copulations of animals, but what the senator and the Cheyenne town girl were doing in the shack was strange to her, and therefore frightening. She had run away, never mentioning it to anyone. For a long time she had believed it might have something to do with the girl's being an Indian, and whenever Carlotta's father smiled at her, she had an unreasonable fear that he might be planning something similar for her.

"Poor Carlotta," she whispered in the darkness. "What will this do to you?" Carlotta had no brothers or sisters. The lovely

Martha's fragility had been quite real, and it had prevented Tom Madigan from ever having the son and heir he had craved. Carlotta was It, the Only. She had lost both father and mother in the space of a year, Lee thought, and now she had no one.

Such a loss could be disastrous to an ordinary person, and Carlotta was so very, very, far from being ordinary.

When a man is found dead in an apartment not his own, the logical assumption is that his murderer is probably the person whose name appears on the lease. The person whose name appeared on the lease of the Georgetown apartment was one J. L. Nesbit, and neighbors confirmed that J. L. was a female, very blonde and secretive, who went her own way and was not communicative. She drove a white BMW. The voice that alerted the police to Madigan's presence in the apartment had been both female and hysterical over the phone, and its owner was arrested in Pennsylvania shortly after midnight.

Joly Lorraine Nesbit had promptly surrendered herself to the police and accompanied them back to the District of Columbia. She had been driving toward New York in a half-hearted attempt at escape. The police did not release her name to the press until noon the next day. Television screens were full of her face from that time on. It was a face destined to be much in the public eye for weeks to come.

Cotter and Rachel Vere saw Joly's face on the cover of a bloodthirsty tabloid in London. SENATOR CARVED UP IN WASHINGTON LOVE NEST screamed the headline and, beneath the picture of Joly, *Ex-Showgirl was Senator's Long-Time Mistress!* Cotter bought the tabloid and brought it up to their suite in the Park Lane.

"Listen to this," he said excitedly. "Reliable sources claim that Miss Nesbit and Senator Madigan had been intimate for at least ten years."

"For heaven's sake, Cotter," said Rachel. "How can you read that tripe?"

"I thought you'd be interested." He was instantly on the defensive. "After all, she's *your* friend, darling."

Rachel sighed. She had had a terrible hangover before she'd even heard about Carlotta's father, and now, with the revelation of each horrible new detail, her head felt it might burst. "Precisely because she *is* my friend," she told her husband, "I find it very offensive when you gloat over half-truths in the gutter press."

She had used her most patient voice, which never failed to make Cotter's lips curve in a sullen pout. She had thought his mouth so pretty before they were married, and now it often seemed sullen and peevish—the mouth of a weak man.

"How do you know they're half-truths? How about the libel laws?"

"Oh, Christ, they barely exist. I knew Senator Madigan very well, and I doubt very much if he would bother with a woman like that for ten years. For one night, maybe, now that his wife is dead, but I can assure you that bleached blonde was never his mistress." She picked up the paper and studied Joly's face again, noting the heavy eye makeup, the doughy little nose, the sensual mouth that appeared almost black with lipstick in the tabloid photo. "Never," she said firmly, handing the paper back to Cotter.

She slouched back in the chair again, massaging her temples and making plans. She would call Carlotta in Washington and find out when the funeral was to be. Then she would have Cotter arrange to have their tickets changed. Tomorrow she would have her hair done, and a manicure, and there would be time to shop for something really smashing in black. She might even have her hair lightened just a little, go from tawny to honeyish, just for the contrast.

"Well, well," said Cotter in a nasty undertone. "Miss Joly has added attractions not featured on the front page." He held the paper open to the second page, where a full shot of Joly, presumably from her show-girl days, revealed a female body even Rachel found hard to criticize. She stared in fascination at a woman clad only in high heels, a g-string and pasties, and an enormous crown of feathers. She had long, lovely legs, a tiny waist, and high, melon-like breasts that didn't look like implants. Of course, Rachel told herself, *she* wouldn't want a body like that—those huge bazooms would ruin the line of any dress you put on. It would be impossible to look high-fashion. Still, naked . . .

"Come on, Rachel," said Cotter in his most annoying voice, "admit you wouldn't mind a little more on top? Just a little?"

"Go fuck yourself, darling," said Rachel, and then promptly burst into tears. Cotter was instantly repentant, thinking he had wounded her, and she was trying to explain why she was crying while he caressed and comforted her. "It's not what you think," she sobbed against his shoulder. "Oh, Cotter—I know I'm horribly selfish and self-centered, but I'm not a monster, am I? Oh, poor Carlotta, poor Carlotta! This will just kill her. We've got to go home, right now, today. Carlotta needs me."

Although Rachel tended to babble when she was upset, a part of her was most sincere when she wept that Carlotta needed her. Who else left living could possibly understand what Tom Madigan had meant to his daughter? Carlotta herself didn't understand.

"Oh, it would have broken your heart," she said to her husband. "If you could have seen her at school, in Switzerland, the way she had her father's picture on her desk. Most of us had pictures of our boyfriends, of course, and there were a few deadly dull girls who had photos of both parents—but Carlotta? No mama, no boyfriends. Just Daddy. 'Who's that?' I asked her the first time I saw the picture, 'the Marlboro Man?'"

"What did she say?" asked Cotter, who was dutifully bending over the pigskin carry-on Rachel used for stowing her drugs.

"Well, really, Cotter, how could I possibly remember? She indicated that the man in the photo was her father, and I said the truth—that he was the handsomest daddy I'd ever seen. Just a Valium, I think, sweet. I need to keep a clear head."

"What for, Rachel?"

"To plan for the *funeral*," Rachel screamed. "Haven't you taken any of this in?"

"It'll probably be private," said Cotter, pouring some pepper vodka into a crystal glass and handing it, together with the pill, to his distraught wife. "Chances are, she won't want you there."

"She'll want me," said Rachel. "She'll definitely need me. You can stay in London, Cotter, but I've got to leave. I've got to get to Montana."

Rachel rose to her feet and went toward the bathroom in search of a cold cloth to lay across her forehead. She was genuinely flushed and hot from her tears, but as always, she feared that the reality of the moment was not enough. She swayed, lurching a little, as if with a grief so great she could not be depended upon to steer a straight course, and cast a furtive look in the mirror to note Cotter's reaction.

"You must have one hell of a hangover," was what Cotter said.

"Your insensitivity is monumental," said Rachel, changing her mind about the cold cloth and altering her course. "I'm going out shopping. There's no time to have anything made— I'll simply have to find something suitable for the funeral. Please see to my reservations, Cotter. Anything in the next twenty-four hours will do." She spoke as imperiously as possible, under the circumstances. She could hardly leave the suite without fluffing her hair and searching out the fun-fur fox she had bought in Chelsea. It was, she felt, so very Kings Road.

"Anything?" said Cotter. "How about a Norwegian fishing boat?"

She shot a withering look in his direction, but then she had to giggle. Just when Cotter seemed stupidest—like a member of her own family, in fact—he redeemed himself with these little flashes of humor. Cotter—who was Rachel's mother's idea of the ideal husband and who had once been Rachel's idea of the same—was not a complete loss.

Mayfair bored Rachel. At this point in history, it was not a place for the young. Elegant it might be, but it held no promises for her. She was not interested in good little dressmakers, or window displays that featured gold cigarette lighters reclining on pillars of black velvet, and so she told the taxi driver to take her to the Kings Road, in Chelsea. She liked browsing in the demented shops, being assaulted by the ear-splitting rock music they piped in, and having for a clerk some haughty young English beauty who refused to defer to her. She and a Cockney clerk were bound to be equals, if only by virtue of their youth and good looks.

"Something for a funeral, actually," Rachel murmured, and then laughed delightedly when the inevitable black leather mini-dress was presented.

Carlotta had never been like that at all. Clothes didn't interest her, nor did the idea of improving her appearance. Carlotta had never expressed her dislike of the Swiss school's uniform, and that alone would have made her interesting to Rachel. Carlotta was perfectly capable of dressing in the bulky, gray, shapeless skirt and blazer every day without showing her disgust. She never tried out different hairstyles, or experimented with her makeup. It was as if, being born perfect, Carlotta felt no need to tamper with her reflection. By day or by night, whether she was clothed in the ugly school uniform or one of her chaste, white nightdresses of batiste, Carlotta looked beautiful.

What had always tormented Rachel was this: If Carlotta, so effortlessly, had already attained that which Rachel aspired to, why wasn't she happier? Was perfection, in fact, not enough?

She might have been tempted to hate Carlotta, except for one fact. Carlotta was beautifully, stupidly, innocent. Rachel had the upper hand as far as experience went, and felt superior, naturally. How could any normal sixteen-year-old hate a self-confessed virgin who kept a photo of her father in the place of honor, enshrined on her desk? Pity, perhaps, for one so lovely as Carlotta, but never hate.

So long as she could remember, Carlotta had had no other friends at school. The other girls seemed rather in awe of her, and although they had been friendly enough, most of them, Rachel was the only one to get close. Carlotta confided in Rachel, just as so many people did. Rachel smiled at her image reflected in the boutique's silver panels. The secret of getting people to confide in you was simple: you simply poured out all your own secrets, holding back nothing, and eventually the other party felt obliged to respond in kind.

There had been plenty of confidences exchanged at the school in Neuchâtel—what else had they had to do? The courses weren't very demanding, and if you were at all smart, you could finish your assignments in half an hour and devote the rest of study hall to gossiping. This was made possible by the fact that Madame Calvet, the monitor, was deafer than her superiors knew. As long as you kept your face turned away from her and pretended to be addressing an open book, you could get away with anything.

"I decided to get rid of my virginity two years ago, when I was fourteen," Rachel had explained to Carlotta in study period one evening. "It was a very conscious decision, nothing romantic about it. I didn't even have a candidate."

"Did you go out looking for one?" Carlotta had asked. Say one thing for her: Carlotta wasn't a prude, not about other people, anyway.

"As it turned out, it wasn't necessary. It was Easter vacation, and my horrible brother Anthony came home with a friend from Harvard. He was nice-looking enough—he looked a little bit like Richard Burton, only younger, of course. It was tough, but I got him to come around."

"Why was it so tough?"

"Jesus, Carlotta, don't you know *anything?* It's against the law. He was eighteen, and I was underage. He could have gone to jail. I just kept on after him, though, until he surrendered."

"What sorts of things did you do?" Carlotta asked, her eyes wide with interest.

"Put my hand on his legs under the table at dinner, mainly. I let him know that he'd be welcome in my room; I told him when we were playing mixed doubles at tennis. Another thing—I told him I was really seventeen going on eighteen. I said the whole family lied about my age because I was so slow and kept failing in school."

Carlotta shook with laughter. "He couldn't have believed that," she said.

"Shhhh!" hissed a studious girl from Belgium.

"Sorry, Marie-Thérèse," said Carlotta. And then, shyly, "When it happened—did you like it?"

"Not very much. It hurt, and it was sticky and messy, and there was blood on my sheets. But that's not the point, Carlotta. You have to get it over with, and then it gets better. Even then, I could see it had possibilities."

"Did you ever see him again?"

"Don't be a romantic."

"Shhhhhhhh!"

"Up yours, Marie-Thérèse."

Yes, Carlotta had been an excellent confidante, but she had very little to offer in return. In exchange for the tales of Rachel's defloration, two expulsions from private schools in America, and various experiments with drugs, Carlotta could only provide admiring stories about her all-powerful father. Daddy had addressed the senate, warning of the folly of involvement in Vietnam. Daddy had bought an Arabian stallion and broken him himself. It was, in some respects, like talking to a little girl.

Rachel had understood that Carlotta missed her life in Montana and Washington, and missed the only friend she seemed to have, an Indian girl called Lee. She tried to be patient with Carlotta, but she herself had been in private schools since the age of eleven. She could not remember being homesick.

"It's like being in a prison," Carlotta used to say, and Rachel would merely shrug. The school was in a chateau, isolated from the town by its position on a hill. There was a panoramic view of mountains from every window, adequate food, and a regime that was not too strict. Rachel hated it, and Switzerland, because she had no freedom, but it wouldn't have occurred to her to complain. Being in boarding school was what you did until you were old enough to make your own decisions.

The girls at the Académie came from all parts of Europe, with a sprinkling of Americans from the eastern seaboard. The American girls were, like Rachel, from old-money families, and since Carlotta was neither, strictly speaking, old money or from the East, she was something of an anomaly. Snobbish Marie-Thérèse had once suggested to Rachel that the school was going down if they were admitting politicians' daughters. "What an *incroyable* ass you are, Marie-Thérèse. Her father is a gentleman rancher as well as a very powerful United States senator. His ranch is probably bigger than all of boring Belgium." Marie-Thérèse had beetled her heavy, unplucked brows and gone off muttering.

Where was she now, Rachel wondered, attracted by some black boots with spiky heels; where was that dowdy, unpleasant girl? Nowhere very interesting, that was certain. She indicated that she would like to try the boots on, and arched her foot prettily so that the young clerk could admire her legs. It was wasted effort, since he was so obviously not attracted to those of the opposite sex, but she liked to keep her hand in. "My foot, in this case," she said out loud.

"Beg pardon, love?" said the clerk.

"Nothing, really." Rachel stretched her leg out so she could admire the effect of the black boot. Kinky, quite kinky, the way the supple leather went up so far. With a mini, the combination would be devastating. "What do you think of these for a funeral?" she asked.

The clerk laughed wildly, and then, when he saw that she was serious, assumed a crafty look. The boots cost nearly 200 pounds, and he certainly didn't want to put her off. "Super," he said. "I mean, they make a statement."

Suddenly Rachel thought of a black mantilla, a particular one a girl whose name she had forgotten wore on Sundays, for her devotions. She had been very pious, and the mantilla had greatly improved her appearance, covering her beaky face and giving her an air of mystery. Rachel did not want to cover her face entirely, but mightn't a wispy black mantilla, more transparent than the pious girl's had been, be just the thing?

She hadn't thought so much about her school days in years. She wasn't one to dwell on the past, and there were much more interesting things to contemplate now. Graham, for example, a rock musician from the same general area the Beatles had come from. She had met Graham at a party, and he had informed her meaningfully that he would soon be touring in America. It was about all he could do, Cotter having been very much in evidence.

The King's Road boutiques didn't seem to be offering mantillas, so Rachel beckoned a taxi and asked to be taken to Harrod's. She was wondering where to go if Harrod's disappointed—a religious supply store?—when the name *Erna Stott* leaped into her head. For a moment she thought she was hallucinating, but since she'd taken nothing but Valium it seemed unlikely. But yes, of course, Erna Stott had been the pious girl who had worn the very article she was looking for now.

"Thank you, Erna," said Rachel. Erna Stott, good lord, what a hopeless case. At least she had not had to endure Erna as a roommate. The girls slept in chaste, narrow beds, four to a room, and Rachel had been subjected to some fairly awful roommates. The first year the serpent in her nighttime garden had been the detested Marie-Thérèse, who suffered from adenoids and snored deeply. Marie-Thésèse also had difficulty with her periods and regularly, each month, moaned rhythmically, like a woman in labor. Rachel's sleep that year had been punctuated by the noises issuing from Marie-Thérèse's bed; as a consequence she dreamed of buzz-saws and lowing cattle, and awakened cross and out of sorts.

The second year had been better, but far from perfect. She and Carlotta had requested to share a room, and the request had been granted, but there were always the two unknown quantities. Rachel had been the first to arrive. She had acquired a fondness for grass over the summer, and she was just about to extract a baggie of fine, Colombian Gold from her shoe bag when she heard the tapping of feet coming up the corridor. Hastily, she thrust the baggie back.

The owner of the tapping feet was a chic, friendly Parisienne called Laure. Laure had brought champagne, and proposed to open it immediately. "Our last year confined," Laure said in accented but perfect English. "This cries out for a celebration, does it not, Rachel Windolm?"

Rachel and Laure had been drinking the champagne, swigging it straight from the bottle, when Carlotta had burst into the room. She was taller, more radiant, than she had been a mere few months before, and Rachel knew, taking her in—the heather-colored Scottish suit, the hair gathered into a French twist that called the exquisite bone structure into dramatic relief—that Carlotta had lost her virginity at last. What she had not been prepared for was the burst of emotion she felt on seeing Carlotta again. Goofy, gorgeous, naive Carlotta, sent once more back into exile in Switzerland, nearly moved her to tears.

Rachel had understood something important on that day. Despite her dozens of friends, Carlotta was the only one who really mattered, because she was the only one who made Rachel happy. She wasn't sure why this should be, but she never questioned it.

Later, when the fourth roommate arrived, the giddy mood brought on by the champagne was instantly dissipated. Trudi, a matronly young woman from Geneva, plodded in clutching a framed photograph of a youth wearing horn-rimmed spectacles.

"Which is my desk?" she inquired in a sing-song Schweizer-Deutsche voice. "I shall want to write to my fiance immediately."

All that school year, the melancholy face of Jacob, the fiance, regarded the four roommates with seeming disapproval. Even Carlotta, who hadn't a mean bone in her body, said she pitied Jacob and Trudi's future children.

Five years had passed since their school days, and they had remained friends through everything. Rachel still did not understand what made Carlotta so special to her. Because hers was not a close family, and because the only other person she had ever cared for was an old nanny she had not seen for years, she failed to recognize the emotion Carlotta called up in her. It was simply unconditional love, innocent and enduring.

Love was something Rachel talked about a great deal, and understood almost nothing about.

Clutching the long box that contained her bulky new boots, hurrying in to Harrod's, Rachel had a vague feeling that perhaps the mantilla was a bit too much. The feeling was quickly replaced by a vision of the dignified Jacqueline Kennedy, her face veiled, walking in her husband's funeral cortege.

Carlotta lay, sedated, in her bedroom in Washington. She was no longer asleep, but in a drugged state where she wandered freely in and out of shallow unconsciousness. She was aware of the people in the house, whispering, tiptoeing when they passed her door, and of the opening and closing of the door downstairs on Q Street. She was here, in her father's house in Georgetown, and the world had come to an end. Addie Sharpe, her father's personal secretary, had met her at the airport. One look at Carlotta's face and Addie had cut short her words of sympathy and brought her home.

How long had she slept? The effort of turning her head to the bedside clock seemed too great. Anyway, what did it matter?

"What does it matter?" she said to her father on a summer day years ago. "Who cares, Daddy? What does it *matter*?" She had been passionate in her argument, had felt close to tears. They had been discussing the matter of Carlotta's going to school in Switzerland. She had always known she would have to go, when she reached a certain age, but on that particular day, jouncing along beside him in his Land Rover, traversing the remote north quadrant of the ranch, the idea had seemed unbearable. Switzerland! So far away from the bulking, blue mountains of Montana (never mind that there were even better mountains in Switzerland) and everything she knew and loved—it was unthinkable. That was when she had begun to argue and plead, but he was so much wiser and stronger, so much more skilled in dissecting a subject and providing answers, Carlotta had been reduced to the idiotic chorus of *What does it matter?*

The words had angered him. "How can my daughter ask me of what importance her future is to me?" he had asked softly. "If you think your future doesn't matter, Carlotta, you are very sadly mistaken." She had sneaked a sideways look at him then, and seen that beneath the anger he was hurt. She hadn't meant to imply that he didn't care about her future. The angry tone had made her tremble, but the wounded one lurking beneath had a double-edged effect: it made her grow almost faint with remorse, but at the same time she felt . . . what could it be? A small thrill of pride, she guessed. That was it. Pride that her daddy cared so much what she thought.

"I don't want to go away," she had said, calmer now.

"It's only for a few years, sweetheart, and you'll be back with us on your holidays."

Us! "It's mother's idea, isn't it? Easterners all send their kids to boarding school."

Her father had chuckled, easy and offhand, as if she had said something amusing. "Baby, don't you know me well enough by now to understand *anything?* Do you think I'd let your mother send you off to school if I opposed it?"

Betrayed, Carlotta had stared out the Rover's window, fixing her gaze on a jackrabbit who was fleeing from the oncoming car. Her father was going on about how he wanted his daughter to grow up with some knowledge of the world beyond the United States, how trips abroad were only pleasant intervals and a really first-rate European education was invaluable.

Still following the escape of the jackrabbit, her rebellious mind had come up with several arguments. One was that a girls' boarding school in Switzerland was hardly likely to make her a Citizen of the World. Another was so disloyal she scarcely knew how she could put it into words—if her father were speaking on the floor of the senate, wouldn't his words seem downright un-American? In any case, none of this was important, really. The issue was a simple one. *Wouldn't he miss her?* She was longing to ask him, scream the words, in fact. *How can you do without me? How can you be so casual about it?*

And then, in one of those moments so familiar to her she wanted to cry, their perfect chemistry meshed. Senator Madigan, as if hearing his daughter's unvoiced cry, reached across and pressed her hand. "Of course, I'm going to miss you something fierce, Carlotta," he said. "But if I'm willing to make the sacrifice, why not you?"

Feeling ashamed, she had bent her head and nodded. He was, as usual, right. He knew what was best, and she was being unattractively childish, with her silly suspicions and grievances, her feeling that she was being sent into exile for her parents' convenience—she was self-centered and foolish, and the angry emotions still boiling inside her had to be repressed.

They had held hands all the way back to the ranch, except for a few times when Tom Madigan had been obliged to use both hands to negotiate some dangerous turns.

How well he drove. How wonderfully well he did everything! Watching him, on the last few miles home, she felt a yearning so powerful it seemed to her a kind of madness. It was not enough to be his daughter and best companion—exalted though such a position may be, it was not enough. She thought, hurtling down the homestretch, that she would like to be Tom Madigan himself. It was such a peculiar thought that Carlotta had giggled nervously.

"What's so funny, baby?"

"Nothing, Daddy. A jackrabbit . . ."

How long had she been here? How long, lying in this bed? A day, two days—she sank into a little oblivion only to waken with a jolt. How could she have thought it didn't matter. How could she leave people like Addie Sharpe and Mrs. Pine, the housekeeper, to take care of things? The last thing she could do for her father was to behave as his daughter should. There would be time later to retreat into herself and mourn; for now she was obliged to act like a Madigan. She could not *become* her father, now that he was gone, but she could show the world what it was to be his daughter.

She called down to the kitchen and asked Mrs. Pine to send up a pot of strong tea, and then she went into her bathroom and turned on the shower. Her head felt light as a helium balloon, but she was determined to put herself right and act with dignity. The shower and the tea helped. She selected a black cashmere dress and black high-heeled shoes, swept her hair back, and twisted it severely atop her head. She looked pale, drawn, but very much in command.

When she entered the drawing room she was amazed to find at least fifteen people present. "Good afternoon," she said. "Are you being looked after?"

There was a low, collective rumble. Everyone looked embarrassed. "This is Miss Carlotta Madigan," her father's lawyer, James Haley, announced to the people she did not know. Some of them, she thought vaguely, might be detectives. "The senator's daughter," Mr. Haley explained unnecessarily. Heads were respectfully dipped.

"Carlotta, dear, are you feeling any better?" Addie Sharpe asked, and then blushed.

"I am sorry to have slept for so long," Carlotta told them in her curiously formal way. "If I had known how strong the sedative was I would certainly have refused it. Has there been an arrest?"

One of the men began to speak, but James Haley stood. "I would like to have a word with Miss Madigan in private," he said. "Perhaps in the library, Carlotta?"

The library was the worst place for him to have chosen, since of all the rooms in the Washington house it was the one most bound to remind anyone of Tom Madigan. It was completely masculine, with huge leather chairs in shades of tobacco brown and bottle green. Its dark wood paneling and tall bookshelves were gloomy without their master's presence to liven things up. Carlotta chose a chair that would not force her to look at her father's portrait—his second favorite, the favorite being back home in Montana—and waited to hear what Mr. Haley would say. He was clearing his throat awkwardly and looking miserable.

"Carlotta, my dear," he began, "I would give anything if I didn't have to tell you this. It is very unpleasant, but there is no way on earth to keep it from you. I'm so very sorry."

She stared at him. What could be of the slightest importance compared to the fact that her father had been murdered? What else mattered?

Then he told her about Joly Nesbit.

"I'm sure there's been a mistake," Carlotta said, her mind refusing to register what he had said. "My father didn't know anyone by that name."

Mr. Haley sighed and handed her the late edition of the Washington *Post*. There she read for herself the outlandish claim of one Joly Lorraine Nesbit, 35, to have been her father's mistress for the past ten years. Her apartment in Georgetown was paid for by Senator Madigan. Miss Nesbit had been arrested in the matter of the senator's murder, and since only her fingerprints had been found on the handle of the carving knife . . . Carlotta put the paper down.

"This can't be true," she said. "Anyone can claim to be the mistress of a public figure. And of course her fingerprints

would be on the knife in her own house." Even as she spoke
she knew she had no case, and for that very reason she rushed
on, lying desperately.

"I'm sorry, Carlotta," said Mr. Haley gently. "Your father
was found in Miss Nesbit's apartment."

And then Haley gave a long speech about how regrettable
it was, and how Carlotta was to remember the many good
things the senator had accomplished during his lifetime, and
how she was never to doubt how much he had loved her and
her mother. At the mention of her mother he faltered, but
Carlotta was barely listening to him. She was repeating three
words ceaselessly to herself, trying not to scream them. *How
could you?* Oh, God, how could he?

TWO

THOMAS MADIGAN WAS BURIED, AS HE HAD ALWAYS SAID HE wanted to be, on his ranch. Under the circumstances, there was no great state funeral. No crowds passed by his casket to say a final goodbye. The spokesman for the Madigan family —which now consisted only of Carlotta and her Aunt Harriet, a woman of sixty-five—made it clear that the funeral was to be a private affair. No flowers arrived. The world stayed away out of embarrassment, and those who would have come from curiosity were barred. Even the press showed little interest; they were occupied in speculation over the fate of Joly Nesbit. A famous lawyer, one who liked challenges, was rumored to be taking her case.

The president sent a message of condolence, as did most of the senators and congressmen, but these were merely a matter of form, and meaningless. Most of the telegrams that came pouring in were oddly impersonal, not even addressed to Carlotta herself but to the ranch, as if the senders did not know who to try to comfort. The few people who took the trouble and time to write to her personally she vowed to remember. The rest she counted as enemies.

The actual burial was a bleak affair. An autumnal wind was blowing down from the mountains, even though the sun was high and glaring, and the words of the service were caught in the currents and seemed to dance around and repeat themselves.

The ritual spadeful of earth full on her father's coffin with a horrid finality. She had gone through it before, of course, when her mother had been buried, but Martha, for reasons of her own, had stipulated burial in the Carshaw mausoleum in Philadelphia. Death had seemed remote there, amidst all those manicured green trees and little winding, pebbled paths, but here—on the rolling plains east of the Continental Divide beneath the vast Montana sky—it was not at all remote. Her father was to lie beneath the earth, here, forever.

They were a small group. Addie Sharpe sobbed unashamedly. Her little cries sounded not quite human in the hugeness of the place, like the peeps of a wounded gopher, but Carlotta was grateful for Addie's grief. Unlike the mournful High Church priest, whom she had never seen before, Addie was truly mourning.

Another person who inspired her gratitude was Charlie Redwing, Lee's father. He had come, although no one had thought to invite him, dressed in a dark suit and looking, to Aunt Harriet, so sinister she gave a little gasp when he appeared. Charlie had been her father's ranch manager, and the sight of him propelled her into the past so powerfully she nearly broke. The copper-beechnut skin, the black eyes that could seem so impassive to whites, who didn't understand, were much more comforting to her than the president's telegram. Charlie Redwing made his way to her and communicated, without the slightest movement, his sorrow and regret.

It was to Charlie she looked when the words of the Christian Rites of Burial overpowered her most, and it was from Charlie she took her cue. The others were looking into the raw wound of the grave, but Charlie was staring steadfastly at the mountains.

Carlotta wished she were part of an ancient tradition, a religion old as time, as Charlie was. She wanted to believe that her father's spirit had entered a cottonwood tree or a circling hawk, or had ascended to the timber line of the mountains. How could a spirit as great as his simply cease to be? She shut her mind away from the manner of his death, and tried to think of him as he had once been.

The ordeal was not over with the burial, Carlotta discovered. From the windows of the great front hall, when they had returned, she saw a black limousine gliding up the road toward the ranch. It was a private road, and security guards had been posted to prevent the curious from gaining access to the Madigan property. She stared at the approaching limo with dread—who was coming to disturb her now? The door of the car opened, across from the driver's side, and one of her own security men got out.

"I'm sorry, Miss Madigan," the man said at the door. "She says she's your friend. I told her the funeral was over, but she wouldn't go away. Says she's come all the way from London."

"Did she give her name?"

"A Mrs. Vere," said the man doubtfully. "A Mrs. Cotter Vere."

"What is it?" cried Aunt Harriet, coming into the hall.

Before Carlotta could reply, the back door of the limo opened and they were treated to the sight of an almost mythic figure. Rachel was dressed entirely in black; she embodied mourning, and Carlotta felt sick. Damn Rachel, anyway. She saw this as an opportunity for high drama, and was resolved to be a major player. She was walking toward the house, trying to be sedate in her black dress and London boots, but her step was unsteady. She nearly lost her footing on the steps to the veranda, but she righted herself and, with a gesture that would have done credit to Sarah Bernhardt, drew the lacy black veil from her face. Her eyes were dilated and tragic. She was, Carlotta knew, drugged. She had a brief vision of the pills—blue, white, yellow, red, black—that kept Rachel going.

"Oh, Carlotta," Rachel whispered, "you knew I'd come."

"What an extraordinary young woman," Aunt Harriet murmured. "Is she really your friend, dear?"

But an odd thing had happened. Rachel's air of mystery had disappeared. Gone was the studied grace of her dramatic arrival. As she stared at Carlotta she became subdued, contrite, as if she had only now been awakened to the reality of Carlotta's loss. "Oh, Carlotta," she said in a wondering voice, "I'm so sorry." She threw open her arms in an awkward gesture and embraced her friend with all her strength. There was a measure of true comfort in the pressure of those slight arms, and Carlotta leaned against the smaller woman gratefully.

She would always remember the strangeness of it: Rachel, appearing from nowhere—"all the way from London," as she put it—hugging her on the veranda, only to get back in her limousine and drive off, mission accomplished. It was a measure of her own grief and confusion that she did not ask Rachel to stay for a bit. It was also true that she wanted nothing but to be alone.

On the day after the burial, she lay on the wide window seat in the game room. All around her, the glass eyes of her father's trophies glittered in the light of the fire she had built in the huge grate. Elk and brown deer stared from the walls, and the snarling lynx leered at her from his place on the mantel. As a child, she had loved the lynx, and played at putting her fingers between his sharp teeth. Now he seemed unpleasant.

It occurred to her that her father had put an end to the lives of all the creatures in this room. It was an odd way of phrasing it—everyone hunted, and thought nothing of it—yet once *she* had thought of it she could think of nothing else. The taxidermist's services were required regularly at the Madigan ranch, because her father had liked his trophies mounted.

How Inga had hated dressing venison! Carlotta could still remember the odd noises that came from the usually goodnatured cook when she was engaged in that activity. She realized now that Inga had merely been cursing in her native Swedish, but at the time there had seemed to be something powerful and incantatory in those little explosions of sound.

Carlotta could remember a time when she had liked venison, despite the unpleasant little bits of buckshot that could never be completely removed. She had stopped liking it during the hunting season of her twelfth year. She remembered, because it was the only time in her life she had had bronchitis. Her family had always flown back to the ranch for every weekend of the deer-hunting season. It would have taken something monumental, a war or assassination, to keep the senator in Washington at the time, and Carlotta could remember the exhilarating feeling of leaving the coolish, gray air of a Washington autumn and re-entering the dazzling world of what was already winter in Montana. Usually, there would be snow, and the air would be so cold and pure that inhaling it was like filling your chest with icicles.

There was a special, mystical quality to riding horseback in the snow. She and her father often went on wintry rides, and the muted thump of the horses' hooves on the packed snow was a sound that had thrilled her. Sometimes the overburdened limbs would creak and groan, and then, riding beneath great pines, a little puff of wind would envelop them in a powdery snow squall. Once, a mound of snow had begun to move, had taken flight before their approaching horses, in the shape of a white rabbit.

That year, her twelfth, he had promised, over Martha's objections, to take her deer-hunting with him for the first time. Charlie and Lee were to come along, too, and Carlotta had looked forward to it all autumn. She didn't mention the cotton-wool feeling in her head on the plane, and when the sore throat started she concealed that, too. She wanted nothing to spoil the promised treat, and vowed that she would die before letting her parents know.

On the long ride to the ranch, she silently cursed Susie Barker, the daughter of the secretary of agriculture. Susie sat near her at her private school in Washington, and for the past week Susie had been emitting great, wet sneezes. Carlotta hadn't cared at the time, but now, her head throbbing and chest tightening, she thought the very least Susie might have done was to stay home rather than infect everyone else. Soon after Susie had been forced to take to her bed, Mercedes Guerrero, daughter of the Brazilian ambassador, had come down with similar symptoms.

She had gone straight to bed, hoping that she would feel better in the morning, but when she awakened she was hot and dizzy, and the cotton-wool feeling was ten times worse. Nevertheless, she dressed herself for the hunting expedition and came down to breakfast hopefully.

Her father was at the sideboard, helping himself to steak and eggs. Martha had not yet arisen. "You'll want to eat a good, big breakfast," Daddy said. "It's cold out there, and you need stamina."

Carlotta opened her mouth to reply, and her body betrayed her in the worst possible way. Out of her mouth there came ripping a horrible, barking, rasping cough. She tried to speak over it, but her whole body was seized with a series of wrenching explosions, each one worse than the last. She sounded like a seal begging for a fish.

"What's this?" Daddy had said, his brows furrowing with alarm.

"Nothing," she had sputtered, her body bent double to forestall another seizure.

But he had set his plate down and come to her, placing his

big hand on her flushed forehead. "You have a fever," he said. "Why, sweetheart, you're sick."

Then Martha had appeared, wearing the purple robe that made Carlotta think of the Greek goddesses they were studying in her mythology class, and all thoughts of going out deer-hunting were automatically dead.

The memory of the doctor from White Sulphur Springs, the memory of her mother nursing her long after her father had been forced to return to Washington, the sting of the penicillin-shot needle and the furtive, frightened murmurings of the word *pneumonia*—all these were mere blurs. She remembered with perfect clarity the moment when she had crept from her bed, kneeling dizzily on her little chaise before the windows, to witness the departure of the hunting party.

Lee was wearing something scarlet. Her black hair streamed across the back of the bright coat, and even from such a distance Carlotta could see the white slash of Lee's smile in the bronze face. Charlie was already mounted, but Lee and Daddy were waiting for Jack, one of the ranch hands, to lead their horses out. Her father's bay stallion was the first to appear, but for some reason he did not get into the saddle. He stood, his gun strapped to his back, holding the stallion's reins and talking to Lee and Charlie.

When Carlotta saw her own pony, Sundance, being produced for Lee, she was prompted to a fresh seizure of coughing. It wasn't, she told herself, that she begrudged Lee the loan of her pony, but why Sundance? There were plenty of ponies Lee might have ridden, and Sundance had been her father's present to her on her tenth birthday.

Lee laughed again, and went to mount the pony. Carlotta, with her hot head pressed against the cold glass of the window, watched while her father did an amazing, a totally unnecessary, thing. He caught Lee in his arms, scooping her up as easily as if she had been a puppy, and flung her into the saddle. Lee rocketed forward, lying out across Sundance's mane, and quickly righted herself. Then Carlotta's father sprang onto the bay's back, and the party of three cantered off without a backward look.

Carlotta watched them until they had disappeared from sight, and then crept back to bed, coughing. She had a vague and muzzy feeling, a feeling that she wasn't being missed. Her presence was not important enough.

For the first time, she hated Lee. Later, when the doctor

came, she blamed her tears on the fever. It was an odd time in her life, she who had always been so healthy, and she had never hated Lee again. Only in that instant when her father had held Lee in his arms, seeming to protect her just instants before he flung her into the saddle, had Carlotta felt cold and hateful.

She and Daddy had often played that game, and that he should play it with anyone but his own daughter seemed a violation, but a violation of what? It had all been too much for her to puzzle out, and she had retreated gratefully, into the shell of her illness.

Two bucks had been shot that day, and Inga cursed softly in the kitchen, and ever afterward Carlotta had disliked the taste of venison.

By the time she was thirteen, her father had a new passion —the buying, and breaking, of Thoroughbred horses.

She wondered what would happen to Amir Lateef, the prize Arabian stallion her father had bought last year. No one was allowed to exercise him but her father and Ted, the groom, when Tom Madigan was in Washington. She shut her eyes, remembering how Daddy had looked on that magnificent and dangerous beast, grinning as he acknowledged the stallion's willful spirit, and then, proceeding to master it. The image changed to one quite different and so disgusting that Carlotta gave a low moan of pain and outrage. What she had seen bucking and arching under her father's powerful, straddled legs was the body of a white voluptuous woman. Joly Nesbit. She had seen the same photograph that Rachel had seen in London, and had never hated the sight of anyone so much in her life.

Carlotta sat across from James Haley, trying to make herself pay attention to the long legal phrases. The only other person present at the reading of the will was Aunt Harriet. Her father was generous to two of his most faithful employees, bequeathing $50,000 each to Addie Sharpe and Charlie Redwing. There were smaller bequests to the cook and other longtime servants, and "to my dear sister, Harriet Madigan Blount," he left three oil paintings, among them a Fragonard, and a collection of valuable first editions. This, too, was generous, since they had never been close and Aunt Harriet was rich in her own right.

Haley droned on, full of pursuants and heretofores, and

then looked up, paused, and read something it took Carlotta several minutes to comprehend. The ranch, all of the land and the house and the livestock, was to be sold. The proceeds were to be used to found a Foundation for the Rehabilitation and Betterment of the American Indian People of Montana. It was to be named in honor of the senator, and he hoped it would "stand as a measure of my esteem and sympathy for the original inhabitants of the state I loved and served."

Everything else went to Carlotta, as she had known it would. Haley read the long list of assets out, mentioned something about yearly income, detailed an excruciatingly complicated series of trusts. Something, she wasn't sure what, would come to her on her fortieth birthday. He was also leaving her a piece of Chinese sculpture, a little T'ang Dynasty horse she had always loved.

When Mr. Haley stopped reading, there was a profound silence in the room. She became aware that he and Aunt Harriet were looking at her oddly. "Is there anything you would like to ask me, Carlotta?" Mr. Haley said. "Do you understand the terms of the trust in your name?"

Carlotta nodded, not much caring.

"I know it must be a shock, rather," he said. "Your father had spoken to me about altering the will, softening up the terms, but—" He spread his hands, as if to say that Tom Madigan had not been expecting to die so suddenly.

"Why would he alter the will?" Carlotta asked, having a sudden dread that her father had planned to make her share his money with his mistress.

"Ah—well, you see, under the terms of the trust funds, to put it very simply, you can touch neither the interest nor the principal until your fortieth birthday. He has created another trust, the interest from which will bring you $20,000 a year, but I'm afraid that is all. Of course, the house in Georgetown is yours, and there is the little T'ang piece, which I believe is quite valuable." Mr. Haley cleared his throat. "I would advise you to sell the Washington property, my dear, and live in the cooperative apartment in New York."

He went on, explaining that the maintenance of the house and staff in Washington was too great for her to manage, and outlining various courses of action. All she could think was that she never wanted to see the Fifth Avenue apartment again. She could never enter that bedroom. She thought she would sell both places and go away where no one knew her. After she'd used up all the money, she would have to live on $20,000 a year. It didn't sound so bad to her. It sounded like quite a lot of money, and she couldn't understand why Mr. Haley was being so solicitous.

Like most very rich girls, she had no real concept of money. Everything had been done for her, so that money never changed hands. She supposed that was about to change, like everything else.

When she returned to Washington, she became acutely self-conscious. She imagined that people were staring at her, wherever she happened to be, whispering and snickering as soon as she was gone. Sometimes she was right. Once she was driven out to Nieman's to buy some note paper, and found herself handing over her charge card to a smartly dressed salesclerk with knowing eyes. The woman withdrew, and Carlotta could see her murmuring to another clerk in passing. When she returned, the woman said: "If you'll just sign the slip, *Miss Madigan?*" She seemed to want everyone within fifty feet to know who her customer was, and when Carlotta walked off she thought she heard the sounds of muted laughter.

At first she didn't go out socially. It was a strange sort of limbo she lived in, seeing only Mrs. Pine and the rest of the staff. They knew they were losing their jobs and treated her with the remote courtesy of people already thinking of the future. The house in Q Street had been placed on the market, and Carlotta sometimes encountered the woman realtor from the Elite Agency shepherding prospective buyers through the rooms. She shrank from such meetings, and from the curious glances of the well-heeled clients and the professionally sympathetic agent.

When two weeks had passed, she began to receive invitations to dinners and cocktail parties. She was flooded with them. It was the party season, and all the hostesses who had once invited the senator now invited his daughter. Carlotta separated the invitations into three piles. The first contained invitations from those who had always included her, if she was at home. The second was from the people who were making an effort to be kind, she thought. The third—and by far the largest—consisted of invitations from people she had never heard of who wanted to capture her as a sort of trophy.

These she tossed into the fireplace, but she wrote gracious and graceful regrets to all the hostesses from the first two categories.

In Mid-November a new scandal rocked Washington—something to do with the arrest of a New England senator's son on charges of drug-peddling—and Carlotta felt grateful. It made her feel small and cheap to revel in someone else's difficulties, and reminded her of how low she had sunk. Her father would not be proud of the timid, shrinking creature who hid herself on Q Street and let the world go by. He wouldn't even recognize her as a daughter. A Madigan ought to rise above the petty scum of scandal and go forth and conquer!

Armed with these thoughts, she decided to go to a large party on Foxhall Road, the home of a congressman from Wyoming and his charming wife. The problem had to do with what she would wear. Given the year, and her age, a mini was in order, but she didn't want to remind the guests of long legs and pliant flesh. Nothing about her should suggest the whorish, gaudy aura of a Joly; it was important that she seem dignified and beyond reproach and also gallant and adventurous. Her father's daughter.

"Hello, there, honey," said the elderly senator from Oregon, who had always liked her. "What a sight for sore eyes you are." Surprisingly, he hugged her hard, then held her at arms' length. "What a pretty outfit that is," he said. "Unusual, too. What do you call it?"

"Evening pajamas," said Carlotta demurely.

"Well, well, evening pajamas—what will they think of next?"

Carlotta took a glass of champagne from a passing tray and took several gulps to cover her confusion. How nice it had been to be hugged, even by an old man in his seventies! Nobody had touched her for so long, she'd forgotten how good it was to feel arms holding her with affection.

She felt safe with Senator Geering, but she knew she wouldn't be allowed to remain with him for long. Already her hostess was bearing down on her with a smile of triumph. "Carlotta, dear, how lovely you look!" she cried. She was a large, capable woman, known for her ability to get the right mix for her parties. She was wearing a long scarlet dress and ropes of jet, and she sparkled with electric efficiency as she maneuvered Senator Geering into a conversation with the secretary of the interior's wife and bore Carlotta off in the direction of the fifteen-foot Christmas tree. It was hot and noisy in the packed room, but Carlotta felt cool and poised. The jade green silk of her evening pajamas swished pleasingly against her legs, and when she caught her reflection as they passed a long mirror she knew her hostess had spoken the truth. She did look especially lovely. Good. No one could say, *That poor Madigan girl—you can tell how she's suffered.*

"Ah, here they are," her hostess said brightly, steering her up to a group of younger people, her daughter among them. "Joan, dear, introduce Carlotta to your friends."

Joan was a year younger than Carlotta. She was a pleasant but plain girl, and they had never had much to say to each other. She was wearing a striped mini-dress and staying very close to a blond young man whose eyes widened with interest at the sight of Carlotta.

"This is my fiancé, from Princeton," Joan said nervously. The young man held Carlotta's hand longer than necessary, and Joan grew more nervous. She introduced Carlotta to the others. They were college kids, pleasant and clean-cut, and Carlotta regarded them as children. One of the girls, on vacation from Vassar, kept staring at her with wide, sad eyes. Joan's fiancé was murmuring in her ear—something about going on to a club to dance, later, and wouldn't she join them —when the girl interrupted in a loud voice.

"Excuse me," she said. "Are you Senator Madigan's daughter?"

Everyone stopped talking and Joan blushed. "Vicky!" she reproved. But Vicky went right on. "I just wanted to tell you I sympathized," she said. "What a terrible thing for you. I know how you must feel, and if nobody else is going to mention it—" She seemed to run down.

"Thank you," said Carlotta coolly. Her hands were trembling violently and she thought she might spill her champagne. She turned to leave and heard one of the boys call after her: "Don't mind Vicky, she's stoned."

She hovered at the fringes of a group, calming herself, and then went into the long, mirrored dining room. A well known reporter from the Washington *Post* was filling his plate at the buffet. He looked up, saw her, and his eyes flickered with recognition. She fled from the room before he could speak to her. There were dangers everywhere. She took another glass of champagne, turned to avoid the lecherous eyes of a man who had something to do with the Italian embassy, and ran straight into another man, spilling champagne on his arm.

"Carlotta!" he cried. "I had no idea you were here!"

She looked up and saw that it was Hugh McManus, son of one of the most powerful lobbyists in town. She had dated him, briefly, when she'd first come back from boarding school in Switzerland, and then Hugh had gone off to Harvard. She had heard he was practicing law in Cambridge now.

"Hello, Hugh," she said. "It's been a long time." He must be nearly thirty now, she thought, and he was greatly changed. He had been a reedy boy, over-anxious and too diffident. The Hugh standing before her now was confident and attractive. He was still thin, but now he seemed lean rather than gangling. His dark hair was glossy, and the new, longer style suited him. His lips were quirked in a little welcoming smile, and the eyes which had once regarded her with awe now appraised her with lazy admiration.

"Shall I get you a drink? Most of yours is on my arm," he said. Old Senator Geering passed by, winking at her, and she remembered his hug. "Hugh?" She knew she was about to surprise herself, but it would surprise Hugh even more. "I have a better idea. Why don't you take me home?" His blue eyes darkened, and he nodded.

Outside on Foxhall Road, a few snowflakes were dancing in the air. She lifted her face to feel their coolness on her burning cheeks, and shuddered a little as Hugh McManus took her arm.

She had promised him champagne, but by the time they were standing in the drawing room on Q Street, champagne no longer interested either of them. Hugh brought his hand to her cheek, stroking her face so lightly his fingers might have been feathers. It was hypnotic. His thumb traced her cheekbones, caressed her jawbone, passed over her lips. Carlotta closed her eyes and sighed. His other hand was toying with her hair, sifting through the silky mass of it. She felt he was worshiping her.

"Carlotta," he whispered, trailing his fingers over the green silk that covered her breasts, "how beautiful you've become." She felt her nipples harden and ache beneath the teasing fingers. His hands continued their exploration, sliding over her flat belly and stroking her thighs. His touch was still so light she might have been dreaming it, except for the turmoil in her body. She was burning, trembling, and when she felt his lips so softly on hers she gasped and clutched him to her, arching her body to him and thrusting her tongue into his mouth. Now he was gasping, too, and in one swift movement he simply picked her up, holding her to him as he might a child, except that when she wrapped her legs around him she had never felt less like a child.

On the huge divan near the fireplace, she lay stretched out, whimpering with impatience while he stripped away the evening pajamas. Her nerve endings seemed laid bare, so that his slightest caress made her shudder with pleasure. Her breasts felt swollen, as if they might burst, and when he bent to them and she felt the hot point of his tongue against her nipples she cried out so loudly she frightened herself. She had never felt this way before, never so passionately eager. Never had so much pleasure seemed to be available to her.

She sobbed a little, feeling his soft hair tickling her belly, and then his clever fingers were softly hunting out the source of her ache, stoking it to a white heat what would devour her. Now his tongue where his fingers had been. *Mustn't make so much noise . . . the servants . . .* She turned her face against one of the satin pillows, muffling the cries she could not hold back. A great dam seemed to be bursting inside her and she was afraid she would drown. Her back arched as if it would break and her heels dug into the divan as she felt him leave her hovering on the brink of that cataclysm. She cried out to him as he began to strip off his clothes, revealing his hard male body, withholding it from her just when she needed it most.

Then he was with her again, inside her now, driving toward that bursting dam within her, causing her belly to contract in agonizing spasms of pleasure until no higher plateau could possibly be reached and she was fragmented into a million points of ecstasy. She sobbed into the pillow at the wonder of it.

There were no words between them. A little while later, Hugh McManus kissed her on the forehead, got dressed, and let himself out. Carlotta was glad, and grateful to him for understanding so instinctively. He had sensed her need, filled it, and gone discreetly away. There was nothing else between them, and never would be.

She crept up to her bed and lay between the sheets, her body still reverberating from its pleasure, and fell into a deep sleep, untroubled by dreams.

The next day she felt bitterly ashamed at her behavior. She wasn't worried about what Hugh would think of her. Everybody went around sleeping with everyone else these days, and she had known him for years anyway. Hugh wouldn't talk about it to a soul, but he would walk around for the rest of his life believing that she was an extremely passionate woman. He would never know that he had been the only man to provoke such tumultuous feeling in her. Well, let him. She felt very kindly disposed toward him and there was no way to tell him that last night's passion had less to do with him than it did with her.

That was what bothered her. Where had it come from? It was as if some other woman's soul had inhabited her body—the soul of someone low and coarse, who kicked and scratched her way to whatever she wanted. It frightened her that day, but on the following day she had already begun to tell herself she was exaggerating the whole business. She invented many glasses of champagne, substituting them for the one she had had before spilling the second on Hugh, and decided that she had been drunk and overly imaginative. By the third day, her ecstasy with Hugh on the couch had been reduced to the usual grapplings she had experienced, only rather nicer.

She didn't want to go to any more parties—they were clearly dangerous to her in her present state. It was very quiet in the big house on Q Street now. She and Mrs. Pine were the only people left, and soon Mrs. Pine would go, too. The woman from the Elite Agency had called to say that an Englishman from the World Bank was very interested in the property. He had a wife and five children, and Carlotta was not to be surprised if he made an acceptable offer some time during the first week of the new year.

It was very cold now, and there were constant brief snow squalls. She felt a prisoner in the very house she would soon be forced to leave. Often she took out the letter she had received from Lee Redwing and reread it. Lee said, right at the start, what no one else had articulated. *I feel such pain for you*, she had written in her bold hand, *because I know this is the worst thing that could happen to you. Nothing else could make you suffer as this is doing—in my own life I can find no standard of comparison.*

Bleak words they were, and harsh, but they were more comforting to Carlotta than anything else, because they were the truth. She and Lee had grown up together. They had met at such an early age that their different stations in life had made no difference. They had been inseparable for years, and by the time Carlotta realized how unusual their friendship was— white Boss's daughter and red-skinned wild papoose of the Boss's underling—nothing could have strained their friendship. Nothing but banishment to school in Switzerland.

You will always be the great friend of my childhood, and that is a powerful and unbreakable bond, wrote Lee from Berkeley. *I will think of you always, from time to time, and hope you are safe. That is more than most people can hope to have—a true friend for life.* She had signed it: *Your friend, L. Redwing.*

Oh, Lee, Lee! Lost forever, studying to be a lawyer in far-off, dangerous Berkeley. Nothing prevented Carlotta from hopping a plane and flying to California in search of her childhood's sister, but she was sure Lee would have returned to Montana for the holiday, and Carlotta no longer had a home in Montana.

Two days before Christmas, she was overpowered by a sudden, vivid image of Christmas on the ranch. Her mother had had a talent for making holidays beautiful and festive. No room escaped her attention—even the deer and elk in the game room sported wreaths of holly and mistletoe—and the whole house smelled of fragrant pine boughs. From the enormous kitchen would come another delicious smell compounded of gingerbread and hot spiced wine. All of her senses had delighted in those Christmases of her childhood. The thick blanket of snow, the magic of frost-diamonds, the clean, blue skies of winter, the pine and candle glow would cast a spell on her and, at the center of it all, causing it to happen, were those charmed and golden people, her parents. She had secretly believed, especially at Christmas, that their family was the happiest and luckiest on earth. The source of that happiness must be, of course, her father.

There were, in fact, two Christmases on the Madigan ranch. The first took place on Christmas Eve, when the Redwings and all the ranch hands came from their bunkhouses and dwellings to participate in a Madigan Christmas. They came at a prescribed time—seven in the evening—and always left by nine. There were presents for all of them under the huge spruce in the drawing room, and there was a huge buffet supper, and hot wine. Martha had always prohibited strong spirits, saying that American Indians, in particular, reacted to them badly. Only Charlie Redwing, who was, in fact, an abstemious drinker, was slyly given a generous measure of whiskey. He nursed it all evening.

The ranch hands were all bachelors, or men who had forsaken their families so long ago they could no longer remember them, and the only children at these events were Lee, her brothers, and Carlotta. Although Mrs. Redwing tried to keep her sons in order, Raymond, the eldest, always seemed to succeed in making trouble.

Once (she couldn't remember how old she had been), Ray had insisted on Lee's kissing the stuffed moose, because there was mistletoe on the moose's antlers, and Lee had wandered directly beneath. Jim, the second son, was adept at gulping the remains of the adults' drinks. At the age of ten, he had drunk himself into a stuporous state. Lee, Carlotta, and Ray had been obliged to plunge Jim's face into cold water in the kitchen, while Inga looked on and laughed. Baby Dominic was too young to cause trouble that particular year, and merely sat in his mother's lap, the lights of the Christmas tree making patterns in his wide, dark eyes.

Where were they now—Ray, Jim, and Dominic? Carlotta saw them frozen in the tableaux of long ago, and wished she could free them. She could picture Lee in Berkeley well enough—distinguishing herself among scholars, winning a name for herself—but what had become of her brothers?

Mrs. Redwing was dead and gone, that she knew. Lee's mother had died, of a sudden and virulent cancer, when Carlotta was in Switzerland. *Poor Ruth has gone,* her mother had written. *She died peacefully, in the hospital in Butte, where your father arranged for the very best care for her, last Saturday. I thought you would want to know, dear.*

Who was Ruth? Carlotta read and reread her mother's letter, hoping for enlightenment. It came to her in a classic burst.

Ruth, said Charlie Redwing's voice in her mind, *where's the new fertilizer?* Carlotta had always had too much respect for Lee's mother to think of her as "Ruth." The idea of Mrs. Redwing's mother having a first name would have seemed strange to her, back when she was only a child. Charlie was Charlie because she heard Daddy call him that about a hundred times a day.

She had realized something odd that day, holding her mother's letter and feeling grief for Mrs. Redwing. Often she thought of her mother as "Martha," yet Lee's mother had not needed a name to identify her. She was so palpably a mother, someone you came to when you had bee sting or a badly skinned knee. Carlotta's mother was flustered whenever Carlotta incurred some little injury. She could not bear the sight of blood, and usually wanted to phone for a doctor no matter how trivial the hurt might be.

It had been simpler to go to Lee's mother, who always knew exactly what to do, and made you feel better while she was doing it. She was always calm, always reassuring. Lee's mother knew many Indian remedies, and was able to prepare mysterious medicines from unlikely sources, such as blackberries and mud, but it wasn't her Cheyenne sorcery that was so soothing. It was something quite different, which the older Carlotta now knew was simply instinct, and a liking for children. Martha Madigan was ill at ease around children. Their noise, needs, and unpredictable sorrows unnerved her; she represented order, and they were firmly planted in the camp of chaos.

It was partly because of the presence of so many children that Carlotta's mother tired so easily during the Christmas Eve edition of a Montana Christmas. Directly after her guests departed, she made it a habit to go straight to bed, even though it was early in the evening. Carlotta always lingered hopefully, thinking that she and Daddy might have one of thier solitary evenings together, but generally the senator went down to the bunkhouse, or even to Charlie's place, where he continued the seasonal festivities.

Once—she had been very young—she had wakened to the sound of raucous singing in the middle of the night. She had crept to the window, shivering, and looked down to see a solitary figure standing in the snow. There had been a little, hard half-moon, the color of a dime, and by its light she had recognized her father. Dressed in his sheepskin coat, a bottle in his hand, Daddy was striding toward the big house. He was singing "The First Noel" in his deep baritone.

1-in fields where-aire they lay-ay, keeping their sheep, bellowed the senator, raising the bottle to his lips. She had laughed, as at the antics of a clown. Daddy was in a very happy mood. She wished she could be out there with him, under the light of that timid little moon, singing Christmas carols.

No-o-ell, No-o-ell, No-o-ell, No-o-o-nell-ell! boomed her father, gaining access to the veranda and passing from her sight.

Born is the King of Is-ry-ay-ell!

Outside, on the landing, there was a small commotion. Her mother had fluttered anxiously out to confront the caroler. She heard the sound of shattering glass, as if Daddy had thrown the bottle across the tiled hallway, and then her mother's tense and pleading voice: "Tom, for pity's sake!"

The second Christmas at the Madigan ranch was strictly a family affair. Inga served breakfast to them on trays in the drawing room, so they could open their presents beneath the lights of the great spruce. Her natural, child's greed had made her wild with pleasure on these occasions. Wonderful things would emerge from beneath the colorful paper and gilt bows —things she had not even known she had wanted! Hooded jackets of arctic fox-fur that were softer and more protective than any jacket she had ever heard of; huge stuffed animals from FAO Schwarz in New York; marvelous, undreamt-of toys and games; chemical sets that would enable her to make her own perfume; a set of bow and arrows made entirely of Western African ivory!

The best was always saved for last. Carlotta would open a small envelope and find that she was now mistress of some amazing object to be found in the stable or paddocks. Usually it was a pony, added to the string she already owned, but once her daddy had fooled her and had given her, instead, a tankful of gorgeously colored salt water tropical fish.

The fish had been a mistake. Senator Madigan had ordered them to be flown in from San Francisco. They were peculiar and entrancing creatures, electric blue and acid yellow, and they had all died, belly-up, within a week.

Carlotta, flushing the lovely, inert things down the toilet, had reflected on the cruel nature of imperfection. The fish died because they were not able to acclimate themselves to a Montana world. Their inability to adapt marked them as an inferior species.

Wasn't she an inferior species, also, running to Lee's mother whenever something attacked her? She hoped her father would never find out that she had been stung by bees, or bruised by boulders in a running stream. For him, she wanted to be perfect. His perfect daughter, immune from the random calamity that strikes lesser mortals.

At Christmas it was easier for her to be perfect, because there was so much pleasure. It had even been a pleasure to go to church, after the opening of the gifts. Normally, she did not enjoy church. Her mother went nearly every Sunday, and when they were in Montana Martha attended the Episcopal church in White Sulphur Springs. Her father was something known as a "lapsed Catholic," but, as she had once overheard him explaining to someone, a man in politics could not afford to be a lapsed anything. On important church holidays, Christmas and Easter especially, Senator Madigan always appeared in church with his wife and daughter.

Everyone in White Sulphur Springs, whether they were Democrats or Republicans, loved living in such close proximity to a United States senator. Church attendance swelled to such overflow proportions on Christmas that little folding chairs had to be added in the back of the nave, and cynics said the people came in such numbers not to be near to God, but to be near Tom Madigan.

All Carlotta knew was how proud she felt to be sitting with him in the pew. He was forced to sit quietly beside her—there was no way he could leave her, not in church. Sometimes, when the minister droned on for too long, he would catch her eyes and almost, but not quite, wink. And after the service was over, when everyone wanted to shake his hand and get close to him, it was wonderful to know that she need do nothing to get close to him—all she had to do was exist!

Once her mother had been forced to stay away from church, on account of a number of guests who had come to stay with the Madigans over Christmas. Carlotta resented them, even though one of the women, Mrs. Harrow, fascinated her. The holidays were supposed to be a private time for families, and the six added adults seemed an unnecessary intrusion. Nevertheless, the situation had one very attractive bonus. She got to go to church with her father alone, and afterwards, when he greeted his constituents on the steps, she stood in the place normally allotted to Martha. She felt nearly dizzy—perhaps it was the overpowering smell of the dozens of extinguished candles—and she leaned against him a little.

"You know my daughter, Carlotta," he would say, and Carlotta would smile and shake someone's hand, trying to do it as gracefully as her mother did, hoping not to fail him.

Now she remembered something unpleasant, lurking somewhere in this happy memory, something that had happened later in the day. It had vaguely to do with Mrs. Harrow, whose fascination for Carlotta lay in the fact that Mrs. Harrow was the only grown-up lady she had ever seen who behaved exactly like a child. Alicia, that had been her name, but everybody called her Leesie. She had very black hair, and she wore it perfectly straight, like an Indian, but Mrs. Harrow's hair was so fine it looked like silk. She had big, greenish eyes, and talked in a tiny soprano whisper.

Although she wore many jewels, like the other women, they only made her look more childish, as if she were a little girl who had borrowed her mother's jewelry. Although she smoked incessantly (her cigarettes fitted into a pearl holder) and drank whiskey sours, she seemed closer in age to Carlotta than the others. She had a habit of sitting on the floor, hugging her knees, and looking up at whoever was talking with wide eyes and parted lips. Sometimes she bit her bottom lip in excited wonderment.

Carlotta had known Leesie Harrow in Washington, and the first time she had seen her, she had honestly thought there had been a mistake. The tiny creature who had been presented as Mrs. Harrow could not be a grown-up. She must be Mrs. Harrow's daughter, a girl a few years older than Carlotta, who had been ten at the time. But moving closer she had seen the amazing proof of Mrs. Harrow's adulthood: tiny lines radiated from the corners of her eyes and bracketed her unpainted mouth. The face might be a doll's, but it was not a child's. Carlotta had been disappointed, and then—when she saw Mr. Harrow—relieved. He was bald and jowly, as clearly adult as his wife was not.

On the Christmas when she and her father had returned from church alone, the drawing room was full of their houseguests. She could hear the clicking of ice cubes and smell the smoke of their many cigarettes before they even entered the room. Leesie Harrow was kneeling in front of the fire, dressed in red velvet, and she was holding her glass up to be refilled. All of them appeared to be drinking scotch, even her mother, except for Bertie Craig, Martha's personal maid. Bertie was always included at Christmas dinners, because of her loyalty and devotion to Mrs. Madigan. Bertie and Martha shared secrets, Carlotta knew, but she could not imagine what they were. Bertie was sipping the hot mulled wine Inga had made in a huge pot, and on the bosom of her gray suit was pinned a little brooch of holly.

The tension in the room escalated when her father stepped into it, and everyone seemed to be shouting for attention. Some jokes were cracked about his religious duties, and an immense drink was poured and put into his hand. He drank it off in one long gulp, and another appeared. Belatedly, everyone *ooooh*ed and *ahhhh*ed over Carlotta, and a man named Harry Spence came lurching over and demanded a kiss on the cheek. He smelled of whiskey and nicotine, and when Carlotta placed her lips obediently against his prickly cheek, he smiled idiotically.

"How old are you now, Carlotta?" Harry Spence asked.

"Thirteen."

"You're going to be a heart-breaker, isn't she, Vera?"

Mrs. Spence, who hadn't heard him, merely smiled and waggled her fingers in Carlotta's direction. As an afterthought, she blew Carlotta a kiss, crinkling her eyes in that way of adults, mistakenly thinking that squinched-up eyes denoted affection and sincerity.

Leesie Harrow was the only one who did not try to make a fuss over Carlotta. As always, she ignored her, unless their paths crossed directly, and Carlotta felt grateful for this honest expression of disinterest.

Even in the drawing room, the smells of the turkey and Inga's chestnut stuffing were deliciously strong. Carlotta was hungry and thought that surely they would be called to table at any moment. Twice Inga appeared, and twice she was sent away, as fresh drinks were poured. Martha's face began to stiffen. Her smile became the painted-on grimace of goodwill Carlotta had seen before, and her eyes darted furtively around the room, lighting on her husband. The senator was having a fine time, drinking his whiskey and holding forth to various clumps of people. The tray of hot hors d'oeuvres had long since disappeared, and Carlotta seized a stalk of celery stuffed with blue cheese and gnawed at it hungrily. Her stomach rumbled in an embarrassing way, but the noise in the room covered it.

When Inga appeared for the third time, looking desperate, the senator was hunkered down near the fire, talking to Leesie Harrow. He had his arm flung around her in a friendly sort of way, and when he heard Inga's imploring voice he looked up in irritation.

"I do think we should go in, Tom," Martha said coldly. "Turkey dries out so *frightfully,* you know."

Bertie Craig nodded.

Carlotta saw something frightening in her father's face then. It seemed to her that he was about to say something, heedless of her presence, that she would rather not hear.

"I'm starving!" she cried into the silence. "Daddy, I'm just about to die of hunger."

It worked. Her father's eyes came into focus, sliding away from her mother, from Inga, from Leesie Harrow in her red velvet dress, and met his daughter directly. "We can't have that, princess," he said, rising to his feet in one long motion. He gave her his arm, crooking it elegantly, and led her in to the dining room.

In some way, a way she could not grasp, she thought she had saved the day. The turkey was a little drier than any other Christmas turkey she could remember, but it was edible. None of the grown-ups seemed to notice, anyway. After the long meal, they went horseback riding or took naps, according to their dispositions. She escaped to Lee's during the long, dull, anticlimactic hours of the late afternoon, and when she saw the houseguests again they were dully nibbling at the cold buffet supper and announcing their intentions of early retirements to bed. Even the galvanic Leesie seemed subdued and morose.

Carlotta, too, went to bed early. If she hadn't awakened toward midnight, and gone out along the landing to determine who was still awake, she would never have heard the muffled sobs from behind the closed door of Bertie's room. Why was Bertie crying?

"Now, Martha, dear, don't carry on so," Bertie's voice said

strongly, lovingly, from beyond the door. "It will all look different in the morning, dear. You know it will."

The sobbing abated a little, and Bertie's voice had lowered to an inaudible pitch. She was making comforting sounds, inarticulate cooings. The weeping woman was Carlotta's mother, then. It could be no one else. Carlotta had fled back to her room, feeling that she had heard something she had never been intended to hear. Her mother's sobs affected her powerfully, but she told herself that they had to do with something she was not meant to understand. It had to do with the outsiders, Leesie and her group, who had invaded a Madigan Christmas and spoiled it.

They had stepped across the invisible boundary, and robbed this Christmas of the magic and harmony a Christmas on the ranch was made of. It was not their fault. They didn't know any better.

Remembering those enchanted Christmases in Montana, she began to feel crushed by loneliness. The disparity between what she remembered and the reality of the present—the empty house in Georgetown, its lord cut down—was too great. She didn't know she was crying until a tear fell on Lee's letter, dimpling the surface of the paper. Another followed, and another, and she thought of the mistletoe twined in the elk's antlers, and the time she and Daddy had snowshoed together on Christmas Eve, and then she was weeping as a small girl might, noisily and with real despair. It was the first time she had cried since her father's death, and she allowed herself the luxury because she couldn't stop herself.

When she had cried herself dry, she blew her nose, doused her red face in cold water, and went to the phone to call Rachel Vere.

THREE

"YOU MEAN YOU REALLY DON'T KNOW ABOUT *POPPERS?*" Rachel, who had been reclining indolently on her plum-colored chaise longue, sat up indignantly. Her big dark eyes were wide with shock. "Crickey, Carlotta, where have you bloody *been?*"

Carlotta smiled at her friend's outrage. She also smiled at the "crickey" and the "bloody." Rachel had taken to peppering her speech with English expressions, so that at times she seemed to be all the Beatles talking at once. She knew Rachel had learned these mannerisms from her rock-musician lover; Rachel had always been wonderfully adaptable, like a chameleon, and was able to take on any identity she liked with ease.

"For your information, love, a popper is something you inhale, sort of. It's amyl nitrate, for heart patients to use when their hearts go all wonky. You simply snap this capsule open and breathe it in and your heart beats like there's no bloody tomorrow! See?"

"Not really," said Carlotta. "Why would you want that to happen?"

"Give me strength," Rachel sighed, sinking back to her languid position. She put one arm over her eyes, as if the brilliance of Carlotta's ignorance had blinded her. "In orgasm," she said, speaking from behind the lace sleeve of her see-through kimono, "the heart naturally accelerates. If a person inhales a popper on the brink—the very *brink*—of climax, then the orgasm is much more powerful. It sort of beats, and beats, like the wings of a huge bird. Right?" She peered out from behind her sleeve hopefully.

"I don't know," said Carlotta. "It sounds kind of awkward."

"How like you to characterize sex as awkward."

"I don't mean sex," protested Carlotta. "I meant the popper thing. There you are, having terrific sex, and suddenly someone has to leap up and snap open a capsule and press it to your nose. It's not very romantic."

"Good sex has nothing to do with romance," said Rachel wearily. "Haven't you learned that yet?" She sat up again and fixed Carlotta with the same baleful stare Carlotta remembered from their school days in Switzerland. Even at sixteen, Rachel had been an educator. She had a passion for teaching. "Whores have always known about poppers," she said. "We could all learn just *volumes* if we studied the techniques of prostitutes."

Carlotta, who had been quite amused by her friend's sexual ramblings, was brought up short at the thought of prostitutes. They reminded her of Joly Nesbit, and the sorts of people she had never expected to encounter at Rachel's sedate east-side apartment in New York. Rachel and Cotter had settled into the privileged life for which they had always been intended—a life circumscribed by social events which were later written up in *W* and offered to the public as proof that an American aristocracy did still, in fact, exist.

Rachel came from old money, and Carlotta, who had met her family many times, always wondered how people as dull as the Windolms could have produced a daughter as vibrant and eccentric as Rachel. They were perfectly ordinary people, aside from their vast wealth, and so conservative that they had disapproved of Rachel's friendship with the daughter of a Democratic senator. It was possible that Rachel's very wildness was a reaction against such rigid and boring parents, but the Windolms were too stupid to notice, and she had, in the end, pleased them by marrying the Right Sort of Husband.

Cotter Vere was handsome, young, rich, conservative, and a banker. He was also, Carlotta thought, rather uninteresting, and showed signs of being a bit of a bully. His weapon was sulking.

"Do you and Cotter use those popper things?" she asked.

Rachel whopped with laughter. *"Cotter?* Are you daft, love? Cotter thinks he's having a big, pornographic time if I get on top. He talks a lot about sex, but he's extremely limited when it comes to performing. No, Graham is the one who introduced me to them. I can hardly wait for you to meet him. He's marvelous."

Carlotta had seen photographs of Graham, the rock musician from Lancashire, and didn't consider him to be marvelous at all. He had long, white-blond hair, like an albino, and a sneering mouth. The group he belonged to was called Yobbos, and they had one hit single, "Toad in the Hole." She didn't think Mick Jagger or Paul McCartney were losing any sleep over Graham.

Rachel had taken a joint from the little malachite box on her dressing table. "Do you know," she said, lighting it and inhaling deeply, "do you know that when we were first married Cotter wanted to know how many lovers I'd had? I said three, and he was very annoyed. Can you imagine?"

Carlotta laughed. She knew Rachel had had more than three lovers before she was sixteen. It was one of the first things Rachel had told her. She would never forget their first meeting. She had been wandering aimlessly in the school gardens at Neuchâtel, homesick and whiling away a free period before her Latin class. A trio of clannish French girls had just passed, paying her no mind, and she had been thinking that Switzerland, for all its beauty, was too tame and neat to please her. She preferred wider spaces and broader skies.

"Hello," a voice had said, "what on earth are you thinking about?"

"Montana," Carlotta replied, searching for the owner of the voice.

"Jesus—why would you want to think about a thing like that?"

There, half-hidden in a grape arbor, had been a small girl with exquisite features and extravagantly curling, tawny hair. She was wearing eye makeup, which was against the school regulations, and she was also smoking, which could get her expelled. "I'm Rachel Windolm," she said. "I come from New York City, where a girl has no trouble getting laid whenever she wants. Switzerland is awful, don't you think? I had five lovers last year, and now all of a sudden I'm supposed to be celibate. How about you?"

"My name is Carlotta Madigan, and I'm from Montana and Washington, D.C."

"No, no—" Rachel had shrugged impatiently. "How many lovers have you had?"

She'd considered lying, but she was a very poor liar. She tended to blush. "None, actually. I'm a virgin."

The huge, dark eyes had regarded her with pity and contempt. "That's very unhealthy, you know. I hope you masturbate, at least."

Carlotta had been outraged, but you couldn't be angry with Rachel. She simply didn't allow it. Within minutes she was enlisting Carlotta's help in an elaborate plot involving a seduction of Monsieur LaPointe, the choirmaster, and before the end of the day they had become friends.

Of course, Monsieur LaPointe had merely been a joke because, as Carlotta soon found out, he was elderly and rotund and sported an immense, burgundy-colored nose. There had come a time, during their second year at the school, when Carlotta had had to help Rachel out of a Monsieur LaPointe-type scrape, but in the early months of their friendship Rachel had been all talk and no misdeeds.

She had confided endless secrets during study hall, telling Carlotta the most intimate details of her personal life, things which, if Carlotta had had similar stories to relate, would have caused her to blush with shame. Yet she did not judge Rachel, or think badly of her. Rachel made her feel tame and dull by comparison, and whenever Rachel said something that really shocked her, she found excuses for her.

Rachel, unlike herself, had not been sheltered by her parents. The Windolms were terribly rich, and nothing had been spared to see that their daughter had the finest clothes and toys and private schools. This was true of Carlotta, too, but there the resemblance ended. Rachel, she thought, had had no love. From what Rachel told her, Mr. Windolm was vague and rather dim, and he disliked touching his daughter. Mrs. W was a bit warmer, but Rachel maintained that her mother was a foolish woman who spoke entirely in cliches. As for Anthony, her brother, Rachel could not abide him.

"Anthony is a sadist," Rachel had said.

"What's that?"

"Someone who enjoys inflicting pain, *ma pauvre*. Jesus, but you're ignorant, Carlotta. Haven't you ever heard of the Marquis de Sade?"

For the next ten minutes, Carlotta had been regaled with the most harrowing details from the Marquis de Sade's erotic life. "I'm sorry, but I really don't believe you, Rachel. I don't believe your brother ate dinner on your naked back."

"Of course he didn't, stupid—a sadist merely takes his name from the Marquis de Sade. Anthony is more a psychological sadist. For example, when I was twelve, he warned me that soon I was going to die from a rare disease. He said I would start to bleed from deep inside. 'In your thing,' was how he put it—he's not very bright—but what made it so ugly was the look on his face. He was hoping to scare me to death."

"How cruel," said Carlotta, whose own mother had prepared her for her menses in a calm, rational, if slightly embarrassed, way.

"Well, of course it didn't work. I knew all about it, because the school nurse at my first boarding school told us."

"What else?" Carlotta asked, filled with morbid fascination. "What else did Anthony do?"

"He used to tie our old cook's shoelaces together, sneak up on her, crawling on his hands and knees, and then give a scream and she'd jump and fall over on the floor. He was also fond of calling people and saying their children had been killed in accidents. One time he killed a garter snake, in Newport, and put it in the toilet of my mother's private bathroom. She screamed for simply hours. I could go on, Carlotta, but I'm sure you get the picture. Anthony is *not* a nice person. I think it's because my mother is obscurely descended from Oliver Cromwell."

"What are you laughing about so privately?" the grown-up Rachel asked with asperity.

"It was a silent laugh of horror," said Carlotta. "I was remembering when you first told me about your brother."

"Darling Anthony. I'm so glad he's been removed to the Orient. He's supposed to be involved in world banking, but I think Daddy pays him to stay away."

"How are your parents, Rachel?"

"Much the same. My father moves in a perpetual alcoholic

haze, and Mummy is still the Queen of Cliche. Once, when I tried to intimate that my marriage was not all it might be, she gave her silvery laugh and said, I swear, 'Marriage is not a bed of roses, dear. It is a matter of compromise.'"

Rachel had perked up briefly. Possibly the hostility she felt for her family had dispelled the drugs, or held their effect at abeyance, because she said, quite lucidly, "I was thinking about our school days, too. In London, it was. There was an entire afternoon when I could think of nothing else. Laure, Trudi, Marie-Thérèse, deaf old Madame Calvet . . ."

"And did you think of Monsieur Burotti?"

"Him? Oh, Christ, Carlotta!" Rachel giggled and selected another joint. Languidly, she lit it and inhaled deeply. "Actually not," she said in her former, dream voice. "I was thinking more pristine thoughts. About friendship. You."

She didn't doubt that this was so. She had forgiven Rachel for many things because Rachel was a true friend. Beginning with M. Burotti, and culminating in her visit to Montana— they had never spoken of it, and perhaps Rachel had been so stoned she had managed to forget it—Carlotta had made allowances for Rachel's outrageous behavior.

She wondered if Rachel would ever change. At the present time, she seemed exactly like the schoolgirl who had captivated her in Switzerland. Rachel was as small and childlike as she had been at sixteen. Her hairstyle might be different, but she was still a wicked little girl, in spite of the fact that she was married and the mistress of a large and imposing domicile.

Mrs. Cotter Vere, stoned out of her mind and clad in an Oleg Cassini, was no different from Rachel Windolm, dressed in a gray school uniform and intent on shocking Trudi with some sordid bit of sexual esoterica. They were one and the same.

The current Rachel spoke airily of poppers; the earlier had delighted in shocking Trudi with mention of such things as French ticklers. "I should think you would want to tell Jacob about them," she would say, and Trudi would turn the color of brick and announce: "Our relationship is chaste."

"Bertrand," Rachel now said in a druggy, bemused voice; "I hadn't thought of him in years."

Bertrand had been Monsieur Burotti's first name. It sounded Italian, the "Burotti," but he was from Corsica, home of Napoléon Bonaparte. Monsieur Burotti was dark and passionate-looking, and none of the girls at the Académie could understand how he had slipped by. Did the authorities imagine that the girls would not take note of his considerable charms? He was short, it was true, but Napoléon had been likewise short. Lack of stature in no way implied lack of virility, and Monsieur Burotti was endowed with qualities which the lithographs of Napoléon clearly missed.

He had the kind of black eyes which were invariably referred to as "flashing," an abundance of wild, black hair which could only be regarded as romantic, and a compact, muscular body quite remarkable for its ability to look sensual in riding clothes. He could not be more than thirty years of age, and he was, dear God, the new riding master during Carlotta and Rachel's last year at the school. (The old riding master, a leathery and homosexual Englishman, had retired.)

The riding lessons offered in Switzerland were of the kind that bewildered Carlotta. The emphasis was on jumping, and something called *dressage,* during which the horses were required to mince and execute peculiar, constricted movements. It was not an activity she chose to enlist in. The saddles were Eastern, or English, as they were called at the school, and since riding, for Carlotta, had a wild, free, Montana feel to it, the riding in Switzerland did not appeal to her. She avoided the twice-monthly events called *gymkhanas,* and pined for Greyling, the mare who had replaced her pony, Sundance.

The Corsican, Monsieur Burotti, instructed the girls in horsemanship at every conceivable level. His stellar pupil was an English girl named Philippa who liked to hunt. She had brought her hard hat and pink coat from Oxfordshire. How, Carlotta wondered, had the wild, dark Monsieur Burotti—who reminded her of a slightly shorter edition of Heathcliffe from *Wuthering Heights*—schooled himself in such a restrained form of horsemanship as the county hunt?

"Don't be such a child," Rachel said. "He needs a job, and he knows which side his bread is buttered on. He'd teach needlepoint if it would bring in the bacon. Oh, Carlotta, don't you think he's *divine?*"

Rachel, who had learned to ride when she was a child, and who had always hated it *(those big, pumping haunches, and all that snorting, and the big, windy farts)* had enrolled in Monsieur Burotti's riding course as a rank amateur. She pretended not to know which foot to put into the stirrup and exhibited a pretty confusion as to whether her boot should point up or down. At first it seemed that Monsieur Burotti treated Rachel no differently than any of the other girls, but one day she returned from her lesson so flushed and excited that Carlotta felt sure progress had been made.

They locked themselves in the bathroom they shared with the girls next door and Rachel confided that she'd had a break-through. "We made real eye contact," she whispered. "Not the kind when he shouts 'Heels down, mademoiselle,' but a long, burning stare. I didn't look away and neither did he. It seemed to go on forever."

She demonstrated the way she had stared back at the riding master, and really Carlotta couldn't imagine how the man could resist her. Those immense, dark, yearning eyes, seeming even larger in Rachel's fox-like, delicate face—how could a hot-blooded Corsican ignore them? Carlotta had qualms, foresaw how calamitous it might be if her friend really did succeed in seducing Monsieur Burotti.

"I've decided that I'll have to act fast now," Rachel whispered. "He'll never do anything unless I initiate it. I think it has to do with some moral conviction or other. Probably he thinks it would be sinful to take a student to bed."

"But just think—if he were discovered he'd lose his job and you'd be expelled."

"I wouldn't care. It would be worth it."

"But *he* might care, Rachel. Jobs for riding masters must be scarce."

"Then we'll have to make sure we're not caught."

"*Alors!*" shouted Laure from the other side of the door. "*Je dois faire pipi!*"

That night in study hall, Carlotta's worst fears were confirmed. Rachel's idea of taking the initiative involved falling from her horse, faking an injury, and, while Monsieur Burotti carried her to the infirmary, propositioning him outright. Since it was all top secret, Rachel for once wrote Carlotta a note instead of simply speaking out loud.

Carlotta wrote back, warning Rachel that she could really be hurt and might not have to fake the injury. *At least let me show you how to fall properly,* she wrote.

In the end, Rachel's loony plan worked without a hitch, and all she suffered in her mock fall was a bruise on her right hip. She told Monsieur Burotti she was unable to walk, and when he picked her up in his arms she threw her arms around his neck and laid her curly head on his breast, where his heart was pumping wildly.

None of it would have worked if not for the fact that the stables and riding ring were in an isolated part of the school grounds, quite close to the gates and not observable from the chateau itself. "Don't take me to the infirmary, monsieur," she whispered in a low, thrilling voice. "Why not, mademoiselle," he inquired, "are you not injured?" Rachel swore she had said her heart was injured on account of loving him, and then she suggested he take her to his rooms above the stables and make love to her.

After a panicky, initial reluctance, dispelled by Rachel's hands, which were caressing the nape of his neck, Monsieur Burotti had done exactly as Rachel requested.

In the locked bathroom, after the others were asleep, Rachel concluded the tale of her triumph. "It was perfect! No one saw us but the stableboy, and Bertrand sent him to go after my horse. Then, when the boy was out of sight, we ran up the stairs to his rooms. Oh, Carlotta, he's so passionate! He called me *chérie amour,* and we rolled right off his bed. He has quite a lot of black hair on his chest. I've never slept with a hairy man before—it's like mating with a bear or something. Oh, how divine, not to be bored at school anymore!"

The affair went on for six weeks before the inevitable happened. It was always a risky business, since Rachel had to wait until the stableboy's attention was distracted before she could dart up the stairs. Once or twice bloody Philippa, the horse freak, had spoiled things for her. She had been hanging around the tack room on one occasion, and on another she was actually volunteering to help muck out the stalls. "Insufferable bitch," Rachel said to Carlotta. "I'd like to wring her neck."

Carlotta didn't like the danger or the intrigue itself, but she took to going down to the stables when Rachel's lessons were concluding. If Philippa was there, she would involve her in equine conversation, drawing her aside so Rachel's path would be clear. She babbled on about her father's Arabians, asked if Philippa had ever ridden a Tennessee Walker, and made the English girl wonder, aloud, why the knowledgeable American didn't ride more.

"I mean, if you're so keen," Philippa said, "it seems a pity you don't take more of an interest."

"An old injury, Philippa. I don't ride anymore."

"Bloody hell," said Philippa. "Were you frightfully smashed up?"

From the depths of the tack room, Carlotta saw Rachel go speeding across the inner courtyard. Safe. Carlotta shut her eyes and breathed a sigh of relief. "I don't like to talk about it," she said sadly. "If you don't mind."

It was rumored that Bertrand Burotti had a wife and several children stowed away in the town of Neuchâtel. Every Saturday, when the girls were allowed to descend to the town in Charibancs for an afternoon of relative freedom, Rachel speculated about Madame Burotti. Bertrand was elusive about the subject, implying at times that he was indeed a married man, and at others that he was a widower. It didn't matter to Rachel, who had no plans to marry a Corsican riding instructor, but it did rouse her curiosity. Bertrand was never on the school grounds on Sundays, and it was their theory that he went home to his shadowy wife, attended Mass with his family, and then paid what Rachel called a "conjugal visit."

"She could be any one of these women," Rachel would say, sipping at the thick chocolate in their favorite cafe, indicating the milling women on the broad avenue. "That one, for example," she would snicker, nodding in the direction of a fat young matron wearing unfashionable shoes.

"Or that one," Carlotta said on one occasion, stung by Rachel's seeming callousness. She was indicating a pretty blonde who was strolling by with a lovely little girl of about eight.

Rachel merely shrugged.

"Aren't you ever jealous, Rachel?"

"Well, of course not, Carlotta. What peculiar ideas you have."

"But you said you were in love with him."

"That doesn't mean I want to own him."

"Not *own* him—that's ugly. But don't you care if he sleeps with another woman, even if it is his wife?"

Rachel licked the little smear of chocolate from her upper lip. At that moment she looked particularly, endearingly, childish—angelic, even. "Not as long as he saves enough for me," she said.

Carlotta had a thought, an embarrassing thought, and bit her lip to keep from voicing it. Nevertheless, it came popping out a few moments later. "If I ever love a man, really and truly and wholeheartedly, I'm sure I would want him all to myself. I don't think I could bear having to share him. Not ever."

"Spoken like a true virgin," said Rachel. "When you've had a little experience, sweetie, you'll see it my way."

And then there had come a day when they had actually seen Bertrand's wife. There could be no doubt that the pleasant-looking, auburn-haired woman was Madame Burotti, because, along with the two young children walking with her, there was the incontrovertible evidence of the riding master himself, whose arm she held. They were laughing together, and Madame Burotti had—Carlotta would always remember —a silk flower pinned in her long, rippling hair.

Carlotta turned to Rachel, and saw in her friend's face a look of bewilderment. She thought Rachel was beginning to see that her lover had a life quite separate from the hasty and forbidden encounters in the quarters above the stable, but all Rachel said was: "What's he doing in town on a Saturday?"

The end of the affair had come unexpectedly. On a day in late April, when the snows were beginning to melt from the high peaks and the sun shone brightly on the grounds of the Académie, Carlotta left her last class of the day, Latin, and walked slowly down to the riding stables. Senior girls were allowed a measure of freedom, and nobody accompanied her. Today was one of Rachel's riding lessons, and Carlotta had a feeling of foreboding. It was Philippa's interference she feared, but when she got to the inner courtyard of the stables they were utterly deserted. Horses whickered from their paddocks and she could hear the dull thumps of their stamping hooves, but no humans were in evidence, not even the stableboy. Good, then. Rachel and Monsieur Burotti were already safe in the haven of the upstairs quarters, and she was not needed to act as spy or diversion.

She was about to turn around and make her way back to the chateau when she heard the chuffing of an automobile passing through the gates. It was still a removed sound, but something told her it was an important one. Many vehicles passed through the gates of the school, but they came at regulated times. Deliveries occurred in the mornings, and visits from family came on weekends. Rarely was there any traffic in the late afternoons.

The road was such that she could not see who the driver of the car was until the old green Renault was nearly upon her. Madame Burotti sat at the wheel, her face composed along grim lines. Her hair was drawn back into a no-nonsense bun, and she went wheeling into the stable courtyard with a practiced air. She was alone; no children accompanied her.

Some tragedy had occurred, Carlotta felt sure. One of the Burotti children was desperately ill, perhaps, and the riding master's wife had come to inform him of it. The lines were down at the school, as they so frequently and mysteriously were, and she had come to fetch him.

She pitied Madame Burotti and wished to help her, but at the same time she thought of what it would mean to Rachel— sweet, fragile, loveless Rachel—to be discovered naked in the riding master's fierce embrace. She would be expelled, sent home in shame for the third time, and obliged to pretend it didn't matter.

"Madame Burotti!" screamed Carlotta, loud enough to be heard by the sinners. "Madame Burotti, oh, please, help me!"

The riding master's wife, caught in the act of getting out of her Renault, turned an anxious eye in Carlotta's direction. "Mademoiselle?" she inquired courteously, clearly allotting her a small portion of time to make her case before she ran up the steps to her husband's apartment. Already she was headed in that direction. Her "Mademoiselle" was perfunctory.

Carlotta thought that Rachel, with her quick, supple way of moving, was by this time concealed in a cupboard, or underneath the bed, but she could not be sure. What if lovemaking rendered one incapable of movement, or worse still, deaf? Bertrand would surely have heard. His guilt must make him quiveringly alert. Carlotta cursed her lack of experience, and noted that Madame Burotti had gained the stairs. What if? What if?

She threw herself down on the ground. She tried to emulate the behavior of a girl from New Zealand who occasionally suffered *grand mal* seizures during chapel, and it worked. Madame Burotti came hurrying to her side, a deep furrow of concern marring her placid face. She knelt by Carlotta's side, and, foraging in her purse, produced a pencil, which she thrust into Carlotta's mouth.

It was very uncomfortable, and though she knew Madame Burotti was only trying to make sure she didn't swallow her tongue, it made her stop the charade instantly. "I'm going to be all right," she tried to say, and Madame Burotti withdrew the pencil.

"I'm so sorry, madame," Carlotta said. "Sometimes they are over almost immediately."

"Let me help you to rise," the woman said in heavily accented English. "I will take you to the place for the *malades*, in my car. It is only up the hill, yes?"

Carlotta did not want to go to the infirmary, but it seemed the perfect way to remove her benefactor from the stable area. She allowed Madame Burotti to lead her to the car, and when they were inside the riding master's wife turned to her and said, "How did you know my name?"

"I saw you in town with Monsieur Burotti once, madame. Your children are lovely."

Madame Burotti smiled, a small, secretive smile, and then said something so completely unexpected that Carlotta felt doubly guilty. "Bless you, mademoiselle. Another one is on the way now, or you noticed perhaps?"

At the infirmary door, a side entrance to the chateau that looked as if it had once been the entry to a dungeon, she climbed out of the car and thanked Rachel's lover's wife. She waved until Madame Burotti was out of sight, and then walked back to the main entrance.

A few moments later, Rachel came sauntering into the large and gloomy lounge, or common room. Not a hair on her head was out of place. "I hid in the tack room when she came back, until she'd gone up to Bertrand's quarters," she whispered. "What on earth happened? I heard you screaming."

They withdrew to the most remote and dim corner of the room, where Carlotta explained. Rachel stifled giggles, her face flushed with admiration. "I love you, Carlotta," she said. "I owe you a favor, anything at all, so long as we both live."

"We don't have to wait that long. I'm calling it in now." And then, fully aware of how righteous and pompous she sounded, Carlotta explained that Rachel was not to see the riding master again. At first, Rachel was indignant, but when she heard about the new life in Madame Burotti's body, she became, by turns, angry, pensive, and finally pliant.

"Okay," Rachel had said in a small voice. "I suppose you're right, Carlotta. The bastard always told me he never touched his wife. I didn't believe him, not really."

"We'll be out of here in two months, Rachel. It's not such a sacrifice."

"Too true, actually. I was getting tired of all that body hair—he was like a horsehair sofa. And there was another thing, a thing I never told you."

"What was that?"

"He smelled of garlic."

At the end of term, Carlotta Madigan and Rachel Windolm flew back to America, and freedom. They parted at JFK airport, where Carlotta was to take a connecting flight to Montana, and Rachel was met by a chauffeur who would drive her up to Newport. Like veterans of a violent and grueling foreign war, they held each other close in the arrivals section of the customs hall.

"Friends forever," Rachel had said. "Right?"

"Right."

"No matter how much time goes by, no matter what happens. Through thick and thin, and all that shit."

"For richer or poorer . . ."

"I don't think it will come to *that*," said Rachel.

"Poor Carlotta," Rachel said now, her voice a little slurred from the marijuana. "No dope, no sex . . . What keeps you going?"

"You know I get a headache from grass," Carlotta said. "I just don't enjoy it. And as far as sex is concerned, I keep my affairs to myself. I'm secretive. For all you know, I could be having a wild thing with Wu."

Wu was the Veres' Chinese cook, and Rachel laughed so hard at the thought that she rolled off the chaise longue. Cotter chose that moment to return from his work, and when he saw his wife howling and stoned on the floor, he gave Carlotta a look of disgust.

"Do you see what I have to put up with?" he whined.

"It's my fault," said Carlotta loyally. "I made her laugh."

"Oh, shut up, both of you," said Rachel. "We have some serious partying to do tonight."

Carlotta wakened at noon, feeling unrefreshed. Harsh winter light poured into the pretty guest room, and she could hear rock music pounding away in some other part of the apartment. She stretched, wincing. The serious partying, which had involved another couple and the inevitable spare man for

her, hadn't ended until six that morning. They had gone out to
dinner, and on to Aux Puce for dancing, and then everyone
had come back to the Veres'. Cotter had gone off to bed, and
Carlotta's last memory was of Rachel trying to organize a
game called Truth Strip.

"You say something you've done, something sort of unusual, like actually making love in a taxi, and then everyone
who *hasn't* done it has to take off an article of clothing."

Carlotta stayed for three rounds. Since she had never slept
with someone of the same sex, danced topless on a table, or
harbored incestuous feelings for a sibling, she had been
obliged to remove both her shoes and her necklace. "I'm
going to bed," she told them. "At this rate I'll be stark naked
in ten minutes."

She thought it was time to move on. She loved Rachel for
their shared past, but Rachel's life was as alien to her as life
on the moon. Her friend had provided a haven when Carlotta
was at her lowest ebb, and she appreciated it, but she had been
at the Veres' apartment for six weeks now, and she could not
remain as a sort of permanent guest.

In Washington they were selecting a jury for the trial of
Joly Nesbit. Rachel had hidden the paper from her, but Carlotta knew. She had passed newsstands, seen the banner headline on the *Mirror:* CRIME OF PASSION—A JURY FOR JOLY!

More than anything she wanted to escape the trial and all
the foulness that would be heaped on the memory of her father, but she was not a coward. She felt it was her duty to
remain until Daddy's murderess was brought to justice. Then,
and only then, could she be free to disappear. When Joly was
shut away forever, Carlotta would go to Europe and begin a
new life. She could not imagine what that new, free life might
be, but she knew she had to return to Washington for the trial.

It was a matter of honor.

Honor thy father. A dry, unhappy little laugh escaped Carlotta's lips as she sat up wearily in the bed. Could you honor
your father if he committed adultery and got himself killed for
his sins? It seemed you could. She went to the dressing table
and began to brush her hair. She dragged the brush listlessly
through the long, heavy masses. How much simpler it would
be to have shorter hair, even though the current fashion was
for long. Nearly ten years ago, she had wanted to cut it and

wear it in the pageboy style so many of the girls in Washington were sporting. She smiled now, remembering.

"Your hair belongs to you, honey, and you can do whatever you like with it," her daddy had said. "But personally, if I were a little girl I wouldn't cut my hair, ever. Not for as long as I lived."

"Never? Why not?"

He had crossed the room and taken the brush from her hand. "Because," he had told her, "then you wouldn't be able to do *this.*" Slowly, gently, he had brushed her hair, from the crown of her head to the ends of each tress. He gathered it up in his hands, as if it were some precious, rare fabric, and sifted through it reverently. "Such beautiful hair, Carlotta-girl. I sure would miss the sight of it."

Carlotta heard her mother tap at the half-open door. "Tom?" her mother called, "Are you there?"

Carlotta thought her father would stop brushing her hair when Martha came in, but he went on with his task, almost dreamily. She moved away a little, sensing that her mother would not find the scene to her liking.

Martha came in, her little social smile in place, but when she saw what was happening her lips pursed.

"We were just talking about whether I should cut my hair," Carlotta said. "What do you think, Mother?" She was trying to draw her mother in, make the hurt look go away, but her attempt misfired.

"What I think is that you are old enough, *quite* old enough, to brush your own hair, Carlotta. You should not require your father's services to groom yourself."

The senator chuckled and gave a few more strokes with the brush. "Calm down, Martha. She didn't ask me to do it. I had a sudden impulse. See how beautiful your daughter's hair is?"

Martha's hair had darkened to a still-lovely auburn, but unless she were to dye it, it would never again have the fiery brightness of Carlotta's. Suddenly, she could see into her mother's thoughts, and knew Martha was forcing herself not to touch her own hair.

"I don't care about my stupid hair," she said, feeling confused and saddened. For the first time she could see that her mother was no longer young. She was far from old, but the face Carlotta automatically saw when she looked at her mother was no longer the face she wore. Martha's lips seemed to have grown thinner, her nose sharper and, although she had no lines or wrinkles, there was a parchment quality to the skin of her forehead and throat. It was winter in Georgetown, and the harsh light made her seem unnaturally pale.

"I think it might be a very good idea to have your hair cut," Martha said. "As it is, it's just growing wild, and there are so many attractive new styles."

"No," said her father. Just like that. *No*.

"Why not, Tom?" The tone of her voice implied that she was fully aware of his reasons.

"She doesn't want to, so why should she be forced?"

"Carlotta just said she was thinking of cutting her hair, surely. How do you know she doesn't want to, when she's just implied she did?"

"She has changed her mind, darling. It is every woman's prerogative, and every little girl's. Isn't that right, Carlotta?"

"I guess so," she said. "I don't care." How could anything so simple have become so complicated? She felt a brief, rebellious flash of the feeling that sometimes came over her when her father was telling her what she wanted. She imagined herself shaving her head and knitting him a sweater of her hair. He could wear it every day, if he liked it so much, and nobody would have to quarrel about what to do with it.

She felt a heavy, dragging sensation in her lower belly, and knew that *it* would soon be here again. It had first happened that summer, when she was in Montana. At first she had thought she was getting stomach flu, but when she felt the wetness she knew. Martha had carefully prepared her for what would be happening any day now, and she raced to the little dressing room that adjoined her bedroom.

There, in the bottom drawer of a small chest containing underthings, was the pink belt and pad her mother had prepared for her. She peeled her panties down, noting with distaste that there was a rusty-looking stain, and carefully stepped into the belt. The pad felt huge and cumbersome between her legs, but she was grateful for it.

She couldn't imagine what to do with her ruined panties. Since it wasn't winter there were no fires to burn them in, and she couldn't ask the ranch's laundress to wash them for her. If she washed them herself, there was the problem of where to dry them without a maid seeing them. It seemed she had failed again. A cleverer girl, forewarned about the signals, would have put the pad on before any damage could be done. In the end, she cut her panties up in very small pieces and flushed them down her toilet. It took a long time, and when she had finished, the real cramps hit.

Indignantly, she paced her room, doubling over in outrage when a really bad one squeezed at her. Martha hadn't mentioned this part of the deal—she had said there would be "discomfort in the tummy region," but she hadn't added that it would go on and on.

She was afraid to go to her mother, knowing how fond Martha was of doctors. She thought she would rather be tortured to death than have white-whiskered Dr. Aul come over from White Sulphur Springs and peer at her *there*, if that's what they did. Lee might have been able to help, but she was in Butte with her older brothers, visiting some cousins. Anyway, Lee had come down with this business at the beginning of the summer, and was quite cheerful about it. It didn't seem to bother her much.

Lee's mother was the natural choice. If she could bring herself to tell Mrs. Redwing what was happening to her, Mrs. Redwing would be able to brew up a Cheyenne remedy. Maybe she could even reverse the whole process.

"You're looking pale, dear," Martha Madigan's voice said in the bedroom in Georgetown. "Is anything wrong?"

"No," Carlotta mumbled.

"Nonsense," her father said, rising from her side and going to his wife. "Carlotta looks wonderful, Martha, and so do you." She watched in the mirror while he drew Martha closer, his arm around her now. All three of them loomed in the looking glass. They were a lovely tableau. His arm was around his wife's still-slender waist, and even as Carlotta watched, his other hand came to cup her cheek in tender fingers. "My beautiful girls," Senator Madigan said, "my beautiful girls." What had been on their three faces in that moment? Martha had smiled, but beneath the smile there seemed to be fright. Carlotta could not know her own expression, but suspected it to be one of confusion. Daddy's look was one of pride and possession. It was his hands that were important, though. The hand that lay on the silk shantung of Martha's dress was relaxed, while the one on Carlotta's cheek was tense.

Carlotta closed her eyes. Mrs. Redwing *had* brewed her

something to drink, although it wasn't very exotic, and she had stroked her forehead and smiled into her eyes. "Congratulations, honey," she had said. "You're a woman now, you know."

They were common words, even, as Carlotta later understood, a cliche. Yet they had matched her need, were, in fact, infinitely more suitable than Martha's words, a day later, when she finally told her. "Well, for heaven's sake," Martha said.

When she opened her eyes, Martha was drawing her father away, speaking of the need to dress for dinner. There were going to be guests. Her hair was apparently, blessedly forgotten, and she watched them leave the room together. For her mother's retreating figure she felt a kind of respect. Martha had been a woman for a much longer time than she had. She deserved sympathy, but Carlotta wasn't sure her father knew how to be sympathetic when confronted with imperfections.

She felt it was a flaw in his character, but try as she might, all she could feel for him was overpowering love.

Such beautiful hair, Carlotta-girl. I sure would miss the sight of it.

A decade later, the hair was still there, more of it, even, and he was gone. "I suppose," she said to her reflection in the mirror, "I can never cut it now."

Even a trial lawyer as brilliant and celebrated as Jeremiah Tompkins found the matter of assembling a jury for Joly Nesbit difficult. The average woman was never going to sympathize with Joly, and men, while they might admire her more obvious charms, were bound to regard her crime with loathing. What would the world come to if every mistress whose man refused to marry her decided to take a carving knife to him?

That's what it came down to. Joly Nesbit had murdered the senator because, even with his wife out of the way, he did not intend to change their relationship in any way. How phenomenally naive she had been, thought Jeremiah Tompkins, to imagine that Tom Madigan would ever marry her. She had no proof of her assertion that the senator had promised to marry her if ever he became free, and Tompkins didn't believe it for a minute. If Madigan had been foolish enough to promise her marriage, he certainly hadn't put it in writing. All of his communications to his mistress had been short and businesslike, and they consisted of invitations to join him on trips to various out-of-the-way cities where he could stash her in a hotel.

Tompkins was puzzled by his client. The enormity of her crime, the impossibility of her thwarted hopes, indicated that Joly Nesbit was either criminally stupid or mentally ill, but she was really neither. Diminished capacity due to insanity would be laughed out of court. Miss Nesbit was not only sane, she was clever enough to perceive that the only way to save her skin was to let Jeremiah Tompkins mold her into a creature of pathos.

And she was attractive—a thousand times more attractive than any of the flashy pictures shown in the tabloids. Her beauty was of the frankly sensual kind women jurors instinctively disliked. Even if he dyed her platinum hair mousebrown and had her appear in court in a shapeless dress and oxfords, the beauty would show. She had been blessed with a double row of dark eyelashes, so that her eyes naturally appeared to be made up, and her fair skin was just as naturally radiant. These very blessings could prove her undoing. As if they weren't bad enough, she had the sort of body that managed to look sexier in the unbecoming prison garb than most bodies did dressed in their finest.

Jeremiah Tompkins was attracted to her, as he knew any man would be, and he thought Senator Madigan must have had some wild times in her bed. The male jurors would surely desire her, but that could cut both ways—some of them might feel so guilty for having a hard-on for a murderess they could go extra-rough on her. The ideal jury for Joly Nesbit was one he couldn't assemble in Washington, D.C. It would consist of twelve Las Vegas show girls who had all been the mistresses of famous, powerful, married men.

He laughed at the thought, startling his wife. He had forgotten she was in the room. "What is it, dear?" she inquired pleasantly. When he told her of his ideal jury she sniffed and said she didn't think anything to do with Joly Nesbit was amusing in the least. "I hope they gas the little whore," Mrs. Tompkins said with uncharacteristic crudity. When Jeremiah pointed out that they didn't gas people in the District of Columbia, his wife muttered darkly that death was too good for the Nesbit creature.

He had begun to think he would have to make Joly's sexuality work for her. If he could convince the jury that the woman before them was a victim of extreme passion, that she had lived for love of Madigan and nothing else, and that when he had dashed her dreams so cruelly she had reacted with the same extreme emotionality that before had gone into loving him, what then? He thought there was more than a little of the truth in that scenario, but he knew he would have to paint Madigan as a greater villain than he'd been. Madigan would have to taunt Joly in those fateful moments, perhaps call her low names, rubbing salt in the wound. What he had really done to arouse her murderous rage was laugh.

"He laughed at me," she had told Tompkins. "Not that big, booming Montana laugh he used in public, either. It was a mean, snotty little laugh. He was trying to get this sentence out—'Marriage is out of the question' was what he was trying to say, but he was laughing so hard it was like 'Marriage—ha ha, is out, oh, ha ha ha, of the *haw*—question.' It made me see red, Mr. Tompkins, the way he was so goddamned *amused*. I mean, we had been together ten years, right? Tommy was crazy about me, couldn't get enough, if you'll excuse me for saying so. That should have gone for *something*. He could have been nicer about it."

"And did you really believe, after his wife had died, that he would marry you?" Tompkins had asked.

"Not right away, of course. But later, after a decent period of time. Yes. I did. Why not? His daughter was grown up, and it's not like I could have tarnished his image. He was so popular he could have done *anything*, and they'd still love him and send him back to the senate every four years." She had asked for a cigarette at that point, and he couldn't help noticing the way she pouted her lips when she exhaled. It made him think of all the things that mouth could do.

"And did you love Senator Madigan?"

She had laughed, showing her pretty white teeth and shutting her eyes as if in the throes of orgasm. "Sure I did," she said. "I fucked—excuse me—him *exclusively* for ten years, didn't I? Women like me don't stay loyal to a married man for ten lousy years unless we love him."

"And you were, ah, loyal? There was nobody else in all that time?"

"Nobody," Joly had said with determination. "I devoted myself to that man. I considered I was married to him."

"And did you believe that he loved you?"

She had frowned, choosing her words carefully. "I was never sure about that. Like I said, he was crazy for me. Sexually, he adored me. That I know. I'm not sure he *could* love a woman, not in the way you mean. He respected his wife, but he didn't love her. He loved his daughter, but that's not the same thing. In the end, Tom really only loved himself. Himself and his ranch. But I'll tell you one thing. I'm the closest he ever came to loving a woman. I'm it. That's why it made me mad enough to kill him when he laughed at the thought of marrying me. It was so *stupid*, you know?"

Tompkins thought he understood. It wasn't an argument that would make a jury compassionate, but she had given him what he needed. From the rather crude intelligence of Joly Nesbit, he would construct a pitiable figure. A little girl from North Dakota (true), who had been abused by her step-father. (Partially true.) A little girl who had run away to Las Vegas at the age of seventeen and fallen in with mobsters and hucksters and made a disastrous early marriage to a compulsive gambler. (True—she had kept his name. Her real last name was Sorenson.) A distraught young wife who had become a show girl to pay off her husband's gambling debts, and then, when she had finally got rid of him, stayed on in the profession because it was all she had known how to do. Her beauty had been her undoing, and evil men had taken advantage of her. When she met Thomas Madigan at the Democratic convention (this was troublesome, since Joly had been working the convention as a call girl), the confused little girl from North Dakota at last met the man of her dreams. The powerful senator had dazzled her, and she had been content to be his back-street woman because of the overpowering love and gratitude she felt for him. At last the little girl saw some meaning in the life that had been so hard, and pledged her own life to the man she loved. For ten years she lived only for him (true, apparently, although hard to swallow) and was content to inhabit the shadowy world of the illicit mistress, while the Great Man's public love flowed toward his wife, his daughter, and his country, not to mention the great state of Montana. And, ladies and gentlemen of the jury, when this man's wife died, and his young mistress dared, *dared*, timidly, to suggest that one day the man who professed to love her might marry her—what happened? Did she answer her suggestion with the respect and affection her position in his life would seem to have merited?

Or did he, in the gentlest possible manner, inform her that a United States senator could not, in all probability, marry an uneducated girl whose naked body had graced half the runways in the strip joints of Las Vegas? Or, again, did he assure her that he had no plans to remarry but that she would always hold a special, treasured place in his life? He did not. The great and privileged senator did not respond in any of these ways to the anxious little show girl who had loved him for a decade. What did he do, ladies and gentlemen of the jury?

He laughed.

Carlotta stared at Joly Nesbit with a horrible fascination. It was as if her eyes refused to rest anywhere but on the face of her father's killer. Joly was so much smaller than she had imagined. Where was the monstrous sensual creature whose photograph she had seen so often? Joly wore a black dress with a little white collar, and her blonde hair had been twisted in a chignon at the nape of her neck. She was pale, yet somehow radiant, and Carlotta's hatred—so strong and bright when she entered the courtroom—had nothing to feed on. Was it really this *girl* (for Joly looked not much older than herself) who had taken up a carving knife and stabbed her father to death? Was it she who had opened her legs and received Carlotta's daddy time after time, for ten years? It didn't seem possible. Joly Nesbit sat very quietly, hands folded like a good schoolgirl, listening with apparent intelligence to medical evidence about the angle at which the knife had entered the dead man's body.

Carlotta felt that *she* was the fugitive, and could not understand how such a thing could be. She was staying at a little hotel up in back of DuPont Circle, where she wasn't likely to be recognized. She had thought she would follow the trial from afar, watching television and reading the papers. She had believed that nothing could lure her out to the courtroom, where prying reporters might shout their noisy questions in her face, yet here she sat. There had been the need to see Joly Nesbit, and it had been so strong she could do nothing but obey it. She had thought that some of her hatred might be purged, in some primitive way, by laying eyes on the woman she wanted dead. Instead, she found herself confused and sickened.

It was almost as if she had *known* Joly at some time in her life, but this was clearly an impossibility. Her father would never have brought the two of them together, and if she had ever glimpsed her by accident she would remember. It wasn't that Joly was familiar to look at, so much; her face brought forth no memories and she looked like no one Carlotta had ever seen. Yet there was that feeling that she had spent time with Joly, spoken to her, even. She felt, unreasonably, that when Joly spoke, if ever she took the stand, it would be in some other language than English.

Jeremiah Tompkins, the celebrated attorney, was rising for cross-examination.

"Dr. Blye," he purred in his most ingratiating voice, "you have testified that the wounds to the deceased's chest seemed almost randomly inflicted. Would you say that the pattern of attack was quite unlike that of an attacker conversant with the lethal properties of a sharp knife?"

"I'm not sure what you're getting at," said Dr. Blye.

"I am suggesting," said Jeremiah Tompkins, "that the stab wounds inflicted on the person of Senator Madigan were the result not of murderous intent, but of hysteria."

"Objection!" shouted the prosecuting attorney. Joly looked down demurely at her hands.

"Looks like butter wouldn't melt in her mouth," whispered a woman behind Carlotta to her companion.

"Bet the senator did, though," snickered the second woman.

Carlotta felt bile rise at the back of her throat. It had been a mistake to come here. She rose and left the room blindly, climbing over people's knees and not bothering to apologize. It might be her duty to know what was going on at the trial, but she would never come to the courtroom again. She didn't want to be in the same room with Joly, or overhear the vile, disgusting comments of the cold-hearted people who saw the trial merely as a lewd entertainment.

Before going out, she tied the plain scarf over her bright hair again, and put on a pair of big dark glasses, the kind Jackie Kennedy wore. She had never exactly been a public figure, and she hoped to elude reporters. She thought they were all back inside the courtroom, anyway, but she couldn't be too cautious.

She stepped out into the cold air gratefully. A damp wind was blowing off the Potomac, making her shiver. She headed for a taxi, glad that no reporters seemed to be loitering.

By the end of the first week of the trial, the reporters had discovered her hotel. No matter what hour she exited or returned, a little knot of reporters would be lying in wait. "Miss Madigan! Miss Madigan!" they cried out, at first eagerly, then piteously, and finally with anger. Carlotta simply refused to acknowledge their presence in any way. She stared straight through them, and once, when a particularly insistent little man blocked her way, standing between her and the door, she pushed him aside with all her force.

She had made an enemy of him by that action, and he abandoned all pretense of civility and bleated out questions like: "Did your father have other girlfriends besides Miss Nesbit? Were you aware of his reputation as a lover-boy?"

Finally, she stopped going out altogether. She took all her meals in the hotel dining room, and paid the porter to buy all the newspapers for her each day. She was a prisoner in the hotel, and she would later look back on the two weeks of the trial as the strangest in her life.

She read the newspaper account compulsively, devouring every word, and also the lurid articles in the magazines. At six o'clock in the evening she turned the television on and listened to an investigative reporter's account of the day's happenings in the matter of the State vs. Nesbit. Her father's trial was taking precedence over everything—even the war in Vietnam. It was the hottest scandal to hit Washington in years.

"Today," the reporter would begin, nearly licking his chops, "Joly Nesbit, the shapely blonde show girl accused of murdering Senator Tom Madigan, took the stand. In answer to Defense Attorney Jeremiah Tompkins's questions about gifts given to her by the late senator, Miss Nesbit itemized a lengthy list of jewels, furs, and automobiles."

Sometimes, to the background of a court artist's sketches of Joly and the two lawyers, the announcer would repeat, verbatim, Joly's answers to the questions asked of her.

"And did you love Senator Madigan, Joly?"

"He was the only man I ever loved."

"And did you believe that he was in love with you?"

"He told me he loved me. I always believed that he did."

Carlotta's nausea at the exchange was even greater when Joly was asked how frequent her sexual relations with the senator had been. "When he was with me, in Washington, we made love every day at least once, sometimes more. He was very active for a man of his age."

When Tompkins moved on to Joly's tragic childhood and her early, pathetic young womanhood, Carlotta burned with indignation. He was trying to make them feel sorry for Joly, of course. It was glaringly obvious, and in the hands of a less skilled trial lawyer, it would have been ridiculous. But Tompkins was the best. He could wring tears from a stone. He could, and did, paint her father as a ruthless kind of man who had taken advantage of a confused young woman from a different social class.

If it hadn't have been for for Bertha Craig, Jeremiah Tompkins would probably have managed to get Joly off with a very light sentence indeed. He was not aware of the existence of Bertha Craig, or of her fanatical loyalty to the late Martha Madigan. Bertha did not step forward until quite late in the game, and when she did, she went to the prosecuting attorney.

Thus it was that Bertie, whom Carlotta had not seen since her mother's death, stepped reluctantly into the limelight and told the court that Joly Nesbit had been responsible for more than one death. She had also killed the senator's wife, albeit indirectly.

According to the newspaper, Bertie Craig wept a little on the stand, and said she had never intended to tell a living soul. It would have gone with her to her grave, but now she thought she had to speak out. Mrs. Madigan had been a fragile woman, but her stroke, at such an early age, had always seemed out of the ordinary. It was Bertha who found her that day, lying on the floor of her bedroom. The mail had been delivered, and Mrs. Madigan was still clutching a thick envelope in her hand. The envelope contained half a dozen prints of what Bertha referred to as obscene and pornographic photographs. The lovers had posed together, naked, for a time-exposure portrait of their fornication. *You can't give him what I can* said the neatly typed sentence which was the sender's only message. Mrs. Madigan had lived for two more days.

When Bertha was asked who the naked couple had been, nobody was surprised when she said it was the senator and Miss Nesbit.

All of Jeremiah Tompkins's brilliant strategy went out the window with her testimony. No juror would ever believe that Joly had acted in an unpremeditated and uncharacteristic fit of violence. Not now. Not a shred of sympathy could be mustered for her, in light of what Bertha Craig had told them.

For Carlotta, who had thought the worst had already happened, a whole new pit of suffering had opened up. For a while she thought she wanted to die, but she hardened herself with hatred and contempt, and after a while she felt nothing at all.

FOUR

Malcolm Fitzroy Kitson was a good-looking specimen of the English aristocracy and, what was more surprising, he was intelligent. He had taken two firsts at Cambridge and, at thirty, had just published a book on British foreign policy which men twice his age had praised. As the younger son of the Earl of Northumberland, this paragon was only the Honorable Malcolm Kitson; his brother, Lord Rupert, was the heir to the earldom. This had never bothered him, since he knew he was vastly superior to Rupert, and of an independent frame of mind.

Malcolm had smooth, pale hair and long gray eyes. He was lean and tanned and naturally graceful and athletic. He was engaged to Lady Belinda Muir, one of the beauties of her season, and there was no reason why he should not be perfectly happy and at peace.

Nevertheless, something was bothering him as he sat at the window overlooking the long garden in Northumberland. It had taken hold of him the very first time he had ever seen the girl, and it wouldn't let him rest. She was the friend of his younger sister, Fiona, an American Fiona had met in one of the noisy dancing clubs in London. Probably Annabelle's. Fiona had just fallen in love with her on the spot, declaring her the most original and wonderful female on the face of the earth. His sister was susceptible to these strong attachments, because she was insecure, but even Malcolm had been bound to admit, on meeting the American girl in London, that Fiona was right for once. Something in that cool, carefully composed little face had wrung his heart.

He looked for her now in the crowd of Fiona's friends holding a garden party on the fabled lawn. They were all drinking more than was good for them. Some of them were openly smoking grass, and a stoned game of croquet was taking place near the spot where a portion of the old Roman wall, Hadrian's Wall, crossed his father's property. The Honorable Julia Phipps seemed about to puke all over his mother's famous white rose bushes, and her younger sister, the Honorable Emily, was shrieking and hooting with delight while a chinless man dropped wild strawberries down her blouse.

His eyes moved away from that particular tableau. Caroline Moore would never be part of anything so juvenile. He saw his sister, plump and solemn, close in conversation with a group of aspiring playwrights from her London life. That was not the place where Caroline would be, either. His impression of her was that she was neither juvenile nor pretend-intellectual. He saw her as a misfit. She was about Fiona's age, twenty-four or -five, but unlike Fiona, she carried secrets with her. She was a mystery.

Malcolm's gray, English eyes located her at last. Caroline was leaning languidly against a yew tree, holding court. Three men surrounded her. At this distance he could not see the expression in her eyes, but he could see the way the white, Greek dress lay close to the curves of her body, and noticed how it complemented her long, smooth arms and legs, burned almost to the color of caramel from her sojourn in Sardinia. Her thick, reddish hair was loose today, streaming around her shoulders and running down her back. He thought there was something wild about her attitude, the way she lay against the ancient yew tree and accepted the admiration of her circle of admirers.

Who was she? Who was this troubling girl who roved around the world without any visible care? Her coldness of manner had led Malcolm to think, when Fiona had first introduced them, that Caroline Moore was one of those American heiresses one met from time to time. But she neither giggled nor seemed interested in advancing her position in English society; she was curiously old for her age, and Malcolm couldn't tell if Caroline were so innocent she did not understand her power over men, or whether she was so decadent she didn't care.

He toyed with an erotic idea. She was a courtesan who managed to seem well brought up, aristocratic even, and who had been sent to torment him and disturb the balance of his perfectly ordered life. For a while, this idea charmed him. But it took only another look to convince him that the object of his secret passion was neither predator nor professional. She was a victim, and every gallant instinct of chivalry rose up in him to convince him that he would be her savior. Everything that ailed her, he would cure. He would unravel the mystery that held her captive.

She dreamed she was diving into the sea, back in Sardinia, from a white, gleaming boat. Her body arched and soared through the blue air, and then she plunged down and the warm waters of the Mediterranean covered her. She swam straight down to the ocean's floor with the ease of a mermaid, and became aware of a beautiful sound, as of cathedral music. Brightly colored fishes and vivid coral surrounded her in her underwater paradise, and she swam on, following a dim figure that beckoned to her. Her heart seemed to beat with anticipation as she approached the figure, and then he turned in the water, smiling, and held out his hand to her. It was her father. His black hair waved like sea grass, and the tender love in his blue eyes was unmistakable. The lovely music swelled as they swam off together, side by side, turning to smile into each other's eyes. It was wonderful how perfectly in harmony they were. It didn't matter that they could not speak underwater—there was no need.

It went bad when the light began to fade and the water grew murky, and colder. She had trouble seeing him now, and felt afraid that she would lose him. She thought he was just ahead of her, and she struggled frantically to catch up with him. He was disappearing. She saw him give a little kick with his powerful legs, and then he was gone. She swam to where she had last seen him, and found that he had entered a black cave. Nothing was friendly now, or beautiful. The cave was full of menace. Each time she tried to swim into its entrance, the sea beat back at her, preventing her from going in. She was in despair now, and terribly afraid, and horrible dark shapes were moving toward her. She swam up, seeking the surface now, unable to find it. Slimy things brushed her body, teeth pricked at her, and she swam on, desperately, until she rose back to consciousness.

It was dawn, or just after. She lay in the huge bed, gasping for air, as if she had really been almost drowned. The horror of the dream seemed very real to her still, but she was no stranger to nightmares, and it was not the horror that would prevent her from going back to sleep. It was the peculiar sweetness of the earlier part of the dream, when she and Daddy had swum together in such tender harmony.

She got up and went to the long windows. Her room faced the garden, and she forced herself to become distracted by beauty. Everything—the leaves on the yew trees, the soft, clipped lawn, the closed petals of the roses—seemed etched in silver at this early hour. Later, when the summer sun burned down, the garden would be luscious and improbably green. Bees would drone and everyone would exclaim on their good fortune at having such fine August weather, there in the north of England, where it rained so often. Now was the magical time, when no one else could see the dawn-silver garden.

She splashed her face with water and hastily slipped out of her sheer nightdress and into one of the light Greek caftans she had bought during her time sailing the Aegean. It slid over her naked body with a feathery touch. She was so eager to feel the dewy grass beneath her feet she was out the door in seconds, combing her tangled hair with her fingers, speeding soundlessly down the long hallway, past the closed doors of Fiona and the many houseguests.

No one would be up for hours, not even the servants. She ran along beneath the stern eyes of generations of Kitsons, whose portraits lined the corridors and staircase, went scuttling through the morning room and drawing room to the library, where she knew there were French windows that would lead her to the garden.

The cool, moist grass felt just as she knew it would on the naked soles of her feet. Alone in the silvery morning, she ran the length of the garden, then spun in circles. It was a treat for her, something she had never done. Back home you never went barefoot, on account of rattlesnakes, and in Washington only the hippies did it. She had been barefoot on the decks of yachts, but never in the cool turf of England, and she found it delicious. When she grew tired of playing, she leaned against the smooth, cool trunk of an ancient yew and regarded Fitzroy Hall. She understood the English halls and castles. They were not so very different from the ranch in Montana. They were older, and they were draftier, but in the end they represented the same thing—the power of owning land. Fiona, whom she had befriended one night at a Knightsbridge disco, was the English version of herself as far as her heritage was concerned. But Fiona was still blessedly unaware of the tricks life could play, even on privileged daughters. Fiona had not been cut adrift.

She closed her eyes, willing self-pitying thoughts to fly away, and felt the cool dawn air caress her skin. Maybe if she remained in this exact position, she would be turned into a silver statue, immune from pain.

"I beg your pardon," said a cultured voice, quite near, and her eyes snapped open. Malcolm, Fiona's older brother, stood not five feet away, attired in a shabby-looking dressing gown. His feet, like hers, were bare. She felt a mild alarm.

"Are you Aurora?" Malcolm asked, coming closer.

She blinked, shook her head, straightened herself against the tree trunk. "No," she said. "I'm Caroline." It still felt strange to call herself by that name. On several occasions, she had failed to answer to it.

Malcolm smiled. "Aurora is the goddess of the dawn," he said. "I saw you from my window, and I mistook you for her."

"That's a terrible mistake," said Carlotta, smiling with the hard, bright smile she had perfected. "I'm no one's goddess."

"How do you know? You might be mine," said Malcolm.

It was a typical comment for a man who was gearing himself up to a major approach, yet she didn't take offense. There was something she respected about Malcolm. He was different.

"Do you have insomnia?" she asked. "What brings you out at such an early hour?"

"I like to write before anyone else is up," he said. "I was scribbling away when I happened to look up and catch your dance." He smiled again, and leaned one arm against the yew tree. "Do you perform it every morning?"

"Of course not," said Carlotta. "If you must know, I had a nightmare. I woke up and looked down on the garden. It had a soothing effect."

"A nightmare? How distressing. What was it about?"

"Oh, I don't remember. It's not important." In one blinding moment of clarity, she understood that Malcolm was in love with her. She had understood this about many men in her life, and particularly since she had become an exile, but Malcolm was the first man she felt as her equal. Here was a man worth trifling with! She felt desire rise up inside her, like sap in the twig. It was the desire to make a fool of this nice, handsome brother of Fiona's, to enslave and captivate him until he had no will of his own. She was dismayed and baffled by her own cruelty, but she could not deny it—she wanted to punish Malcolm for having such a happy life.

"Do you often have nightmares?" he asked gently.

Carlotta put her arms behind her head in a gesture designed to inflame him. The thin cloth of the tunic strained over her breasts; she might have been offering her body to him. "Dreams are something everyone has," she said. "It's boring to discuss them."

He nodded. "As it happens, I agree with you," he said. "I expect we agree on a number of things. I only asked because you interest me, exceptionally. Anything to do with you, any slightest thing, is of interest to me."

He was so frank and aboveboard it was hard to score off him. She smiled sweetly, showing him the pink point of her tongue. "It's also boring when men are interested in me," she said.

"Of course," he agreed, "because it happens so often. I've always thought that beautiful women must have a terrible time of it—all those men trying to think up original techniques to seduce them. But I'm not trying to seduce you, Caroline. I'm engaged to be married, you know. I am only determined to become your friend, because I want to help you."

"Do I look like a person who needs help?" she asked sarcastically. His words had annoyed her, especially the part about being engaged. It was as if he had thrown down a gauntlet.

"Yes," he said gently. "To me, you do."

Score one for Malcolm. She felt her color rising. For one terrible moment she thought it was possible he had found out her true identity. She had taken such pains to make sure no one in Europe could gossip about her, pity her, snicker behind her back. And if Malcolm knew? She felt a shiver pass over her body.

"What is it, Caroline?" He moved still closer, touched her cheek with gentle fingers. "Let me help you. You'll find I make a very loyal friend."

"I'm cold," she said. "That's all." She tossed her head to remove his hand. "I'm going back to bed," she said. "The garden was much nicer when I had it to myself." She walked away, back up the long lawn toward the French windows. She was aware that he could see the lines of her body through the thin cloth and felt his eyes on her back. She resolved to win the next round in their battle, and thought that in the end he would be very sorry he'd ever crossed swords with her.

She continued to feel his eyes on her in all the days that followed. Fiona had invited her to stay at Fitzroy Hall for the entire month of August, and she saw no reason to go away on Malcolm's account. The life here suited her very well. She had begun to grow tired of the Mediterranean and the Aegean, the predictability of the hot, white sun, the foolish people on the yachts who were only interested in drugs and sex. She had returned to cool, sensible England, and she did not want to be forced out by the Honorable Malcolm. She was convinced he knew nothing about her, after all, and she amused herself by tormenting him.

"I read of a most unfortunate thing in the paper this morning," Lord Kitson said one night at dinner. "There are terrible brush fires raging in southern California. Apparently they are most difficult to extinguish." He looked down the long table and singled Carlotta out with a sympathetic glance. "That is your state, isn't it, my dear? I hope no harm will come to your family's property."

"Daddy, Caroline is from *northern* California," said Fiona. "Those fires are simply miles away from San Francisco."

"Quite," said Lord Kitson, looking rebuffed.

"But how kind of you to be concerned," Carlotta said. "I do appreciate it, m'lord."

He brightened. "My geography is not what it should be, Caroline. I know Europe, of course, like the back of my hand, but I have only been in the eastern part of the United States."

Partly because she liked old Lord Kitson, and partly to tease Malcolm, Carlotta spent an hour with the earl after dinner, poring over an ancient atlas he had produced. She was wearing a summer dress with a round, low collar, and knew

Malcolm's eyes were struggling to stay away from the sight of her partially revealed breasts as she bent over the atlas. Lady Kitson was reading a glossy magazine, and Fiona and her other young guests were arguing about whether to drive to a pub in Morpeth, where there was dancing, or drop in on The White Stag in the village. Malcolm stood near an open window, staring out into the moonlit garden. She looked up often to make sure he saw how charming she was being to his father. She laughed sweetly at Lord Kitson's little witicisms, and occasionally their hands brushed as she pointed out Rhode Island or indicated Illinois. The earl was becoming innocently intoxicated by her proximity—so much so that Lady Kitson became alarmed.

"Andrew, dear, you must not monopolize Caroline's evening. I'm sure she is longing to go off with Fiona and the young people."

"Ah, yes, quite." He flushed and snapped the atlas shut. Fiona's party went off to Morpeth, but Carlotta pleaded a headache and remained behind. Soon she found herself alone with Malcolm, which was what she wanted. She picked up a magazine and pretended to read, crossing her bare, tanned legs conspicuously. She would make him say the first word.

"You're pretending to read," he said at last. "Just as you were pretending to flirt with my father."

"I like your father," she replied. "I wasn't *flirting* with him. What a typically male thought."

"Perhaps you like much older men, even if you don't like the rest of us?"

"That's a possibility," admitted Carlotta.

"They don't pose any threat."

"I can't be threatened."

"The person who can't be threatened in some way or another has not yet been born."

"Well," said Carlotta evenly, "at least you don't give up. There you stand, still trying to threaten me with your friendship, which I don't want."

"What do you want?" He was regarding her very intently, as if his life depended on her answer.

"Tell me about your fiancee."

Malcolm blinked in surprise, then came to sit in a chair near her. "Belinda is twenty-seven years old. We've known each other forever. She lives in London, helps run a shelter for battered wives in Chiswick. She has a title, and is considered a great beauty."

"Is she prettier than I am?"

"No one is," said Malcolm with a sigh. "You're very different. Belinda is small, and has black hair."

"Do you love her?"

"I should not be about to marry her if I didn't."

The garden by moonlight was even more beautiful than it had been at dawn. Carlotta and Malcolm seemed to move through liquid mercury as they strolled down between the rose bushes. The heavy odor of the flowers still lingered; it was almost too powerful to bear.

In a little ornamental pergola behind the stand of yew trees, Carlotta lifted her lips and kissed Malcolm gently on the cheek, as if he were a child. She was sorry for what she was about to do, but that did not prevent her from putting her palm in motion. Malcolm trembled at her touch. "You were lying when you said you didn't want to seduce me," she whispered. "You want me more than you want Belinda. More than you've ever wanted anyone. You're so dishonest, Malcolm."

He caught her to him roughly, and by the trembling of his body she knew he had at last been provoked beyond his endurance. She stared into his eyes, a half smile on her lips. His heart was galloping, and he gave a little moan and slit his eyes as if Carlotta were a devil he must not look at. "Who are you?" he whispered.

"Your destiny," she said with a little laugh. "Your downfall."

Score one for Carlotta.

Malcolm knew himself to be fatally afflicted, and understood there was nothing he could do but see the game through to the finish. He could not imagine what the outcome might be, and he thought it well might ruin him, but he had no alternative. The girl, Caroline, needed him. She didn't know it, but he was important to her in ways she could not begin to understand.

Her nasty, teasing little game—something he would not have forgiven in most women—seemed merely to underscore her need. She had been right when she called him a liar, but not entirely. When he had told her he would be her friend he managed to make himself believe it; some absurd, English, code of honor which he still obscurely subscribed to had prompted him to offer those chivalrous words. He had proposed himself as her knight, and she had rejected him. Was it because she felt only scorn for a man who could lie to himself about wanting her?

He did want her, of course, but not in the way she imagined.

He wished it were the eighteenth century, when he could buy her from her father and then marry her and force her to love him. It would be the only way to capture Caroline—to build a prison of love for her and force her to accept it. She had been wounded in some way, he guessed, and until he knew the nature of her injuries, he would have to proceed with infinite care.

On the day after she told him she was his destiny and downfall, he drove to London to confront his fiancee. Belinda listened gravely to what he had to say, and although she grew very pale when he described his obsession, she never reproached him. He felt a great love for her, the love he might feel for a sister he cherished a hundred times more than his real sister, and wanted to lay his head in Belinda's lap and beg for forgiveness. He could not even speak of this love, because he would have been obliged to add that the emotion he felt for Caroline Moore was so mysterious and powerful it could alter the entire course of his life.

"You're bewitched," Belinda said. "My poor darling, you're bewitched."

"I suppose I am."

"If she takes the spell off, remember me. I shall still be here."

He had driven back that night, his mind a jumble of images as he roared up the motorway. He saw the calm and lovely face of Belinda, whose husband he had planned to be, and mourned for the happy life they might have shared. But just when his sorrow seemed greatest, Caroline's presence filled the car and overwhelmed him. He saw her in all her guises—stretched languidly against the tree at dawn, pretending to pore over the atlas with his father, taunting him in the pergola . . .

Who are you?

It seemed clear to him that he must take her away, cut her off from the foolish, giggling company of Fiona and her friends. In some quite foreign place she would be dependent on him, and forced to surrender her secret.

"Tell me the truth, Caroline," he said to her, on the second day after his talk with Belinda. "Aren't you getting rather bored here?"

"Why should I be bored?" she asked coolly, favoring him with a falsely sweet smile. They were together in the dining room, the first to be down for breakfast.

"Because," said Malcolm, "my sister Fiona is a giggling little girl, despite her chronological age. Whatever you may be, you are not a giggling little girl. You don't have anyone to interest you here."

Caroline broke off a bit of toast with a dainty, distasteful gesture. "A nice way to speak of your sister," she said. "I'm quite fond of Fiona, actually."

"I love her, *actually*," he said, stressing the word to mock her. "Yes, Caroline, I love my little sister, but I should be driven to despair if I had to endure more than fifteen minutes of her company."

"Is this your roundabout way of suggesting I leave?"

"No, suit yourself. If endless, jolly rounds of croquet with the squealing, overgrown children of the aristocracy please you, who am I to suggest a break in the routine?"

Caroline sipped her coffee, eyeing him over the rim of her cup. She was interested, definitely, and it was a part of what he saw as her essential—if deeply buried—niceness that prevented her from masking that interest. She was not the bitch she appeared to be, but it was a role she could play to stunning effect.

"Where do you suggest I go?" she asked.

"Oh, Paris, I should think."

"Nobody goes to Paris in August."

"Exactly. We'd have it all to ourselves."

Caroline laughed, putting her chin in her cupped hand and narrowing her eyes with scorn. *"We?* Is that what you're proposing, Malcolm? To rescue me from boredom by taking me to Paris, when you know I find *you* boring? From the frying pan into the fire?"

"You don't find me boring," Malcolm said, trying to keep his hands steady as he buttered his toast. "You don't like me, I grant you that, but you're not bored. Nobody is bored by the prospect of being a man's downfall, Caroline. It must be rather exhilarating."

Caroline rose from her chair and went to the sideboard

where all the food reposed in large silver-covered dishes. She idly lifted a cover and selected some ham. Normally she ate rather sparingly, and he knew she was feigning interest in the food to cover her confusion. She returned to the table and looked at him with an unreadable expression.

"Look," she said, "forget all that. I'm sorry, Malcolm. If you want me to go away, I'll be glad to." She spoke in the candid tones of a thoroughly nice, American girl, and it broke his heart. "I can always fake a telegram—a sick aunt or something—and be gone in no time. That downfall business, well, it was just a stupid kind of joke."

"But I don't want you to go away. Not without me." He tried to speak steadily. "I can't forget what you said, because I have a sort of notion it might be the truth. I hope I can turn it around."

"And what about your fiancee? What about Lady Belinda? Does she allow you to take off for Paris with American strays?"

"I have spoken to her. I've told her about you."

This seemed to outrage her. "Why? I have nothing to do with you! How dare you hurt her when I haven't a single shred of feeling for you?"

"I have already done it; it can't be undone. I didn't want to have any secrets from Belinda."

"Or maybe you have an *arrangement?*" Caroline spat. "Something terribly civilized, where you have everything to gain and she has everything to lose? How gallant, Malcolm, how dignified."

Her disgust seemed so deep that it crossed his mind to wonder if Caroline were fleeing a marriage of the sort she described. It was possible, and he chose his words carefully. "No," he said. "We have no such arrangement. I don't approve of such things. I never dreamed you would come into my life, but now that you have, everything has changed. You have certain responsibilities toward me, Caroline, like it or not."

"And I suppose one of them is sleeping with you? I'm just not interested in that, Malcolm. It isn't only you—I'm not like other women; I don't care about that. I can live quite well without having some man pawing at me. I'm immune to all that."

"My dear Caroline," said Malcolm, retreating into his Englishness, "that is entirely a matter for you to decide. We shall have separate rooms, of course. I would never dream of forcing myself on you."

Fiona burst into the room, clad in a peppermint-striped dressing gown. "I woke up with the most frightful craving for kippers," she cried. "Do, *do* tell me there are kippers this morning?"

She was followed by Lord Kitson, who inquired, on seeing two of his offspring and a guest in the room: "Dear me. What have you young people planned for today? I believe there's a fete and gymkhana a few kilometers from here . . ."

Malcolm saw a look of tedium briefly cross Caroline's face, and he saluted her over his coffee cup to underscore his point.

The next day he went to London, ostensibly to spend some time with his fiancee, and a telegram arrived in Northumberland, informing Miss Moore that her first cousin, Lucy, had been taken ill in that city and would appreciate Caroline's presence. Malcolm flew to the deserted city of Paris, took two suites in the Georges V, and hoped desperately that he had done the right thing.

When Caroline arrived, she telephoned him from her room, saying she was dead tired and planned on retiring immediately. Hearing her voice, his body convulsed with relief. This was a war in which very small victories were important. She was here, in Paris, and even if she planned on maintaining that peculiar, teasing aloofness, he had succeeded in moving her across the English Channel.

Here, where his father could not come doddering in, where his sister could not lay claims to a friendship which did not, in fact, exist; here, in this neutral territory, he had a chance of discovering her.

"I haven't been here since I was a child," she told him the next morning, when they met for breakfast. "We used to come to Paris fairly often, and we always stayed in this hotel."

"Do you mean with your family?"

"Yes, or sometimes just with my father."

"What is he like, your father?"

She tensed at the question, and then said: "Just like everyone else." Then she picked up her cup of chocolate and ended the conversation.

It was hot and sultry outside, and Paris was, as they had

known it would be, nearly deserted. The chestnut trees along
the Champs Elysées looked dusty, and the few American tourists appeared hot and out of sorts. Caroline never complained
of the heat, and never looked less than fresh and composed.
She walked beside him in her high-heeled sandals, wearing an
endless procession of sliplike summer dresses that left her
lovely throat and arms bare. Surprisingly, she requested to go
to the Louvre, which she had last seen at the age of fourteen,
and insisted they spend the entire afternoon.

She became quite vocal about the paintings, and Malcolm
let her talk, even when she was telling him things he already
knew, for the pleasure of hearing her speak on a subject that
excited her. "We mustn't forget the Gauguins," she said solemnly. "They're out in back, in the Orangerie, if I remember."

She stood in front of one of the Gauguins for a long time.
It was a young Polynesian girl, bare-breasted and holding a
plate of fruit. "Is that your favorite?" he inquired gently.

"She reminds me of someone who was once a great friend
of mine, like a sister."

"A Polynesian friend?"

"An Indian. A Cheyenne."

This surprised him, but he knew enough now not to probe
the small confidences she offered up. She would withdraw,
become resentful and aloof. Instead, he asked her if she had
ever wanted to become a painter.

"But how could I?" she said. "I have no talent. The world
doesn't need any more untalented artists."

At Notre Dame, she climbed the shallow, endless stone
steps to the roof, saying she wanted to see the gargoyles
again. He knew he would never forget when, finding the exact
gargoyle she had come to see, Caroline leaned out and placed
her hand on the monster's head, smiling a small, secretive
smile. He would always be able to see that smile, the look of
her young, slender hand—so smooth and fragile against the
ancient stone—as she patted the gargoyle's head. And something else. A bitter look had passed over her face, her hand
had dropped away, and she had turned and said to him in a
toneless voice, "Let's go back down now."

Sometimes, sitting in cafes and sipping Pernod or Cinzano,
she would open up a bit. He had earned her confidence by
being the perfect friend, demanding nothing, and parting from
her at night without so much as a hint of regret about not

being admitted to her bed. It was a gradual process. At first she questioned him about his book. Had it been very difficult to write? Did he enjoy the writing, or did he see it as a chore? She listened attentively to everything he said and occasionally, shyly, offered small insights of her own.

She was most relaxed at dinner, at the end of a long day, and then, warmed by wine and slightly flushed, she sometimes regaled him with anecdotes about the school in Switzerland she had attended. She could be quite witty, and Malcolm laughed with delight when she mimicked the earnest, singsong pieties of an insufferable roommate. Caroline laughed, too, and it was a natural, gleeful laugh that made him ache with love for her.

He guessed that her childhood had been a lonely one, except for the friendship—never alluded to again—with the Gauguin girl, but he could not ask about it. At the end of four days and nights, he knew only that Caroline had no brothers and sisters, was fond of great art, liked avocados and could not abide caviar, and had been to school in Switzerland. Nevertheless, he was far from discouraged. She now trusted him enough to take his arm in traffic, and she was even affectionate, in a removed sort of way. She scolded him for smoking too much, and once, in a heart-stopping, casual gesture, had plucked a leaf from his hair. They had been strolling in the Tuilleries at the time, and she had simply reached up, as if in an embrace, and extricated the leaf that had fallen on his head.

"Vine leaves in your hair, Malcolm. Won't do."

"Ibsen, Caroline."

"Something I had to read at school. I didn't like it much."

The prelude to his downfall had come on their fifth night in Paris. She had retired to her room, and he, as usual, had gone to the bar for a nightcap. He ordered a large brandy and soda, and drank it down so quickly he felt the need to order another. The brandy, coming on top of all the wine they had drunk, sang in his veins and asked a question. *Who am I? What am I doing here? Why am I—a man happily engaged to be married—spending a fortune to try to get close to a disturbed American who offers me nothing? Who is she, and what has happened to my life?*

He drained his second brandy and, full of love and misery, went to her suite. He pounded on the door with more force than he had meant to employ. When she answered, dressed in a thick bath towel and obviously fresh from her bath, he behaved badly. Like a man in a bad dream, he knew that what he was doing was exactly wrong but, like the man caught in the dream, he could not prevent himself.

"Oh, Caroline," he heard himself moan. "I do love you so. Won't you love me back?"

Her eyes were wide as she stepped, backwards, away from him. Her hands clasped the edges of the towel that was knotted over her breasts, and he saw that she had gathered her hair in a great clump at the crown of her head. Little tendrils had escaped and snaked about her head and neck. She looked very lovely, and more than a little frightened.

Malcolm hated himself, knew he had undone, in this one impulsive act, all that he had accomplished in their time together in Paris. There was no way out. He couldn't turn and walk and hope that she would pretend it never happened. He could only go forward now.

"I'm so sorry," he said miserably. "I didn't mean to barge in on you like this. I literally couldn't help myself."

"Isn't that what rapists say—that they couldn't help themselves?" She was beginning to look angry instead of alarmed.

"Dearest girl, you can't mean that. I would never harm you—surely you know that?"

There was no answer. Her catlike eyes regarded him with contempt.

"Is that it?" Malcolm asked gently. "Is that why you are so guarded, Caroline? Did someone rape you?"

"Oh, don't be so melodramatic. Of course not, Malcolm."

"What is it, darling? What ails you, makes you so unhappy and lonely? Who hurt you so terribly?"

Caroline sat on the edge of her bed and laughed, so softly he thought it a sigh at first. "I never said anyone hurt me," she said. "You talk like something out of a woman's magazine, Malcolm. I've always been very fair and aboveboard with you. I told you, right from the start, that I neither needed nor wanted your friendship, but you wouldn't listen. Isn't that true?"

He nodded. Her words were the sort that would hurt him terribly the next morning, but for now he felt so wretched and foolish that nothing could escalate his pain. "Perfectly true," he whispered, and even as he half-hated her for her cruelty, he knew his estimation of her as someone who had been wounded was correct. He had to forgive.

"Then is it any wonder that I don't appreciate it when you come stumbling in, babbling about love? You promised nothing like this would happen. You *promised*." Now she was sounding like a little girl, and he could see that she was blinking back tears.

"I was beginning to trust you," she said. "I even liked you, Malcolm, and then you had to ruin things. I thought we were becoming friends, but I suppose men and woman can never be anything as nice as friends."

"I'll be your friend," he said humbly.

"Until the next time you think of how much fun it would be to poke me," she said bitterly.

Her crude use of the word "poke" shocked him, because it was so unlike her. "Is that what you imagine I want?" he asked. "To poke you now and then, whenever the need arises, as it were?"

"I think we'd better go back to England. I have to collect my things from your parents' house and say my thank-yous. We shouldn't arrive on the same day, though. There's still time to patch things up with Understanding Belinda, isn't there? I think I'll fly back tomorrow."

"Whatever you like, Caroline, of course." Her bare shoulders were glowing in the lamplight, and he could see a few droplets of water in the hollow of her throat. "Understand one thing, though. What you believe of me is not true. I would wait a year before so much as touching you, if that was what you wanted, and when I did touch you, it wouldn't be a poke. You may laugh at me, call me old-fashioned, but what I want is the chance to cherish you."

She drew her knees up, cushioned her chin. She neither laughed nor appeared to offer any sympathy; indeed, she seemed to be working something out. Calculating. "All right," she said in a dreamy voice. "Cherish away, if that's what it'll take to prove how wrong you are. But not tonight. The night after tomorrow will do."

The blood pounded audibly in his ears. He felt thick and stupid. "What do you mean?" he asked.

"I mean," said Caroline, speaking patiently, as if to a child, "I'll wait for you in my room at Fitzroy Hall two nights from now. Come to me there, late, when everyone's asleep, and I'll cure you of your passion."

"How?"

"You'll see."

"Caroline—"

"I'm tired," she said. "If you'll excuse me?"

He returned to his suite in a state of dread. The euphoria of his brandies had long since departed, and he felt cold and shaken. He wondered how he would get through the next two days, and pictured the mixture of anticipation and revulsion he would experience when he crept to her room—a felon in his father's house. He knew he would go, though. It was the only thing he was sure of. Nothing could keep him away, because it was the last chance to capture her.

He came to her when everyone in Fitzroy Hall was fast asleep and owls were hooting out among the yew trees. She was waiting for him. She lay naked on the bed, arms behind her head and one knee cocked in a classic whore's pose. She had left the curtains open, and moonlight bathed her body. Malcolm closed the door and came toward the bed slowly, his eyes devouring her. She stared at him without expression as he stripped away the robe to stand naked before her. He had an athlete's body: muscular arms and chest tapering to small, lean hips and long, powerful legs. She supposed he was very handsome. Certainly he was more than ready for her. Probably he had been in that state since his return from Paris.

He lay beside her on the bed now. Wonderingly, he placed his hands over her breasts, cupping them like chalices. He touched her everywhere with that same, worshipful calmness, as if his own need would have to wait until he had adored her. She felt his hands on her thighs, between her legs, everywhere, and it didn't seem to matter. She allowed him to investigate her most intimate parts as if he were a doctor, not a lover. Obediently, she offered up her body, but without any sign of joy. She made no sound, spoke no word, but her attitude might have drawled: *Well, get on with it.*

She had felt this numbness before, in Sardinia, when she had allowed a handsome Frenchman to make love to her. It all went on somewhere beyond and outside of her. The Frenchman had been so aroused he hadn't even noticed her coolness. She remembered her distaste when, some minutes after his orgasm, he had turned to her and said: *"Alors,* did you geet off, Caroleen?"

But Malcolm was not like the Frenchman. There was despair now in the touch of his hands and she willed him to feel her lack of desire for him. She thought it possible that he might not even be able to complete the job unless she hurried matters along, and that would never do. If Malcolm did not actually spill his aristocratic seed inside her body, he would be able to tell himself that he had remained faithful to his fiancee; Belinda would be uncompromised and the church bells would ring out and everybody would be just too happy for words.

Carlotta pressed herself to him with enough counterfeit energy to restroke his waning passion, and then she rolled over on top of him and imprisoned him deep inside her body, riding him like one of the fine English horses Lord Kitson kept in his stables. He cried out her name despairingly when he exploded inside her, but she displayed the same amount of interest she might if he had asked her to pass him the newspaper at breakfast.

Then she climbed off and lay beside him, resuming the old pose. She looked into his sad eyes, resisting the tiny twinges of compassion that she felt, and thought, *Game to Carlotta*.

FIVE

THE TROUBLE WITH BEING A STOREFRONT LAWYER, THOUGHT Lee, was that every sorry sight on God's earth passed before your eyes. Junkies and amateur prostitutes, runaway hippies so wired on acid they couldn't even remember having set fire to some building, poor, misbegotten creatures all—the flotsam and jetsam of the Age of Aquarius.

It wasn't that she didn't want to help these people. She had resolved to be a criminal lawyer when she passed her bar examination, and to represent people who were powerless and broke. She knew she was idealistic to a fault, but she couldn't bear to admit that she had made a mistake. The people who came to the storefront law office were not those she had dreamed of defending. Instead of redressing the wrongs of those whose race or poverty made them the victims of society, she was dealing with people like the girl who had just left. Maybe it was Berkeley that did it; perhaps she should go somewhere else.

"Like, wow!" the girl had said. "Far out. An Indian! That's beautiful, man, and so totally far out. It blows my mind."

She had come for legal advice, with a vague thought of suing her landlord. He had evicted her, along with her old man, from a two-room apartment they had inhabited for a year. He had objected to the noise, she explained, but it happened that Teeg, her mellow boyfriend, could only get into practicing on his guitar in the middle of the night. The landlord had also objected to the smell of the eleven cats that lived in the apartment.

"That's why I was so freaked when I saw you were, like a Native American," the girl had said, pawing at her long, greasy hair in her excitement. "It's like I knew you would understand about the cats. I believe cats are the souls of people who have, like, died. It's uncool to ignore them. Isn't that what your people believe?"

Lee had sighed, sympathizing with the landlord. She told the girl to bring her a copy of the lease, and she'd see what she could do. The very idea of a lease was so complicated and alien to the girl that Lee saw with relief she would never be back.

Mike Golden, one of her lawyer colleagues, was shaking with silent laughter. As soon as the door had closed behind the girl he called to Lee, "Counselor Redwing, would you like to, like, have this incredibly mellow, far-out dinner with me at Rimini's tonight? Or do your people believe that the souls of the departed live in, like, old Chianti bottles?"

She sailed a paper clip at him and smiled. Mike was from Brooklyn, the product of an Italian mother and a Jewish father. He was short and compact and nice to look at, though far from handsome, and he made her laugh. She had been sleeping with him for over a month.

He came to her desk and bent close to whisper, "Afterwards, we makeum beast with two backs. Heap good. Plenty exciting."

She reached up and tugged painfully at his long, droopy moustache to reprove him for this impertinence, but, as usual, she laughed. Some of the more militant Indians at Berkeley disapproved of her affair with Mike, calling her an "apple" behind her back—red outside and white inside. This was not the case, and she couldn't see how sleeping with Mike Golden meant she was being disloyal to her race. If she were to confine her sex life to carnal knowledge of the few Indians at Berkeley, her choices would be narrow indeed.

"Sure," she told him. "If nothing comes up to take me to the courthouse."

She had her own apartment now, and it suited her. She had secretly felt suffocated by life in the communal boarding-house, and treasured her new freedom and independence. She had been a scholarship student, so poor that there had been days when she could afford only one meal. It was ironic, she thought, that Carlotta's father had changed all that. His generous bequest to her own father had astounded her, but even more amazing was the huge amount of money the sale of his land and his ranch had brought to the newly created Thomas J. Madigan Foundation for the Rehabilitation and Betterment of the American Indian People of Montana.

As the girl with the eleven cats might have said, it blew her mind. That a man she had always regarded as evil could give his most precious possession up, even after death, to benefit her people, forced her to re-evaluate her picture of him. She did not think him evil because of the long-ago escapade she had glimpsed through the windows of the shack on his ranch. The girl from White Sulphur Springs, had been a prostitute. There was nothing evil about the senator's pleasure as he lay back, arms folded behind his head, while the girl's shiny black hair rippled and bounced as her head bobbed between his legs; he had only been behaving in the weak, decadent, sly manner which had been his nature. It wasn't his fault that she had later run off to Hollywood and eventually died of an overdose of heroin—that had been *her* nature.

No. What Lee could not forgive him for was the way he encouraged Carlotta to worship him. He played her like a speckled trout in a stream, inflaming the little girl's natural affection for a glamorous father, gloating in his ability to make her glow from a casual caress, a cocky smile. It was as if Tom Madigan did not recognize boundaries. He seemed not to understand that his daughter was not in the running. She, like every other pretty female creature on the face of the earth, was his for the taking. Even at the age of seven, Lee had known this was wrong. By the time she was old enough to understand and articulate the feeling, Carlotta was so far submerged beneath her father's spell that any warning would have had tragic results.

Lee had been present at the beginning of Carlotta's very first romance, and she'd been around for the end of it, too. The boy's name had been Jesse Carson, and during the summer when she and Carlotta had been fifteen, Jesse Carson had come to the Madigan ranch in search of one of Lee's brothers, Jim.

It was easy for her to picture the boy's face, because it was a memorable one, and because Jesse Carson had been so pale. His pallor was caused by a long bout of mononucleosis, from which he had just recovered, but they didn't know that then. All they saw was a lanky boy with unruly brown hair and a pale face, climbing out of a pickup truck and walking up the path toward the Redwing house. They had been sitting in the kitchen, drinking lemonade. Carlotta had been telling Lee about her trip back East, where she had been to some boring garden parties with her mother's relations.

"Who's that boy, Lee? He's coming to the house."

"Don't know, never saw him before."

They were alone in the house. Charlie was in the high pastures with the senator. Ray had run off to California on his eighteenth birthday, Jim was working as a short-order cook over in Butte, and Mrs. Redwing had taken Dominic in to town to buy him new sneakers.

The unknown boy, who appeared to be about seventeen, had tapped at the screen door, seeing them inside. "Excuse me," he said. "Excuse me, ladies, but I'm looking for Jimmy Redwing?"

"How come?" Lee asked. "What do you want him for?" Her older brothers were, sadly, notorious troublemakers, and she didn't want to deliver Jim into the hands of the law. The boy didn't look like a lawman, but you could never be sure.

"I'm from the Carson ranch, about forty miles north of here," he said. "Jim's father used to be my dad's ranch manager, and we were pals when we were only little. I ran into him in White Sulphur Springs in January, and I promised to come see him."

"What kept you so long?" Lee asked drily.

"You're Leana, aren't you?"

"Lee. Nobody calls me Leana anymore. I don't remember you."

"Well, how could you? You were just a baby when your father left for the Madigan ranch. Jim and I were eight, I reckon. Ray was about ten."

Lee felt hostile toward the son of the Carson ranch, remembering the descriptions her mother had volunteered of their housing there. What right did he have to come poking around, looking for the companion of his childhood, just because he and Jim had met up, by chance, in White Sulphur Springs?

"He's over to Butte," she said grudgingly. "You'll find him

flipping flapjacks in a place called The Big Sky Kitchen."

"I thank you, Miss Lee," said the voice from beyond the screen door. "I forgot to introduce myself. I'm Jesse Carson. I would have come before now, but I've been sick."

"Would you like some lemonade?" came the voice of Carlotta.

"That would be mighty refreshing," said Jesse Carson, peering through the screen to discover who the owner of this new voice might be.

Carlotta turned on Lee a look that was both apologetic and wheedling. She apologized for offering hospitality in a house not her own, and begged for favor.

"Why?" Lee whispered.

"Because he sounds nice," Carlotta said.

Lee had gone to the door and unlatched it. Jesse Carson's long, slight figure had entered the kitchen. Close up, she could see that he was someone to be reckoned with. He had long, pale eyes that sluiced around the room and radiated both intelligence and humor. He was courteous and somehow at home in the Redwing kitchen. He showed class. Jesse Carson sank into a kitchen chair and waited for Lee to pour him a glass of lemonade. When she brought it to him, she noticed that he was having trouble taking his eyes from Carlotta. Well, that was to be expected. She knew Carlotta was very beautiful, and he was, after all, a boy.

"Thank you," he said. "Cheers."

Carlotta was wearing white shorts and the strange kind of cotton shirt her mother always stocked up on when they went back East. It was thin cotton, but with a collar and a pocket, and this one was pale blue. Her breasts seemed rather prominent, and Lee saw now that Carlotta had kept on growing in that area, whereas Lee had stopped. They had compared breasts a few years back, and found to their delight that they were exactly the same—a nice B cup. They were too old, at fifteen, to compare, but Lee judged Carlotta to be a C now. She would have to ask sometime when they were alone.

"Carlotta," Jesse Carson was saying. "That's a pretty name. You're Senator Madigan's daughter, aren't you?"

Mention of Daddy brought a big smile, Lee noticed. "Yes, I am," she said. "Do you know my father?"

"Not to speak to, but I've seen him, of course. I admire your father, Carlotta. I think he's a fine man."

"Yes, yes he is," she agreed, pushing her hair back with a graceful gesture and continuing to smile. There was an awkward pause, and Lee felt she might as well not be in the room. She wasn't hurt, but she was fascinated at what was going on before her very eyes. Her friend, her funny, unawakened friend, was feeling the lure of the opposite sex for the first time! Lee had been feeling it for some time now, had even had a crush on one of the wranglers, a state of affairs Carlotta had found incredible.

"You said you had been sick," Carlotta offered timidly. "What did you say it was?"

"I didn't, but it was mono. Mononucleosis."

"The kissing disease," said Lee wickedly.

Jesse colored a little, and grinned. "Don't I wish, Lee. That's not how I got it."

"How did you?" Carlotta's eyes had gone all misty with compassion.

It seemed that Jesse had become run down due to studying too hard. He was in his first year of college, at the University of Montana, even though he was not yet eighteen. He had skipped a grade, and he had been majoring in anthropology when the mono struck him down. "I want to be an archeologist," he said modestly.

The clanging of the heavy, cast-iron bell that summoned people home to meals on the Madigan ranch was heard. Carlotta was being called home to lunch. She rose to her feet, looking unhappy. "I've got to go," she said. Another girl, faced with a boy who intrigued her, might have ignored the bell, but not Carlotta.

"I'll drive you home," Jesse Carson said, springing to his feet.

"It's only a few hundred yards," said Carlotta, brightening.

"Doesn't matter. I have to be going, anyway. I want to drive to Butte and say hello to Jim."

From the door, Lee watched Carlotta climb into the cab of the pickup. It was as if her friend was ascending into a new realm Lee had imagined denied to her forever. Carlotta was attracted to a boy, and all of the senator's fabled power could not stop the headlong rush of nature. The truck went rattling off toward the ranch, and Lee's brief, optimistic thought was darkened by a cloud of doubt. The senator could not prevent his daughter from feeling the natural emotions of a fifteen-year-old girl, but he could surely take steps to make sure they were not gratified. He could turn everything sour.

I hope I'm wrong, Lee whispered to the screen door. But even as the words left her mouth, she knew she was right. Senator Madigan would never stand by idly while his princess was in thrall—however temporarily—to another man. He required absolute loyalty, and unqualified adoration.

At first things went smoothly enough. Carlotta was granted permission, by her mother, to go to the movies in White Sulphur Springs with Jesse. He was, after all, the son of a prominent rancher, although his father's position was, in relation to that of Tom Madigan, the place of an outer star to that of a brilliant planet. Jesse was clean, intelligent, well-mannered, and good-looking, and nobody could find fault with him. As a potential candidate for Carlotta's hand, he was thoroughly unsuitable, but as a first and harmless romance, he seemed perfect.

"My father says Jesse looks unhealthy," Carlotta told Lee on one occasion. "Daddy's always very nice to Jesse, but later, after he's gone, he sort of makes fun of him. I can't think of an example, but he does. Oh, I don't know, I can't explain."

"I can imagine," Lee said. "All fathers are jealous of their daughters' boyfriends."

Carlotta had bitten her lip. "Jealous? Oh, no, Lee, certainly not *jealous.*"

"Don't listen to him. You just make up your own mind about Jesse. I think he's just fine."

It was obvious that Carlotta also thought Jesse fine. She could no longer carry on a conversation without mentioning his name, and Lee was sure that Carlotta and Jesse did the same things in the pickup truck that she and a friend of Ray's had done in the front seat of his Chevrolet. Hot, open-mouthed kisses, trembling, massaging hands, cries of no, no, and the strategic blockading of certain parts of the body. . .

"He says he loves me, Lee."

"Well, probably he does. He's older, remember. Do you love him?"

"I don't know. No. Well, maybe. I think I might."

There had been an occasion when Jesse was invited to dine at the ranch. According to Carlotta, her father had drawn him into a conversation about archeology. Jesse had held forth brilliantly, pouring out his ideas, expressing his passion for the concept of learning from bygone civilizations, and at the end of it Senator Madigan had given a little smile and said:

"It sounds a bit dead and dusty to me, Jesse, but I suppose someone has to do it. I'm more interested in the future, myself. I should think you'll end up teaching, wouldn't you say? Only a handful of anthropologists end up working in the field, you know."

It was at the same time that boarding school was introduced as a suitable move. Boarding school had loomed on Carlotta's horizons, but she had always been able to postpone it before. She had turned up her nose at the idea of a school in Massachusetts, protested against one on Long Island, and rejected a horsey establishment in Virginia. Now her parents were talking Switzerland.

Lee saw it as a conspiracy to remove Carlotta from the sphere of Jesse Carson's influence. The Madigans were lenient enough to keep her in private school in Washington, long past the time when Martha thought it appropriate for a young girl to be "finished," but with the advent of Jesse they saw Carlotta as a wild colt who had to be broken in the more civilized atmosphere of Europe.

The end of Carlotta's little rapture occurred quite abruptly. It happened near the end of the summer, and it was brutal.

Only the day before, she had confided to Lee that the business of looking for Jim had been a ruse. Jesse had been no more than six when the Redwings left for the Madigan ranch, but he had to use the long-ago friendship between the two little boys to find some excuse for driving onto the senator's property. He had seen Carlotta in town with her mother, and fallen in love with her on the spot. "You do forgive him, don't you, Lee? For lying?"

"It was for a good cause."

On this day in August, the day that was to mark the end of Carlotta's puppy love, Lee could see the lovers from her bedroom window. They were on horseback, riding down from the stream. Carlotta was on Mr. D'Arcy, a haughty, spirited Tennessee Walker, and Jesse was mounted on the broad, reliable back of Bingley, a sensible, dun-colored regular from the Madigan stables. Lee had often ridden Bingley, and knew him to

be an even-tempered, rather unexciting horse. She suspected
that Carlotta had chosen Bingley for her true love because, as
she told Lee later, Jesse had once been thrown, when he was
quite young, and had ever since distrusted horses that were
skittish. It had been a bad fall, resulting in a broken leg and
collarbone, and Jesse had nearly been trampled beneath the
horse's hysterical hooves.

Even as she watched, the riders slowed from a brisk canter
to a walk. Jesse reached out and caught Carlotta's hand, kissing it, and Lee turned away, feeling it was wrong to see them
when they believed they were alone. She had been shucking
ears of corn, her baby brother Dominic pretending to help,
when she'd heard sounds that alarmed her. The senator's deep
voice was borne to her on the wind, and also the powerful
whinnying of a horse that could be neither Bingley nor Mr.
D'Arcy. She went to the door and saw, with a deep, unex-
plained foreboding, that all three of them were congregated at
the ring Senator Madigan had had constructed especially for
the breaking of his Arabs.

Dominic was winding corn tassels around his plump
fingers, intrigued by the loss of blood flow he could produce
if he pulled them tight. She told him to quit it and scooped
him up and deposited him on the porch. "Stay here," she
instructed, "where I can see you, okay?"

He sensed the urgency in her voice and nodded solemnly.
Lee went running to the ring, sure that her presence would not
be welcomed by the senator, but unable to prevent herself.
Something momentous was about to occur. Something evil.

"I don't think he should, Daddy," Carlotta was saying as
Lee arrived. Her face was pale and strained. Her eyes darted
anxiously from the face of her father to that of her love.

"It's all right, Carlotta," Jesse said, but his voice was un-
certain.

"That horse is dangerous," Carlotta said. "You're the only
one who can ride him, Daddy. Jesse's fine on Bingley. We
were just fine, really."

Lee took it all in at a glance. Carlotta's father had arrived
on the scene like a crusader. Mounted on his raven-black Arabian stallion, a beast so newly broken it still reared and
bucked like a bull at rodeo, he had surprised his daughter in
the company of a male so deficient he would condescend to
ride old Bingley.

"Bingley!" snorted the senator. The word exploded contemptuously. "Bingley is a woman's horse, Carlotta. If your mother, God bless her, ever decided to go for a ride, I'd mount her on Bingley. He's no fun at all for a young man, right, Carson?"

Lee saw the look on Jesse's face. It was the look of one who was damned either way. If he agreed, he would be forced to ride the murderous Arabian stallion; if he demurred, he would forever be the butt of the senator's jokes—a man too timid to ride a Real Man's mount. A man who rode horses designated for women and children.

"Don't!" shouted Lee, but she was not an essential part of this particular drama. The players were locked in so tightly they barely noticed her.

"Don't," said Carlotta. "Don't, Jesse."

The senator shrugged, looking amused. *Well, of course,* he seemed to say, *if it's all too much for you . . .*

"I will," said Jesse. "I think I'll take you up on your offer, Senator."

Lee would never be able to forget the sound of Jesse's voice. Beneath the bravado lay the most abject of fears, but in his young face there was a steely determination. He knew exactly what game it was he was being asked to play, and he was willing to play it for the sake of Carlotta. Between Jesse and the senator there flowed a current of perfect, hateful understanding.

I'll play your silly game, Jesse might have said. *For the sake of Carlotta, I'll risk my life. I am willing to do it to break the spell you have over her, you old bastard.*

Do your best, boy, the senator's eyes telegraphed back. *You'll lose. You haven't a hope in hell of winning, and you know it.*

The senator swung easily out of the saddle, holding the reins of the snorting stallion. "Best ride him inside the ring," he said. "He's used to that."

"Jesse," Carlotta said in a small voice. "You don't have to do this. I wish you wouldn't."

"Don't nag him, baby," her father said. He undid the horizontal bars and led the horse inside, speaking reassuringly to it, gentling the huge, glistening flanks. Lee thought the horse seemed calm enough, but she was apprehensive all the same. "You want to keep a fairly tight rein on him," the senator said to Jesse. "He has a mind of his own, even now."

Looking even paler than on the first day they had met him, Jesse crossed the space that separated him from his adversary. He mounted the stallion without any difficulty, accepted the reins from Senator Madigan, and gave Carlotta a courtly little salute.

"He's called Jamil," the senator said.

"Okay, then, Jamil," Jesse said, "let's see what you can do."

He walked Jamil halfway around the ring without any trouble, although the horse continually danced sideways, aware of the unfamiliar presence in the saddle. Then they trotted uneventfully enough for the return lap. The senator was lounging against the posts of the riding ring, smiling a little as if in anticipation of events to come. Lee could see that Jamil's ears were laid back, and his eyes rolled oddly.

When Jesse got him into a canter he cut a fine figure in the saddle, but Lee could see the control slipping away as surely as if it were she who sat astride the Arabian. Jesse was no longer in control, but at the horse's mercy. Jamil reared mightily, coming to an abrupt halt and pawing straight up into the air, but his passenger stayed on, brought him down again, and cantered off. Lee became aware of Carlotta's ragged breathing; Carlotta, too, was feeling that she was in that dangerous saddle.

This time the horse refused to round the ring at the far end. He reared again, wheeled around, and galloped furiously in their direction. "He's going to jump the fence!" Carlotta shouted. Jesse seemed to understand, because he threw his weight forward to avoid losing his balance, but when the great beast went thudding over, he was slammed so hard against the pommel that Lee guessed the wind had been knocked from him. Jamil came to an eerily total halt, shrugged, and rid himself of the unwelcome burden on his back. Jesse had been hit in the solar plexus and had no strength to resist. He landed flat on his back and lay gasping for breath.

Carlotta reached him first. There were tears in her eyes. The senator was laughing his big, booming laugh—that manly laugh which was supposed to convey to Jesse a sense of male camaraderie, but which in fact conveyed something quite different.

"Well, well," he said, between bursts of laughter. "No bones broken, I presume?" Jamil whickered softly at the sound of his master's voice, as if to highlight who was in charge here. The senator offered a hand to Jesse, which was declined. Jesse, still bent almost double, struggled to his feet on his own. There were tears in his eyes, too. Lee knew they were tears of rage, but he appeared to be just what the senator had wanted Carlotta to see: an inept crybaby. He couldn't seem to look at Carlotta, and he certainly didn't want to look at the senator, and so he stared into the distance.

"Sorry about that," the senator said. "Bingley is the horse for you, right, son? I misjudged—all my fault."

It was at that point that Jesse Carson simply walked to his pickup truck and, without a backward look, drove off the Madigan ranch and out of Carlotta's life forever.

"I hate you for that," Carlotta had said, turning on her father and speaking in a quiet, deadly voice. "I hate you."

"Don't say things you'll regret, baby," the senator warned. "There's a reason for everything I do. You'll thank me later."

So far as Lee knew, Carlotta had never thanked her father for his humiliation of Jesse, but eventually she was won over by him again. Seduced. Jesse's name was never mentioned, and life went on as usual, as if Carlotta had never known what it was to be loved by a boy close to her age. Still, she had meant it when she said she hated him. Many women must have hated the senator, Lee thought. All the women who had loved him in his lifetime must eventually have come to hate him, and now one of them had killed him.

Lee had followed the trial of Joly Nesbit with repugnance and fascination. At first she had sympathized with Joly, swayed by the brilliance of Jeremiah Tompkins. When poor old Bertha's evidence had come to light, however, she had felt the same revulsion for Joly she had always felt for the senator. They were two of a kind, although Tom Madigan's superior wealth and power had enabled him to operate more smoothly, and Lee was glad when Joly was sent away for life.

Carlotta was on her mind more and more lately, although she had disappeared from the face of the earth. It was more than a year ago that her father had written that Carlotta had gone to Europe, according to the lawyer. She had vanished soon after the trial, and Lee had never heard from her.

She had meant what she had written to Carlotta, about being her friend for life. She would always worry about her, even while Carlotta's father's generosity made her own life easier. She was very much afraid that the senator had created a monster, and she wished she could tell the world—Carlotta's world—that the monster was really a very nice girl, and could not be blamed. It was not her fault.

Rachel, too, was thinking of Carlotta, but for very different reasons. Cotter had just rolled off her with a satisfied grunt and sunk into sleep like a stone hurled into a pond. Her body had been satisfied, but her mind was whirling. Little spurts of adrenaline fed her consciousness and kept her wide awake. She conjured up the image of Carlotta's beautiful breasts— Montana breasts, high, wide, and handsome, with pale pink nipples that hardened wonderfully in the showers at school in Neuchâtel. Then there was Carlotta's pubic hair, a pale frost of strawberry-colored fur.

Rachel sighed. It wasn't going to work. Carlotta was ravishingly beautiful, but she didn't arouse her. Carlotta was her friend. Somehow she couldn't get the hots for someone she had known since her sixteenth year. She summoned up other women, women nearly as lovely as Carlotta. The tootsie from Ecuador who was currently dating Cotter's friend Blake, for example. Gorgeous, long legs and the kind of ass where you could always see the divide, no matter how she was dressed. Little sharp tits, high and demanding. Big, glistening lips. No. No dice, as her father said. It wasn't in the cards.

Rachel turned, pounded her pillow with disappointment. She was not used to being denied what she wanted, and it seemed terribly unfair. Bisexuality was *in,* and she wanted— oh, so very much—to be attracted to a woman. It was such a *small* thing to ask. Graham was bisexual, as she had discovered the time she'd walked in on him with the drummer that night in Newport. Why couldn't she be?

There had been that business back in Switzerland, but she didn't think it really counted. It had been the year she met Carlotta, when they were both sixteen, and it had only happened because there were no men around. Rachel smiled in the dark, remembering how Carlotta had brought up the riding master, Bertrand! Trust Carlotta to remember every detail when Rachel had practically forgotten the whole episode.

In the year before Bertrand had come to the school, Rachel had thought she would die of frustration. When she was being honest with herself, she would admit that it wasn't the sex *itself* she missed so much. No. It was the delicious play of it all—the flirtation, the reading of admiration in the other person's eyes, the clandestine, dangerous, wonderful nature of having a love affair. The other part, the payoff, you might say, she could achieve quite easily by herself, beneath the covers. She didn't even need to wait until her suitemates had fallen asleep; once, in an especially horny mood, she had given herself quite a nice little orgasm while pretending to study her Latin textbook. She had done it by folding one leg under her and sort of rocking around on her foot, and the odious Marie-Thérèse had been sitting five feet away and never knew the difference!

But it wasn't much fun, when it came down to it. All of the things she so loved were missing, and at the very top of the list was the admiration business. Rachel thrived on admiration. Where was she supposed to get it in a chateau filled with people of the same sex?

Oh, she had her following, all right, but the girls who admired her were pleased by her daring, sophistication, and neat way with foul words. Nobody was particularly thrilled by her beauty. Homely girls envied it, and pretty ones saw her as a potential threat in the outside world.

Someone (she was fairly sure it had been Marie-Thérèse) had complained to the floor mistress about Rachel's blatant flaunting of the no-makeup rule. She had had to endure a lengthy interview with Madame Portier, during which time the kindly, humorless lady had endeavored to explain why it was that the young ladies of the Académie were forbidden the use of cosmetics. Beauty, counseled Madame Portier—as if she had just coined the phrase—was only skin deep. The fortunate girls who were privileged to attend the school at Neuchâtel were there to expand intellectually and spiritually. Surely Mademoiselle Windolm could see that painting her face did not contribute toward these goals?

"Life without beauty would be intolerable, don't you agree?" Rachel had asked.

"Ah, my dear young lady—of which beauty are you speaking?" gasped Madame Portier, switching into a stilted, arcane English. "I refer to the higher beauty, while you, I fear, have recourse to that beauty which may be cheaply purchased in a shop."

Not for you it can't, Rachel, had thought, wounded. Aloud, she said: "Human beings are beautiful sometimes. Any living person who has any shred of beauty owes it to himself, and to everyone who has to look at them, to enhance that beauty. That's what I think, madame."

"In your case, my dear child," said Madame Portier, "you are simply gilding the lily."

It took a moment for Rachel to realize she had been given a compliment. She felt gratified, and there was something else. Madame Portier, by speaking in English and mouthing cliches, was reminding her of her mother. She felt a grudging pang of affection, and promised that she would throw her artful cosmetics away.

It was a challenge, in a way, to make herself up while avoiding detection. She had to use a very light hand with mascara and blusher, and she discovered lip gloss. She applied the lip gloss to her eyelids as well as her mouth, and was pleased with the results. She won hands down the contest sponsored by the racier girls, to see who could use the most makeup and appear to be bare-faced.

In those early days at the school, it was Carlotta whose admiration she craved the most. Carlotta was by far the most beautiful girl at the school; if there was anyone whom she could regard as more than her equal, it was Carlotta Madigan. If she could excite the hoped-for admiration in Carlotta's eyes, she thought she would be happy.

But Carlotta, for all her breathless admiration during the study hall confessions, seemed oblivious to Rachel as a physical entity.

"Do you think I'm pretty?" she asked Carlotta once, as they were filing from chapel to history class.

"Of course I do," Carlotta replied, as she might to a question about the indigestibility of last night's Brussels sprouts.

"I mean, *really* pretty? Or just passable?"

"Really pretty," Carlotta said firmly, "but you know that, Rachel. Why ask me?"

Rachel had lowered her eyes in a studied movement, and then glanced up from beneath lowered lashes. It was an expression guaranteed to make strong men tremble, and she was offering her best profile, hoping the lip gloss on her eyelids was enhancing her eyes the way it had in the mirror three hours ago. She was carried away by her own performance; in that moment she was actually trying to act in a seductive manner toward the woman who would become her best friend. What should she say?

"I am asking you," she said sadly, "because I value your opinion. More than anyone else's, Carlotta. I feel so alone at times, and I can always depend on you for a straight answer."

Carlotta had assumed a stricken look, a look of genuine sympathy and solidarity. She had assured Rachel once again that she was wonderfully pretty, beautiful even, and hoped that Rachel would not feel alone. It was a heartfelt speech, delivered with stammering sincerity, but it was not what Rachel had hoped for. No kindling of prurient interest flashed in Carlotta's eyes; no awakening of desire bloomed there. She was merely concerned, in a sisterly way, at what she no doubt perceived as Rachel's lack of self-esteem.

Rachel saw that Wilhelmina was her only hope. Willi was a Dutch girl, reputed to be a lesbian because of her towel-snapping antics in the public showers after hockey games, who was forever perfecting her body. Her roommates complained of being awakened too early by the sound of Willi doing jumping jacks. She boasted of taking cold baths and had the hearty, hale-fellow-well-met sort of personality Rachel tried to avoid. Still, she was attractive, with her long, brown limbs and fringe of yellow hair; she reminded Rachel of a Choate boy she had known. Willi it would have to be.

She devoted all her energy to the task of attracting Willi. She sent her long, languishing glances during chapel, and then averted her eyes as soon as their glances met. She willed herself to blush whenever they came into direct contact, pretending the Dutch girl was the boy from Choate. Whenever Willi's eyes were on her, she moved with an awkward, self-conscious gait that suggested suppressed sexual longing. Soon Willi's gaze, whenever it alit in Rachel, reflected the admiring, hungry passion so essential to Rachel's well-being. Willi wanted her.

On a moonless night in October, Rachel had found herself creeping out of her room as soon as Marie-Thérèse's snores began. Her other roommates had been asleep for ages, and it had been terrible, having to wait until the grampus sounds started up from Marie-Thérèse's bed. Terrible, but necessary, for she was the one girl who would have reported Rachel immediately. Part of her agitation had been about what she was going to do, but she also feared that Willi would have given up on her and left their meeting place and gone back to bed.

At first it had seemed creepy that Willi should propose meeting in the kitchen. *Meet me tonight in the kitchen, as soon as you can get away,* the note had said. *I will wait for you.* It wasn't signed, but since Willi herself had passed it to her, there was no need for a signature. There had been no burning glances, no romance, just the workmanlike little note summoning Rachel to a rendezvous in the kitchen.

At the head of the broad marble staircase, Rachel shivered a little. Her feet, bare for silence's sake, were literally getting cold. On a demi-landing she passed Madame Portier's door, which was ajar as always, so Madame could hear if any of the girls needed her in the night. She passed, silent as a ghost, and ran lightly down, past the floor of senior girls to the main floor. She wished she had been foresighted enough to buy a wispy negligee on the Saturday trip to town; it somehow ruined her image of herself—a girl in a castle, running to meet her lover—to know that she wore a regulation white flannel nightgown.

The marble of the great hall's floor was even colder than that of the stairs. She saw the vast receiving rooms, dark and full of old couches and settees, and wondered why Willi had chosen the kitchen. Wherever would they do whatever it is they were going to do in the kitchen? Still, she supposed it was safer there. No giggles or rapturous cries could float up to waken the housemistresses.

She pushed open the heavy, ornately carved doors to the dining room and groped her way among the many tables. The long curtains had been drawn, and it was pitch black. She bumped into a table, heard the gentle clashing of silver. The tables had already been set for breakfast. Twice she blundered into the walls, her hands searching for the swinging doors that led to the scullery and kitchen. Christ, at this rate it would be dawn before she even *got* to the kitchen!

At last her fingers felt baize and she pushed, was rewarded. She was standing in a big, dark pantry that smelled of cinnamon. From somewhere ahead gleamed a watery light, and she walked toward it, feeling apprehensive now, and not at all sexy or romantic.

In the enormous kitchen the light seemed to beckon her on, like a will o' the wisp. She passed a table on which two dozen pies, freshly baked by their smell, were cooling. She had the eerie feeling that the kitchen staff had only recently vacated the premises, might still be lurking close by.

"Rachel," hissed Willi's voice. "Over here."

Willi was sitting on the edge of one of the scrubbed work tables, swinging a little pocket flashlight in an arc. "Have you no torch?" she asked.

"Excuse me? Torch?"

"This," said Willi, tapping her flashlight. "Without one you can have a blind voyage in the dining room. It will be heavy weather."

Rachel thought Willi was even more nervous than she was, because normally her English was quite good. She saw that the Dutch girl was eating a slice of pie. There was a fine sprinkling of sugar on her clean-cut upper lip. "Come," she said. "Sit, Rachel. I have a square of pie for you. It is apple, very tasteful."

Rachel sat on the table and regarded the pie intended for her. It was clearly sliced from the army of pies she had seen, and she wondered if the staff would notice in the morning. How could they not?

"I see you thinking," Willi said. "You are not to be worrying, Rachel. I will take whole pie up to my room, afterwards, and they will never notice one is missing."

Afterwards? Had Wilhelmina summoned her to eat pie, and not what she had thought? Perhaps it was a bizarre ritual at the Académie, something she hadn't understood. She picked up her wedge of pie and bit into it. It was quite good, and tasted of the cinnamon she had smelled in the darkened larder.

"You see," said Willi dreamily, "quite often I am hungry here. I am so active, and my body requires much food. I am here three years now, always hungry. Last year I discover there is food in the kitchen at night, and I think *why not?* My parents pay good money for me to be educated here—is it not my right to eat?"

"Damned right," said Rachel, feeling she had wandered from a vision of outlawed love into the pages of *Alice in Wonderland*.

Willi played the flashlight's beam straight into Rachel's face. "We are the daughters of the rich," she said. "Is it fair I should have less to eat than the daughter of the greengrocer back home in Rotterdam?"

"Definitely not fair," said Rachel, shaking her head vigorously.

"I like you," said Willi. "You are so special, and so pretty. As well, you like me, I can feel it. We will be friends this night, and then no more, you understand? I am older than you, eighteen, and I am to be married at Christmas, okay? Okay, Rachel?"

It was not what she had bargained for. Willi's broad, wholesome face loomed close, and then the little flashlight went rolling away, across the table. Willi's sugary, cinnamon-scented lips sought hers and found them. Gone was Rachel's wild impulse to surrender herself to hot, illicit love, thereby alleviating her boredom. Instead she found herself clasped in the white-flanneled arms of an identically clad schoolgirl who seemed to know no more about the mechanics of illicit love than she did.

They kissed, open-mouthed and panting, and held each other close. They touched each other's breasts with great timidity, and called it quits when Willi, frankly and unashamedly, began to cry.

"I don't want to be married," she sniffled against Rachel's left ear.

"Then don't," said Rachel, whispering into the darkness of the kitchen.

"It's expected," said Willi. "It's all arranged."

"Don't let them bully you." Rachel felt very tired. The adventure was already over, and nothing much had happened. She hadn't minded the kissing and groping, but neither had it thrilled her.

"You don't understand," Willi protested. Her hand had dropped back to Rachel's thigh, which she rubbed methodically, more in agitation than lust. They sat on for a time, uncomfortable with each other now, and at last Willi sniffed and said, "Come, Rachel. I think we go back now."

With her flashlight in one hand and the pie tin in the other,

Willi led Rachel back through the dark dining room and up the stairs. They parted on the senior girls' landing, and Rachel climbed the last flight alone and dispirited. She had been planning to tell Carlotta all about her night of lesbian love, had been looking forward to shocking Carlotta, perhaps even making her jealous, and now there was nothing to tell.

She had even been a little afraid. Had Wilhelmina found her insufficiently exciting? Was that why she had become distracted and morose? She kept her fears to herself, and didn't mention her night wanderings to Carlotta at all. It had been the only secret she had ever kept from her.

Rachel moved fretfully about in the bed, feeling jittery and anxious. She told herself that she was a married woman, an adult, and ought to concern herself with things more important than being bisexual. She imagined what Madame Portier would have to say on the subject, and wondered if poor Willi had indeed married the boy she did not wish to marry.

"Stop thrashing," mumbled Cotter in his sleep. She slid from the bed and stole to the box where she kept her Seconal. She swallowed two pills, washing them down with white wine. She walked aimlessly from room to room, her mind fixed on Carlotta again. In eighteen months she had received four postcards. One from London, one from Sardinia, one from Scotland, and the last from Barcelona. They were brief and relentlessly cheerful, and they contained no address where Carlotta could be reached. Rachel wondered how long her friend was planning to frolic in Europe, and whether she was ever coming back.

She missed Carlotta, and was pained that she had no way of corresponding with her. There was no one to call for information. Once she had called the house in Georgetown, about a month after Joly Nesbit's conviction and sentencing, and a strange woman had answered. She and her family had just moved in. She had no idea where Miss Madigan had gone, and had never even met her. She gave Rachel the name of the realtor, who was equally uninformed. Carlotta had succeeded in vanishing.

Rachel had dozens of friends, but no one she could really confide in. She could never tell Daisy Burgess, for example, of her failure to even conceive of being attracted to another woman. Rachel was Daisy's heroine—she would be crushed to discover how pedestrian Rachel was at heart. Carlotta was the only woman she had ever felt to be her equal, and the only one she'd ever told the truth to, always. Losing her was like losing a sister.

Big, handsome Tom Madigan came drifting into her mind. She saw him as he had appeared on an evening five years ago, when he had taken Carlotta and Rachel to dinner at "21." He caused a stir just by walking into a room. All eyes fastened on the senator as if he were a movie star and, indeed, he was better-looking than most of the men up there on the silver screen. Even in his mid-fifties, he radiated a kind of mythical sexuality. Rachel remembered feeling almost dizzy that night, sitting with him at the table. The gray in his black hair only made him handsomer, just as the little lines that radiated from his ice-blue eyes when he grinned at her accentuated his rugged appeal. His big hands on the stem of his wineglass thrilled her. *Black Irish,* her father said with patrician contempt when he referred to Senator Madigan.

"He's no better than those Kennedys," Mr. Windolm was fond of saying. "A few generations ago his people were squatting in a bog."

Rachel thought her father might take lessons from the Black Irish, if Carlotta's father was a fair representative of that group. The senator really noticed women, down to the smallest detail, and appreciated them. "That dress is very becoming," he had said to her, referring to the lemon linen shell she had been wearing. "You are as lovely as a wood sprite in that dress. And the earrings? Topaz, are they?"

"Yes, topaz," the young Rachel said, touching her lobes in agitation.

"They bring out the golden flecks in your dark, gypsy eyes. Have you noticed, Carlotta, that Rachel has sparks of pure gold in her eyes?"

"Yes, Daddy," said Carlotta dutifilly, flashing a pained smile, "Rachel has wonderful eyes."

It would have been corny if the senator had given the subject his undivided attention, but all along his own eyes were roving the room, and addressing themselves to his wineglass. He made you feel that his admiration was genuine, yet at the same time he managed to imply that it was impartial.

Her own father was as incapable of paying a compliment as he was of making a direct statement. He didn't seem to notice anything. When Mrs. Windolm had sported two black eyes as the result of minor cosmetic surgery, Rachel's father wondered aloud as to whether his wife had not been struck by an errant tennis ball.

"Sport can be dangerous," was what he had said.

Of course, her father's dimness was partially a result of his drinking so much, but the senator was hardly a teetotaler. Covertly, she counted up the number of drinks he had at "21" that night: three big whiskies before dinner, most of the bottle of wine they had with dinner, and a brandy afterward. He never got confused or slurred his words like Mr. Windolm, who frequently called her "Rashl" when he was in his cups. She concluded that Carlotta's father really was superior to other men. He was better-looking, more famous, and infinitely more charming; he could out-talk, out-drink, and probably out-screw them.

Rachel couldn't remember what she had eaten that evening, but she remembered it had been an early dinner, because they were going to see a Broadway show, a musical. The senator had helped them into their coats at the hat-check, and she had felt kind of shivery when his hands brushed her shoulders. He was so big! She felt him towering, unseen, behind her, and it wasn't the same sensation she would have if, say, some Yale football player were helping her on with her coat. The Yalie might be just as big as the senator physically, but he would lack Tom Madigan's authority.

On the street they walked three abreast, the girls linking their arms with his. Carlotta walked much closer, of course. Rachel had seen how protectively the senator had draped the coat over Carlotta's shoulders, how he had gathered her hair and spread it over her collar so lovingly. Carlotta stood still as a statue, and Rachel had the sudden image of Carlotta as a perfect doll, a doll for her father to play with.

Although he had a car and driver, the senator announced that they would walk to the theater, which was only a few blocks away, because it wasn't good to be idle right after a big meal. Again Rachel had to admit that the man was superhuman. Any other parent, suggesting a walk after dinner, would sound like her mother—"Movement keeps the circulation going, dear"—but Carlotta's father managed to make even the dullest pronouncements sound glamorous, the tamest adventures thrilling.

Earlier, Carlotta had confided that she would have pre-

ferred to see a play, *A Taste of Honey,* but her daddy had his
heart set on the big, glittering musical they were going to see.
It was the biggest hit on Broadway, and tickets were almost
impossible to obtain.

"Why isn't your mother going?" Rachel had asked.

"She doesn't like musical comedies."

She doesn't like musical comedies. The words had a dreadful ring, with hindsight. Had Martha known, even if she
hadn't allowed herself to acknowledge it, that her husband
was keeping a former show girl? Did the strutting, long-
limbed chorus girls remind her of her competition? If so, she
was wise to pass up the entertainment at the Wintergarden
Theater that evening, because there was enough bare flesh on
stage to drive a prim woman into a fit of hysterics. By today's
new standards, it had been very tame, but Rachel could still
remember a daring scene in which the second leading lady had
re-created Salome's dance of the seven veils. By a trick of
lighting, the actress appeared to be utterly nude when she
whipped off the last veil and sank to her knees, and the image
was so erotic that the audience applauded for several minutes.

Rachel sneaked a look at the senator to see if he was enjoying it, and was surprised to see that he had a small, cynical
smile on his lips.

The love interest in the musical was Tony Blake, a Hollywood actor whose earlier pictures Rachel and Carlotta had
seen when they were children. He sang in a cracked, out-of-
key fashion, but what did it matter? He was Tony Blake; he
was an icon. From the stage he looked exactly as he had in the
movies. His hair gleamed black and abundant, and his
shoulders were broad. Only by his slightly cautious movements could Rachel tell that he was really quite old.

"Would you like to meet Tony Blake?" the senator asked
when the curtain had fallen and the cheering had died.

Tony Blake had admitted them immediately to his dressing
room, pumping the senator's hand and producing champagne
from a cooler. Carlotta and Rachel sat on a couch and watched
while stars like Carol Channing and Ethel Merman drifted in
for quick kisses and hugs. Rachel had never known anything
like it. She was used to society parties, where show-business
folks almost never made an appearance, and found it pure
magic. They were so much more interesting than her parents'
friends, and Carlotta's father seemed as much at home with

them as he did on the floor of the senate. Rachel allowed her glass to be refilled many times, and nobody seemed to care. Carlotta drank less, and looked tense.

At one point, the actress who had played Salome wandered into the dressing room. Her stage makeup had not been removed, and the extravagant black lines around her eyes made her seem predatory and unreal. She was wearing a silk Japanese kimono, and Rachel could tell she was naked underneath. The sway of her high, full breasts proclaimed it, and when she accepted a glass of champagne and bent over, the kimono parted and showed a brief glimpse of light brown pubic hair.

"Hi, Tom," she crowed, seeing the senator for the first time. She moved toward him, balancing her champagne in the palm of her hand, exaggerating her sexy walk to the point of parody.

The senator did something with his eyes, something sly and secretive, and the actress turned. "Oh," she said. "Little girls. Which one is yours?"

They had left soon afterward, but not before Rachel had seen the senator's hand give a furtive, affectionate tap to the actress's ass. He managed it well, and Rachel wondered if Carlotta had seen it, too.

Rachel's father's remarks had come back to her that night at "21" and she had thought, "He can squat in my bog anytime," and then—to her horror—burst into uncontrollable laughter. But it didn't matter. The senator liked laughter, just as he liked drink and pretty women and fast horses. He flirted all evening long with Rachel and Carlotta, bathing them in the radiance of his supremely masculine aura. My God! Imagine having that man for a father!

The Seconal was beginning to do its work. The last coherent thought Rachel had before lurching off to bed was a curse for the senator. Damn the old bastard anyway for what he had done. It was his fault that Carlotta had disappeared. His fault that Rachel no longer had a confidante.

Carlotta's London flat was on Sloane Street, in Chelsea. For a quite outrageous sum she had a small sitting room, a tiny kitchen, a bedroom, and a bathroom that was, for some reason, larger than any other room in the flat. For a while, it amused her to buy things to beautify the place. It was fun to go to the Portobello Road and hunt for eccentric antiques. In one day alone she had bought a nineteenth-century leather-covered bellows for her fireplace, a cranberry glass pitcher, and a wastepaper basket made from an elephant's foot.

Gradually, however, the charm of decorating palled. The Sloane Street flat was not her home—it was merely a place where she lived when she was in London. She stopped the beautification process as suddenly as she had begun, and as a result the flat had a half-finished quality. It didn't matter. She didn't entertain, choosing always to go out, and no one saw it but her charwoman, Mrs. Hooks.

Mrs. Hooks was a cheerful Cockney who came to clean three times a week. She was very talkative, and loved to tell Carlotta about the appalling lives of her three grown children. Her son, Stanley, was in prison at Wormwood Scrubbs for forging checks. Her other son, Alf, had married a shrew of a girl who carried on with other men and never minded the house. Daughter Betty, who was only thirty, had been told she would have to undergo a hysterectomy, a process Mrs. Hooks referred to as "having her works out."

On a dull, rainy day in February, six months after she had lain in the moonlight with Malcolm Kitson, Carlotta sat reading a travel book about Portugal. She was thinking of going there to escape the damp, dismal climate. Mrs. Hooks was changing the linen in the bedroom, occasionally poking her head in to say things like: "Our Stanley must be suffering dreadful in prison, with the damp. I expect he'll 'ave rheumatism before long, and him only thirty-two. But life's a vale of tears, Miss Moore."

When it was time for Mrs. Hooks to have her lunch, which she always brought with her, Carlotta went to the kitchen and asked if she would like a warming glass of sherry. Mrs. Hooks always sat reading a paperback book when she ate. She favored romances with voluptuous heroines in ripped bodices on the covers, but she also liked lurid true-life detective stories. Carlotta sneaked a look to see what she was reading today, and nearly fainted. She must have cried out, because Mrs. Hooks was staring at her with alarm.

"Whatever is it, miss?" she asked. "Are you having a turn?"

Carlotta gripped the sherry bottle, trying to calm herself. The title of her char's paperback book was *A Fallen Hero: The*

Life and Death of Tom Madigan.

"Maybe I'm getting the flu," said Carlotta carefully. She poured out the sherry, trying to keep her hand from trembling, and then asked casually, "Where did you get that book, Mrs. Hicks? It looks interesting."

"Betty loaned it to me, dearie. It's just come out. I expect it's in all the bookshops." She smiled and downed some sherry. "It's ever so fascinating," she said, "all about a big politician from the States and his fancy woman who murdered him. But you must know about it, Miss Moore. It happened in your country."

"Oh, I recall something about it," said Carlotta.

"Ever such a scandal, wasn't it? This Madigan was a terrible man, but I will say this for him. A finer-looking specimen you'll never see. He could take any woman in."

Carlotta's mouth went unpleasantly dry. "Do you mean there are pictures in that book?" she asked, her voice a whisper.

"I believe you *are* getting the flu," said Mrs. Hooks. "Your voice is that hoarse."

"Pictures?" Carlotta repeated. "Photographs?"

"Oh my, yes. Plenty of those. Say what you will about the Irish, they produce good-looking men. Look at Erroll Flynn."

Carlotta sat at the table and looked with dread as Mrs. Hooks opened the book to the section of photographs. They were grainy and badly reproduced, but they were as dangerous to her as a ticking time bomb. "You just have a look at those and I'll make you a hot lemon drink," said Mrs. Hooks. "Good for your throat."

The first was the photo everyone loved best, the one she had seen on the television screen the night of his death. It was followed by a photo of Martha, and then one of their wedding day. Now Carlotta began to appear, first as a baby in her father's arms, then at the age of five or so, riding her Indian pony. Daddy was on the bay gelding. *With his daughter, Carlotta, on the ranch in Montana,* the caption said.

Carlotta was afraid she would see herself grow up and become recognizable, but she refused to skip ahead, and studied each picture in the proper sequence. The senator was shown with various luminaries—*Senators Madigan, Kennedy, and Jackson at a State Department reception, 1953*—and with Martha in Paris, and then with Charlie Redwing on the ranch.

The last picture of Carlotta had been taken in 1959, when she was fourteen: *With his daughter in Washington.* She knew the picture well; it had been part of a series of photographs called "Famous Fathers and Their Daughters" which had been published in *Life* magazine. She remembered posing for it, wearing a red velvet dress with a white lace collar and sitting on the arm of his chair in the library. Mother had assured her that the red of the dress complemented her hair rather than clashed with it.

She studied the photograph, submitting it to the closest scrutiny imaginable. Could anyone who knew her as Caroline Moore look at the girl in the picture and see that it was she? It had been reproduced in black and white, and she had, naturally, changed greatly. A huge relief began to sweep over her when she realized that it would be impossible to identify her. The relief was so great that she felt like crying. Or maybe she felt like crying because of the expression on the face of the fourteen-year-old girl—a look of perfect love and trust, a look that would make her even more unrecognizable since it never appeared on her face these days.

The rest of the pictures were of Joly Nesbit at various stages of her sordid career. Never did she appear in the company of Tom Madigan. At least he had been careful about that. The very last one was of Joly in prison. Carlotta snapped the book shut.

"'Ere's your 'ot lemon," said Mrs. Hooks, setting a steaming cup on the table before her. "I expect it's the flu, Miss Moore, because your eyes are all watery now."

Carlotta said thank you to Mrs. Hooks and took her tea and went directly to her bedroom. She had not really seen the char, just as she was now not really seeing the familiar items in the book; an extraordinarily vivid image had sprung up, engulfing her with its power. She wanted to hold on to it as sometimes, after a pleasing dream is interrupted by wakefulness, all people will try to creep back into the enchantment of the dream images.

It had been prompted by the photo labeled *With his daughter, Carlotta, on the ranch in Montana,* but she was not now in the time of that photograph, merely in the place. She was not a child of five, but an older girl, ten or eleven. She still rode an Indian pony, but her father was astride the first Arabian he had bought, long before the days of Amir Lateef, and there were no photographers to record the event. She was alone with him, the way she liked best, and they were cantering along a trail that led ever upward, as if to draw them along to the Continental Divide and pull them up to the roof of the world.

She could feel the rocking between her legs—the steady, surging motion of the horse as he pursued the senator's black Arabian. She heard the creaking of the leather saddle, and smelled a wonderful mixture of odors. There was the clean, nose-prickling smell of pine and beneath it, borne by a breeze from below, the tang of sage. There was also the smell of the horses, warm and friendly and lathery. Oh, it was glorious! She wanted to ride on forever, deeper into the Montana landscape, until it swallowed her up.

Like a child who thinks, if she stares long enough at a beloved illustration in a book that she will be able to melt into it, Carlotta tried to follow her father's horse up the steep trail and into some undefined infinity of happiness. She gripped the pony's flanks with her knees and forced her heels down in the stirrups, but these physical actions pushed the wonderful image away. It was fading, the sounds and smells were growing fainter, and suddenly she was standing in a room in London and hearing the rain drum at her windows.

She set the untasted cup of tea on the windowsill and threw herself on the bed, face down. She squeezed her eyes shut and tried to will the image back, but it was no good. It was as if, by closing the book so abruptly in her relief at being unrecognizable, she had banished herself from a kind of paradise.

Had there ever been such a day in her actual life? Of course, there had been hundreds of times when she had ridden with her father on the ranch, and beyond—but had there been the particular day she had been reliving, or was it an hallucination?

She fell into an uneasy half-sleep, always aware of the texture of the pillow beneath her face and the sounds of Mrs. Hooks moving about in the next room. Just as the half-sleep threatened to plunge into the real thing, her father's voice was proposing a holiday. It boomed unnaturally in her ears, and she was instantly awake. The room seemed still to resound with his mammoth words: JUST YOU AND ME, BABY, NEXT SUMMER!

They had reined their horses in, and were idling in an al-
pine pasture after the hectic ride. Yes, it was real; it had happened, just like this. Wild columbine was blooming all around
them, and Carlotta's pony was snorting with his exertions.

"Won't Mummy come, too?"

"No, sugar. Mummy doesn't feel up to a major trip just
now. Just you and me this time." Her father had smiled, and
Carlotta had thought his strong, white teeth capable of eating
up the universe. The blue eyes were gentle, though, and
pleading for her to accept the plan. He lounged in the saddle,
his body completely at ease, but Carlotta could tell that the
holiday was of supreme importance. She loved their holidays
together, and would have gone anywhere with him, but it
seemed a part of his plan that she should hang back a little, be
mildly suspicious.

"What kind of holiday?" she had asked, turning her boot in
the stirrup and trying to look unconcerned.

"On a yacht, Carlotta. A boat."

"Where?"

"Sardinia."

The word *Sardinia* reverberated throughout the room, as if
her father repeated it in his strange, booming, dream voice,
and then she really was asleep.

When she woke up, it was already dark, and Mrs. Hooks
had gone.

Malcolm Kitson, in New York to promote the American edition of his book, was invited to attend a big publishing party
in his honor. The publishers explained that the hosts of the
party had nothing to do with publishing. It was common practice, in the case of distinguished books, to prevail upon some
very social New Yorker to lend his name and home for the
festivities. The name of the man who was hosting Malcolm's
party was Cotter Vere.

The Veres lived in great splendor in a vast apartment on
Park Avenue. The parquet and marble and carved oak had
prepared him for a sedate, older couple, and his surprise on
meeting Cotter and Rachel was great. He was several years
Malcolm's junior, and his wife was a little sprite with masses
of lion-colored hair and wicked eyes. She was quite beautiful
in a way that did not move him, and his overall impression
was one of privileged children playing house.

Malcolm did not like parties of this sort, but, being the guest of honor, he chatted with the various amiable Americans who seemed to want to make him feel at home. He ate the peculiar hors d'oeuvres passed to him by smiling waiters, and dutifully answered questions. When a minor movie star made her entrance, he pretended to be thrilled, although her capped teeth and artificially implanted breasts depressed him.

There were copies of his book placed strategically in every room in the Veres' apartment, but he noticed that people did not bother to examine them. The few who picked the book up glanced at the author's photograph and the favorable quotes from famous people, and then put it down.

Malcolm wandered through the endless rooms, pausing to speak to the few writers he recognized and admired. He felt quite lonely, and thought with mixed pleasure and apprehension of his impending marriage to Belinda. He was wondering why he could not feel happier at the prospect of wedding such a lovely and worthy woman, a woman who loved him whole-heartedly and was, beneath her cool, English exterior, passionate and inventive in bed. He came to what he could only think of as a sub-library, since it was a smaller and more feminine edition of the main one. The chairs were covered in chintz rather than leather, and the curtains at the windows were canary yellow. There were several shelves of books, and a number of framed photographs. He thought it was the Rachel person's private retreat, but there were half a dozen people inside, so he entered.

An elderly woman dressed in mauve lace turned to him with well-bred enthusiasm. She wore an old-fashioned diamond brooch on her ample bosom, and reminded him of his Aunt Ariadne. He was astonished to find out that she was Rachel Vere's mother.

"I trust you're not finding this a bit too *hectic?*" Mrs. Windolm asked. It was obvious that she had retreated to this quiet room because her daughter's parties assailed her nervous system. Probably it was the loud music. "My daughter is a great believer in the value of excessive noise as a means of insuring pleasure at public gatherings," she said peevishly.

Malcolm was assuring her that he found the party charming, when his attention was caught by one of the photographs just beyond Mrs. Windolm's mauve shoulder. A somewhat younger Rachel laughed into the camera, while her companion, a girl of the same age, merely smiled. Both of them seemed to have posed outdoors on a breezy day, and their hair was becomingly tossed. It was the smiling girl who mesmerized him. He stared at the shape of the lips, the hollow of cheekbones, the delicate line of jaw and pure, clear brow, and knew in his bones who it was. Caroline.

"I beg your pardon," he said to Rachel's mother, "can you tell me the name of the young lady in that photograph? The one with your daughter?"

She wheeled around ponderously and allowed him to lead her to within a few inches of the picture. "Why, that's poor little Carlotta," she said. "Such a dear friend of Rachel's. They were great chums for years." Mrs. Windolm smiled, addressed his attention to another picture. "There they are at school together, in Switzerland, where they met. Mr. Windolm and I thought that Carlotta was not a proper companion for Rachel, but the girls were inseparable. And then, of course, there was the unfortunate business, and I don't believe they've seen each other since it happened."

Careful, Malcolm told himself. *Steady on.* Long experience in dealing with skittish old ladies like Aunt Ariadne prepared him for the ordeal he would have to endure in order to coax the story of the "unfortunate business" from Rachel's mother. He pretended to be uninterested, which fueled Mrs. Windolm's need to talk, and he inserted innocent questions just when she was most frustrated.

Soon she was like a broken dam, overspilling herself with a flood of information, and Malcolm was told of the glamorous senator's appetites, his total lack of regard for his wife and child, his predictable and sordid end on the floor of a Georgetown love nest.

"And poor Carlotta Madigan?" she said histrionically. "Who cares for her, or remembers her?"

"Where is she now?" asked Malcolm.

"Oh, here and there in Europe," said Mrs. Windolm. "Rachel told me she gets a postal every once in a while. The girl just wanders from place to place, apparently." She sighed, and made one more confidence before changing the subject. Lowering her voice to a near-whisper, she said: "It was particularly tragic for Carlotta, because she *worshiped* her father. I don't believe in this psychiatry business, but it seems to me that

Carlotta loved her father *too* much, if you see what I mean. It was *unhealthy.*"

Malcolm nodded, remembering Carlotta, so passive and uncaring in his arms, with an aching clarity. He admitted to himself that she was the reason he did not want to marry Belinda, and felt helpless with longing and pity.

SIX

THE ROMAN SPRING CAME EARLY, AND WAS HEART-breakingly beautiful. Soft, golden light bathed the old stones, and the air was full of the fragrance of flowering chestnut trees. At the open-air cafes along the Via Veneto, people sat in a kind of blissful trance, barely bothering to sip their Campari or Cinzano. The Borghese Gardens were thick with couples in love who did not try to conceal it; it was the kind of spring when everyone not in love felt their lives were wasted, and set about to correct the situation.

Carlotta sat on a ruined stone step in the old Roman Forum, feeling the heat collect in the granite and pass its way through the thin stuff of her skirt to warm her thighs. A few early tourists were wandering about, cameras and binoculars weighing them down, but most of the people who passed by were just Romans using the Forum as a shortcut.

She liked Rome, and wondered why American women complained of being pinched, poked, goosed, fondled, and hissed at in the streets if they were unaccompanied. None of these things had happened to Carlotta, and so she assumed the women had been exaggerating, or bragging. She had no way of knowing that her beauty was too extreme, her manner too aloof, to provoke such behavior. She frightened the men, and even those who would willingly have raped her, given the opportunity, did not dare to approach her.

Her peers were another matter. The rich young men who traveled from country to country, and party to party, the younger members of what was called the international social set, homed in on her like pigeons. Last night at a club called Antici she had been propositioned beseechingly in Italian, French, Spanish, English, and Arabic. Some of the men she had met in Sardinia or even in London. If you hung around Europe long enough, the same people kept turning up in the clubs and at parties.

Carlotta sighed. It was a real problem if you enjoyed being around men and required their admiration but didn't want to pay up. Maybe she would strike a bargain with Antonio Fortunado, a good-looking boy (he wasn't more than twenty-two), who admired her extravagantly and yet never came on to her. She suspected that Antonio was a homosexual who was still in the closet, as they said. The very fact that he wasn't owning up to it marked him as very unusual—among the people she knew, nothing was forbidden. But how would she put it? "Tonino, we like each other, don't we? Couldn't we pretend to be madly in love, even if I am a few years older? I don't mean to be immodest, but it couldn't hurt your reputation, being thought of as my lover. What's that? What's in it for me? Well, protection. Protection from all those men who want to get in my pants. It's not that I don't like men, but for the past few years someone has been filling my body with novocaine, so what's the point? Is it a deal, sweet boy?"

Carlotta looked up from her musings to see a child of perhaps four staring at her. He had climbed up on her rock and was studying her so intently she had to smile at his solemnity. He had eyes like black olives, and when she smiled something flickered in those eyes.

"*Buon giorno,*" she said softly. The little boy seemed to come to a decision. "*Que bella signorina,*" he said, and abruptly climbed into her lap, as if sure of a welcome there. He told her that his name was Giovanni, and then he leaned his head against her breast and asked her name. His accent was not Roman, and she wondered what part of Italy he came from.

She was about to tell him that her name was Caroline, when it struck her that her name could make no difference to him whatsoever. *"Mi chiamo Carlotta,"* she said, and felt her name ring in the air between them like the pealing of a huge bell.

"Carlotta," he said, considering it. She could see a woman approaching, picking her way across the stones with haste and agitation. "Giovanni!" the woman called angrily.

She was sorry that the woman was going to deprive her of the pleasant burden in her lap. Giovanni was so warm and smooth, and he smelled of peaches. It was amazing—the pleasure she felt in holding another human being close to her. He climbed down and rejoined his mother, who gave him a little shake and called anxiously up to Carlotta, *"Scusi, signorina."* There was more, but Carlotta's Italian, not so good as her French, wasn't up to it. She thought the woman had said that Giovanni was a wicked boy. She smiled and shook her head to show that no harm had been done. When they were almost out of sight, walking rapidly away, Giovanni pulled on his mother's arm and turned. *"Ciao, Carlotta!"* he yelled.

His voice set up a thousand reverberations, and she heard her name echoing and dancing crazily among the ancient ruins.

The party that night was at a new club called Perugia, for no other reason than that its owner came from that city. It was in a dim alleyway off the Piazza Navona. Carlotta could hear the throb of the music before she had disembarked from her taxi. She was wearing a pale blue shift with a scalloped hem that she had bought in Venice, and the moment she walked down the three steps and entered Perugia, she regretted her choice.

The interior of the club was lit entirely in blue, giving everyone a lunar, corpse-like aspect, and she felt that she had disappeared in the blueness. Apparently this was not so, because a chorus of *Car-o-leen* arose when she appeared, and she was able to make her way to the long table where Jean-Claud, Amelia, Sebastiano, Franco, Jane, Marie-Thérèse, Serafina, Bianca, Ali, Nigel, Eduardo, and Leila were all gathered. She was amazed to find them in such sedentary positions, because they were all tireless and exhibitionistic dancers. Normally, they would be out on the floor, pumping and perspiring, but tonight they sat like senior citizens, their drinks before them, waiting to be entertained.

"You're just in time," hissed Bianca. "It's a special entertainment."

She had time enough to squeeze in between Bianca and Sebastiano, and then the lights dimmed and there was the swelling of music. *Carmina Burana*. Serafina giggled. Carlotta had not seen Antonio anywhere in the club. So much for her scenario.

The lights rose to reveal a nun, dressed in the stern black habit and white headgear of a Benedictine. Around her neck there swung a gigantic cross, and at her waist were rosary beads. The nun seemed not to know where she was. She stared in panic at the audience, shielding her body from their manifold eyes. The orgiastic music bewildered her. Then, slowly, she began to sway to the rhythm, a pensive look overtaking her delicate features.

The audience tittered. "Santa Maria!" bawled a male voice.

Gradually, the nun removed her clothing. The wimple went first, then the coif. She smiled as each article fell to the floor, but she was still so covered that the smile might be thought to be innocent. The rosary beads were plucked off expertly and retained, wound around the stripper's wrist, for a later use.

The club was charged with excitement; it trembled in the air. The sacrilege of the stripper's act combined with her skill to make the viewers dangerously aroused.

There was a breathless hush when the performer began to peel away her habit, teasing the audience with brief glimpses of her naked body, only to hide it again. She had large, dark-nippled breasts that appeared to have been oiled. When at last the habit lay in a heap at her feet she stood before them attired only in her cross and g-string. The black bush of her pubic hair could not be contained by the slender strip of silk, and many of the men moaned and called out to her.

Now she grinned unabashedly at them, a carnal, evil grin. She moved to the music, slowly at first, then more urgently. She ground her hips, fondled her breasts and turned, bending, to show them the smooth, plump cheeks of her rump. "Santa Maria!" yelled the man again, in a real frenzy now. The stripper squatted so that the tip of the cross slithered over her g-string. She pouted her lips and sighed, as if the motion were giving her pleasure, and then, as if she had had a brilliant thought, she unwrapped the rosary beads from around her wrists and held them up invitingly. The audience shouted its encouragement. Beside Carlotta, Sebastiano was breathing hard.

The dancer wetted her lips, threw back her head, and dangled the beads over her breasts. Across the table from Carlotta, Ali shouted his appreciation in Arabic. It sounded as if he was calling on Allah. The rosary beads were descending lower now, and Carlotta saw, with disgust, what was going to happen next. She wanted to look away, but watching the hot eyes of the men around her was worse than looking at the woman. At least the dancer's excitement was simulated; the men's was real. When she passed the beads between her legs and began a sawing motion of her hips, there was a collective shout of approval. She was quite acrobatic, Carlotta had to admit. She was capable of doing a sort of backbend while masturbating with the beads. The muscles in her thighs strained, but she never missed a stroke. When the music reached an orgasmic peak, she gave a great shriek and collapsed on the floor, panting.

The lights went out and the club was in total darkness. The shouting subsided and there was a furtive silence punctuated with little grunts and sighs. Sebastiano grabbed at Carlotta's hand, forcing it beneath the table. She resisted with all her strength, but his power was far greater than hers, and he pressed her hand against his crotch so she could feel the might of his erection. She stamped on his foot as hard as she could, grinding her pointed heel into his instep, and he let her hand go with a cry of outrage.

"Beetch!" he muttered.

The lights came on again, and the nun and all her paraphernalia had vanished. The sounds of Mick Jagger replaced her, and everyone at the table staggered to their feet, the men with visible erections, and went to throw themselves around on the dance floor.

Only Amelia remained behind. She looked troubled, shaken. "What did you think of that?" she asked Carlotta.

"I thought it was repulsive," Carlotta said.

"I guess we are the only ones to feel that way," said Amelia. "It makes me sick to think such a thing can go on so close to the Vatican."

Carlotta agreed, although the Vatican's proximity had not entered her mind. She had been thinking of another naked dancer, and wondering if she had produced the same effect in the man she later killed as the nun had in Sebastiano. It was not a thing she wished to think about, and when the waiter came, she asked for a double vodka and drank it as quickly as possible.

She liked the cool, dark rooms of the flat she was living in; they were all the more appealing because of the deceptive nature of the place. Trastevere, the old quarter across the Tiber, contained many surprises. The building she lived in was made of yellow stone, and was very plain on the outside, like houses she had seen in pictures of Sicily. Inside, however, the rooms were nobly proportioned, even palatial. The floors were an elaborate mosaic of tile which felt cool beneath her feet, and from the windows she looked down on a little sundial in the center of a hidden courtyard. The heat of the day never penetrated the thick walls, and it was possible to sleep the day away if she liked, because of the thick, Mediterranean shutters.

Often she lay until late afternoon in the large, carved wood bed, rising at 4:00 to bathe and dress for the evening's activities. She liked to sit in the cafes on the Via Veneto or Margutta, sipping an aperitif at the delicious hour when the light was beginning to fade. There was always a late dinner party to attend, and dancing, and the clubs. She had made it a point to never return to Perugia, but she and Antonio often went to Antici and danced the night away.

One evening, just as the bells of the Church of the Capuchin Monks were striking six, Carlotta settled herself at a table on the Via Veneto and ordered a Cinzano with ice. She was thinking that she would have to sell another piece of jewelry soon when she heard a familiar laugh. It didn't quite register, only hovered at the edge of her consciousness. She had gone through the money she had received for selling the house in Georgetown, and it was not yet time for her semiannual check. She was wondering how much she could get for her mother's diamond bracelet when the laugh rang out again.

Carlotta looked in the direction of the laugh, and found herself staring straight at Rachel Vere. Rachel was sitting at a table with an older woman, and she had not seen Carlotta yet. It would have been possible to steal away and avoid Rachel, but the sight of her friend had an overwhelming impact. Wave after wave of what she could only call homesickness passed over Carlotta, but she merely sat still, waiting for Rachel to look in her direction.

Rachel had let her hair grow longer and was using less makeup these days, but otherwise she had not changed. She seemed very absorbed by what the older woman was saying. Carlotta smiled fondly when Rachel lit a cigarette, blew a perfect smoke ring, and then crushed the cigarette out. It was an old trick.

When Rachel saw her, she knocked over her glass in astonishment. Her huge eyes widened almost comically and she gave a little shriek. "Carlotta!" she cried, leaping to her feet and running between the tables, "Oh, Carlotta!" And then Carlotta was on her feet and they met halfway and fell into each other's arms, embracing in the middle of the Via Veneto, much to the amusement of the crowd.

"Oh, Jesus," Rachel sniffed, tears streaming down her face. "To think I might have missed you. If the timing hadn't been exactly right—I didn't know you were in Rome."

"I've missed you," said Carlotta. "It makes me so happy to see you, you can't imagine."

And it was true. She felt happier than she had in all the time she'd been partying around Europe. She let Rachel lead her to the table where the older woman sat looking suspicious.

"This is my best friend in all the world," Rachel said, as they sat down, "Carlotta Madigan. Carlotta, this is the Contessa Natalia della Toscana."

"I am pleased to make your acquaintance," said the contessa formally, but she did not look pleased. She seemed about forty, and had the regular but severe features that brand a woman as handsome. She was deeply tanned, and her greenish eyes glittered in the dusk.

"Natalia and I met in New York," Rachel said. "I'm her guest here in Rome."

"Is Cotter here, too?" Carlotta noticed the contessa's eyes narrow at the mention of Cotter.

"No, he couldn't get away just now. I needed some time away from him, anyway."

For the next half hour, Rachel talked a steady stream of gossip, news, and anecdote, and Carlotta listened happily. At last the contessa interrupted. "Rachel, you have not given Miss Madigan a chance to speak at all. If you have not seen her for so long a time, should you not be interested in hearing about her?"

Rachel winked at Carlotta. "She'll tell me when she wants to," she said. "Carlotta likes to be secretive."

They all went to dinner together at a restaurant on a little hill reached by a flight of pink marble steps. The contessa was treated with near reverence, and the food and wine were excellent.

"I haven't much to tell," Carlotta said. "I've just been here and there, leading the usual dissolute life of expatriates."

"Are you then an expatriate, quite literally?" the contessa asked. "Why have you chosen to abandon your country?"

"Oh, Natalia," Rachel said, "Carlotta's just being funny." She telegraphed a mute message of reassurance, and then patted the older woman's hand. Natalia imprisoned her fingers for a moment, then excused herself and went to the ladies' room.

"Rachel," Carlotta said, "I'm known as Caroline Moore here. Please don't call me Carlotta if you meet any of my friends."

"No, oh, of course not," Rachel said, shrugging the question of names aside. "But listen, darling, I have the most marvelous thing to tell you." She hugged herself and gave a little pleased giggle. "Can you guess?"

"I think you'd better spell it out."

"I've discovered I'm bisexual," said Rachel. "Just when I was beginning to think I was boring and straight, I found out the truth. I met Natalia."

"Natalia is your—?"

"Natalia is my lover," said Rachel. "She's just too fabulous for words."

Gradually, Carlotta came to understand Rachel's attraction to the contessa. Natalia della Toscana was one of those women who seem stern and forbidding at first out of a deep-seated shyness, but as Carlotta began to discover, she was an extremely kind and intelligent woman, deeply religious, and possessed of a highly developed moral conscience. Natalia read the newspapers and grieved for all the troubles of the world as if they were her own. She lived in luxury, because she knew of no other way to live, but Rachel had told her that

Natalia gave immense amounts of money to charitable causes.

She did not flaunt her lesbianism, was not promiscuous. She was very much in love with Rachel, but would never have invited her—a young married woman—to visit her in Rome if she had not seen that Rachel was unhappy with Cotter. Carlotta understood that the contessa was just a passing fling for Rachel, although Rachel didn't know that yet, and she wondered if the contessa understood that her beloved was bound to abandon her.

"How calm and beautiful it is here," Carlotta said. "You have created a paradise, Natalia."

"Ah, no, I cannot take the credit, dear Carlotta. The things you see in the villa have been in my family for many generations."

"But you built this pool," Rachel pointed out. "It was your creation."

"True, true," said Natalia, who was rubbing a sun-filtering lotion on Rachel's back, devotedly making sure that the delicate white skin would not burn under the fierce sun.

They were sitting at the edges of the miraculous pool, in the garden of Natalia's villa on the ancient Appian Way. It was irregularly shaped, as a natural pool would be, and so densely planted around with laurels and thick, fragrant bushes that you had to know the way in to even know that it was there at all. If Carlotta lay on her back and looked up, she would see the tall tops of the cypress trees beyond, but otherwise it was possible to believe that she was by the side of an enchanted pool, deep in a forest.

Out of deference to her, she felt sure, Rachel and Natalia were wearing bathing suits. Rachel's was a Rudi Gernreich bikini, but Natalia wore an old-fashioned tank suit, black and no-nonsense. She had a lean, superbly proportioned body, boyish and still young. With her dark hair free from the usual ballerina knot and flowing around her shoulders, she could pass for thirty-five, but Rachel had told her that she was close to fifty.

"There, *cara*," Natalia said, "you are well oiled." Rachel rolled over and smiled and then, in one supple movement, slid into the pool. She dived down into the water and re-emerged a few moments later, laughing and shaking her wet, curly hair as if she were a seal. Carlotta studied the contessa covertly, noticing the look of tenderness that had come into the green eyes while Rachel frolicked. Natalia lifted her glass of wine to her lips and drank, but her eyes never left their subject.

Carlotta envied them. She understood that their very opposite personalities were what had brought them together. Rachel loved what was strong and tranquil and morally good about the contessa, and Natalia loved, despite herself, the good-natured and joyous amorality which had always been Rachel's nature. "She is such a child," she said, still watching Rachel. "She has the energy of a child, as well as the ability to believe that nothing bad will ever happen to her. She *trusts*."

"Yes," said Carlotta. "You've summed her up in just a few words."

"But you, Carlotta, you are very different. You trust no one—I read it in your eyes—yet you are as young as she and just as beautiful." Natalia smiled ruefully. "More, if one could be objective, as I cannot. You are beautiful, and apparently without a care in the world. I say apparently, because you can go where you will and do as you like, but I know you are sorrowful."

Carlotta focused her attention on a swarm of swallows flying in the white sky. "If I seem different from Rachel," she said at last, "it's because I know bad things can happen."

"Ah, *carina,* so do I. I have always known, from childhood, but it has not made me so distrustful that I have withdrawn from life. I have my retreat here, in this villa, along this ancient road, but occasionally I go out into the world and see what is happening."

"That's all I've been doing for two and a half years," said Carlotta. "Going out into the world to see what's happening."

"You mistake me. I do not mean going to nightclubs and on cruises and appearing at the right places with the right people. I mean—how do you say in English?—an *expedition*. An expedition to lead you outside of yourself. To see how the world is faring, and what your place in it might be, and how you might help."

Rachel had swum back to them and was calling for a drink. Natalia poured her a glass of wine, added a wild strawberry to the glass, and handed it to her. Rachel saluted them, bouncing in the water and gulping at her wine. Carlotta noticed that Rachel's body seemed fuller, more voluptuous. The small, pretty breasts—the kind the French pronounced perfect, since they were the size and shape of a wineglass's cup—swelled over her bikini top with a new ripeness. She had a brief, erotic vision of the contessa's hands working some magic on Rachel's body.

"Your vision of the expedition outside myself is a noble one," Carlotta said when Rachel had drained her wine and gone off again. "That's probably because you're noble yourself, and can't understand lesser mortals like me. I thought I was noble once, an American princess, and then I found out that the man I admired most—my father, actually—wasn't even close to being a prince. He was a frog disguised as a prince, but I'm sure Rachel has told you all about it."

A part of her was amazed at this loose-tongued confidence. She was willingly parting with information that she would have guarded with her life in England. Why? She put it down to the contessa's hypnotic presence, and the pagan aura of the place itself. The dusty road lined with ancient tombs, the statue of the goddess Minerva in the garden of the villa had all combined to rob her of her common sense and make her babble.

"Listen," said Natalia with her enigmatic smile. "When I was twelve, my father shot himself. He did it in full view of my mother, whose dress was spattered with his brains. She discovered, after his death, that he had incurred enormous debts at gambling. I have six illegitimate half-sisters and -brothers, whom I try to help financially. My mother died in a villa at Fiesole, so mad that she had to be restrained from eating razor blades. My brother was a Fascist during the war, and he was later shot. One of my sisters became a nun in one of the silent orders, and the other has disappeared altogether. I presume she is dead. But have I decided that their fate will be mine? No. I am my own person, and I will not allow myself to believe that I am a prisoner of fate. I shall survive, Carlotta, because I will it to be so."

No conventional expression of sympathy would do. Carlotta wanted to tell Natalia how sorry she was for so many wasted and blasted lives, but Natalia did not want sympathy. She was trying to be instructive.

"Do you picture yourself in paradise with Rachel ten years from now?" Carlotta asked bitterly. "Is that part of your survival plan?"

"Unhappily, no," said Natalia. "I am not a fool, Carlotta. Rachel will return to her husband quite soon, and I will be left alone again. I knew, you understand, that Rachel was my last love."

"How do you know she'll go back to Cotter so soon?" Carlotta asked, avoiding the all-knowing green eyes and staring at her painted toenails.

"Haven't you noticed?" said the contessa. "You have known her since she was sixteen. She doesn't know yet, because she doesn't choose to recognize such things."

"What things?" Carlotta asked. "What is it that she refuses to recognize?"

"Why, *cara,*" said Natalia, whispering, "it is perfectly obvious to me. Rachel is going to have a child. She is pregnant."

SEVEN

"IT'S STRANGE," SAID THE KILLER, SPEAKING IN A LOW, breathy voice. "You go along, not questioning it, the way things are supposed to be, and then one day you can't take it anymore. It just happens. You can't take it. You *refuse* to take it. You rebel, I guess you could say. It's his life or yours, and you choose your own over his."

The woman was about Lee's age, and she spoke in calm, reasonable tones. She was explaining, in the Butte, Montana, jail, her reasons for shooting her husband to death with his own shotgun in their kitchen.

"He was drunk, you see," said the woman, pushing her dirty blonde hair away from her eyes. "When he was drunk, he was liable to do anything. He knocked three of my teeth out the first month we were married. *Wham!* And there went those teeth, quick as anything, and I had a pretty smile, Miss Redwing. Used to have.

"And it just got worse. He broke my ribs by kicking me when I was down, and he blacked my eyes so often I wore dark glasses. I swear he would have killed me if I hadn't killed him, Miss Redwing. I felt it. He was crazier than usual, and he would have killed me." The woman bent her head and sobbed, quietly and humbly, into her hands. "He wasn't a bad man," she said between sobs, "he was a good man, basically, only there was something *wrong* with him."

"When your husband injured you, Mrs. Carlson, did you go to a doctor?"

"No," said the woman, scrubbing at her eyes. "No, I was too ashamed. I couldn't bear for anyone to know. I was always making out I was having accidents. When I went to the dentist the time he bashed my teeth in, I said I'd fallen face-first on the ice."

"This is very discouraging for me, Mrs. Carlson. What you're saying is that no one can testify in your behalf."

Sally Jane Carlson looked up, her face a mask of misery. "Does that mean you're not going to take my case?"

"Oh, Sally, of course I'm going to defend you. But you have to help me build your defense. I can't do it without you. How about your children? I know you don't want to put them on the stand, but we need everything we can get."

"He was never violent with them. Only me. They're still so young, Miss Redwing—the oldest, Candy, is only six. They never dreamed what he was like."

Lee studied the woman with pity and utter bewilderment. How could she have remained married, for seven years, to such a man? Any woman could make the mistake of marrying a man who seemed kind and good but proved to be violent and cruel, but Sally Carlson had gone on to have three children by him. It was incomprehensible.

How was she to convince a jury that a woman who shot her husband was a victim, not a criminal? Especially when there were no X rays showing broken ribs, no family or neighbors to testify that the dead man had abused his wife? She would have to subpoena the dentist who had repaired Sally's teeth. She made a note on her pad.

"On the night of the incident"—she had noticed that Sally flinched at the word "killed" so she tried to avoid it—"you say he was drunk?"

Sally nodded. Her pale eyes were so swollen from crying they seemed little more than slits. "He was real tanked up," she said. "He had been at The Longhorn—that's where he did his drinking—and when he came through that door, looking so mean, I knew. I knew he would kill me this time."

"Did he have friends he drank with regularly?"

"Sure," said Sally. "But they'd stick together. They'd never admit in court to how heavy he drank."

"It's a terrible thing to say," said Lee, "but I wish he'd gotten a lick at you before the, ah, incident. At least we would have photographs of you with a black eye, or a split lip. When you stop crying, by the time you get to court, you're going to look perfectly normal."

Something happened to Sally's face, a slight flicker of excitement. "There is *something*," she said slowly. "I have some marks, scars now, but they're still there." She got up from the chair and turned her back to Lee, awkwardly lifting her sweater.

"Do you see?" she asked. Lee saw. Sally's back was punctuated with little round, puckered scars. Some of them disappeared beneath the strap of her brassiere, and Lee counted nine. She thought she knew how Sally had come by them, and shuddered with revulsion. "How did they get there?" she asked gently.

"He burned me with his cigarette," Sally whispered wretchedly. And then, as if she still needed to defend the man she had married: "That was a long time ago, though. Roy never did that again. Just the one time."

"Why? Did he give up smoking?" Lee knew it was not her place to speak bitterly of the monstrous Roy Carlson, not until she got to court, but she hadn't been able to keep the words back.

"No, Miss Redwing. He was still smoking three packs a day, right up until, until—"

"Just one more question for now, Sally. Or two, really. How much did Roy weigh?"

"A little over two hundred pounds."

"And how much do you weigh?"

"A hundred four."

"I'm going to get you out of this," said Lee, "or die in the attempt. Sally, Sally, why did you stay married to him?"

"That's three questions," said Sally, showing a sense of humor for the first time. She smiled wanly. Just before the prison guard showed Lee out, though, she called, "I loved him, that's why."

The bartender at The Longhorn Hotel was a big man with sandy hair and a thick, reddish moustache. He had a soft voice, and Lee wondered if he kept it low in reaction to the noise all around him. Hank Snow was blaring from the jukebox, and the customers, who all worked for Anaconda Copper but dressed like cowboys in their leisure hours, whooped and guffawed as they drank their endless beers. There were only two other females in The Longhorn, and both wore skin-tight jeans and even tighter sweaters, and giggled hysterically at anything the men said.

Lee, in her neat business suit, was an unusual sight, and the noise abated a little as they lowered their voices to speculate about an Injun dressed like a white-collar worker.

She ordered a gin and tonic, and in a voice as low as the bartender's, inquired if he had known Roy Carlson.

"Roy? Course I knew him. That was a terrible thing. Terrible. What's the world coming to if a man can't be safe from his own wife in his own kitchen?"

"I guess he'd had a lot to drink that night," said Lee, as if admiring Roy Carlson's capacity. "He was a real good-time guy, huh?"

"Who are you? Why all these questions?" The bartender backed off suspiciously.

Lee handed him her card. It would be nice to pretend she was a prosecutor, but that would be unethical. "I'm defending Mrs. Carlson," she said.

The big bartender looked at her with distaste. "You want me to make out Roy was drunk? So what? Is that a capital crime? A man has a few and his wife mows him down. Is that it?"

"No," said Lee. "I just want to know how much he had to drink that night. I want to hear it from you."

"Oh, just a coupla beers, as I recall. Nothing heavy."

"If I subpoena you, and you say that in court, you're going to look like a liar. I'm sure you wouldn't want that. The coroner's report will show the exact level of alcohol in his blood, you know. We already know that Roy Carlson came here straight from work and stayed until half past ten. He was killed at 11:20, so he couldn't have had much more to drink after leaving The Longhorn. It's a twenty-five minute drive from here to where the Carlsons lived."

"Well, ain't you smart," the bartender sneered. "Yeah, I reckon Roy was lubricated that night. So what?"

"Stick around and find out," said Lee.

When she left, one of the men called to her. What he said sounded like, "Come on over, Suzy-Q, and I'll buy you a drink." Lee knew he was saying Siouxsie; it was an old joke.

"Cheyenne, honey. Me no drink with paleface."

The dentist was an unexpected ally. Dr. Robert Morse told Lee that he had been suspicious about Sally Carlson's injury. For one thing, young healthy women who were used to Montana winters didn't go falling on the ice, straight on their faces. Not unless they drank, and Sally didn't. He knew, because he had been her dentist all the years of her life.

"But more importantly," he said, leaning back in his chair and assuming a scholarly look, "the nature of the dental injuries was not consistent with a fall. They were, I thought at the time, caused by impact."

"What sort of impact?" Lee asked.

"Impact with Roy Carlson's fist, if you ask me." He got Sally's X rays from his files and, using a great deal of technical jargon, explained how the X rays were identical to ones of people who had been in a fist fight. "It's a sad thing," he said, "to suspect that a young woman is being victimized like that. But if she won't admit to it, what can anyone do?"

"Would you be willing to testify on her behalf in court?"

"You bet," he said. "More of that sort of thing goes on than people realize. It might be a good thing to get it out in the open."

Lee felt like kissing him.

The name of Lee Redwing was the last Carlotta expected to hear on Antonio's lips. In fact, when he spoke it, she thought she had misunderstood at first. She was lying in the big bed in her Trastevere rooms, sleepy and pleased with herself. Antonio sprawled at the foot of the bed, outside the covers, reading the *Rome Daily American*. He read it every day, hoping to improve his already excellent English.

Carlotta and Antonio were lovers now, after a fashion. It had all come about quite naturally, and there had been no need for her to recite the little speech she had rehearsed in the Forum that day. Antonio wanted to be with her, and because he was so gentle, she did not fear him at all. The surprising part was the lovemaking business. It had surprised them both.

They had been at a party at the Via degli Artisti, and neither of them knew the hostess or quite remembered what had brought them there. The woman who seemed to be the hostess was a tall, vampiric creature who wore long velvet robes and drifted from room to room, carrying a silver candelabra. The only light came from flickering candles, and the only music to be heard was a wild, Arab lament. Everywhere, like bowls of peanuts, lay great silver trays filled with pills of every sort. There were uppers and downers, Seconal, Tuinal, Preludin, looking, with all their mixed, bright colors, like jelly beans. "She is rumored to be a heroin addict," Antonio had told Carlotta. "She is very, very decadent." And he had sighed, as if so much decadence bored him.

A girl in a silver shift had approached them at one point. She had long, rippling hair like Botticelli's Venus, and looked as divinely innocent. "You are both so beautiful," said the lovely girl in a soft, musical voice. "I would like it if you would take off your clothes and make love while I watch. I wish to see you fuck."

It had been so unexpected that both Carlotta and Antonio burst into laughter. The girl, offended by their response to her erotic suggestion, went drifting off, and soon the vampire-like hostess came to reprove them. "It seems you expect to enjoy my hospitality without repaying it," she said. "You have hurt Claudia's feelings." This made them laugh harder, and then, of course, they couldn't stay. They had found themselves back on the Via degli Artisti, and Carlotta had invited Antonio to come home with her to Trastevere, as she might have invited a woman friend.

How had it started? They had talked for a long time, drinking tart, icy white wine. Antonio told Carlotta of his desire to become a filmmaker, a rival of the great Fellini. He also told her that he would never be a great success in Italy because he was not an ideal Italian male.

"I am not capable of looking at women as they do," he had told her. "I do not regard a woman as something to be caught and pinned down and violated, so I can tell my men friends all about it the next day. They see a woman and think only one thing—sex, as hard and quick and brutal as possible—while I look at a woman and see only another person. Sometimes nice, pleasant, attractive—sometimes not. Rarely do I desire one, and this makes me very odd, no?"

"Maybe if you lived in a different culture," Carlotta had

told him, "a culture that didn't insist on men being so eternally macho, maybe then you would find yourself desiring women more."

They had begun to be very sleepy, and gone to lie on the huge bed together. Like children settling in for a nap, they lay holding hands, still laughing about the vampire and the angelic girl who had wished to see them fuck. They drifted into sleep, and somehow into each other's arms.

She had awakened at one point, and found her head against Antonio's chest. He smelled of limes, and she supposed it was his aftershave. His dark, smooth skin where the collar of his shirt lay open was so attractive she unbuttoned the shirt completely and laid her head on his naked chest. He was such a pretty boy, so candid and gentle and intelligent, and she felt such affection for him. She kissed his chest. Soon she felt his hands sifting through her hair, caressing her neck, and when she lifted her head she found him staring at her with a strange expression.

Tentatively, they had begun to caress one another. Their lips met, clung sweetly, parted. She felt his body quickening, but for a long time it was as if they were only playing. Their clothes came off, somehow, and they admired each other's bodies.

"Ah, Caroleena, you are so lovely," Antonio would say, arranging her hair over her breasts and then sweeping it away to plant a shy kiss on one rosy nipple. "You, too," was her sincere reply as she smoothed her hands over his hard, wonderfully round buttocks. They felt, she thought, like marble warmed by the sun.

When Antonio entered her body it was not with a hard thrust, but gently, almost playfully. They moved together in easy, rocking rhythm, and when Antonio's orgasm came he merely sighed with pleasure, murmuring her name. For Carlotta it had been so loving and sweet that she didn't at all mind her own lack of passion. There had been great pleasure just in being so close to another person again, and in giving him pleasure.

Sometimes, in the days that followed, she felt little echoes of pleasure when she and Antonio lay on the bed and played. It was a little, fluttering sensation, as if a school of minnows had gone swimming through her, but that was all. She understood that if her response had been the violent, ecstatic one she dimly recalled from the night with Hugh McManus, Antonio would have been frightened and repelled. *He* understood that if he had taken her with all the fiery, driving passion of an Italian lover, she would retreat back into her mysterious, sorrowful coolness.

On the morning when he lay reading the *Rome Daily American*, Carlotta lay between sleeping and waking, her body warm and vibrant from their childlike lovemaking. Occasionally the bed would shake a little as Antonio laughed at something he had read. He found American names very amusing, and he would repeat the ones that took his fancy, and laugh. Mamie Eisenhower was a name he never tired of, and Walter Cronkite and Katharine Hepburn were great favorites.

The bed shook softly. "Dean Rusk," said Antonio with delight. Carlotta was just falling asleep when she thought she heard him repeat Lee Redwing's name, but that was impossible. Nevertheless, the very thought prevented her from going back to sleep.

"What did you say, Tonino?" she asked lazily.

"A name, *cara*. I think it must be an Indian name. Lee Redwing."

She was now wide awake and fearful. "What about Lee Redwing?" she asked.

"I am reading about her," he said. "It is a very sad thing."

Carlotta sat bolt upright. "What?" she cried. Her voice was so urgent that Antonio's eyes widened. "Has something happened to her?"

"No, no. Not to her. She is the lawyer who is going to defend the sad one. A woman who has killed her husband. He was a brute, it say he beat her—" His English was deteriorating due to Carlotta's initial, almost hysterical response to the name of Lee Redwing. "Here," he said, handing her the paper. "You read it for yourself. I will go make the coffee."

Apparently the case of Sally Carlson was becoming a *cause célèbre* in America. Miss Lee Redwing, attorney for the defendant, had refused to plea-bargain and was entering a plea of not guilty. Her client, said Miss Redwing, had acted in self-defense. Feminists all over America were taking an interest in the case in remote Butte, Montana, Carlotta read, and if Miss Redwing succeeded in winning a verdict of not guilty, a sort of precedent would be made. The trial was just beginning, and it was expected to last a long time.

Carlotta let the paper drop, and lay back against the pillows. She was proud of Lee and wished her success. When Antonio came back, bringing coffee and fresh pomegranate slices on a silver tray, she was smiling again.

He set the tray down and climbed back into bed beside her. He twined one leg cozily with hers and tied one long strand of her hair around his wrist. "Is it all right, then?" he asked.

"Yes," she assured him. "Lee Redwing was a very good friend of mine once."

"Va bene," said Antonio. "But pity the poor Signora Carlson. Here in Italy she would be stoned, probably. Here a man who kills his wife is still considered a hero, so imagine what is thought of a wife who kills her husband!"

His lips were very red from eating pomegranate, and he looked like a young Roman god. She put her hands beneath the bedclothes and found his rosy maleness, sleeping against his thigh. She fondled it until he became very hard and the bedclothes rose as if by magic.

"Do you know?" Antonio whispered, turning to her, "I think I could get used to this."

"Me too," said Carlotta.

Antonio came with her to the Excelsior, where she was to have a drink with Rachel and the contessa. She could see Rachel, fetching in white linen, a crimson silk flower in her hair, but no contessa.

She introduced Antonio, and Rachel's eyes registered her approval, but she said, "Would you mind if I talked to Carlotta, I mean Caroline, in privacy? Just for a few moments."

"Of course," said Antonio, withdrawing politely.

"Where did you get *him?*" Rachel asked, rolling her eyes. "He's fabulous. Oh, sly Carlotta. You always surprise me."

"I'm very fond of Antonio. Since you've banished him, you could at least tell me what we have to talk about in privacy?"

Instantly, Rachel's features rearranged themselves in an expression of great solemnity. "I've got to go home," she said. "I wasn't feeling too great the other day, and I went to Natalia's doctor, and what do you think?"

So the contessa had been right. Carlotta waited for Rachel to tell her.

"I'm two months pregnant! Can you imagine? Cotter

knocked me up a month before I came to Rome, while I was having an affair with Natalia in New York. I should keep better track of things, don't you think?"

"What are you going to do?"

"Natalia was terribly shocked when I mentioned an abortion. She doesn't believe in it, you know. The odd thing is"—she looked apologetic—"neither do I, really. Cotter and I had been trying to have a child, and then Natalia arrived on the scene, and I'd had my IUD taken out..." She spread her hands, as if proud of the chaos of her life. "Well, the thing is—I can't really bring up a baby with Natalia, can I? A child needs its father, too. So I guess there's nothing to do but go back and have the baby."

"Poor Natalia," said Carlotta.

"Yes, that's part of what I wanted to talk about. She's going to be pretty lonely at first. Could you sort of go out to the villa, now and then, and cheer her up? She likes you, but don't worry, she won't make a move on you. Take Antonio if you like. Just check up on her now and then?"

"Of course I will. I would even if you hadn't asked."

"Well, that's taken care of, then," said Rachel cheerfully. "I'm leaving tomorrow. Just think—a baby! Do you think I'll be a good mother? I'm looking forward to it, now that I've made my decision. And I do wish you'd come back home, Carlotta. I'll need moral support, and I want you to be the baby's godmother." She was speaking very rapidly, even for her, and Carlotta could see that Rachel was running scared. It was characteristic of her that she already thought of Natalia as someone who could be "cheered up" by a visit or two.

"Now that everything's settled," said Rachel, "let's bring back your darling Antonio. I want to measure his eyelashes."

After Rachel flew back to New York, Carlotta waited a day and then went to the villa on the Appian Way. It was locked and deserted, and no servant came when she rang. She looked at the statue of Minerva, and ached with sympathy for the contessa. She might be as wise as the goddess, but wisdom could not drive away pain.

A few days later, she received a note from Tangiers:

You are the only person in all the world who knows what I am feeling, dear Carlotta. I shall recover, but at present I require solitude. If you have left Rome before I return, take my best wishes with you always. Just now—*odi et amo*.

Natalia

Carlotta looked at the phrase in Latin, a language she and Rachel had studied in Switzerland, and thought the contessa had summed the situation up perfectly. *I hate and I love.*

EIGHT

THE FIRST FEW DAYS OF THE TRIAL IN BUTTE WENT WELL FOR Lee, even though the prosecutor, a tough little man named Garnett, had amassed a regular army of men willing to testify to Roy Carlson's good character. They were mainly Roy's drinking buddies from The Longhorn, but neatly dressed and sober-looking, they seemed quite respectable.

"Yes, sir," they answered Garnett, "Roy was a hard worker who provided for his family. A God-fearing man. Friendly, decent, and loyal."

Lee simply asked them all, on cross-examination, if they dropped in at The Longhorn more or less every night. They admitted it was so, and looked perplexed and angry at the question. It made them uneasy that she asked nothing else of them.

Through it all, Sally Carlson sat meekly, her face pale but unmarked, wearing the modest but sleeveless dress Lee had selected for her. She wanted the jurors to see how thin and fragile Sally's arms were. How powerless.

Lee was feeling at her combative best. The jury was neatly divided—six men and six women. Garnett believed he had the advantage, since two of the women were from a funda-mentalist sect that believed the man of the house to be one step removed from a god, and Lee allowed him to feel triumphant. He had managed to get two good ole boys into the group of six males, but he had not been able to prevent her from sneaking in two sympathetic men—a landscape gardener who clearly disliked the good ole boys, and a retired schoolteacher, unpopular in Butte, who had spoken out against the war in Vietnam. The other two men could go either way, but she was confident of the women. Even the fundamentalists were women first, believers second.

Lee gave a great deal of attention to her appearance. She didn't want to appear in court as a defiant emissary from America's Third World, but neither could she pretend to ignore that she was a Cheyenne. The former would arouse anger, the second contempt. At first she relied on her old hair style for going to court: a severe, swept-back look, with the mass of her hair coiled at the nape of her neck. When she saw her face on the local television broadcasts, she realized that it would never do. She looked too fierce. Reluctantly, she cut bangs, and allowed some of the hair to lie in soft wings against her cheeks. It gave her a fashionable, sex-kittenish look which she hated, but if it would help Sally Carlson, so be it.

She needed the softer look when she examined the coroner, a sweet-looking old fellow, and asked him about the alcohol level in Roy Carlson's blood. It was a question the prosecutor had avoided, concentrating on the fatal wounds which had deprived Roy Carlson of his life, cutting him down in what the D.A. was happy to call "the flower of his manhood."

The lovable old coroner had shuffled through his report— it was the last question he had expected to be asked—and finally divulged, in highly technical terms, the information.

"Will you explain to the jury what a blood alcohol concentration of .32 percent means?" Lee asked.

"Well," the coroner drawled, playing to his audience, "it means Roy Carlson had had a few."

The courtroom exploded with laughter.

The coroner was less comic when she asked him to tell the court what the legal level was in Montana, and by the time she produced her expert witness, the court became thoughtful. Roy had definitely passed the falling-down drunk stage, he testified. A blood alcohol concentration, of .30 to .40 percent generally led to stupor, while one of .40 to .55 percent resulted, in most cases, in coma.

"And a .60 percent or greater BAC?" asked Lee.

"It would be fatal."

She got him to explain that an habitual drinker of Roy's body size could pass into the stuporous stage at the lower limits and still be capable of violent and dangerous behavior. There were many calls of "Objection!" but Lee maintained that Roy's BAC on the night of the fatal shooting was at the heart of her defense, and most of the objections were over-ruled.

She had to fight every step of the way. Dr. Morse's testimony about Sally's smashed teeth interested the jury, but was ultimately ruled inadmissable on the grounds that the dentist was conjecturing. She submitted, for evidence, the X rays taken of Sally in jail that showed old wounds to the ribs and spine, but the prosecutor was able to plant a seed of disbelief in the jury.

"Why," he said, "I broke three ribs when I was a boy, falling off a Palomino that hadn't been broke, and I defy medical science to tell you when those injuries happened."

Her greatest triumph came when she introduced into evidence the photographs of the scars on Sally's back, and produced a doctor who testified that the scars had been caused by burning. It was about that time that the TV crews began to arrive from New York, and Sally Jane Carlson's pathetic, tortured back became a national sensation.

Lee was glad of their support and interest, but she was not deceived. The media interest would not save Sally. It might make her an object of curiosity for a time, and rouse feminist ire, but it would not cause a jury from Butte, Montana, to judge her not guilty. If anything, the presence of the Easterners was an irritant. Butte felt it was on trial, which was unfair. The sort of thing that had happened to Sally happened in every city of every state of the Union—something Lee intended to emphasize in her summation.

When she put Sally in the box, all hell broke loose. Defendants in the witness box were always an unknown quantity. No matter how well they had performed in private, or in the pretrial hearings, you never knew how they would do when it came to the real event. Poor, spiritless Sally proved to be a natural.

"You have told the court that you 'knew' your husband had murder on his mind when he came into the kitchen," said

Garnett on cross-examination. "How are you privileged to 'know' such things? Do you possess an intelligence so far removed from most of ours that you can 'know' the future?"

"No, sir," said Sally. "I could only know Roy."

"And knowing Roy, what made you fear for your life? Was he armed as he stepped into the kitchen?"

"No, he wasn't armed."

"We know that the shotgun, which he had been cleaning, was in the portion of the kitchen where you stood. Even the carving knives, Mrs. Carlson, were in your territory. All the weaponry was on your side. We have had testimony proving that your husband was nearly in a stupor, and there you were —sober and fully armed. Is that an accurate assessment of the situation?"

"I wasn't *armed*," said Sally indignantly.

"It would appear otherwise," said Garnett. "Dismissed."

"Sally," began Lee on re-direct, "Mr. Garnett had suggested that all the potentially lethal weapons were in the portion of the kitchen where you stood. Is that true?"

"Yes, ma'am," said Sally. "That is certainly true."

"Will you tell the court why, in view of those facts, you felt your life to be in danger?"

"He didn't need weapons," said Sally.

"Objection!" shouted Garnett. "Council is leading the witness."

"Overruled," pronounced the judge. "I will hear this."

Lee, with mounting excitement, repeated the question.

"He could kill me with his bare hands," said Sally. "I used to wonder why I was still alive."

"And did you want to stay alive?"

Sally looked surprised, genuinely so, as if she had never considered the matter before. It was an unrehearsed question.

"Yes," she said. "I did. I wanted to go on living."

Carlotta followed the case as best she could. She no longer read about it in the *Rome Daily American*, for she had fled Italy when true summer came on, and returned to her London flat. Antonio had been sentimentally tearful when she left, but he had promised to come see her in England. She missed him, as she had known she would. She missed the sweet, intimate nature of their puppy-lovemaking especially, but she could not spend her life dallying with a pretty boy in a bed in Trastevere. She was going to have to sell the apartment in New York, and such things could be accomplished more easily from England. The English understood the realities of money and real estate and misguided legacies, and she would find a solicitor to handle the business for her; in Italy it would have been nearly impossible.

England was almost as interested in the Carlson case as America seemed to be. It had something for everyone. The gutter press had a field day on the subject of battered wives, and the serious papers and thoughtful television talk shows took up their cause, too. A BBC crew had been dispatched to Butte to make a documentary film. Maybe, thought Carlotta, someone would tell them it wasn't pronounced "But."

She felt she had passed into a new period of her life on her return to England. She felt calmer, less driven. It no longer seemed important to her to dance the night away, or make sure that every evening was filled with frenetic activity. If she glanced at her diary and saw empty spaces, indicating nights without an invitation, she almost felt relieved. She no longer saw Fiona, but Jane Wiley, the English girl she had met in Rome, had become a friend, and through Jane she had met a whole new set of people. She would be twenty-six in the autumn, and it seemed time for her to become absorbed in something more serious. But what?

One evening she saw, by chance, a group of people discussing the Carlson case on television. A distinguished British barrister, a Sir Henry Prior, was explaining that, much as he sympathized with battered wives, a not-guilty verdict in the case of Sally Jane Carlson would spell havoc for the civilized world.

"I must agree," said a rumpled man with a red face, "that such a verdict could mean that every woman with a grievance against her husband would feel perfectly within her rights to simply . . . *remove* him. We are on dangerous ground here."

"Let's hear from Lady Belinda," said the moderator, turning in the direction of the only woman on the panel. "You have participated in the maintenance of a shelter for battered wives in Chiswick for three years," he said. "How widespread is the problem?"

The cameras came in for a close-up. *Lady Belinda Muir*, said the identifying words at the bottom of the screen. Carlotta sat up straighter, wondered where she had heard the name, made the connection. Malcolm's fiancée. Why wasn't she Belinda Kitson by now?

"It is much more common than any of us would like to believe," said Lady Belinda. "It extends to all portions of our society, although the women who come to our shelter in Chiswick are mainly from the working class. It is a problem as old as time itself, and the only way to attack it is to make people so aware of its existence that they can't afford to ignore it, or pretend it doesn't exist, ever again."

She was lovely. Her delicate face fairly glowed with dedication. It was a face meant to be photographed lovingly and placed in the glossy pages of a society magazine—*Lady Belinda at Home with her Sealeyham Terriers*—yet the possessor of the face concerned herself with women from another world. Unfortunates—women she would never have been allowed to meet when she was growing up in her sheltered youth. Carlotta admired her, and wondered why Malcolm had ever given *her* a thought when someone like Belinda Muir was around.

"I must disagree with Sir Henry," Belinda said. "A verdict of not guilty is the right one in the American case. Contrary to encouraging women to kill their husbands, I believe it might have a much more constructive effect. When men realize that it is *not* their unalienable right to brutalize and torture the women they have married, which they would have to do in the event of an acquittal for the American woman, they will think twice before they do so. Isn't that an advance?"

There was a great amount of squabbling and shouting then, and shortly after that the program ended. Carlotta turned the set off, feeling troubled. She sympathized with all her heart with that miserable girl in Montana, but what would Lady Belinda—and, more importantly, Lee—have to say about Joly Nesbit and her father? How far did this go? Where did it end?

"Miss Redwing," said one of the BBC crew, "you were the daughter, *are* the daughter, I should say, of the man who was once ranch manager for Senator Thomas Madigan, isn't that correct?"

Lee, who had been expecting it for ages, nodded. "Perfectly correct," she said.

"Do you think it possible that the bizarre death of the senator"—here he inserted a compact synopsis of the reasons for Tom Madigan's murder and the subsequent trial and conviction of the murderess—"have influenced you to champion the cause of Mrs. Carlson?"

"Not at all," said Lee, with perfect composure. "The two cases have absolutely nothing in common."

"Nothing? A woman kills her lover in Washington, another woman kills her husband in Montana. Except for the legality of the relationship, what's the difference?"

They were making it easy for her. They were on her side. Lee relaxed, and gave them the answer they had been expecting.

Even in the best of worlds, Lee knew, Sally would have to go to prison for a time. Sally in prison was not an image she wished to dwell on. It pained her that the best she could do was to reduce Sally's time. In the beginning, she had envisioned a fantastic, triumphant moment when the foreman of the jury would stand up and declare that they found the defendant not guilty, and Sally would go free. She no longer believed that would happen. No matter how sympathetic some of the jurors—the women, mainly—were, the fact remained that a human life had been taken. They would probably return a verdict of guilty with mitigating circumstances, and include a recommendation of mercy.

"Mrs. Carlson," Garnett was saying on cross-examination, "even if we had proof that it was your late husband who put those scars on your back—and as far as proof goes, we have none but your word—and even if you had good cause to be afraid of him on that night, couldn't you have protected yourself in some other way? Could not less drastic means have been found?"

Sally looked up in bewilderment. "What means?" she said. "How, sir?"

"If I thought someone was entering a room, intent on harming me, there are a number of things I could do. I could go to my neighbors, for example. Did it occur to you to run outside the house and seek help?"

"My closest neighbors live three miles away," said Sally.

"How is it that you have never gone to the police, then,

and asked them to restrain your supposedly violent and dangerous husband? There are no records of your ever having done so."

"No, sir," said Sally. "I never did. If I could have called them that night, I would have, but there wasn't time."

"And so you preferred to pick up your husband's shotgun and blast him to death?" said Garnett, cutting a little look of amazement toward the jury box. Lee automatically objected, and the judge sustained. "Rephrase your question, Mr. Garnett," he said mildly.

"Did you believe that using the shotgun was the best way to save yourself from rough treatment?"

"I thought it was the only way to save my life," said Sally.

They adjourned for lunch then, and Lee breathed a sigh of relief. Sally was doing well, and Garnett was not making a favorable impression. Still, he scored with some of the jurors when he harped on the matter of proof. He made it possible for several of the men to believe that some earlier lover of Sally's had been the brute, or even someone she had adulterously loved while she was married to Roy. If only Sally had confided in a single soul, wept on the shoulder of a sister or mother or friend from church, Lee would have some leverage. But Sally had told no one, keeping it to herself all those years.

She was crossing the courthouse square, heading for the luncheonette where she grabbed a hasty sandwich every day, when a woman approached her. "Miss Redwing?" she said in a nervous but determined manner. "I got to talk to you."

She was a tall, thin girl with coppery hair and close-set, anxious-looking eyes. "I come all the way from Bozeman," she said.

Lee had an excited, instinctive feeling that the woman from Bozeman was going to be her savior, and Sally's, too. "Of course," she said. "I'm just going for lunch—will you join me?"

"I need to talk in private."

"We'll get a booth in the back," said Lee. "No one will overhear you."

When they were settled in the rear of the luncheonette, the woman began to pleat her paper napkin nervously. "I'll just have coffee," she told the waitress. She waited until they were alone again, then heaved a sigh and began. "I've been following the case," she said. "Right from the beginning. I wanted to talk to you all this time, but—" She shrugged. "My husband. You know how it is."

Lee waited patiently, allowing the woman to take her time and wiggle her way into her story from whatever angle she liked.

"My name is Doris Neely," she said. "That's my married name, Neely. My husband will probably divorce me for this, but I felt I had to do it."

The waitress brought Lee's sandwich and two coffees. Doris added an astonishing amount of sugar to her cup, stirred, sipped. "The thing is," she continued, staring into her coffee cup, "I was engaged to Roy Carlson ten years ago. I was eighteen and he was twenty. I thought there was no finer guy in the world than Roy. I was working at a coffee shop pretty much like this one, back in Bozeman, and Roy would drop in for a cup of coffee and a piece of blueberry pie. That was his favorite, blueberry pie with a scoop of vanilla. We would talk, and he would kind of tease me, and then we started dating. He was real handsome ten years ago. The pictures I've seen in the paper, well—he must have put on weight. Too much boozing, I suppose. Anyway, I reckoned I was in love with Roy, and when he asked me would I marry him, I was on cloud nine."

Doris Neely smiled at the old-fashioned expression, and then lapsed into silence, as if she had completed her narrative. Lee ate half of her sandwich and the silence continued. Sometimes it was necessary to give a tiny nudge. "But you didn't marry him?" she asked.

"No, no I sure as hell didn't. Something happened that made me change my mind. That's why I'm here. If I could tell you something that would back up what his wife's been saying, would that help you?"

"I'm sure it couldn't hurt, Mrs. Neely."

Doris took a deep breath. "I broke up with Roy because he got real drunk one night and started punching me around. For no reason, Miss Redwing. We weren't having a fight. It was like Roy suddenly went crazy and couldn't stop himself. I fought back at first, but he was so much stronger. He blackened my eyes and split my lip, and when I fell on the ground, he kicked me. This was in a parking lot, Miss Redwing, the parking lot of a roadhouse, and I couldn't believe it was happening. Some couples came out and saw what was happening. The guys started for Roy, but he just got in his pickup and roared off.

"When my daddy saw my face he pretty nearly went out of his head. He was ready to kill Roy, and I guess Roy got wind of that, because he left town for good. I'll tell you this, though. Even if he'd stayed and apologized on his bended knee and sworn it would never happen again, nothing could have made me marry him after that. There's something really wrong with a man like that, like some wires get crossed in his brain and he blows a fuse when he drinks too much."

Lee tried to keep her hand still as she lifted her cup to her lips. "Would you be prepared to testify to that in court, Mrs. Neely? All you'd do is tell your story the way you've told it to me."

"Oh, Jesus," the woman said, "I was afraid of that. Can't you just tell them for me?"

"I could submit your sworn statement to the judge, and protect your anonymity," said Lee. "But that wouldn't have the same effect as if you appeared in court and told the jury."

Doris Neely was stubbornly silent, but her hands had resumed their shredding of the napkin. "Look," said Lee gently. "The D.A. is trying to get the jury to believe that somebody other than Roy Carlson stubbed those cigarettes out on Sally's back. Your testimony is the only one in *existence* that proves Roy liked to beat up on women.

"I know it's hard for you, but *you* didn't do anything wrong. You wouldn't be uncovering anything shameful about yourself, Mrs. Neely, only about Roy Carlson. I'm begging you to testify, and for only one reason—Sally. You could save her from a long prison sentence, and if anyone ever needed saving it's that poor girl. She wasn't as smart as you. She stayed with him for seven long, painful, wretched years. She's suffered enough already, don't you think?"

Doris lowered her eyes. "Yeah," she said tonelessly. "And she's got three kids, too. Shit. Oh, shit."

Lee held her breath, crossing her fingers so hard the nails turned blue.

"Okay," said Doris. "I've got to do it. I couldn't sleep at night if I didn't."

"Congratulations," said Lee gleefully. "You have just become what very few people get to be in real life."

"What's that?"

"A surprise witness."

NINE

RACHEL'S ENTHUSIASM OVER BEING PREGNANT BEGAN TO PALE very quickly back in New York. In Rome, the mystique of it had seemed overwhelmingly attractive, but at home she merely felt increasingly awkward and uncomfortable. She seemed to do everything exactly opposite to most pregnant women; her biological makeup just screwed her at every turn.

The morning sickness, for example. Here she had gone for two months, in total ignorance of her condition, without a twinge. Then, in her third month, just when most women began to get rid of it, morning sickness descended with a vengeance. *So—you thought you were special, huh? Expected to get away scot-free? We'll show you.* That was what the sullen waves of nausea seemed to say as they woke her each morning, and woke her far too early.

And then there was the matter of her nice, new, larger breasts. It was fun having tits people noticed. At first. Now they ached and seemed cumbersome, and she searched them every day for blue veins and stretch marks. Her friend Daisy had prescribed cocoa butter to minimize the visibility of stretch marks, and Rachel dutifully rubbed it on her hurting breasts, wincing, twice daily. Her stomach had not grown perceptibly larger yet, but she knew, being small and small-boned, that she would be one of the unlucky ones who ballooned grotesquely quite early on. By September, she calculated, she would be actually unpresentable, and the baby wasn't even due until January.

To make matters worse, her obstetrician had given her a boring list of things she must not do. It included drinking more than two cocktails, smoking heavily, taking drugs, salting her food, and—but not for many months yet—having sex. The sex part didn't especially bother her, not at the moment, anyway. How could you feel sexy when your morning started with retching over the toilet bowl, and your last physical sensation at night was the pain of accidentally rolling over on your boobs?

At first, Cotter had been willing to forgive her anything on account of her being pregnant and giving him the son and heir he wanted. He never doubted that their child would be a boy. In the days of her first week back, he dramatically laid his head on her belly and talked to his embryo son through her navel. It was weird, really, but if she laughed he looked wounded. He was also pleased with her larger breasts, but she made him understand that they were tender, and he handled them with great respect. For that first week, she had been treated like a goddess.

Then, as she had prepared to go off to her parents' summer place in Newport, leaving him to slave five days a week in the sultry city, he had grown belligerent. They sniped at each other listlessly, Cotter accusing Rachel of infidelities in Rome, and Rachel accused him of the same in New York. When Cotter spoke of these imagined infidelities, of course, he pictured her partners as insatiable Italian males. He had never suspected Natalia; he lacked the imagination.

On a perfect summer day, Rachel lay in a reclining lawn chair on the long green stretch of garden that sloped down to the blue ocean. The Rhode Island air was bracing and salty. She had just had an excellent lunch of crabmeat salad and was sipping the last dregs of the one glass of wine she was allowed at noon. Before her, on Rhode Island Sound, were the myriad white sails of boats: behind her, in her parents' mansion, was a devoted staff pledged to make her life as easy and painless and full of delight as possible. She wanted to scream.

How could it be? Less than a month ago, she had been a free agent, cavorting with Natalia in the enchanted pool off the Appian Way—a glorious, juicy, beloved creature of boundless daring and pleasure, adored and, in her way, adoring. That wondrous sprite was now a sluggish, aching, earthbound woman who lay in a lawn chair worrying about varicose veins. Who puked at dawn. Whom no self-respecting man, or woman, would want.

It worried her that she did not really miss her contessa. It was not Natalia she longed for, but the feelings Natalia had forced her to have. She closed her eyes and remembered the night when she and Natalia and Carlotta had all dined together at the villa. In those days she had been so used to ecstasy that it had seemed her due, her right. The candlelight, the good tastes of food and wine in her mouth, the strange, new condition of her body—which she had not then attributed to pregnancy—had all combined to make her wild.

She had run from the table like a mad thing, across the dining room and through the shadowy, connecting rooms, past the tapestries and sculptures and huge, carved Renaissance furniture, her high heels clicking on the cool marble as she sped to the bedroom she and Natalia shared. Inside, in a fever, she tore her clothing off and lay on the bed, her head turned toward the door, waiting. She knew Natalia would follow, anxious to know what had driven Rachel from the convivial table.

She had been two people in those moments, waiting for her lover—the woman on the bed, reduced to the state of an animal, her entire being nothing more than nerve endings, and the woman who hovered above the bed, watching and observing. The fact that one half of her watched the other only made her more wildly excited. It was as if she was about to make love to herself and observe it all.

Where was Natalia? What was taking her so long? In her frenzy, Rachel began to tease her fevered flesh. Ever mindful of the self that was watching, she arched her back and allowed her long fingernails to trail over her newly sensitive breasts, whimpering at the sensation in her nipples. She was too inflamed to be subtle; if Natalia did not come to her soon it would all be over.

She had raked at her body, and the light scratches had remained for some time after to remind her of her lust. On her breasts and belly and thighs there had been red tracks to show how, in her demented passion, she had tried to control her hands and keep them from flying to the hot, wet center of her pleasure.

"*Cara?* What is it—are you ill?" Natalia had burst into the room, crying out her fears at the moment when she could wait no longer. Rachel was writhing on the bed, her legs spread wide. "Hurry," she begged, turning her head mindlessly back and forth on the pillow. "Now!"

Natalia had looked shocked, but she obediently knelt by the side of the bed and lowered her head. Rachel's body was already contracting orgasmically, and at the first contact she rocketed into a climax that was almost agonizing, screaming her ecstasy, her hands clutched in Natalia's hair.

The whole incident had lasted no more than three minutes, and they had gone back to the table as if nothing had happened. Carlotta was far too polite to say anything, although she must have heard the almost inhuman yowling, like that of a cat in heat.

Rachel remembered its minutest detail. She could still recall how she had felt at the table, smiling and sipping her wine, while all the time she could feel the little throbbing aftermaths rippling through her, like a delicious secret. The memory and the warm, caressing sun combined to make her horny now, and she squirmed a little in the lawn chair. It was no good, though. It had all happened to someone else. The lithe, beautiful creature who had demanded pleasure was not the same person as the swollen, sluggish woman who lay on a lawn in Rhode Island. The part of her that watched would not be excited at what she saw, and so she could not really become aroused.

"Yoo-hoo! Rachel, dear!" She opened her eyes and saw her mother walking toward her. "I just wanted to remind you that the Prices are coming for tea at four."

"Oh, Christ," moaned Rachel. "Who gives a flying fuck?" She spoke softly, to herself. To her mother she merely grunted in a particularly ungracious manner. The Prices were the most boring people she had ever met. They were very rich, and their combined ages exceeded 140. She shut her eyes again, wondering if Cotter was behaving himself in New York. He would be here on Friday night, as usual, and that wasn't too thrilling, either.

"Mother, do you suppose I could find a doctor who'd put me to sleep for the next six months!" she asked.

Mrs. Windolm laughed uneasily. "The things you come up with," she said. "These are precious times in a woman's life, dear. You must savor them."

"Did you take a course at Vassar, Mum? I mean, where exactly did you learn to be so trite? Was it Triteness 101? It must be an acquired skill."

It was an old game she played with her mother. Mrs. Windolm was so thick-skinned she never took offense, and always countered with another cliche. Rachel waited to see what this one would be.

"Things that sound trite to you are bound to be true," her mother said merrily. "People have said them so often precisely because they *are* true. Otherwise they wouldn't be trite."

Well-satisfied with her wisdom, Mrs. Windolm went back to the house. Rachel felt too tired to get out of the chair and move into the shade, so she closed her eyes and allowed herself to go to sleep. Her last thought, before she dropped off, was that even her dreams would be boring.

In the summer, Antonio came to visit her, as he had promised he would. Carlotta and Antonio went up to Scotland and, because he had a passion for ruined castles, she took him to every one she could think of. He insisted his interest in the ancient ruins had to do with the location he dreamed of in which his first film would, some day, be shot.

They took the ferry from Mallaig to the Isle of Skye so Antonio could check out a noble ruin in the northern section. The island, full of shifting lights and wild glens, seemed haunted. "This is where the witches used to gather, I think," Carlotta told him. "They would hop on their broomsticks and fly here once a year for a grand reunion."

He laughed at her, but later, standing in the shadow of the castle, nothing could induce him to walk out on a rampart, even though it had a guardrail. "Something evil has happened here," he said dramatically. "I can feel it." The castle stood on a sheer cliff, half of it having crumbled away some centuries ago. Hundreds of feet below, the gray northerly sea boiled and foamed on the rocks. "Are you afraid of heights, Tonino?" she teased.

But he was genuinely afraid, so much so that he replied to her in Italian, unthinking. What he said was: *I am afraid of tragedy.*

"You are superstitious," said Carlotta.

He nodded gravely. "Oh, yes. Very much."

Later, they found a little guidebook that told of the history of various places in Skye. Carlotta felt a chill pass over her when she read about the castle, for Antonio had been right. It had been abandoned by the family who lived in it, after the death of an infant child. A nursemaid had been bathing the infant, and the little, slippery body had wiggled out of her arms and gone plunging to its death on the rocks at the base of the cliff. The mother, distraught with grief, had insisted on leaving.

"You see?" said Antonio. "I feel these things."

Back on the mainland of Scotland, he rejected this castle as being too modern, that one for lacking the proper atmosphere. They stayed in the prettiest hotels and inns they could find, eating salmon and drinking malt whiskey. At Loch Ness they hoped to see the monster, but he did not oblige. The castle there, Urquehart, was a horizontal ruin rambling over the grassy shores of the Loch, and Antonio needed a vertical ruin.

Something in their relationship had changed. He was still as friendly and amusing, as affectionate, as he had been in Rome, but in the privacy of the bedroom in all those inns from Ullapool to Inverness, he seemed shy and ill at ease. Carlotta did not press him; she understood that he was moving into the true area of his own sexuality, and that between the time she had last seen him and now, he had had an affair with a man. His love for her was deep and loyal, but it had become the love of a boy for his adored older sister. By mutual consent, without talking about it, they began to take separate rooms.

One night, in Edinburgh, he came to her room for their nightly drink before retiring. Holding her foot in his right hand and a glass of Glenfiddich in the left, he said: "Ireland. I think we must go to Ireland to find my castle."

"My father was Irish," she said, the words popping out unbidden. "He used to go there now and then, but it was one of the places he never took me."

Antonio propped himself up on an elbow. "Your father was from *Ireland?*" he asked incredulously, as if she had revealed something fantastic.

"He was American, Tonino, but his people before him came from Ireland. His great-grandfather came from there. Something about a famine, when people starved."

"Is very odd," said Antonio. "I always thought you were an aristocrat." He tweaked her toe to show it didn't matter.

"But I am! America is a very young country. We have

instant aristocracy. Here, in Europe, you have to prove your roots for at least a thousand years. We're so new that three generations makes you a patrician. Four makes you royalty."

They had laughed at the absurdity of it, and wound their arms around each other, and rocked together on Carlotta's bed. She felt, locked in his embrace, the beginnings of those weak flutterings she had experienced in their love nest in Trastevere, but he disengaged himself with infinite grace when their contact became too intimate, and retreated to his own room.

On the east seacoast, just north of the border with England, Antonio found his castle. It was called Tantallon, and ever afterwards she was unable to remember whether it had been the stronghold of the clan of Douglas or of Bruce. What she did remember was the dizzying height of the eroded, green cliffs, the view of the sea beneath, and the hump of pale rock she glimpsed between the battlements glimmering like a jewel in the turbulent, jade-green ocean.

Bass Rock. That, and the sea birds screaming heroically. "This is *it!*" Antonio had shouted.

"It's time for me to go home," Carlotta told herself. Experimentally, she matched her friend's shout, calling the words in her strongest voice, but the high wind on the sea cliff snatched the words back and sent them down her throat, where no one could hear them.

In actual fact, she was nearly broke. The Fifth Avenue apartment had not yet found a buyer willing to meet with the asking price. She had been selling her mother's jewelry piece by piece as the need arose, and was down to the beautiful pearls, a lustrous, triple-strand necklace, which her father had given to Martha, and which Martha had particularly loved. Carlotta felt sentimental about those pearls, and also the emerald collar, and didn't want to sell them. Back in a safety deposit vault was the beloved T'ang horse, and that she had vowed never to part with.

By September, she was faced with an unpleasant truth. When she returned to New York she would have to get a job. She didn't object to working, but at what? Who would hire a woman who had been trained for nothing but life as a rich man's wife? She knew how to plan and give dinner parties, how to arrange flowers to perfection; she knew the correct titles for diplomats, and also for the titled. She could sail, ride a horse, dance, and be decorative, and she was fluent in French and all right in Italian. That was it. She could not type, work with figures, or take shorthand. Teaching was out, because she had no degree.

For the first time she felt bitterness at her father's lack of interest in her future. When she had come back from school in Switzerland, at the age of eighteen, there had been vague mentions of college, but the senator had laughed at the idea. "Carlotta's got brains—she's as smart as she needs to be," he had said to Martha. "I want my little girl to have fun while she's young." It seemed a feudal attitude, looking back, and it shamed her to realize how little resistance she had offered. Whatever her father thought was right—she never questioned him. She knew now that he had expected her to have a whirl in New York for a couple of years, and then become the adored wife of some rich and powerful man selected, probably, by Tom Madigan himself. She would go from the protection of her father to the protection of her husband, and never have to fend for herself. It accounted for the peculiar terms of his will.

But how did all of it square with his fervent desire for her to have a "future"? She remembered again the time in the Land Rover, when she had nearly begged not to be sent away to Switzerland, remembered how he had chided her for saying "what does it matter?" He had spoken fine words about the value of a European education back then, but what had it all been intended *for*? Had she been sent off into exile merely to improve her value on the marriage market?

The thought disturbed her, and she found that the kid gloves she had been examining on a counter at Harrod's were shaking in her hands. She dropped them and selected another pair, but she could not be distracted from the headlong plunge of her thoughts.

Carlotta's got brains—she's as smart as she needs to be. Needs to be for *what?* To marry some young diplomat and speak French well enough so as not to embarrass him with guests at the dinner table? Yes, that was it, or a part of it—college was out for Carlotta because she wasn't one of those unfortunate young women who had to entertain hopes of a career in medicine or the law in order to distinguish herself and rise above the lackluster level of her parents. Carlotta was special, and therefore not much time need be devoted to her. She had it made. All she had to do was obey her loving daddy and obligingly marry the right young man, in whose arms she would dutifully be ground against the bed approximately three and one-half times a week. *That* was the grand future Tom Madigan had pictured for her when he spoke so persuasively in the Land Rover.

Her mother had often spoken of her days in boarding school as the happiest in her life, and the impact of those sad little excursions into nostalgia now hit Carlotta for the first time.

"What fun it was," she heard Martha saying, "how delicious it was, the time Helen Griggs and I crept down to the kitchen and stole two lemon pies. We shared them with the other girls, of course, and the next day, at chapel, the headmistress told us the entire class would be punished until the culprits confessed. All our little privileges revoked, you know. But since we had all partaken of the pies, we all felt equally guilty, and we agreed to suffer the consequences. Such loyalty, Carlotta! It's the sort of thing that one only encounters when one is young."

How innocent her mother had been. Carlotta absolved her completely. Martha had seen all of life as a matter of teamwork, and longed for the days when it could be demonstrated on the hockey fields, or in defiance of the headmistress. But the senator? No. Daddy had been a man of the world, a man whose lips had curved cynically—she now realized—when his wife revealed her essentially innocent nature. Had he been blind enough to place Carlotta in the same category?

"You were *wrong*," she said aloud. "You think you're always a few jumps ahead, don't you? So goddamned confident you are. You. *You*."

A concerned saleslady was making her way toward Carlotta, her mouth pursed in disapproval. Carlotta dropped the gloves and hurried off. She should have known what would have happened if she allowed herself to lose her temper. It wasn't allowed, particularly where Daddy was concerned. She told herself these things as she picked her way through the crowded main floor in search of the exit, and then, when she finally emerged to a drizzle of light rain, asked herself what on earth she meant. She didn't have a temper. Irish temper. How perfectly ridiculous!

She got into a taxi and gave the address of her flat. Something was troubling her, but it lacked form and substance. Like a large and ugly fish, it circled in the muddy waters of her consciousness. She told herself that her peculiar behavior in Harrod's was all part and parcel of her need to leave London, and Europe in general.

All in all, she could see no reason for returning to America, but ever since that day at Tantallon Castle, she had known she would do so. Three years of exile was enough. Her father's death was no longer a juicy scandal, and no one would care when Carlotta said her name was Madigan. It would be lovely in New York just now—autumn was the best time— and nothing held her in London. Rachel wrote to her frequently, begging her to return and stay with them as long as she liked. The letters from Newport had been morose, complaining of boredom and nausea and utter uselessness, but now that she had returned to New York for the fall season, Rachel seemed cheerier.

"Being six months pregnant is much better than being three," she wrote. "I feel fine now, and I am having divine maternity outfits made for the fall parties. Of course I have a belly like Alfred Hitchcok now, but at least people can *see* I'm pregnant. Before, I just felt slightly fat and pasty and wanted to murder every skinny woman in the world. Hurry back before my present bloom wears off and I am like a huge, beached whale."

It wasn't only Rachel's letters that made her homesick, it was the feeling that a great change was taking place in America and she was missing it. The dippiness of the sixties had worn off, but the political commitment they made had stuck. More politicians were speaking out openly against the war in Vietnam—something her father had done before it was fashionable—and more women were seeking positions of dignity. Look at Lee, who was now famous for having won her case in defense of the pathetic, battered woman who killed her husband. The verdict of not guilty had broken precedent, and Lee had succeeded in much more than just freeing the Carlson woman. She had forced the country to see that wife abuse was a common and widespread practice that had to be acknowledged before it could be eradicated.

In the international *Time* magazine, there had been a picture of Lee, looking lovely and strong and dignified. They had quoted a section from her now-famous summation to the jury:

We do not condemn those who kill to save their own lives, if we are quite sure that their assailant is seriously capable of inflicting lethal harm on them. We do not condemn a soldier who faces his opposite in battle and does what he must to survive. How can we condemn Sally Jane Carlson for wanting to live? She was a soldier in a kind of secret war in which she had remained a pacifist for too many years. The fact that her enemy was her husband is sad beyond words . . .

Carlotta had written to Lee in care of the Montana State Bar Association, but she had no way of knowing if her old friend received the letter. The act of addressing a letter to Montana also made her homesick, as everything seemed to. When even the sight of the president, Tricky Dick Nixon— one of her father's political enemies—produced nostalgia, she began to pack her things.

TEN

BRENDAN DELANEY HAD AN EYE FOR BEAUTY, BOTH INANI-mate and warmly alive. He was the owner of a famous art collection, and both of his ex-wives had been collectors' pieces, too. There were many things he appreciated about women, in addition to their beauty, and they sensed it and flocked to him, even now, when he was in his late fifties. It didn't hurt that he had a reputation as a lover, and that middle-age had not robbed him of it.

The girl stepping into the first-class cabin of the BOAC jetliner had attracted his attention. Covertly he studied her, but his close scrutiny only backed up his first impression: she was as lovely as any woman he had ever seen. If he had not been averse to cliches, he would have said to himself: *That is the most beautiful girl I have ever seen.*

And she was a girl, not a woman. It wasn't her youth that made him judge her so, but something else. Just as there were many twenty-year-olds who were women already, so there were dowagers who had remained girls. She was tall and poised, and everything about her spoke of money, from the tips of her Italian shoes to the crown of her bright head. She looked a trifle tentative as she handed her ticket to the stew-ard, as if she could not believe she was entering the plane, about to fly from London to New York. He could scarcely believe that a girl like that was unfamiliar to travel. He would have deduced that this was her first trip to the United States, but he could have sworn she was American. Her clothes were European and her poise seemed English, but her legs were American. Maybe she had been away from home for a long time.

She walked down the aisle now and settled in the seat across the way from him. He could smell her fragrance, a very light perfume that had probably been privately blended for her. There weren't so many people in the first-class cabin on this flight, and the girl had no neighbors. She also had no magazines or carry-on bags. She simply sat, very still, taking no notice of anyone around her.

Delaney looked forward to this transatlantic flight. He knew his own powers, and he was sure that he would know a great deal about the girl by the time they arrived in New York. He would proceed very slowly and gently, though, because she would not be easy to win over. Another man might have inquired, when the plane arose over Heathrow and headed toward Ireland, if she would care to have a drink with him. Delaney, patient and full of guile, would wait at least an hour before he spoke to her.

Carlotta noticed the man across the aisle when the stewardess brought her drink. He was very powerful-looking, she thought, in both senses. She wanted to study him at her leisure, but of course that wouldn't do. He would think she was trying to flirt with him. She thanked the stewardess for the drink and turned to the window and a view of blue ether. His hair had been totally silver, but she knew it had once been black because his well-shaped eyebrows were black. She thought he must be well over six feet tall. An interesting-looking man.

She began to regret not having bought a book, or magazines, to occupy her time. She rang for the stewardess and asked for a magazine, and then she had a chance to look at him again. He was definitely in his forties, perhaps even fifty. His clothing was expensive and understated. A man as big as that would have to have things specially tailored for him, as her father had.

The magazine didn't really occupy her attention, and when

she looked at her watch and saw that only an hour had passed, she sighed.

"Excuse me," said the man across the aisle. "I have more than my share of magazines over here." He had a deep voice, but it was also very soft. He was holding a sheaf of magazines, fanning them out for her consideration. "We have *Life*, *Time*, *Paris Match*, and the *Saturday Evening Post* to choose from. Or shall I let you have them all?" He smiled. A nice smile.

"I'll have *Paris Match*, please," said Carlotta. She realized that she sounded like a customer at a newsstand. The man handed it to her, and she found herself looking at his hands. They were large and beautifully shaped, and unadorned by rings. One of the few things about Antonio that had disturbed her was his penchant for gaudy jewelry.

About a quarter of the way across the Atlantic she realized that she was more apprehensive about returning to America than she had admitted to herself. That accounted for her desire to talk to the man, she thought. It would prove more distracting than reading. It was odd, because normally she detested conversations with strangers on airplanes, and always managed to stay aloof. When the stewardess brought them a tray of little sandwiches, she returned the magazine to him and said, inanely, "Oh, good. I'm hungry."

"In that case, you're welcome to all my sandwiches," said the man.

"Oh, no, no thank you," said Carlotta, alarmed. She didn't want him to see her as childish and greedy, and when she unwrapped the sandwiches she found she wasn't so hungry after all.

"Airplane food," she said, "always tastes like cardboard."

"Except on Air France."

"Do you travel a lot?"

"Enough. I enjoy all things in moderation." He smiled, to show her it was a joke. "The trick is to leave a place before you've exhausted it. That way you'll always be glad to go back."

She glanced at him in surprise. "You're right," she said. "I think I overstayed my time. I like London, but right now I don't care if I ever see it again."

Gradually, they were in a real conversation. Because the man's voice was so soft, she found herself leaning toward him, and then, of course, he came and sat beside her. She explained that she had been living in Europe for three years, described how, standing on a cliff in Scotland, she had realized it was time to go home. "I started out in Sardinia because my father took me there once, when I was a child, and I had pleasant memories. I saw a bit of Spain, and lived in Rome for a while, but my home base was London. I just got tired of being—"

"In exile. No matter how pleasant."

"Yes." And then, because she felt she had talked too much about herself, she asked what he had been doing in London.

"I was only there for two days. I spent most of my time in Ireland. I have a house there, in Donegal."

Carlotta said she had never been in Ireland, and the man described his farmhouse on the wild Donegal coast so captivatingly that she felt she had been there. Looking at him again, she decided that he was probably Irish. An Irish-American who had made enough money to buy a house in the mother country. Her father had spoken of buying a house in Ireland, but somehow it had never come to pass. There had been some political reason for it, something that had happened when she was very young. She had never been told.

"My name is Brendan Delaney," said the man. He extended his hand and Carlotta took it, finding the slight pressure of his fingers pleasant and reassuring.

"I'm Carlotta," she said, speaking her name, which had become unfamiliar to her, as she had once done to the little boy in the Roman Forum. "Carlotta Madigan." She wondered if she had imagined the slight tightening of his fingers, but when she looked to see if his expression had changed, it was completely neutral.

It was with great restraint that Delaney refrained from reacting. That his seatmate, the little beauty whose mystery he had determined to unravel, should turn out to be Tom Madigan's daughter seemed astonishing at first. And then, he began to see how neatly it fit. Her poise and her carriage were, after all, that of someone whose family had once been regarded as American royalty. It solved the mystery of why she was a girl. Big Tom's Little Girl, poor thing, whose enchanted life had been shattered to bits when that show girl picked up the carving knife. No wonder she had fled to Europe. He resisted any impulse to show sympathy, sensing that she preferred to think herself anonymous now that more than three years had passed.

"With a name like Madigan I should think you'd want to visit Ireland," he said. She had seemed to enjoy his description of Donegal, so he rambled on some more about the beauties of Ireland. She listened intently. Her blue eyes, Tom Madigan's eyes, grew soft and dreamy, and her lips parted slightly, as if for a kiss. She aroused him immensely, but he was a careful man who would make no false moves. He knew it would be a long time before he could become Carlotta's lover, and he would simply have to wait. He never doubted that it would happen, only lamented over the fact that it would be weeks, months, maybe, before he would be able to turn her into a woman.

"I never knew people still spoke Irish," she said.

"They do in Donegal," Delaney told her. While he explained the Gaeltecht to her—those pockets in the west of Ireland where Irish was still spoken as a first language—he thought of how innocent she was, despite her apparent sophistication. She was quite intelligent, he thought, and capable of fine things, but no one had ever taken much time with her. She believed he did not know who she was, for example. Fair enough—for thousands of Americans, who had had new scandals to absorb them while Carlotta had been in Europe, the name would ring no bell. But how in the name of sweet, suffering Jesus could she think that a wealthy Irishman of an age with Tom Madigan could have forgotten? He had met Tom once, at a party for young Kennedy. Both dead now.

It saddened him to think of how many good men had been brought down since those days. It seemed a lifetime ago that he had stood in that bayberry scented drawing room in Georgetown, but he could remember certain details very well.

Scented candles, so common now, had been a novelty in those days. The hostess, a short, pug-faced woman—what was her name?—had been renowned for her initiative. There were many Kennedys in the festive room—old Joe and a kid brother and a Kennedy sister or sister-in-law, he couldn't remember which, wearing a gown of Christmasy red taffeta. He could still see her strong white teeth biting blissfully into a canape. Over by the fireplace, leaning against the mantel, Adlai Stevenson was politely conversing with a blonde belle who had done her level best to resemble that year's most celebrated film star, Brigitte Bardot. Barbara Howar? No.

There were others at the Georgetown party who were destined to assume a major role in the future, for good or ill. Lyndon and Lady Bird Johnson, General George T. Tomlinson, the renegade senator from Oregon, Wayne Morse, and, most obviously, the red-haired senator from Massachusetts and his darkly lovely young wife.

He had thought no one could compete with them for sheer glamor and elegance, until the late-arriving senator from Montana and his wife entered the room. Here was a man like himself, a black, black Irishman who commanded center stage by genetic largesse. Because he was better-looking and more conversationally gifted than anyone else in the room, and made good use of it.

"Hello, Jack," he had shouted across the room at young Kennedy. "All the best!"

Delaney found himself studying Madigan throughout that evening, and studying, also, the lovely Mrs. Madigan. She had none of her husband's magnetism, and seemed content to bask in his reflected glory. She was elegantly, perfectly dressed, and her manners were impeccable, of course, but she seemed out of place in a room so full of unbridled ambition. She performed her social duties very well, but her eyes were always fretfully skittering off in the direction of her husband. Unlike young Mrs. Kennedy, who glittered on her own, Martha Madigan's inner light seemed to glow only when she had the senator's undivided attention. Delaney thought she was lonely. Ordinarily, the sight of a beautiful and lonely woman would have moved him to action, but he had no wish to poach in *that* territory.

For one thing, he would never dream of intriguing with a woman married to a man so much like himself, a man he respected; for another, he sensed that Martha was not open to sexual advances. She would never find solace in an adulterous affair.

He had had only one brief conversation with the senator from Montana on that evening, and it concerned Kennedy's chances for winning the presidency one day.

"If Jack isn't in the White House by 1964 at the latest," Madigan had said, "I'll have to sell one of my horses."

"How's that, Senator? Have you a running bet?"

"Several," said Madigan. "Arabians don't come cheap,

you know." He laughed ruefully. It was a part of his charm that he could pretend that the loss of several hundred thousand dollars might ruin him; it was also a part of his charm that he would make private bets—doubtless with other members of the senate—as to the future presidency of his country. The object of the bet was, at that moment, bending somewhat stiffly to light the cigarette of a Texas oil heiress.

Kennedy, Delaney, and Madigan—three of a kind. They would go their separate ways, but they were in some way alike. Delaney felt a special kinship for Madigan. They were of an age, for one thing, and their ambitions had a limit. Not for them anything so tedious as the presidency, which would, when all was said and done, curtail their activities and make them accountable to some degree; no, Madigan and Delaney wanted to stop before they had become so famous as to be enslaved by public opinion. They wanted to have fun. Madigan was perilously close to the dividing line, while Delaney, in his cleverness, remained within shouting distance.

If anyone had asked Delaney what would prove to be the senator's undoing, he would have replied, unhesitatingly: women. Sexual indiscretion. Even if he had not seen Madigan in action with the Bardot look-alike, sliding his big hand along her lithe, bare arm while they discussed water rights in the far western states, he could have diagnosed his fatal trouble. *He'll go too far, in his position,* Delaney considered. *He won't be able to stop himself, he'll go too far. Poor Martha, she'll be astonished some day. Poor, lovely girl.*

Martha's hair had been the exact color of Carlotta's.

Carlotta—who was now making fitful movements in her seat, as if preparing to ask him a question and bring him away from his remembrances. How easily she could bring him back from that bayberry-scented Georgetown drawing room, if only she knew! A swift calculation told him she had been nine when that party had taken place.

"Are you a novelist, by any chance?" she asked him.

"Not at all. I'm a dull investment banker. Whatever made you think I was something so interesting?"

"You talk so well. You have a way with words. You don't just describe a thing flat out—you work your way into the heart of it."

"It's an Irish trait, they say. In which case, you have it yourself."

Carlotta sighed. "I'm only half Irish," she said.

On reflection, this seemed a funny thing to say and they both laughed. The trip was going very quickly, and they were becoming excellent friends. The thing was to make her trust him, and he was good at inspiring trust in women.

By the time they had landed at Kennedy, and Carlotta's expensively shod feet were on American soil again, she trusted him enough to accept his offer of a lift to Manhattan. His car and driver were waiting, and she got in without a pause. She was going to stay with friends, temporarily.

During the long, depressing stretch through Queens, with views of vast graveyards and similarly unappealing vistas on either side, Carlotta seemed uninterested in her surroundings, but when they approached the Queensborough Bridge and the Manhattan skyline came into view, she sat forward abruptly.

"Oh, my," said Carlotta Madigan, "isn't that a sight? I'd forgotten." She sounded like any ordinary, average, carefree American girl at that moment. Delaney wanted to hug her—a friendly hug—but he restrained himself from any contact, as he had been doing for six long hours.

She fell into Rachel's arms, or tried to, but Rachel's stomach got in the way. Cotter was fussing with her luggage, making work for himself. Carlotta knew that the affection Rachel so openly displayed for her was a source of embarrassment to Cotter, so she disengaged herself and held her friend at arm's length.

"*Look* at you!" she cried in admiration. Rachel's letter had not prepared her for the radiant, vivid creature Rachel had become at this stage in her pregnancy. The added pounds suited the sharp-boned face, and Rachel's pale skin seemed to have been burnished with roses: She fairly glowed. She was wearing a sky-blue caftan that was trimmed with hundreds of little shells; when she walked across the room she tinkled mysteriously, like some high priestess about to perform a rite. What she was looking for was the champagne cooler.

"Welcome home, traveler," said Cotter. "You're welcome here as long as you want to stay. You'll be company for Rachel."

He had succeeded in making her feel like a governess hired to amuse a pampered child.

Later, she and Rachel retired to the little room with the

canary yellow curtains and settled in to talk the way they couldn't in front of Cotter.

"I've never heard from Natalia," Rachel said. "I guess it's better that way. It all seems to have happened so long ago— frankly, I can hardly remember what she looked like." She poured more champagne for Carlotta but did not refill her own glass. "I'm being very good," she said. "For the baby. No drugs, hardly anything to drink. But there is one thing I absolutely refuse to do, no matter how many women tell me I ought to. I will *not* have natural childbirth, with that horrible Lamaze business. Can you imagine? Every woman I meet babbles about the wonderful experience of natural childbirth, with their husband right *there* in the delivery room! Could anything be more grotesque?"

"Well," said Carlotta, who approved of natural childbirth, in a vague sort of way, "it *is* difficult to picture Cotter in a delivery room."

"Especially since he's going to want to kill me. You know how much he wants a boy. He's got the name all picked out— Walter Windolm Vere. That way he sucks up to my father *and* his. No child of mine will be named Walter, not while there's breath in my body. And anyway, I just have this feeling, this *conviction*, that it's a girl."

"How can you tell?"

Rachel placed her hands on the mound of her belly and gave a secretive little smile. "I just can," she said. "When she kicks it's a very *feminine* movement."

"Poor Cotter," said Carlotta, laughing.

"Poor Cotter, my ass," said Rachel. "Can you imagine saying to the baby nurse: 'Was Walter's stool firm today?' No man should be named Walter until he's sixty years old, and possibly not even then."

"How about Brendan?" Carlotta asked.

"Brendan? What an odd name. Irish, probably. Why do you pop up with Brendan?"

"No reason," said Carlotta.

"Do you know what really bothers the hell out of me?" Rachel lay back in her chair, holding her belly as if it were a beach ball on her lap. "Women keep coming up to me at parties and telling me the most dreadful things. It's as if they can't stop themselves. At the Dennisons' the other night this tub of a woman started to describe how she'd been in labor for thirty-six hours. She didn't leave anything out—the pain, the fatigue, the anxiety and agony—Jesus! Then Jo-Jo, you don't know her, came over and I thought I was going to be rescued. But what did Jo-Jo do but launch into a story about how her afterbirth wouldn't come out and the doctor had to practically crawl up inside her to get it. Are these women sadists?"

"Just walk away from them, Rachel. Just—"

"But wait! You haven't heard the worst. Two days ago I was in Bonwit's to buy some gloves, and this utter stranger comes waltzing up to the counter. She's all solicitous and tender, comes on with a big sisterhood act about the heroism of women having babies, and before I know it she's telling me—in *excruciating* detail—about something called post-partum labor pains. The baby's out, happily drinking its bottle in the hospital nursery, and the labor goes on anyway. There you are, writhing away, but nobody cares because the main event is over."

Carlotta laughed, as she was meant to do, but she sensed that Rachel was genuinely disturbed. Not by the prospect of giving birth, for she had true physical courage, but by the impulses that led women to repeat horror stories to someone about to have her first child. "None of that will happen to you," she said softly.

"It fucking well better not," said Rachel, "because I won't stand for it."

A few moments later, mumbling an apology, Rachel dropped into a light sleep. It was something she did frequently these days, and at odd times. Carlotta watched her with affection, and willed her to be safe.

In the grip of jet lag, she stepped from the shower, dried herself, and fell into the bed. The effort of unpacking a nightdress seemed too great. She had thought sleep would come instantaneously, but she was wrong. She kept seeing Brendan Delaney's face—the shock of the blue eyes beneath the black lashes—and the courteous but commanding way he had of doing everything. He moved in the unmistakable aura of power, which was something Carlotta could recognize.

He had asked, when the car drew up in front of Rachel's building, if he might have the pleasure of her company at dinner some night in the future. It was very casual, the way he asked, as if it didn't matter whether she said yes or no. In the same offhand manner, she had given him Rachel's number.

When she fell asleep at last, it was to confused and solemn dreams. She seemed to be in Ireland, searching for her father's house.

ELEVEN

BRENDAN DELANEY'S FAMILY, LIKE THOMAS MADIGAN'S, had been in America for several generations, but unlike Madigan, Delaney had been the first member of his own family to be both rich and respectable. Well, respectable enough.

His grandfather's people had immigrated from County Donegal in the wake of the Great Famine that had killed two million people. Either they starved to death, dropping in the fields and hedges, or they contracted plague-fever, or they died on the foul coffin ships bringing them to a new life in America. A quarter of the entire population of Ireland had been exterminated, and in the middle of the nineteenth century, when such things were not supposed to happen in Europe. A medieval plague in Victorian times. It had not been an auspicious beginning, the circumstances of his grandfather's arrival at Ellis Island. Weak with hunger, dazed with seasickness, mourning the death at sea of his father and an older sister, the twelve-year-old boy who had been Delaney's grandfather had stepped onto the ground of the new world with no reason to feel hope.

His mother would soon die, in quarantine, and the boy, Stephen Patrick, would become the sole survivor of a family that had once included seven. His father and sister were buried at sea, his mother would be buried in a pauper's grave in

America, and the other brothers and sisters lay in a mass grave in Donegal. There had been too many corpses, and no man had the strength left to dig, and there was no money for coffins.

But against all odds, insanely, even, Stephen Patrick *had* felt hope. He later told his own son of that absurd surge of whatever it is that invades the bodies and souls of men destined to survive against all odds. His own son told Brendan Delaney, even though poverty and despair were, by then, things long since banished. Delaney remembered hearing the story as if it had all happened a thousand years ago and finding it exotic. When he got a little older, he understood his father's motives in keeping the story alive. He had two children of his own, one from each marriage, and he had passed it along with the same urgent message: *Don't forget what you have come from. Remember the past.*

His family's past included many unsavory episodes. Civil War intrigues and Tammany politics and whiskey distilleries and a particularly high-class brothel owned and operated by his great-uncle Joe all made up the patchwork quilt of it. Never mind. Who can afford to inquire too closely into what has passed to make a family rich and successful in America?

Delaney was a whiz at making money and seeing that it perpetuated itself. His father, newly rich, had been uneasy with money. He had spent too lavishly in an effort to prove that he was at home with the rich, and Brendan had profited by his father's mistaken notion that *they* had to be reminded, at all times, of a fella's wealth in order to accept him. His father's frenzy had taught him to be low-key. Laid back, as the kids said now. The cooler you played it, the more they came sniffing at your heels. It had worked with the WASPs who were his classmates at Harvard, and it had worked ever since.

For his first wife, he had chosen a Philadelphia deb with the intoxicating name of Marigold.

He sometimes suspected that he was at least as much in love with her name as he was with her—Marigold Savage Westerley. The "Savage" often made him smile, for Marigold was the gentlest creature on earth, and it was merely a family name. Her mother was a Virginia Savage, and the name was perfectly natural among people of Marigold's sort. He could make her blush charmingly by calling her Savage Marigold when they had finished making love; it gave her the impression that she was a wild, unfettered thing in the throes of passion, and this pleased her even as it made the blood rush to her cheeks.

He had first seen her at a house party in Philadelphia. She was the youngest daughter of the house, and not included among his contemporaries, but he noticed her from the start. She was a tall, delicate, flaxen-haired girl, pale as a moonbeam and cool as first frost. She fascinated him because he had never before seen a female whose outward fragility so belied her inward strength.

Marigold's strength came not from intellectual power or spiritual goodness but from the certain conviction that whatever she did was right. She was very rich and very (naturally) blonde, so how could she make a false move?

Delaney didn't know at the time that Marigold was caught up in the exhausting whirl of her coming-out season. He would catch glimpses of her as she sped down the stairs in ball gowns and disappeared into the night, bound for some destination he falsely imagined was romantic. Later, she would tell him of the excruciating agony of those endless parties, dancing with spotty boys and trying to be, as she put it, "loaded with personality." In the early days, Marigold had been blessed—or cursed—with the wit to poke fun at the customs of her own class, while still basking in its light un-self-consciously.

Several years had passed before he saw her again. Often, during those years, an odd, vivid image of her would recur to him. He would see again those tiny, rounded wrists. They were not like the thin wrists of poor girls, whose meager dimensions spoke of malnutrition. They had a rounded, polished look to them, as if some master craftsman had worked them on a lathe. Marigold was sumptuous in her fragility, voluptuous. Her wispy flaxen hair, so innocent, was ten times more alluring to him than the costly, manufactured coiffures of the women he slept with. If a man were to put his two hands around her small waist and squeeze, Delaney was convinced that nothing but blue ether would escape her parted lips.

She was twenty-one when she next crossed his path, but he was sure she had lost none of the innocence which had first drawn him to her. Undoubtedly she was no longer a virgin, but no one had truly touched her. Marigold, oblivious of the fact that her fine, pale hair was escaping from its French knot, was still flicking at her cigarette, there in the old Delmonico's like an unbroken pony. She had not been touched, no matter what. No heavy hand had laid a claim, and in that single moment—there in Delmonico's—Delaney had resolved to marry her.

Nothing could have been easier. In spite of the fact that Mrs. Westerley disliked him on principle, that Mr. Westerley, although liking Delaney as a man, distrusted him as a potential mate for his beloved Marigold, nothing could sway Marigold herself. From the moment he approached her table that night in Delmonico's, smiling and reintroducing himself as a friend of her older brother, she had fallen in love. She was a girl who had been waiting to fall in love now for some four years. Ever since the hectic season of her debut she had expected the right man to turn up at any moment. Her mother archly assured her that "that certain someone" was surely lurking in the wings, but he had certainly eluded her so far.

There had been some nice boys who had obligingly fallen in love with her and once or twice she had pretended to herself, trying to believe, she was "in love" with Dickie Prescott or Ted VanDam, but she wasn't adroit at self-deception. She experienced none of the emotions she had been led to expect from magazine articles and novels—no breathless expectation, no wild swings of mood depending on the loved one's behavior, no feeling that life could not be lived if Dickie, or Ted, were not beside her.

Delaney understood this very well, even though he could not know the particulars, and he presented himself at her table with complete confidence. He might have been saying: "Look, here I am, Marigold, your savior. I will rescue you from the terrible boredom of a romantic rich girl's life."

He was only six years older than Marigold at the time, but in matters of experience he might as well have been twice her age. He was the dark, impossibly handsome, slightly dangerous hero of her romantic novels come to life—here, at last, was a man to make her feel breathless. That certain someone.

During the months of their courtship, people whispered unpleasant things: Delaney was out to marry a WASP in order to better himself; Delaney needed old money to augment his very decidedly new money and make him safe; Delaney wanted to marry a Philadelphia deb just to prove he could. Although Delaney was, in fact, perfectly capable of behaving in the manner polite society ascribed to him, his pursuit of Marigold was quite sincere. He wanted her for herself, and if what Marigold *was* could not be separated from the forces which had made her that way, he was not at fault.

He continued to be besotted by his love's pale, patrician aura, just as she continued to adore the dark and desperate glamor of the knight who had come to rescue her from the Teds and Dickies.

Right up until the moment of the wedding, Mrs. Westerley had tearfully told her husband her worst fear: that Brendan Delaney would lie low for a year and then—in one great, evil swoop of connivery—convert Marigold to the Roman Catholic faith. Mr. Westerley, more worldly than his wife, laughed this fear off as ludicrous; what he did not tell her was his much more reasonable reservation about the marriage: young Brendan would tire of Marigold sooner than she tired of him, and break her heart with his philanderings. Henry, the older brother who had brought Delaney to the Westerleys' in his younger days, smiled uneasily and said very little. He had never paid attention to his younger sister.

In Bermuda, on their honeymoon, Marigold had at last discovered the true rapture so endlessly hinted at in her romanting reading. She believed it to be a sensation reserved for two people who were (that phrase!) *in love,* and regretted having lost her virginity to a Dickie or Ted. While she knew Delaney to be far from innocent, she thought he, too, regretted any previous contact, and felt a sense of pride in knowing that so marvelous a man had forgone the pleasures of the flesh during their courtship. Delaney had contented himself with kisses and respectful caresses before they were married; how was Marigold to know that he, like a skillful juggler, had been balancing several strenuous affairs during the time he was winning her hand?

In the early days of his marriage, Delaney was faithful. He had resolved to be so, putting behind him all the excesses of his youth. Marigold would be enough for him, at least for many years to come, and there would be heady business propositions, and the births of children, to smooth out the boring bits. Both of them wanted many children, but they had agreed to wait a few years before getting down to it. Marigold was, after all, a month shy of her twenty-second birthday when they married. There was all the time in the world.

Nearly a year went by before Delaney began to feel uneasy. He was, by nature, a gregarious man, and Marigold unexpectedly revealed herself as a closet homebody. If he wanted to go out to celebrate an occasion, Marigold would invariably unfold a plan for staying at home. "Why go out, darling? We have everything we could possibly need here. I'll just open a bottle of champagne, shall I? There's a lovely fire in the library—Agnes laid it earlier—and we can go in and toast our toes."

The trouble was that he did not want to go into the library and toast his toes over a bottle of champagne. He wanted to stride into "21" or Delmonico's, his lovely bride clinging to his arm, and be back among people again. He wanted to hear his name called from the corners of restaurants and nightclubs, to know that drinks would be ordered and cigarettes lit because he had entered a room. He was a catalyst, someone who made things happen, and as a consequence of his entry there would be conversation and hilarity.

Alone with Marigold, none of that convivial stuff would exist. She would haul out that embroidery, the work she was so keen on, and dig in for a long evening at home. She never seemed happier than when, with Delaney as captive audience, she described scenes from her childhood. She was always embroidering, or knitting, and the sight of her nimble fingers, pursuing their useless work, irritated him mightily. They were not poor, did not have to clothe themselves in the fruits of Marigold's labors, so why in hell did she have to sit there clicking her needles like an Irish granny?

On the nights when he did manage to coax her out, she began to yawn before 11:30, protesting that she needed her beauty sleep, and when they entertained at home their guests, taking a cue from the hostess, always slipped away early. "Alone together, darling," she would say. "That's what I like best."

She was still ardent in bed, and still the same pale, quintessentially blonde girl he had married, but that was about all that remained. She seemed determined to bore him to death, and in the second year of their marriage he understood: the restless, occasionally witty Marigold he had known was the unhappy Marigold, the girl who was searching for something and unsure of herself; the placid, stay-at-home matron he was married to was the Marigold who felt secure and fulfilled. She was a docile, limited person who had been waiting all these years to become what she now was. Mummy came down from Philadelphia twice each month to shop and have tea with Marigold at the Palm Court. As long as she could have tea with her mother, the occasional picture in *Town & Country*, and Brendan in her bed, she was perfectly happy.

When Delaney understood how irrevocable was the nature of his bride, he made a decision. He would have a European-style marriage, whether Marigold acquiesced or not. He would be a good husband, appearing by her side when she needed him, playing the charming host at her dull little parties. He would give her no cause for complaint, but neither would he subject himself to the tyranny of boredom Marigold thought of as bliss.

He invented business meetings late at night, even whole trips to far-off cities, and reverted to his old ways with no effort at all. Several of his former mistresses were glad to see him back in circulation, and there were always new women who begged him to think of their beds as a home away from home. He felt no guilt at betraying the trusting Marigold—hadn't he given her his undivided attention for more than a year?—and actually thought he had worked out a reasonable solution. He no longer returned to their Park Avenue apartment as to a mausoleum, but in the spirit of a good and tender husband. Having satisfied his need for play, he would contemplate his wife with pride and affection. In his utterly sated states, he could actually be twice as nice to her—embroidery hook and all—as in the days when she had suffocated him with domesticity.

It might have gone on forever like that had not a venomous little bird—Mummy, perhaps, whose ear had picked up rumors in far-off Philadelphia?—whispered the truth in Marigold's ear. Then there were Scenes! Scene which embarrassed him terribly, but also moved him, made him feel guilty, and oddly restored Marigold to her former, intriguing self. Happy, she was as dull as ditch-water, but unhappiness suited her. The thin wrists, no longer employed in needlework, assumed allure once more as they beat against her silvery, hollowed-out temples. Her long fingers raked through the spun gold hair, and luminous tears slid from her eyes like precious gems.

She began to drink more than she ever had before. He was touched to see her sitting, her glass pressed against that place where her dress slid up to reveal her classy, slightly bony knees, interrogating him plaintively.

"I do not see," Marigold would say, in the over-precise cadences of one who was intoxicated and didn't know it, "where it is I've failed you. I fail to see it, Brendan. I have been a good wife, haven't I? I would appreciate it very much, indeed, I would take it as a great kindness, if you would explain to me what it is I've done wrong?"

It was during this period that Patrick, their son, was conceived.

Delaney forswore his bad habits while Marigold was pregnant, and was, once more, a perfect husband in fact as well as superficially. He felt a great tenderness for her, and something else—something he never put into words—which came close to being admiration. Marigold was about to do something heroic, bear his child, and she deserved every consideration during the months leading up to the great event.

In pregnancy she proved a champion. She never complained or grew messy and unsightly. She was one of those women who escaped morning sickness and swollen ankles and blotchy skin; she merely grew a hard little basketball of a belly and glowed and appeared, to the casual observer, to be younger than she was. Now there was a reason for her to knit and crochet, and what had repelled him in former days seemed perfectly natural and charming.

The one fly in all this domestic bliss was something he could never have imagined: the more attention he was prepared to give her, the less she seemed to need him. Just when he was falling in love with her all over again, Marigold retreated to some private place where Delaney's presence was, at best, an intrusion. To be sure, it was an intrusion affectionately tolerated, but an intrusion all the same. She and her basketball were the stars; Delaney was only a bit player, the comic relief, perhaps.

Mrs. Westerley, who came to New York more frequently during Marigold's pregnancy, reinforced his feeling of uselessness. He was often tempted, during the last few months, to visit his old haunts and mix with people who appreciated him, but a superstitious quirk prevented him. If he were propping up a bar somewhere when Marigold went into premature labor, mightn't the child be born defective to punish him? And if he were rolling around in bed with Helen, or Bibi, or

Sharon, and came home to long faces and the news that his kid had been born dead, what would he do? How could he live?

In fact, Patrick was born, with no complications, at the Harkness Pavilion. Marigold surrendered his son into the world at the reasonable hour of ten in the morning, after only four hours of labor. She was young and healthy, and the baby was perfect. Delaney found Marigold sitting cross-legged in her hospital bed, checking off a list of people to be thanked for baby gifts.

"Let's have at least five more," she said, frowning slightly. "Do you remember who gave us the Tiffany rattle, darling?"

Patrick became, on his return home, the center of his mother's universe. After only two weeks, she dismissed the Belgian baby nurse, claiming that she, and she alone, was capable of looking after her son. She took Patrick to the park in his pram, mingling with the nannies as if she herself were a nanny and not a former top-seeded candidate for Deb of the Year. This devotion pleased Delaney at first, but in a remarkably short time, it began to seem fanatical.

He liked to play with young Patrick, but the ways you could play with a fellow of four months were limited. It was his special joy to tiptoe into the nursery where Patrick was likely to be humping around in his crib, his behind in the air as his arms and legs worked furiously. Delaney would pluck him out of the crib, hugging the little body to his breast, and he would make growling airplane noises, his hands firm beneath Patrick's solid chest, and whirl him through the air. Patrick enjoyed flying. His face would assume a brief, worried look, and then split into a grin of rapture. Often he would gurgle with pleasure—a genuine belly laugh would erupt from the infant frame, and Delaney, at such times, felt himself a good father. He was a man who knew, instinctively, how to please his little son.

Once, Marigold caught him at play with Patrick.

"Oh, *Brendan,*" she cried in horrified tones, "what are you *doing?* That pressure on his abdomen! He might spit up, Brendan! What on earth do you think you are *doing?*"

Marigold came scuttling across the room and snatched Patrick away, as if he were in great peril. "I know best," she said to Delaney, as the baby began to cry fitfully. "Trust me, dear, a mother always knows best."

"Then why is he crying?" Delaney wanted to know.

"Because you've got him in an overstimulated state," said Marigold.

His flesh and blood; his son. What he saw as pleasure, she interpreted as "overstimulated." She was the mother. It was her flesh that had been stretched and wrung, not his. He was, once again, a minor player in this most miraculous drama culminating in the birth of Patrick. Patrick was not his own son, but Marigold's creation. He was the odd man out.

Delaney thought he would be better able to share in his boy's life when Patrick was a bit older. It was very difficult to communicate with a being who could neither reason nor speak, but in a few years . . . As it turned out, he wasn't able to wait more than a year before life with Marigold became unendurable.

Shortly after Patrick's first birthday, the senior Westerleys made the Delaneys the gift of a house in Virginia. The house was in close proximity to the properties of Marigold's Savage cousins on her mother's side; in fact, it was in such close proximity the Savages might as well have lived in a compound. *Livin' in each other's ear,* the voice of Delaney's long-dead grandmother whispered. The gift was presented as a *fait accompli.* Nobody had broached the subject with Delaney, yet it was a matter of accepted fact that Marigold would dwell in the Virginia house, with Patrick, during all the long months of the unbearable summer. She was delighted with her gift and squealed that delight in a manner more appropriate to her deb years, when she had never, so far as he knew, squealed at all.

He had met the Savage cousins, had endured a week of their hospitality in the first year of his marriage. Cousin Edmund, the oldest, was a deeply stupid man who wrote illiterate memoirs about a Confederacy he had never known. There was one called Whitcomb, who was considered amusing because he got drunk easily and always recited, when in his cups, *The Boy Stood on the Burning Deck.* Whitcomb sailed and, once, under the influence, got halfway to Portugal when he was under the impression that the ship was bound for Florida.

The wives of these Savage men were interchangeable. Both were hearty, short-clipped blondes who were fond, of horses. Over a family dinner they were likely to argue about the most efficient method of administering an equine enema or filing down a hoof.

This stimulating group was rounded out by the only female cousin, Fleur. Fleur was energetic in a nervous and unwholesome sort of way. She loved a practical joke. She pulled chairs from beneath the rumps of dinner guests, pushed fully-clothed people into her pool, and screamed with laughter when her butler, under duress, passed trays of drinks in which reposed tiny, ugly rubber bugs. Fleur's husband was a judge, and it always made Delaney angry to think of him on the bench. How could you expect justice from a man who smiled benevolently while his crazed wife goosed her guests into the pool? *What fun this is,* the judge seemed to be saying. *This gal is irrepressible, isn't she? What spirit—you've got to admit she's got spirit.*

The judge was a good deal older than his wife, and all of them were many years older than Brendan and Marigold. Delaney was not eager for the premature elderliness that contact with the Savages would bring him, and he told Marigold.

"Don't be perverse," she said. "They're family. The Savages are wonderful people, Brendan. Patrick needs to grow up with a sense of belonging, doesn't he?"

That very night he invented one of his business meetings and spent ten hours in the bed of a Eurasian Latin Quarter dancer. He confessed, in the crook of her amber arm, his need for a divorce.

"Dead simple," said the dancer. "I can come in handy here."

"Nothing messy, sweetheart. Not like that."

"I know these society women, how they work. The one thing they can't tolerate is a crossover. They'll turn a blind eye to anything so long as it's discreet. Darling Freddie can be screwing the gardener's daughter, and as long as he does it in the potting shed it's okay. But let him bring her into his wife's world and all hell breaks loose! One little whisper that Freddie and his girlie were seen together at Veau d'Or? Those women go mad—they can't get a divorce quick enough."

"She's just a girl," Delaney said guiltily, remembering Marigold's youth. But if she was just a girl, why didn't she act like one?

"Suit yourself," said the dancer.

Ten days after that conversation, Marigold announced that she wanted a divorce. She swiftly emended her demand, and said she was going to Philadelphia, with Patrick, to "think things over." If Brendan could explain, or justify, his actions, if he could in any way make clear to her why he had been seen in public, and repeatedly, with an Oriental woman of dubious respectability, then she could be reached in the home of her parents. She would listen to anything he had to say.

No agonized confessions or apologies winged their way to Philadelphia, and after a month Marigold repaired to Santo Domingo and divorced him.

He did not see his son again until Patrick was nearly six years old. He had, with a degree of pain, written the boy off. Patrick would grow up a Westerley, all traces of the Delaney side submerged. It was rumored that Marigold had taken to serious drinking, and he imagined that Mrs. Westerley would be the one to shape Patrick's future. Once he had a nightmare in which Patrick, now old enough to have some motor skills, was crocheting a blanket for himself. "I have a sense of belonging," the dream-Patrick said. "They're family."

It was not until Marigold remarried—to a doctor who had treated her for alcoholism at Silver Hill—that Delaney saw his son again. The doctor must have been one of those enlightened members of the new breed—the sort who believed that a boy couldn't have too many male role models—because Delaney was suddenly offered the chance to spend time with Patrick on a quarter-yearly basis.

Four times a year, Patrick would be chauffeured to Delaney's new flat on Gramercy Park and left for the period of one week. Four times a year, Delaney would banish women from his place and drink more moderately. He hired a woman to look after Patrick during those times when he was out acquiring tin mines in Bolivia or advising greedy foreign businessmen to invest in them, and came home with trepidation to amuse and entertain his son.

It was difficult, because they were strangers. Patrick was infinitely polite—good breeding—and called him "Father." On those bleak expeditions to the zoo in Central Park, or the Museum of Natural History, Delaney often felt that their roles had become reversed. Patrick was solemn and protective, a father figure; Delaney, in his efforts to entertain the boy, was unpredictable and wild. The time they spent together was strained and exhausting. Still, a rapport of some kind existed between them. At the end of each session they spent together they would acknowledge the effort they had expended. Like battle-weary soldiers at the end of a tour of duty, they saluted one another with respect.

By the time Patrick was ten, he called Delaney "Dad."

When Patrick left, after one of his visits, Delaney felt both sorrow and relief for a day or two, and then plunged, unhesitatingly, into the life he loved.

He hadn't planned to marry again, but then, in his late thirties, who should come twinkling down the pike but Ivette? Ivette, with her snazzy tits and blue-black hair, who claimed to be the dispossesed heiress to a coffee fortune in Colombia, when all the world suspected she was Mexican? Never mind. Her face was on the cover of *Vogue*, wasn't it? She was a sensation, and she liked Delaney better than any man she'd ever met, and what with one thing and another he'd married her, and she had given him his daughter.

Elena, a carbon copy of her mother, now lived in Paris. He scarcely knew her. She was only, he reckoned, six years older than Carlotta Madigan.

Carlotta was always in his mind lately, more than he could have anticipated. In the four months he had known her she had become his obsession. He had waited a week before calling her, and she had accepted his invitation to dine at Lutece in her cool, offhand way. He had seen her at least once a week since that night, but he still remembered the powerful impact of that first night. Usually women were less beautiful in the flesh than in one's daydreams, and he had been prepared for a slight disappointment when he rang the bell of the Veres' eastside apartment. A servant had answered the door, taken his coat, and ushered him into a room where a small and very pregnant girl sat sipping tea.

"Hello, Mr. Delaney. I'm Rachel Vere, and I'm not going to get up to greet you—too much trouble. I can ring for a drink, or you can make one for yourself. Carlotta will be ready in a minute."

Laughable, really. Brendan J. Delaney, fifty-six years old, being made to feel that he was calling at a dorm for a date. The pretty little creature wasn't exactly the right choice for dorm mother, either. He had poured himself a Jameson's and settled down to charm Mrs. Vere. Whatever her faults, he could see she was devoted to Carlotta, and he liked her for that. He struck up a conversation about the shifty eyes of the doorman in the Veres' building, sensing she liked trivial subjects.

"How clever of you to notice, Mr. Delaney! Yes, I've often thought that Otto could turn into a mass murderer with the slightest encouragement."

"On that day, Mrs. Vere, I sincerely hope you will be miles from the building."

"Do you have children?" She slipped it in unexpectedly, to disconcert him.

"Two. And three grandchildren." Get it out in the open. Something else—if he said it, she couldn't have the pleasure of thinking it secretly—"My daughter is only a few years older than Carlotta."

He had won that match, astounding Rachel Vere, but then Carlotta herself had entered the room, and the sheer power of her beauty reduced him to a schoolboy. He had tried to preserve his dignity under the circumstances, but he was sure sharp-eyed Rachel had noticed the way the Jameson's danced in the glass.

Carlotta was wearing a cream-colored dress that looked rather like the slips women of his generation had worn, and her amazing hair was loose and free tonight, giving her the look of an innocent schoolgirl. Unless, that is, you knew something about women's jewelry. Delaney knew more than a little, thanks to Ivette, and he was willing to bet that the stone at the end of the elaborate, crusted David Webb chain was a .68 caliber Cubochon emerald.

He thought the emerald must have belonged to her mother, a gift from Tom Madigan. The Martha he remembered would never have chosen it for herself, but the senator had been the sort of man to shower his wife with lavish gems, wooing her away from the sedate pearls and discreet diamonds of her choice.

Martha had been like the lady of a medieval knight, her beauty chaste and gentle. Carlotta's beauty was wild and haunting—the kind that toppled empires. The emerald suited her as it never could have suited her mother.

In the silence that greeted her entrance, she came to him, smiling as if she really meant it. "It *is* nice to see you again," she said, as if there had been some doubt about the matter. And Delaney, his senses reeling, had said to himself: *This is going to be more serious than I thought.*

Now, in January, he stood half-naked before his dressing room mirror in Greenwich, Connecticut. He was dressing to take Carlotta to a dinner party. Fortunately, he would not be consorting with a room full of twenty-seven-year-olds, since the Dennisons believed in multi-generational entertaining. He glanced into the mirror, and was well pleased with what he saw. His powerful body was strong and showed no signs of aging. There was no slack skin, no weakening, flabby pockets of the sort he saw at health clubs in men of his age. Although he hated organized exercise, he maintained himself well. Much of his exercise consisted of lovemaking, which he insisted was better for the body than any of that damned jogging business. You exercised all of your muscles when you got, and gave, a proper fucking, and enjoyed yourself at the same time. He was also a strong swimmer and an excellent horseman, but in his heart he knew his superb physique was just the luck of the draw. Delaneys were all well built.

He gave his driver the night off and chose to drive into Manhattan himself. The irritations of traffic would help to take his mind off the continual frustration of wanting Carlotta and not having that want fulfilled. It was not quite the time, and he had to make do with two lady friends of long standing while he waited.

Somewhere on the outskirts of the city, he had an image of Carlotta as an exquisite and ripe tropical fruit, ready at almost any moment to drop from the branch of a tree. Delaney was standing beneath the tree, ready to catch her.

"Oh, go away," Rachel said when Carlotta came in to kiss her goodnight. "You look too beautiful. I can't stand it."

Rachel had decided, like a medieval woman, to remain in her bed in the final weeks of her pregnancy. "I am definitely unsightly now," she announced. "It would be obscene to subject innocent people to my presence." She was not going to the Dennisons' party, and although Cotter complained, he remained loyally at home.

Carlotta did not go away, but rustled in her green taffeta to the bedside, where she bent and kissed her friend's wan cheek.

"Oh, Carlotta, when are you going to go out with someone who isn't a hundred years old? Charlie Babcock is crazy for you."

"Brendan is only in his fifties," said Carlotta. "And as you very well know, he's much more attractive than rabbity Charlie Babcock.

"I'll admit he's attractive," said Rachel. "But if you're seen all the time with him, the younger eligible men will give up on you."

"Good. I'm not interested in them. I *like* Brendan. I enjoy his company."

"Well, then, you ought to get around to enjoying *him*." said Rachel slyly. "He has quite a reputation, you know. I wasn't going to tell you this, but Alice Quincey said her *mother* had an affair with him twenty years ago. She overheard her mother telling a friend that Delaney was insatiable. He was the Warren Beatty of his time."

"Was he indeed?" said Carlotta wryly. She kissed Rachel again and went to meet Delaney, who had just been announced. She had not been telling the truth when she said she liked him. In point of fact, she adored him. His very presence was enough to make her happy and secure. Whenever the old, bad feeling threatened to overtake her, she shut her eyes and thought of Brendan Delaney and was calm and happy again.

Her one fear was that he would, in some mysterious manner, slip out of her life and leave her alone again. He seemed devoted to her, but he had never tried to seduce her in all the time they'd known each other. She was afraid that he didn't take her seriously, that she was just a young, once-a-week diversion for him. For Christmas he had given her a gold bracelet set with sapphires and diamonds. On the inside of the bracelet he had had something engraved, but the words were Irish and totally incomprehensible to her. When she had asked him what they meant, he ginned and said he'd tell her when she was ready to know.

He stood, waiting for her in the parquet foyer, his dark coat lightly powdered with snow. She kissed his smooth cheek and brushed the snow from his hair, trying to blot out the vivid image of Delaney and Alice Quincey's mother rolling around on a bed two decades ago.

After Carlotta had gone, Rachel rang the bell by her bed and summoned Cotter.

"Back rub?" he asked.

"Yes, please." What Rachel really wanted was to talk about

her fear for Carlotta, but a back rub would be nice, too. Cotter had been behaving wonderfully lately, and she felt a great fondness for him. Now that she had been forbidden to have sex, even if she had wanted to, for God's sake, she and Cotter had become friends. Friends waiting quietly together for the birth of their child.

Rachel heaved herself onto her side so that Cotter could lift her nightdress and massage the aching muscles of her lower back. In the middle trimester, she had recovered her sexual appetite with a vengeance, and she and Cotter had discovered a variety of positions to accommodate her ballooning belly. The sex had been lovely, but she and Cotter had resumed their old, quarrelsome pattern of sniping at each other whenever they weren't in bed.

It was all wrong. Couples were supposed to snipe and bicker when they were sexually frustrated, not the reverse. She thought the problem was simple. They had never learned to trust one another. Rachel believed her husband had had an affair or two, and Cotter was sure (and rightly so) that his wife had been unfaithful right from the first. Now that Rachel couldn't be unfaithful if her life depended on it, he trusted her.

"That's nice, Cot," she said, acknowledging the skill of his back-rubbing technique.

Did she trust Cotter? She had tried, these last few weeks, to satisfy him in the only two ways available to her now. It was nearly impossible to perform oral sex because it was difficult to bend her body, and Cotter was too shy to present himself to her in any really original way. About the only way she could have done it was to rig him up on a set of pulleys and lower him from the ceiling. As for the other—there was something forlorn about doing for him something he could do for himself any old time, and probably better.

"I'm worried about Carlotta," she said.

"Why? She seems fine to me."

"Well, Jesus, Cot, don't you see what she's doing? I mean about Delaney."

"You told me they weren't doing anything."

"Carlotta has found her father all over again. It's as if the senator had been resurrected from the grave. Delaney even *looks* like Tom Madigan. There's a very strong resemblance."

"I guess it's a good thing they're not having a real affair," said Cotter. "Carlotta isn't sleeping with him because she knows it would be like incest, is that what you mean?"

Rachel rolled over, sighing. Sometimes he was so thick. "No, darling. The really spooky thing is that she *doesn't* know. If you told her Delaney resembled her father she'd deny it. She'd come up with a dozen superficial ways in which they don't look alike. The lady would protest too much."

"You worry about her a lot, baby. You're overdoing it. She's a big girl—she can take care of herself."

"Christ alive, Cotter. My best friend is happily dating her *father*, to the exclusion of everyone else, and you say she can take care of herself? She hasn't been this happy with a man since Daddy took her to '21.' It's so fucking *morbid*."

"What's wrong with Delaney, to put up with it? Maybe he's queer?"

"We say gay now, Cotter. Delaney, for your information, is one of the better-known studs around town. He's about as gay as a prize bull. That's the other thing that's bothering me. If he's willing to be celibate with Carlotta it's because he has a long-range plan. I think he wants her for keeps."

"You mean?"

"Yes. I told her tonight she ought to go ahead and sample his wares. Not that she ever listens to me, but I thought it was my duty to state my opinion. At least that way, she might come to her senses. He would lose his infernal mystique and she might get tired of him."

"Are you saying you encouraged Carlotta to have an affair with her father?" Cotter looked shocked.

"Oh, give me strength," Rachel groaned. She took Cotter's hands and held them, speaking in level tones as if to a child. "Look, the only thing worse than fucking your father is *marrying* him, right?"

"Right."

"Good," said Rachel, lying back in exhaustion. "That's settled."

Carlotta devoted equal amounts of time to her two dinner partners, as her decorous mother had taught her to do. She might be her father's daughter, but in social matters she reflected Martha's aristocratic training. Anyone watching her might have marveled at her manners. It was rare, in 1973, to see a girl in her twenties who automatically turned from her conversation as each course was served.

She was attempting to have a conversation with an elderly Colonel Dupree at the moment, but it was far from easy. The colonel kept narrowing his eyes at her, as if he suspected they had been seated together by mistake.

"Well, Miss Madison," he said, "you're probably regretting drawing an old fish like myself for a partner, eh? Can't be much fun for you, eh?"

"Not at all," Carlotta said politely. And then, just to see if he had any life in him: "As a matter of fact, I quite like older men."

"You do." It was a statement, not a question, and, if anything, he seemed twice as suspicious. He chewed his fish in an angry sort of way. She had already noticed that the colonel handled his fish knife as if it were a bayonet. "That's unusual," he said when he had swallowed. "These days your generation doesn't want much truck with mine—never trust anyone over thirty, they say."

"Maybe I'm not a typical member of my generation, Colonel."

"Not by the looks of you," he said. "Certainly not. But then, if you looked like the lot of them, you'd hardly be here, would you?"

Carlotta wondered if he were trying to deliver a lumbering kind of compliment and smiled demurely.

"Most of them, Miss Madison, most of you young folks, just seem to make it a point to offend the eye as much as possible. Long, greasy hair. Dirty, unwashed necks. Filthy rags for clothes, and proud of it." He took a large sip of his wine and swiped at his long, thin lips with his napkin. "Shall I tell you a thing or two?"

Carlotta nodded, hoping he would not ruin her appetite with more descriptions of greasy hair and ringed necks. He bent over until she could smell his winey breath. "You hideous young people—not *you*, Miss Madison, but your compatriots —are making yourselves ugly for a very good reason. The hippies know their cause is corrupt, at heart they sense it, and so they present themselves as losers. They know they'll lose, and they're already dressed as refugees."

"Refugees?"

"After every war," said the colonel in a satisfied way, "there are always refugees. Paint 'em any color you like, make their eyes slant up or down, let 'em babble in Hungarian or German, Korean or Vietnamese—it's always the same old story. Refugees."

So they were, after all, talking about the war. Carlotta was glad that Colonel Dupree didn't seem to know who she was. She was the anonymous Miss Madison, a guest, and not the daughter of a U.S. senator who had delivered fiery—and, at the time, unpopular—diatribes against the war in Vietnam.

It amused her to think that her dinner partner had been the enemy of her father. She herself was not political, but she was suddenly able to call up wonderful images of her daddy and Colonel Dupree slugging it out. *In this corner, from the Pentagon, with a fish knife in his hands . . .*

"What are your feelings about the war, Miss Madison?"

"I'm afraid I don't have many, Colonel. I've been living in Europe for such a long time. I'm much more interested in hearing yours."

Colonel Dupree released a laugh that sounded like the harsh, excited barks of a guard dog. "We're there to win, daughter," he said. "No matter what it takes, we're there to win. And we will—may I assure you of that? No matter how many kids try to undermine this government by marching and chanting those idiotic slogans with their toenails curling over their sandals; no matter how many goddamned monks turn themselves into Kentucky fried chicken; no matter how many red-diaper babies turned movies stars go off to Vietnam and give press conferences—it's a lost cause!"

His zeal was frightening, and she nodded politely and wished she had not been placed next to him. Delaney, she noticed, was in a much more congenial spot at the table. While she tried to behave in a manner her mother would have approved, Brendan ate and drank and conversed in his usual mode. Everything was easy on his side. No madmen there, only women.

"What we really ought to do," said the colonel, "is go the hell into Cambodia and bomb." He sounded nostalgic now, and Carlotta nearly giggled. The man got sentimental over bombs.

She was glad when the duckling arrived. It meant she could disengage from Colonel DuPree and talk to the man on her other side, who was a playwright. She had never seen his plays and was not at all attracted to him, but she found him easier to take than the colonel, who had become so agitated at one point that he had missed his mouth and plunged into his cheek with a fork.

"I represent the traditional values," the playwright told her, attacking his duckling and not looking up. His voice was dull and angry from too much wine. "People sneer at well-made plays these days. Grants are given for the most ludicrous projects. Actors masturbating on stage in wheelchairs and worthless, feminist dialogues featuring noble women in factories *enduring*. It's a joke. History will regard it as a decade of lunacy."

"I've been out of the country for a while," said Carlotta diplomatically. "I've lost touch with American theater. What sort of plays do you write?"

While the playwright answered, at great length, she was free to study Delaney. He was entertaining both of his dinner partners, to judge by their laughter, and she wished to be on his side of the table. One was a very old lady in black lace, the wife of a judge. When she laughed, she threw her hands in the air with a graceful movement to show off her rings. The other was an extremely attractive blonde, a little past forty, who showed discreet cleavage. It was the blonde Carlotta worried about, or women like her.

Hers was the face of the enemy. Brendan had been married twice—Carlotta had looked him up in *Who's Who*—and would surely marry again. A man like that was not meant to live alone. Another woman would take Delaney away from her, and she would have no part in his life.

"Life-affirming plays," her partner was mumbling through his mouthful of duck. "Plays that lift the human spirit instead of degrading it! It is not possible to be resurrected in the back room of a pizza parlor. Sausage and anchovies cannot play a part in the redemption of man."

Now Delaney seemed to be in the most intimate conversation with the blonde, who was telling him something in hushed tones. He leaned toward her, one of his beautiful hands holding his wine glass aloft, as if what she had to say was so important he could neither put it down nor drink from it. His black eyelashes—so boyish, those lashes—were half-lowered over the blue eyes, and occasionally he smiled. Once he grinned. What the hell was she telling him? How dare he be so intrigued by it? Wasn't she ever going to finish this interminable story of hers?

"But I suppose I'm wasting my time on you," the playwright told her peevishly. "You're young, dear girl. It's your generation that will be my ruin." He himself could not be more than thirty-two, Carlotta thought, but he affected a world-weary air, and had been prematurely aged by his own bitterness. On her left, a military man who wanted to go into Cambodia and bomb the hell out of the gooks; on her right, a creepy, effete dilettante who probably got more mileage out of complaining at dinner parties than out of writing plays. Then there were the ones like Charlie Babcock, a young lawyer from a Social Register family who wore outdated Nehru jackets and said "groovy" to show that he had—belatedly—caught the spirit of the bygone sixties. Delaney seemed the last real man left on the face of the earth.

He and the blonde were now laughing together, as if they had shared something wonderful. Carlotta did a quick survey of the women at the table and saw that they were all glancing covertly at Brendan. He radiated charismatic beams of masculinity, and every female body in the Dennisons' dining room responded, no matter their age. All of them wished to be the blonde.

He looked up and smiled across the table at Carlotta, raised his glass, and drank to her. She was no exception to the rule. While the playwright grumbled and the colonel raged, Carlotta lifted her own glass and pledged herself—although she didn't know it yet—to Brendan J. Delaney.

TWELVE

WHEN DELANEY FINALLY DECIDED THE TIME WAS RIGHT, about three days after the Dennisons' dinner party, he invited Carlotta to his house in Greenwich. He kept an apartment in town, but he wanted it to happen for the first time in his house.

The ostensible reason for her visit was to lunch with him and see his art collection. The old joke about coming up "to see my etchings, dear" did not apply, because his collection was very fine and Carlotta, somewhat to his surprise, knew about art.

He had sent the car for her and, although he knew it would be at least an hour before she'd arrive, he felt his nerves hum with anticipation. The ripe fruit was about to fall into his palm at last—today he would be rewarded for his infinite patience. He had looked across the table at her that night and seen what he had been waiting for: a possessive look in Carlotta's normally undisturbed face. He could just barely detect it, the little flush of anxiety that meant she was jealous. When he had left her at the Veres' door he had kissed her forehead, as usual, and then taken her gloved hand, peeled the glacé kid back a bit, and solemnly kissed the inside of her wrist. The gesture was deliberately ambiguous. It could have been an act of erotic tenderness, or it could have been, in her mind, a prelude to goodbye. He wanted her to be confused and frightened, so that when he called with his invitation she'd come running. It had worked perfectly.

He moved impatiently to a window. It was a crystalline winter day. The snow blanketed his front lawn all the way down to the gate where Carlotta would eventually be driven to her destiny. A lamb to the slaughter, thought Delaney, except that he only planned to kill her with love. Even love would have to wait, though, for more hours than he liked to think. First there would be his paintings and sculpture, and the carefully planned lunch he had ordered from his cook and man-servant. A light lunch of dover sole in dill sauce, a green salad, and a deceptive wine that seemed light but was, in fact, heady. Such a lunch left the body alert and sensuous—he didn't want his Carlotta to feel sluggish and dozy.

After lunch a walk, perhaps, through the picturesque fields attached to his property, and then back to the house for a warming brandy. Delaney 'walked through to his library to make sure the fire was roaring. He was proud of his house, although some would have called it austere, under-decorated. His art treasures were his decoration, and the lines of the house itself were beautiful. It was built of pale, rose-colored stone, and had high ceilings and tall casement windows. There was a fireplace in each of the six bedrooms, as well as in the downstairs rooms, and a staircase fit for the castle of a baron. Carlotta would love it.

Twice he thought he heard the wheels of the car crunching on the gravel of his long, circular driveway, and each time he found he had imagined it. He was as nervous as a boy. He poured himself a glass of Irish to calm the old system, then thoughtfully poured half of it back. He had a tendency to drink too much—twice in his life he had become a dangerously heavy drinker—and he never wanted drink to come between him and Carlotta.

When the car finally did come through the gates, his heart contracted at the sight of her in the back. She wore a white fur coat with a little hood, and her face seemed like a flower to him in all its lovely youthfulness and innocence. He thought she would forgive him the crafty preparations he had laid to bring her to his bed, if only she could know how desperately he wanted her.

*   *   *

She was glad when he proposed going for a walk in the snowy
fields. She felt strangely flushed and nervous after the delicious lunch, and was afraid she'd been babbling. She could
not seem to stop talking about his paintings, particularly the
small, glowing Tintoretto, and his Etruscan sculpture and
Gauguin sketches and priceless Oriental figures. She was sure
she'd told him about her little T'ang horse twice now. At first
she thought she was talking so much to impress him with her
knowledge of art, but when he suggested the walk she knew
the real reason. She couldn't be in a room alone with him,
even rooms as huge as these. Their contacts had always been
in noisy, public places—restaurants, parties, opera, the ballet.
Here, in this vast house, he seemed—what? *He's too big to
be alone with me,* were the words that danced crazily through
her mind. When he helped her into her coat and his hands
brushed her shoulders she almost jumped.

Outside, it wasn't much better. The cold air calmed her a
little, and the blue-white snow was beautiful, but striding
along beside him, their boots making that wonderful scrunch-
ing sound, she was troubled by some vague memory. He
touched her arm to point out a cardinal, crimson in the snow,
and again half-remembered images came to haunt her. The sky
had been a bigger one then. The sky in Connecticut was deep
blue and breathtaking, but it lacked the grandeur of a Montana
sky.

Usually, Brendan talked to her, soothing her with his soft
voice and clever words, amusing and reassuring her. Today he
was silent in the out-of-doors. She glanced at him and saw
only the face of a rugged man who was enjoying a winter walk
on his property. She shivered deep in her fur coat, but not
from the cold.

She was just as glad to go back in the house as she had
been to leave it. Already the short afternoon was drawing in.
The sky was dark with new snow clouds, and the snow had
little lavender pockets of dusk to remind them that it would
soon be dark.

Back in the library, in front of the fire, he brought her a
snifter of brandy. She sat in one corner of a long leather
couch. He stood with his back to the fire. "What makes the
fire smell so heavenly?" she asked him.

"Peat," he said. "Turf. What they use in Ireland."

He had affected a brogue with the word turf, pronouncing

it as "torrf," and she smiled. Good. He was reverting to his old personality, he was going to entertain her.

"Do you have it flown over?" she asked.

But he didn't answer. He was staring at her now, his expression unknowable. For a moment she thought he was angry, but then she saw it was something else.

"What is it, Brendan?"

"Put your brandy down, Carlotta," he said in a soft and commanding voice. She obeyed him, her heart beginning to pound. "Now—come here to me." The question that formed on her lips was *What have I done?* but that was ridiculous. Delaney didn't mean to punish her. Obediently, she rose to her feet and crossed the room to him, stopping a few feet away. "Closer," he said. She had to obey. She came so close that only inches separated them. What she saw in his eyes was bewildering. There was a look of tenderness and longing, but behind it was something more dangerous. She knew, she knew! She started to speak, but now his hands were lifting her face to his and warm lips covered her own. She resisted, drawing back, but the heat of his body was like a magnet. She wanted to rest her head on his chest and twine her arms around his neck, but that would only stoke the dangerous thing. Her lips seemed to be opening beneath his, and the way her arms went around his neck wasn't the way she'd intended.

"Brendan—"

"Shhh, darling. I know best this time," he whispered. His arms had gone round her, and it frightened her to feel their power. She couldn't escape, even if she wanted to, and he said he knew best—maybe he did—Delaney knew best . . . He kissed her closed eyes and her cheeks and the place on her throat where her pulse was fluttering so, and that was gentle and infinitely pleasing, but there was also the reality of those frightening, powerful arms.

You didn't struggle against such strength. You gave in to it. He kissed her until she was weak and clasped her hands in his thick hair to keep from falling, and now his hands—those wonderful hands she had always admired—were caressing the line of her back and flanks, almost as if she were a pony. It had a mesmerizing effect, and she leaned against him, surrendering.

He picked her up in one effortless movement and carried her in his arms to the staircase and all the way up the curving stairs. Rhett Butler and Scarlett O'Hara, she thought dreamily, because another, more primal pair had popped into her mind and she wanted to erase them. She was still dreamy, like a child being put to bed, when he laid her on the center of a big bed in a pretty room hung with Persian tapestries. There was a fire here, too, and the air was warm and fragrant from the turf mixed with the logs.

He undressed her as if she *were* a child, pulling her woolen sweater over her head, smiling sweetly, and then smoothing her hair back where it had become mussed. He unbuttoned her blouse, and eased her out of the skirt. When she was wearing only her panties and brassiere, he bent and kissed the place where her breasts pressed from the lace and satin. It was a soft little brushing kiss—they were playing. When he unsnapped the little scrap of satin and bared her breasts he made a little involuntary sound, and she saw that his blue eyes had darkened so much they appeared to be nearly black. Good. The sight of her body pleased him. She wanted very much to please him. If she stayed very quietly on the bed, was *obedient*—but no, that was a silly word.

The fear returned when he stood to undress himself. He was so big—his body would block out the light from the windows, she thought. It would fill the whole world. She stared at his body with a kind of terror, knowing it to be beautiful, but fearing it all the more for that. She closed her eyes when he revealed the part that was taboo. She wanted to beg him to let her go, but it was too late. She felt him lie beside her. One of his hands was stroking her hair.

"Don't be afraid, darling," he said. "Carlotta, my sweet love, my little girl."

"No," she whispered, "I won't be afraid." But she was.

His hand stroked breasts and belly as lightly as if they had been dream hands. At one point she thought he might be inventing her, sculpting her, remaking her in his image. She felt her nipples rise as if they wanted to please his hands. At each sign of her arousal he murmured as if to encourage her. The weak little flutterings she had sometimes felt with Antonio were beginning before he'd so much as touched between her legs. He bent to kiss her breasts and she felt his tongue warm on her nipples and a delicious sensation began to flow from somewhere deep in her belly.

It forced her legs apart and made her sigh. It made her

body, wherever Delaney touched it, rise up to meet him. When she felt the light touch of his fingers sliding across the crotch of her satin panties she cried out with pleasure. It was so warm in the room she forgot herself and thought they were lying on the deck of a boat in Sardinia. The gentle rocking, which was the rocking of her body, could be the sea. She was wet from a dip in the ocean—it wasn't her panties he was removing, but her bathing suit.

His tongue was making little rockets explode along her nerve endings and now she was crying out to him, begging him to stop, because the pleasure was too much, but when he did stop it was she who touched him for the first time, mindlessly pulling at him, urging him into her body. The fear returned when she felt the hugeness of him, but she clung to him as if he were a granite rock in a turbulent sea. She felt all of him lodged up inside her and marveled that her body could accommodate him. He moved, gently at first, and then with gathering force, and almost immediately she contracted around him and found herself in the throes of a terrifying orgasm—terrifying because she had not suspected it could be so easy, or happen so quickly.

He waited until the last pulsing throbs had receded, and then he began all over again, hammering this time, so that she had to throw her legs around him and bite his shoulder to keep from screaming in a mixture of fear and delirious, animal pleasure.

"Oh, Carlotta," he whispered a little later, "we're going to be so very happy. I knew it. I always knew it."

She curled into his arms and lay against his chest, stroking his smooth back. "I love you," she said.

He smoothed her hair. "I loved you the minute you stepped into that plane," he said. "Of course, that was only puppy love. This is the real thing."

Carlotta giggled at the idea of Delaney and puppy love. She twined her legs with his and kissed his chest. "All mine," she said.

She stayed the whole weekend. She couldn't think of any good reason not to stay forever. In her first euphoria, she couldn't bear to be parted from him. They stayed in bed all of one day, rising only to raid the kitchen—the manservant had been given the weekend off; the driver slept in his own quarters over the garage—and have picnics in the library. She called Rachel, remembering belatedly, and was surprised to find that Rachel had never expected her to come right back. Since she was sitting on Delaney's lap, wrapped in one of his thick terry robes, she could hardly speak of her new-found happiness. She did go so far as to tell Rachel she was having a wonderful time.

"Imagine that!" said Rachel. "Just like a postcard. 'Having wonderful time—wish you were here.' I bet you don't wish I was there, do you?"

"Not just at the moment," said Carlotta demurely. Rachel laughed her dirty-old-woman laugh, but it lacked the usual verve. "Are you feeling okay?"

"Beached whales never feel terrific," said Rachel, and rang off.

Carlotta showered and washed her hair in Delaney's vast master bathroom, and he insisted on drying it for her. Sitting before the fire, he brushed and brushed her long hair with wonderful patience. She leaned against him and felt perfectly happy. When her hair was dry, and the same color as the glowing peat fire, he stripped away her robe and made love to her on the floor.

Their lovemaking, she thought, was a continual astonishment. She had never known how many ways there were for lovers to please one another, or how many ways pleasure could be felt. Sometimes her ecstasy was as sharp and brutal as a fit of paroxysms; at other times soft and dreamy as the snow which hissed and danced against the window panes.

Delaney's pleasure, too, was important to her. In one weekend she learned more about love than in her entire lifetime. She memorized him—his body, his sounds, his profoundest, and also his slightest, needs. So much love made him very young. Sometimes it seemed she held a strong young boy in her arms. From her furtive perusal of *Who's Who*, she knew that her lover was fifty-six years old, but where, in all the world of living men, was there a man of that age whose bronzed body and long, black eyelashes so belied his age? Age had no concern for her, in any case. He was a miracle.

Once, when she was sated and sleepy and happy, she remembered the Christmas bracelet, with its cryptic Irish message.

"Am I ready to know, Delaney?" she asked, lying on top of

him as if he were a bed. "Has the time come for me to know what it says on my bracelet?"

His eyes crinkled in a smile. "The time has definitely come," he murmured. "The feminists wouldn't approve, though. I warn you." His hands cupped her head, brought it down so he could whisper in her ear. She felt his warm breath as he gave the words to her. They shivered in the inner chambers of her ear and seemed to reverberate throughout her body.

Property of Delaney, was what he said.

She considered, nodded her head. "Yes," she agreed. "Oh, yes, Delaney. It's exactly right."

Chloe Windolm Vere, purple and screaming, came into the world three days later. The baby weighed eight pounds, and her mother was small and the labor had been long, but once Chloe had been cleaned up a bit and Rachel had slept ten hours, everybody concerned was delighted. Even Cotter, so sure he would be getting a son, fell in love with his daughter.

"Let me out of here!" Rachel remembered shouting when a particularly vicious pain had squeezed her body, threatening to break her back. She had meant, literally, that she wanted out of the agony and indignity of labor, but her doctor, turning unexpectedly poetic, told her she was speaking for the baby fighting to be born.

Generally, though, she knew she had been courageous. She was glad she had read some of the Lamaze manuals on the sly—even if she couldn't bear the idea of classes, she knew a little bit about breathing and panting. She'd endured eight hours of excruciating pain before they were able to give her the caudal and then—the blessed relief of going dead below the waist and still being able to help! She had been aware of everything, had seen her daughter popping out of her like a stone from a slingshot, with eyes unclouded by drugs. She had witnessed a miracle. For the first time in her life, she felt heroic.

Chloe was a beautiful baby, perfectly formed, with a light fuzz of platinum hair covering her head and huge, wide-set eyes. Her fingernails were very long, and had to be cut so she would not scratch her face by mistake. All that, Rachel thought, going on inside me!

In her private room at the Harkness Pavilion, Rachel was

happy, even when she had to submit her private parts to a sun lamp situated at the end of her bed. The sun lamp was to hasten the healing of her episiotomy stitches, and she felt like a battered porn queen, spreading for the hot lights. The happiness persisted even though her breasts, tightly harnessed to make the milk dry up, were killing her and her entire *person* down there felt as if it had been mugged with a broken Coke bottle. She was happy because she had accomplished something real.

Chloe was undeniably real, and Rachel loved her in a way that reassured all her doubts about being a good mother. She was going to be a very good mother, even if she did refuse to breast-feed. Rachel knew herself well, and understood that it would be a mistake for her to breast-feed Chloe. It was heaven to feel herself slender and weightless again. Already, she could feel her old vitality returning, and it was her natural vitality that Chloe needed, not her breast milk. If she were to submit to the slavery of breast-feeding—the leaking nipples and rigid schedule, the wholesome diet and outlawed pleasures—she would become cranky and resentful. Chloe did not need to begin life with a cranky and resentful mother any more than Rachel needed to become, at twenty-seven, like those native women one saw in *National Geographic*.

"But *Chloe,* dear?" Her mother, bending over her bed like a stork, had been alarmed. "Where did you think of such a name?"

"It just came to me. I like it."

"No one in our family, either your father's or mine, has had a name like that. Isn't it, well . . . Negro?"

Originally, Rachel had wanted to name the baby Chloe Grace or Chloe Janis, after the two rock stars she had liked best, Grace Slick of Jefferson Airplane and Janis Joplin. She had been mulling it over for months, while everyone else was sure she was carrying a boy. Now that Chloe was a reality, though, it seemed profane to name her after those High Priestesses of drugs. She had pacified everyone with the sedate choice of Windolm for a middle name.

"And what does Cotter think?" (Her mother, still doing her impression of a stork.)

"Cotter knows something he didn't know before, Mum. He knows that I did all the really hard work of getting her born. He doesn't object to the name. He was all set for a Walter."

There were many visitors at the Harkness. They bore roses and Tiffany christening cups and cunning outfits made in Paris which the baby would outgrow before she was three months old. Champagne was uncorked in her room and the bustling, friendly nurses from Haiti or Santo Domingo rolled their eyes and giggled at the goings-on. One of them told Rachel there hadn't been so much fun on Maternity since Jackie Kennedy had popped one out.

Carlotta came, too, and she was the only person who jangled Rachel's state of perfect bliss. Carlotta was like a bride from an ancient fairy tale—radiant with happiness and far too pleased with herself. In her normal state, Rachel would have cross-examined her friend quite ruthlessly, but caught as she was in an unnatural period of exaltation, thinking only of her daughter, she was relatively helpless.

Carlotta couldn't remark on anything without mentioning Delaney. If she praised Chloe's beauty and said she liked the name, she added, "Brendan has a daughter named Elana." She seemed to want to hear his name spoken, if only by herself. Rachel's worst fears were confirmed when Carlotta admitted that she was in love with Delaney.

"Be happy for me," she begged. Rachel looked into the shining face and couldn't bring herself to say what she should. Carlotta had had so little happiness in her life. Who was she to say that an Oedipal affair with a man thirty years her senior could lead, in Rachel's estimation, only to tragedy?

THIRTEEN

LEE HAD THE FATHER FOR HER CHILD ALL PICKED OUT, BUT HE
didn't know it yet. He was only twenty-two, and he worked as
a mechanic in a Butte service station, but he had all the right
qualifications. He was healthy, good-looking, and very intelligent, although undereducated, and he was a Cheyenne.

She'd met him when her Volkswagen broke down on her
before a pre-trial hearing. His name was Victor Rainwater,
and as he poked around in the interior of her smoking car, she
had a sudden conviction—he was the one she'd been searching for.

"I know who you are," he had remarked. "You're the lawyer who got Sally Carlson off."

"Do you think I ought to hang for it!"

"Now why would I think a thing like that? I'd shake your
hand, but mine's all greasy."

"A lot of men around here regard me as the devil incar-
nate," Lee told him. "Men stick together."

"Yeah, well, not the new generation," said Victor Rainwater, grinning. "Haven't you heard about us? We are sensitive and—what's the word? Oh yes, *caring*. Terrible word,
but you get the point."

She'd had plenty of opportunity to get to know him, since
the VW needed so much work, and they had developed an

easy rapport. He was one of eight children, and he had gone to work when he was seventeen, full-time. He was one of those who would have benefited by Carlotta's father's institution but, by the time it was set up, Victor thought himself too old to go to college. He was self-educated, and endowed with brains, curiosity, and wit.

Lee wanted to have a baby, but she did not want to get married. She knew she could raise her child by herself, and was eager to get going—after all, she would be twenty-eight in a few months. She hadn't met any men she wanted to marry, although she had had many pleasant affairs and convinced herself she was in love several times. She was having an affair now with Gregory Piersall, a fellow lawyer who was amusing and considerate in bed, but she couldn't imagine marrying him. He was a trifle weak, and given to overestimating his skill in the courtroom. Gregory would be only too happy to give her a baby, but she didn't want his child. Her baby would have to be Indian, like herself, through and through.

"Victor, why don't you knock off early and buy me a beer?" she said one afternoon, several weeks after the VW was in perfect condition again. She often drove through the station to say hello to him. He looked up, momentarily surprised, and then said, "Give me half an hour, Lee, okay?"

Now, waiting for him in the dim interior of a bar called Gus's Hi-Hat, she considered the ethics of what she was going to propose. She couldn't simply seduce him, go away for a while, and return with an Indian baby and never let him know. She liked Victor too much for that; it wouldn't be fair to him. He would have to be a willing conspirator in her scheme, and she pondered how to make it seem attractive to him. Then there was the matter of getting pregnant. There was no guarantee that she and Victor would hit the jackpot immediately. If he agreed, they'd have to get down to business in three days' time, when she would be at the height of her fertile period.

She sipped at her beer, and then remembered something. At the courthouse, a clerk had handed her a letter which she had stuffed into her attache case and forgotten. Now she unearthed it and, in the dimness of Gus's Hi-Hat, read a printed notice that informed her that Carlotta had married someone named Brendan J. Delaney. On the notice, Carlotta had printed: *I am very happy, Lee. I hope you are, too.*

"You look funny," said Victor, startling her. She hadn't seen him come in. "Anything wrong?"

"An old friend of mine got married."

"You got something against marriage?"

"No, no. I just hope she chose wisely. She's very special."

Lee shrugged away the vague, uneasy feeling and returned the envelope to her attache case. Victor's comment about marriage had given her a good opening, and she began to explain that marriage was fine for some people, fatal for others. She placed herself in the second category, then added that she longed to have a child, all the same.

"You could do it," Victor told her staunchly. "Professional woman like you? Nobody would even question why you're still called Redwing, now that women go by their maiden names at work."

Excellent Victor Rainwater, building her case for her. "There *is* a hitch, though," she said slowly. "I'm no apple. I want my baby to be Cheyenne, not half-and-half. Nearly everyone around here is Blackfoot or Sioux, and I would prefer our people."

Victor nodded, spread his hands agreeably. "No problem," he said. "You're bound to find someone, sooner or later."

Lee continued to look at him, a little smile on her face. When he understood, he put his beer down with a thud. "Oh, man—*me?*" Lee nodded.

"I'm gonna have another beer, Councillor. Gotta think this over." All the way to the bar, Lee saw, he kept shaking his head in amazement.

There were no words to express the beauty of Ireland in the spring, and Carlotta did not try. When Delaney had asked where she wanted to go on her honeymoon she had chosen Ireland without a moment's hesitation, and now she felt happier than she could ever remember feeling in her life.

They were meandering up the rugged western coast, toward Donegal and Delaney's farmhouse, taking as much time as they wanted. She had stood on the gigantic sea cliffs of Moher, in County Clare, and she and Delaney had made love in a hotel room that overlooked the boundless curve of Galway Bay. He had driven her all around the desolate, haunted peninsula of Connemara, where it seemed nothing could live but rock and turf, and through a lush, deep valley into Mayo and beyond.

"Has anyone ever painted Connemara?" she asked him. "I mean done it justice?"

"Thousands have tried, but it eludes even the best."

She looked at him, his gloved hand on the wheel, his sheepskin jacket open, and felt a jolt of love so sharp she gasped. It wasn't fair she should be so lucky. She studied the plain gold band on the third finger of her left hand. She had wanted just such a ring—no diamonds—and he had had engraved, in the minutest letters, the same message that adorned the sapphire bracelet. *Property of Delaney,* in Irish.

They had married very quietly, almost in secret, in Greenwich. She had told no one before the event, and mailed out notices afterwards. She smiled, remembering the night soon after their first lovemaking when she had told him who she really was. She had been trembling and terrified, but of what? He had stopped her, midway through her recitation, and simply told her that he knew, had always known. Hadn't it seemed odd, he asked, that he—a man so much in love—had never asked her about herself, her family, her background? He didn't have to ask, because he knew, and it mattered not a bit. He had once met her father, had admired him. The conversation had ended there, and she had been stunned by his tact and discretion. He had also understood that she feared being the center of media interest, if their wedding were a big, public affair, and agreed to keep it quiet. He was, in all ways, a perfect man.

She told him so now, putting her hand at the back of his neck and caressing his thick hair.

"In order to maintain my perfection," he said, "I am going to take you to lunch at Kavanagh's. We're nearly there."

They were passing through a field so green it hurt her eyes to look at it. Lambs were frolicking and birds were singing, and it was like something from a child's picture book. Ireland played tricks on you, showing you its different beauties at odd moments. Five miles from the lovely field, for all she knew, there might be cliffs so savage that the Atlantic, hurling itself against their base, sent spray up hundreds of feet. Even now, in the lambs' field, something sad appeared. A ruined cottage, nothing now but a roofless heap of stones, stood in the center of the blazing green. The door frame was still standing and, as she watched, a sheep came out. A tree grew straight up where once had been a roof.

"Is that house from the time of the famine?" she asked him.

"No, darling, that would be early twentieth century," he said. "You'll see them all over Ireland."

He knew so many things, her Delaney. In addition to being loved by him, in every way, she was going to learn a lot. She often felt ignorant in his presence, but *he* never made her feel it. No matter how stupid her mistake (the business of her never having sublet the Fifth Avenue apartment, for example, because she didn't know about such things), he was patient and informative.

When they drove up to the Kavanagh Hotel, the man at the door knew Delaney and greeted him with great enthusiasm. The owner came out and seized Brendan's hand, and when Mrs. Delaney was introduced there was general celebration. Mrs. Delaney, who had braided her hair in two long plaits that day for fun, wished she had not.

Passing in to the dining room and a festive lunch of Irish salmon, she caught sight of herself in a mirror. She looked much too young to have captured such a distinguished man.

The farmhouse was on a little hill five miles from the town of Dungloe. From the windows on the second story, she could see the sea. The north Atlantic waters changed colors dramatically, and she never tired of going to the window in the morning and trying to guess what color the ocean would be. If the sun were shining brightly, it was likely to be turquoise striped with darker blue; on dull days it was slate gray. Once it had been the palest shade of green she had ever seen, like a leaf of lettuce close to the heart.

The beach was an astonishment. She had expected rocks and crashing waves, but the beach was a wide crescent of light golden sand, more like something she would expect to find in the tropics. Palm trees grew along the west coast of Ireland, and giant fuchsias. It had something to do with the Gulf Stream, Delaney told her, but she preferred to think it was magic.

On the seventh day of her stay in Delaney's farmhouse, which he had to keep reminding her was hers now, too, she awakened before he did. The large, square room was bathed in golden light, and she appreciated the simplicity of it. Whitewashed walls, wooden floors, large old bureaus, and the bed itself—one of his few concessions to modernity—a king-size one shipped in from Dublin. Beside her, he lay still sleeping, his hair rumpled and a faint smile on his face. Outside, purple moors, neatly stacked rows of turf, and the wondrous sea. She slipped from the bed and wrapped herself in one of his robes. Even in the first weeks of May, it was cold at this hour. At the window, she checked on the ocean. Blue this morning, the shade of cobalt.

There were six rooms in the house, not counting the modern bathroom facilities, and he had left them much as they had been more than a century ago. She went down the staircase and entered the front room, intending to get a good fire going. She was skilled in the art of starting grate fires, something she had been taught in her childhood in Montana, but no one had prepared her for turf. She worked contentedly for a while, building a little nest of coal with a complicated structure of kindling and peat surmounting it. It was like assembling some primitive work of art, and she liked the challenge. When the fire began to go, she went to the door and collected the two bottles of milk that were left in a wooden box to foil the magpies' attempts to peck through the foil tops.

In the kitchen, she put water on to boil on the Primus range, and sliced two oranges into quarters. She boiled two eggs in the water intended for their morning tea and felt quite proud at her ingenuity. She had never been taught to cook, and had no need to, even in Donegal. Bridie, a girl from the village, came in to cook lunch and dinner when she was needed, but breakfasts were a private time.

When the eggs had boiled for twenty minutes, she was satisfied, but there wasn't enough water left to make tea. She refilled the pan and set it to boil while she sliced soda bread, buttering it thickly with the delicious Kerry butter she found in the larder. Outside, the birds were racketing away and the day was growing more golden. She and Brendan might get in the Land Rover and drive along the dizzying cliff road toward a farmers' market, or they might lunch in the little pub in Dungloe where a fiddler sometimes sent sweet sounds into the air, looking neither to left nor right, or they might choose to make love all through the day, and emerge, pale and spent as vampires, to see the sunset along the Bloody Foreland, where the whole world appeared to be bathed in flame. It didn't matter what they did. What mattered was that she was standing in a kitchen in Ireland, assembling a breakfast for her love.

It puzzled her to see that the eggs were gray around the edges, and that the tea was awash with floating leaves, but she carried it up to him anyway, as a proof of her devotion.

He was still asleep, but he had turned over and she knew he would be awake in a few minutes. She went again to the window and thought suddenly, for no reason at all, of a girl she had seen in Dungloe. The girl was the assistant to the postmistress, and no more than twenty. She had raven black hair and misty gray-green eyes, a lovely combination that made her rather ordinary features assume a look of beauty. She had rather thick legs, but they were long, not stubby, and large, round breasts. Carlotta had seen her several times when she and Delaney had gone to town, and there was something about the way the girl said "Good day to ye, Mr. Delaney," that roused Carlotta's curiosity.

Nora, that was her name. "Hello, Nora," Delaney had said, and walked on, almost too casually. Normally he liked to stand and make conversation with the townspeople. He introduced Carlotta to fishermen and publicans and priests and musicians, and after they had talked he would tell her what he knew of their lives. Father Gallagher had a problem with drink . . . Tom O'Doherty's brother had gone down on a trawler off Crohy Head . . . Peter Quinn had once been an All-Ireland hurling champion . . . Why, then, had he said nothing about Nora? Why hadn't he introduced her to the assistant postmistress, who called good day to him so intimately?

Carlotta looked at the bed, and at her sleeping husband. She felt certain that Delaney and Nora had occupied that bed together more than once. Had Nora slept all night in his arms, her black hair fanned over the pillow, her strong legs twined with his? It made her feel weak to picture them together, yet she forced the image. She knew she had no right to be jealous of women he had known before her, but she was. It was a horrible emotion, jealousy, and one that had never touched her before. She hated all the women who had known him sexually, including both of his wives and Alice Quincy's mother twenty years ago and the innumerable others, too numerous, probably, to even reckon up.

Most of all, she hated the jealousy itself. It was irrational and poisonous. Jealousy ate away at you from inside, because there was no way to express it without becoming an unlovable monster. It made women ugly and shrewish, objects of ridicule. Delaney had never grilled her about the men she had known before him, and she wondered if he didn't care. Perhaps he knew that no one else had mattered.

As she was tormenting herself with doubts, he stirred again and opened his eyes. The first thing he saw was the tray she had brought up, the steam from the teapot visible in the cool air. He looked from the tray to the side of the bed where Carlotta slept, and then he found her at the window. He propped himself on one elbow and smiled at her in a way that made all her jealous fantasies fly away.

They breakfasted on the grayish eggs and soda bread, and washed it down with the leafy tea.

"I believe you are the worst cook it has ever been my privilege to meet," he said, kissing her hand.

"I could improve," she told him, sliding back down beneath the covers and pressing against him.

"No," he said. "Don't ever change, Carlotta. Not ever. That's all I ask of you."

On the map, Donegal was the northernmost county in Ireland, yet it was not a part of what was called Northern Ireland. Carlotta's knowledge of Irish history was scant, and she pictured Northern Ireland—so close to her bucolic farmhouse— as a dark and dangerous place where insane fanatics went about killing one another. In January of the year in which she had met Delaney, there had been an event in nearby Londonderry called Bloody Sunday. Crazy, rioting people had been shot down by the British soldiers who were called in to keep the peace. That was the way they had reported it in London. The poor, scared soldiers had been attacked by mad petrol-bombers· and stone-throwers and opened fire to save their lives. Even if some of the people they had shot had turned out to be children, who could blame them when they were confronting terrorists?

Terrorism was much in the news. Planes were being sky-jacked to Cuba and Libya, hostages kept for hours, days, even, and businessmen shot down by obscure, fanatical students in places like Geneva and Munich. It troubled Carlotta that in the little paradise Delaney had claimed in Ireland there were signs of terrorism. BRITS OUT! was a sign she had seen spraypainted on culverts and stones and ruined cottages from Clare to Donegal, but here—not far from the border—the initials of the Irish Republican Army bloomed in the most unlikely places. IRA adorned the sides of buildings in Dungloe and was painted on boulders around the Bloody Foreland, which seemed such a deserted spot she wondered about the people who had come to deface the very rocks with their slogans.

Were they painted by bands of terrorists who crossed the border in the dead of night, or could they be the work of people she knew? Could Bridie and Tom O'Doherty and Peter Quinn and Nora stalk the moors and cliff tops in search of likely places to write their message?

Once, walking on the golden beach, which was called the strand, with Delaney, she had found the initials written in the sand. IRA.

"Who is responsible for that?" she asked him. "Who does it?"

"It might be anyone," he said.

"But what does it mean?"

"It means this country is at war."

She was quiet then, but later she pursued it. She asked him why it was that the people in the north were so fanatical, and why they resented the presence of the British soldiers.

"It's a long story," he said. "It spans centuries." He seemed disturbed by her question. "Have you ever wondered," he said at last, "why your father didn't try for the presidency?"

They were standing on a little rise of land above the strand. It was just before sunset, and the wind had died down. All she could hear was the gentle lapping of the water and an occasional bleat from the band of goats that walked along the road farther up. The mention of her father was so unexpected she felt almost as if Delaney had slapped her. They had never spoken of him, except for the time she had made her confession. She wanted to lay her hand across Delaney's lips and silence him, but instead she waited to hear more.

"It was a long time ago, before you were born," he said. He spoke dismissively. She knew he regretted having brought it up, but it was too late now. "Your father was accused of helping some people ship arms to the IRA. It blew over quickly enough, and powerful sources helped to shut it up, because your father was so well liked. It didn't harm him, ultimately, but it would have ruined him if he'd run for the presidency."

"But couldn't he prove the accusations were false?"

Delaney was silent.

For the first time, that night, his lovemaking failed to sweep her into the state of bliss she had come to expect. Each time she was ready to succumb to it, she was visited with images of her father and the political passion she had not even known he'd had. It seemed wrong to be thinking of her father and experiencing pleasure at the same time, so she pushed the pleasure away. When the time came, she faked an orgasm, but Delaney could not be fooled.

He never mentioned her father again, not on their honeymoon, and soon things were joyful again. The next time they walked on the strand, the tide had come in and erased the letters written in the sand, and the whole incident seemed never to have happened.

By the time they returned to America, the granddaddy of all scandals was emerging with a vengeance. It was called Watergate, and it gave Carlotta a certain pleasure to see Tricky Dick on the run, caught in a maze of his own making.

FOURTEEN

EVEN AS AN INFANT, CHLOE VERE CAUSED PERFECT strangers to sigh and coo; at two-and-half she was so lovely that her mother had to beg people not to make so much of her. She didn't want Chloe to be vain at such an early age.

She needn't have worried. There wasn't a scrap of vanity in her daughter's makeup; her favorite outfit was a pair of Oshkosh coveralls and miniature red sneakers. Dressed in this fashion, her white-gold hair cut to shoulder level, she was so bewitching that even her nanny, a stern Scotswoman named Mrs. MacDougall, found it hard to ever do anything but smile in her presence.

Chloe was inclined to love everything with equal fervor. She loved her parents and her nanny, the doorman and the elevator operator, all of humanity, with quiet intensity. Most especially, she seemed to love Carlotta, whom she had always called "La-la." Rachel was not wounded by this indiscriminate affection, or by Chloe's crush on Carlotta, because she understood that her daughter's nature was as open as her own had once been. She only worried that Chloe would one day encounter someone who did not love her back, although she couldn't imagine who that could be.

If Chloe was vulnerable, she was also exceptionally bright. At the age of one she had sometimes burst into tears because her thoughts were so interesting, and she didn't yet have the vocabulary to express them. "If—if—birds—go—" She would try it again, her face reddening, and finally give way to despair. Long before she'd hit two she had acquired an astonishing vocabulary, and now she could talk with more skill and aplomb, in Rachel's opinion, than either of her grandparents.

Mr. Windolm was continually reeling back in amazement as his tiny granddaughter said things like: "Grandpa, I hope your moustache doesn't have feelings, because you're always biting it." Mrs. Windolm always laughed merrily at her husband's discomfort, but her time had come round just last week. "Someone we know seems to have missed out on the Terrible Twos," she had said in the garden at Newport. Her tone had been so arch that any reasonably intelligent child could have sensed who the someone was. Chloe had come to her grandmother's side and stared up at her with affection and pity. "Never mind, Grandma," Chloe had said, "yours aren't so bad when you cover them up." All eyes had instantly fastened on Mrs. Windolm's crepey cleavage, revealed in a too-girlish sundress. Of course, nobody laughed, it was too dreadful, but quite soon afterwards Rachel's mother had made an excuse to change into her tennis whites.

Rachel stood at the seaward window of the Hamptons summer house, sipping chilled wine and wondering how on earth to curb Chloe without breaking her wonderfully special spirit. None of the books on child-rearing told you how to suggest to a child so young that it was not tactful to pronounce an aesthetic opinion on her grandmother's breasts. She imagined a dialogue with Chloe, who was on the beach with Mrs. MacDougall.

"Chloe, darling, there is something Mama must make you understand. Although you didn't mean to, you hurt Grandma Windolm's feelings the other day." (Enormous eyes look up in pain and grief. It is as if she has told Chloe that Grandma Windolm has been sobbing ever since.)

"How did I, Mommy, how did I?"

"Well, when you said about how she would look better covered up? When she made the remark about Terrible Twos?"

"She said I didn't get them, and I wanted her to feel better. They *do* look better covered up, Mommy. They're not so purple and squishy covered up."

"That's it, my love. Grown-up ladies don't like to be reminded that their bosoms are purple and squishy. It makes them unhappy."

"Oh." (Chloe considers, bites her lip.) "Should I *lie*, Mommy?"

"Of course not, pet. But there's no need to say *anything*."

"Ever?" (A look of horror. Speech, at which she excells, is being taken away from her.) "Or only when Grandma mentions her twos?"

It was quite impossible. If Chloe had been ten, or even five, Rachel could explain the fine art of tact to her easily, but how the hell did you tell a talkative *baby?* Cotter maintained that Chloe's precocity was the natural inheritance of her own cutting wit, but that was too easy. Chloe wasn't trying to be witty, she was simply expressing the truth as she saw it. In fact, wit was not one of Chloe's strong points. Tears came to her much more naturally than laughter, although she never had tantrums. Her tears came from some deep pool of sympathy Rachel had never fathomed. She shrank from cruelty in any form.

Once, Mrs. MacDougall had reported, Chloe had witnessed the teasing, by a band of small boys, of the Kodiak bear at the Central Park Zoo. The boys had tossed firecrackers at the sluggish bear, lobbing them through the bars into the bear's den. At the sharp explosions, the bear had first been alarmed, then maddened. As Mrs. MacDougall described it, the bear had reared up, pawing at the bars with his sharp claws, and given a terrifying roar of rage and indignation.

"It was a horrid sight for a wee one," the nanny explained, "and I brought her straight away, Mrs. Vere. I was afraid of the bad dreams that savage bear might visit on her. But what is it the puir wee angel says to me, through her tears? What is it, Mrs. Vere, but 'poor bear.' Did you ever hear the like?"

Rachel had never heard, or seen, the like. Her daughter sometimes seemed to her like the changelings one read of in the old fairy tales. Chloe was both a miraculous gift and an onerous responsibility. For the first time in her life, Rachel had doubts about her ability to master the situation. Her own baby daughter, the only real thing she had ever produced, seemed too good for the world.

Everybody knew what happened to those who were too good for the world. They passed out of it.

* * *

Carlotta read the article almost by mistake. Their cook was addicted to a new magazine called *People*, and he had left a back issue in the kitchen. She was about to put it in his room when she noticed a familiar face in the middle section. She was so surprised she dropped the magazine and then had to go searching for the face again. She thought perhaps she had imagined it, but no, there was Lee, her hair blowing in the wind, holding the hand of a child who seemed a bit younger than Chloe. *Controversial attorney Lee Redwing with her son, Dominic, 2,* it said beneath the picture.

Carlotta carried the magazine to the table and began at the beginning of the article. It was a two-page spread entitled "Lee Redwing—Crusading Attorney or Radical Feminist?" It seemed to Carlotta that the writer had been out to get Lee, but had changed his mind in midstream and been charmed by her. He began with a rehash of the Sally Carlson case and several others Carlotta hadn't known about. Apparently Lee was the lawyer to call if you were facing a life sentence for killing your husband, and the writer wanted to know if this was a healthy thing. "There are people who maintain that Redwing's success at getting her clients acquitted has given women an open season on men, with free reign to commit murder with impunity." He was fair, though, and let Lee have her say. "I didn't set out to defend battered wives," Councillor Redwing replied. "It just happened, after the Carlson case. I would never defend a woman I suspected of killing her husband out of greed or for revenge or simple jealousy, or any of the other reasons that people usually kill. All of my clients have been almost classical victims of wife abuse. I can assure you I'd be glad to take the case of any petite man whose enormous wife has been battering him for years, but there aren't too many of those running around."

Lee said she thought the term radical feminist was a misnomer in her case. She liked men, and did not agree with those feminists who advocated that women should withdraw from them completely and be sufficient unto themselves.

Yet that, it seemed, was exactly what she had done. There was no mention of a husband, and when Lee was asked why she was so secretive about the matter, she simply said it was no one's business but her own.

Carlotta bent to study the little boy holding Lee's hand with such trust. He seemed a carbon copy of his mother. Except for his hair, cut bowl-style, he looked exactly like a photo of Lee which Charlie Redwing had always kept on his desk at the ranch. Carlotta knew that Lee had named her baby after her favorite brother, but she was shocked to read that Dominic had been killed in Vietnam.

He had been the Redwings' youngest child, a baby in the earliest days of their friendship, and Lee and Carlotta had often played with him. He had been nine when Carlotta went off to Switzerland, and now he was dead. Carlotta felt tears sliding down her cheeks at the memory of Dominic riding on her father's shoulder. Tom Madigan had been especially fond of the child; perhaps the more so because he knew he would never have a son of his own.

Dominic was everyone's favorite, really. Lee's older brothers were somewhat wild and problematical, Jim angry and Ray sullen, but Dominic seemed almost to have been born with a sunny temperament. "Probably an afterthought," Carlotta had heard her mother saying when her father remarked on the infant boy's beauty.

An afterthought? Carlotta was too young to understand, but she felt sure Martha was wrong. Lee's mother looked radiant when she held the baby, feeding him out of her big, reddish brown bosoms (Carlotta hadn't known about *that*, either, and was quite stunned when Lee explained), and not at all as if she were attending to Dominic as an afterthought.

Dominic was born with a quantity of black hair, shiny and soft and Indian straight, and his immense dark eyes quickened and reflected intelligence at a very early age. Both Carlotta and Lee, seven when he was born, would attribute great feats to the infant Dominic, making Mrs. Redwing laugh.

"He called Lee by her name," Carlotta might say, when in fact Dominic, at four months, had smiled at his sister and made a gurgling sound with the letter "e" in it. Or, at six months: "He's ready to walk, Ma—see how he pumps his legs up and down?"

They took turns getting Dominic to chuckle, but it was so easy there was very little glory in it. He was the most agreeable baby imaginable, game for anything, and very slow to tears.

"The world is his oyster," Mrs. Redwing often said. "Whatever that means."

He lost none of his good nature when he learned to toddle, although, being adventurous and reckless, he often came to grief. He barged about his universe, eating cattails or landing on his bottom in a patch of briars, bellowing briefly with indignation, and then—ever the optimist—grinning in anticipation of whatever might happen next.

"That boy will never learn to hold a grudge," Charlie Redwing said.

"Is that good or bad?" Carlotta asked.

"For now it's fine."

"But later?"

"Depends," said Charlie.

During the summer when Dominic was nearly two, Carlotta and Lee appropriated him. He became their most cherished toy, their mascot. They towed him around the ranch in a red wagon, presenting him at the big house for a ride on the senator's shoulders or a treat from Inga's kitchen. They held him up to touch the muzzles of the tamer horses, and took him to the stream where they allowed him to dangle his feet from the rocks.

He was able to pronounce his sister's name easily, but "Carlotta" perplexed him. He called her "Carta," simply dropping the middle syllable, and the name stuck. Long past the time when he was capable of articulating anything he chose, she was Carta, or Car, for short.

"You'll spoil him," warned Mrs. Redwing, but there was little conviction in her voice. She knew Dominic would not spoil.

Carlotta had only one memory of Dominic that made her feel guilty.

It had been when Charlie had promised to take Lee and Carlotta to Bear Butte, clear in another part of the state.

"But I want to go, too," the seven-year-old Dominic said stubbornly. "Why can't I go?"

They explained about Bear Butte, how it was a place sacred to women, not men, but Dominic refused to understand. The fiercer the girls became, the more belligerent were Dominic's demands to be taken along. If the shoe had been on the other foot, if the situation had involved a place sacred to males, he would have understood immediately, but his refusal to find himself excluded, for once, worked a sort of wicked magic in Lee and Carlotta, and they were merciless.

"Bullshit," said Dominic.

"I'll smack you," said Lee. "At your age!"

"Go on ahead, Lee. Smack me—just try."

The expedition to Bear Butte had been made, and Dominic went unsmacked, but it took them all of three days to win him over again. It seemed he could hold a grudge, after all, no matter how briefly.

The last time she had seen Dominic was during the summer when she was about to be sent into exile, to Switzerland. He had become a tall young boy of nine, and she a quivering, neurotic girl of sixteen. Many years had passed since Dominic had been her mascot, still more since he had been her surrogate baby, the delight of her life.

He was exercising one of the horses, his black hair held back with a red bandanna, and somehow—surely—proud of the fact that he was first in his class in school at White Sulphur Springs. He cantered over to the place closest to Carlotta in the ring.

"Hey, Car!" he shouted. "Is it true you're going off to Europe?"

He made Europe sound as far as Timbuktoo—a place too exotic for contemplation in Montana.

"It's true," said Carlotta. "But I'll be back."

"Hope so," said Dominic. "I'll miss you, Car. Good luck, Carlotta."

He had seemed ready for a hug, or kiss, but the imperious hooves of the horse had borne him off, however reluctantly. He had waved to her—goodbye, for now, and that was the last she had ever seen of him.

The grown Carlotta now felt it unbearable that Dominic, who had thought Europe exotic, should have ended his life in Indochina. It seemed a cheat of the grossest kind.

She went to the desk in the morning room and sat down to write a letter to Lee. This time she would include a return address. She had written only a paragraph when she balled the paper up and threw it away. Lee wouldn't want to renew their friendship, not now. Of what interest would a spoiled, useless, nonproductive creature like herself be to the woman Lee Redwing had become?

While Lee raised her son and defended helpless women and gave interviews to magazines, Carlotta's biggest problem was deciding what to wear to the next party. Only her overpowering love for her husband saved her from being like those empty jet-setters she had romped with in Europe. She wrote a brief note to Lee, instead of the long letter she had planned at first. She told Lee how very sorry she was about Dominic, and wished her well, and then she went in search of Delaney.

Beneath her real sadness about Lee's brother, and her genuine feeling that she was Lee's inferior, there was something else troubling her. Rachel had her enchanting Chloe and Lee had her little boy and Carlotta was still childless. At first she hadn't wanted to get pregnant, and then, when she had seen how lovely Chloe was and what a real challenge it might be to raise a child, her dormant instincts had begun to stir.

She thought it was time for them to have a baby.

Why the hell, Carlotta's husband thought, didn't women know when they were well off and accept it? Why did they always want something more? Were they constitutionally incapable of being satisfied? His first wife had wanted him to devote himself to her exclusively. Well, fair enough, that was what many women thought they wanted, but why hadn't Marigold made herself interesting enough to merit such fidelity? He hadn't expected the marriage to his second wife to last and didn't devote much thought to her, but what of all the rest?

There was always some complaint. The married ones often wanted him to confront their husbands and sweep them away, which would have ruined everything. The single ones wanted marriage. Some complained that he didn't take a proper interest in their careers. "You see me only as a cunt, Brendan," a Viennese opera singer had complained to him once. In truth, her voice had not been up to scratch. He had respected her cunt, but as an *artiste* he found her unbearable. Oh, the list was endless. Women who felt slighted if he did not spend exorbitant amounts of money on them, women who were insulted if he did. Yet they all stayed on to the bitter end. It was always Delaney, who had not done any of the complaining, who had to break things off.

Carlotta was the first woman to whom he had been prepared to give everything unconditionally. His name, his worldly goods, his sexual fidelity. She occupied him totally, on every level, and as far as he was concerned, he belonged to her. She would be his last and greatest love. He would die well before she did, and then she was free to do whatever she liked, with his blessing from the grave. But while he lived, he required that she live through, and for, him. He was to be her world. He was the source of all pleasure and joy, as she was to him. A baby did not fit in.

Why did she, a baby herself, need one? Hadn't he given her everything she needed? He had told her to do whatever she wanted with his house, to change it in any way she liked, so long as it made her happy. She had the same liberty in his New York apartment. He had bought her jewels and beautiful clothing and a gray thoroughbred quarterhorse. He had built a paddock for Carlotta's horse and acquired a painting by one of her favorites, Fragonard, for their first Christmas together. He made love to her with all the ardor of a boy, entertained her, taught her, amused her, adored her. Why did she need a baby?

He had seen it coming on; he knew the signs. He was fond enough of children, in their place, but when he'd perceived the look of the Madonna on his wife's face whenever she held or played with Chloe Vere, he could have wished poor Chloe unborn. He had a son to carry on his name, a son he saw once a year or so, and crazy Ivette's daughter, in Paris. Why should Carlotta trouble herself? Delaney neither needed, nor wanted, a child at his age. Carlotta only thought she wanted one, and he had to make her see that it was a passing fancy. A baby would only drive a wedge between them, and prove to be the snake in their Garden of Eden.

Lee received Carlotta's brief note, and smiled sadly. As usual, there was no return address, only a Connecticut postmark where there had once been the stamp of New York. It hadn't taken her long to find out about Brendan J. Delaney. She had always known that Carlotta would marry someone from *Who's Who,* and even in Butte they had copies in the library. Lee had stopped reading as soon as she'd seen the date of his birth. Oh, boy. Father Knows Best.

She snapped her suitcase shut and went to check on Dominic, who was still sleeping. His sooty, black lashes threw shadows on his cheekbones, and he had gathered his blanket in his fist, pressing it to his face. The little fist looked tense. "Hey, Domi," she whispered, "ease up. We're going to Seattle. No need to clutch that blanket so hard. Mama's here."

Dominic's middle name was Victor. Dominic V. Redwing. Victor Rainwater had given her a fine child, and she was grateful. He was married himself now, but he occasionally made furtive visits to see his first-born son. They had laughed a great deal during the creation of Dominic, and Lee hoped some of the laughter had entered into her son's soul. There had been pleasure, too, but mainly Lee remembered the laughter.

Victor, good mechanic that he was, was anxious to do things right. He had read that sperm was most potent when long pent-up, and he had heroically refrained from making love with his fiancee during the three-day period preceding Lee's most fertile time.

Charlie Redwing doted on the boy, never pressing Lee for details about his parentage. Lee's oldest brother, Ray, had moved to Bakersfield, California, and become a swimming pool serviceman. Jim was an alcoholic ranch hand, and Dominic had died in Southeast Asia, fighting a war no one had understood, now blessedly ended. Lee's mother had died of cancer when Carlotta was away in Switzerland. Who else did Charlie have to dote on? Everyone else was dead, or beyond redemption.

"You're it," Lee whispered to her sleeping son.

She tiptoed out of the room and went to the kitchen, where she flipped open a beer and stood drinking straight from the can. She was going to need something stronger than beer to see her through this next trial. The local council in Seattle had called her about this one and asked for her help. It was complicated, because she was not qualified to practice in the state of Washington, but she could argue for the defendant at the Seattle attorney's invitation. The fee was larger than she thought necessary, but now that she had Dominic's future to think of, she accepted it without hesitation.

The article in *People* had bothered her, more than she liked to admit. If people were calling from other states to seek her help, maybe she *was* turning into a one-note lawyer. She had never gone looking for fame and celebrity, and now that it had descended on her, she didn't want to be remembered as a feminist gun for hire. The male lawyers all treated it as a tremendous joke, pretending to be afraid of her, diving for cover when she appeared, and ceaselessly telling her how well they treated their wives.

She had had some hate mail, too. It was always anonymous, and it ranged from semi-obscene ramblings to intelligently worded observations of why Lee was guilty of conspiracy to murder. There had been anonymous phone calls, too, until she got an unlisted number.

Standing in her kitchen, drinking her beer, she suddenly felt a shudder pass through her. It was prompted by a cloud of dread so intense it was almost tangible. The kitchen seemed to darken for a moment, and Lee gripped the kitchen counter hard, as if she were about to fall. The nameless fear receded, and Lee told herself, speaking out loud, that the irrational moment of dread had been brought on by hunger. "You haven't been eating enough," she said. "You're too busy. Even Victor told you he thought you were getting too thin. There's a chicken leg in the fridge, and some potato salad. Put it on a plate and eat it; for God's sake, Redwing, get a grip on things here."

She carried the plate to the front room and ate on the couch, picking at the chicken. After a few moments she put the plate on the table and told herself the truth. She wasn't hungry, although it was true she was getting too thin. The fear in the kitchen had been real. It could have been a warning. Maybe the collective will of all the evil men who enjoyed inflicting pain on their wives had entered her kitchen to scare her off this case. *Stay away from this one. Don't say we didn't warn you.*

She went to the phone and dialed her father in Billings, although it was past his normal bedtime. Charlie answered on the second ring. "Daddy? I'm real sorry to disturb you at this hour, but it's important."

"Not Dominic," her father said, panic in his voice. "Nothing's wrong with him?"

She quickly reassured him that Dominic was fine, but he was, in fact, the reason for her call. When she asked him if he would mind looking after Dominic while she was gone he heaved a sigh of relief and accepted immediately. "That's no favor," he said, "that will be my pleasure."

"I have to leave for Seattle tomorrow," she said, "and I may be gone for weeks. I'll have to fly back and forth. It's a huge favor, Daddy, but I got to thinking. Emotions are going to be high at this trial, and maybe it's not good for Domi to—" To what? "—to be around that sort of thing," she finished weakly. She did not tell her father that she had suddenly feared for his safety.

"That's showing some sense," Mr. Redwing said approvingly. "I'll be up first thing tomorrow. You take care of yourself, Leana, you hear?"

He was the only person who ever called her Leana, and it never failed to make her feel sentimental, even though she hated the name. When she had said goodbye to him, she phoned Dominic's babysitter, who had been planning to accompany them to Seattle. The babysitter, a divorced woman in her late twenties, was disappointed, but cheered up considerably when Lee told her to cash her tickets in and have herself a blast.

Nothing remained to be done except for Lee to get in bed and make sure she had a good night's sleep in preparation for the battle. Sleep, of course, was impossible for a while. She had to shake the effects of that evil cloud. This might prove to be the case she'd lose, but she wasn't going to be frightened off.

FIFTEEN

"EVERYTHING'S SO COMPLICATED FOR OUR GENERATION," RA-chel said. "In the good old days, if a woman wanted to get pregnant 'accidentally,' she'd just forget to put her diaphragm in. *We* have to go to the doctor and get our goddamn IUDs yanked out."

"But I don't want to put one over on Brendan," said Carlotta. "I want him to want the baby, too."

They were lying beside Rachel's pool at the Hamptons house, drinking lemonade and tequila. The sun was very hot, and Carlotta was beginning to feel drowsy. "You know what he says? 'What does a baby need with a baby?' Can you imagine? I'm twenty-nine years old, Rachel. Twenty-nine years old!"

"I'm aware of that. We've known each other for many years, Carlotta—I'm not likely to forget your age, which also happens to be mine. Brendan, on the other hand, from the vantage point of his sunset years, may very well think twenty-nine is young."

"I won't comment on that crack, Rachel. I happen to love him, and it's not very nice to remind me of the fact that I'll outlive him."

"You just commented on it. Have another drink."

Carlotta giggled. "I'm getting drunk. Too much sun and tequila. What else do I have to do? Are you really going to smoke that joint now?"

"Of course. Why not?"

"You have twenty guests coming for dinner."

"Oh, dear, how terrifying. Be serious, Carlotta. It helps me to think clearly. I'm not concerned with my dinner guests, but I *am* concerned with this baby business." She toked, nodded, held up one slim, tanned hand. "Before I get really high, let me add that I hate you for having such a perfect, unmarked body. It is quite possible Brendan thinks you are a baby because you're so unflawed; it is also quite possible that I want to help you get pregnant so you'll have stretch marks, like me."

"You don't have any stretch marks, Rachel. You look wonderful, and you talk as if you were a battered old veteran of ten deliveries."

"Well, they're not too disfiguring, not grotesque, anyway, but see these little funny places?" She looked down at her breasts, placed her fingers on the flesh above the low line of her swimsuit. Carlotta shook her head, seeing nothing. "They're there, all right," said Rachel grimly. "When the light shines right, you can see them. They're sort of silvery, ghostly little trails. Anyway, *I* know they're there, and I have them on my belly too, which is why I don't wear bikinis anymore."

Rachel was wearing a one-piece suit of some sort of clinging, tissue-like material that was cut so low at the bosom and so high at the thigh it was not much larger than a man's handkerchief. Carlotta felt that her own black bikini was modest by comparison. She poured some more tequila into her lemonade and waited for her friend to get high enough to let forth the wisdom she had promised. Delaney was off in the city, doing business, just as Cotter Vere was. Both of them were expected later. Chloe was with Mrs. MacDougall on the beach, and she and Rachel, free of any responsibility, seemed to have reverted back to their schoolgirl days. Carlotta felt vaguely guilty about confessing her problem. It made her feel disloyal to Brendan, and she didn't like Rachel to know that a cloud was now hovering over her so-perfect marriage. The sun and the tequila and the idleness had done their work, and it had just popped out. Now that the damage was done, she was really quite eager to hear what Rachel had to say. It had been a long time since she had spoken of serious things to anyone but Delaney.

"A woman is biologically unfulfilled without a child," Rachel said experimentally, in oratorical style. "No—that won't do. He's far too smart to fall for that. I bet he's known thousands, *millions,* of women who would laugh themselves to death at that line. Besides, it isn't *you.*"

Carlotta trailed her hand in the turquoise water. "Definitely not," she said. "Also, Brendan isn't denying me a child. He makes it seem as if it's a matter of waiting a while, just a year here, a year there, until the magical moment arrives and it's time. Only trouble is, I could be forty before the time is right. He's like a magician. When I'm with him it's a magic carpet ride, but when I'm alone it all seems so strange. Why shouldn't I have a child? It isn't as if we were poor and would have to scrimp and pinch pennies to feed another mouth. There's no obstacle but him."

"I don't mean to be unkind," said Rachel, her voice a bit distant now, "but when you're forty, darling, your lad will be nearly seventy. If you're serious about this thing, you have to get to it soon. Who wants a dad with a walker?"

"Shut up, Rachel, just shut *up!*" Carlotta buried her face in her hands, sorry she'd revealed so much of herself. It had always been like that. Earnest Carlotta, clever Rachel. Why didn't she learn? "Let's change the subject," she muttered. "We could talk about the centerpiece for the table tonight, or what we're going to wear. I'm planning to wear a Greek handkerchief dress, all white, which will enhance my tan. White sandals from Milan. I'm putting my hair up because it's so bloody hot. Your turn." She felt Rachel's hand on her back, soft and tentative, and looked up from her cupped hands.

"Carlotta?" Rachel's face was softened by real concern. "Oh, honey, you're really suffering, aren't you? I'm sorry, I'll be serious. Here's what you have to do." She stroked Carlotta's hair and spoke soothingly. "You have to convince him that you love him so much that nothing will make your life worth living after he's gone, so to speak, except for a little Delaney. Tell him you don't think you could survive without something created by the two of you, something to make your love eternal. Really lay it on thick."

"But it's true," said Carlotta. "I don't have to lie."

"Then do it," said Rachel.

When Rachel went up to her room to shower and prepare for the dinner party, Carlotta went to her own room feeling drugged and sleepy. She had the biggest guest room in the house, and her windows faced seaward. A slight breeze was stirring the light curtains, and it felt delicious, rippling over her heated flesh. She lay on her bed for a moment, still wearing her bikini, and thought of what Rachel had said. She could never broach the topic of his death to the man she loved. Delaney was unsentimental about death and wouldn't be offended; the problem was that Carlotta herself couldn't bear to think of the time when he would be gone. She forced it from her mind and listened to the murmuring of the sea. Far away, she heard Chloe's voice, and then she fell asleep.

In her confused dream, Delaney and her father were talking to Charlie Redwing at the ranch. She and Lee and Rachel, all very young, were sitting on the fence, watching. In the dream she knew that Lee and Rachel had never met, but accepted their presence together. Daddy and Charlie and Delaney seemed huddled in a conference. The little girls could hear the deep rumble of their voices. Now and then they roared with laughter. After a while, Lee impatiently jumped from the fence and ran to her father. Charlie took her hand and led her away. Tom Madigan and Delaney disappeared into the barn where the prize stallion was quartered, leaving Carlotta alone. She sat on the fence and waited, but they never returned. "I'm going to go look for them," she told Rachel, and even though Rachel tried to hold her back, she ran off to the barn. Inside, it was pitch black. She called "Daddy?" over and over, but there was no answer. The stallion's dreadful hooves were thumping and crashing, and it was so dark, and she was afraid the beast had got loose . . .

She wakened, thrashing, and the word *Daddy* echoed in her mind and someone was holding her down, gentling her, saying she had had a bad dream. "Don't be afraid, it was only a dream," he said. "It's all right, darling, my sweet little girl."

She clutched him to her, holding him with all her strength. "Promise me you'll never leave me," she whispered fiercely. "Promise, Delaney."

"You know I won't."

"Say it. Say, it Brendan."

"I, Brendan John Delaney, promise that I will never leave my wife, Carlotta Delaney, so help me God."

And then Carlotta surprised herself. She, who was generally not the aggressor in their lovemaking, wiggled out of the bikini panties and clawed at his zipper. She wanted no soft caresses, no preliminary dallying. She didn't even want to wait for Delaney to undress. She wanted him now, without delay, hard inside her.

When he saw the depth of her desire he reacted just as she had wanted him to. He pushed her back on the bed, spread her legs with ungentle hands, and drove himself into her with the force of a jackhammer. He cushioned her head in his hands so that she would not hit it against the headboard of the bed in the violence of their movement, and Carlotta threw her legs around him and held on for her life.

He had never taken her brutally, and even now he was not brutal, but the fierce violence of his strokes literally took her breath away. She gasped and tried to cry out to him, but the words would not come. His belt buckle was cutting into her tender flesh. She arched up to him frantically and felt her orgasm begin. It was not like the others, where the sensations began to lap at her from a distance and grew gradually nearer, cresting in waves until they overpowered her. This pleasure came like a sharp sword of flame, and stabbed her from belly to throat. She gave one loud cry, and then lay still. Gradually, she began to move a little. Yes, she was still alive. She laughed softly. A man who could make love like that would surely live forever!

"Oh, Brendan," she mumbled into his neck, "you nearly killed me."

"It was what you wanted, Mrs. Delaney," he said.

There were no swimming pools or seaside picnics or candlelit dinners for Lee Redwing that summer. Later, she would think of it as a time when she was always exhausted, but for now she paid no heed to her exhaustion and did what she had to do.

Jane Kurtz, the woman on trial, looked even less like a murderess than Sally Carlson had. She had pale, soft frizzy hair and huge brown eyes. If she had been an animal, Jane Kurtz would be a doe. She was thin and graceful, and she looked as if she might bolt away into the forest at any moment. It was almost impossible to imagine her stabbing her husband to death, yet that was exactly what she had done. What made it even more astonishing was the fact that Mrs.

Kurtz had killed her husband while he was sleeping.

The smart money around the courthouse said that Lee could never win an acquittal for the defendant, because how could she use self-defense when the man had been sawing zzzzzs? Lee tended to agree with them, but she also knew that Jane Kurtz *had* acted in self-defense.

In a way, she had more to work with than she had in the Carlson case. The Kurtzes had lived in a large apartment building, and there were plenty of neighbors to testify to what they had heard. Mrs. Kurtz had tried to get help from various agencies, and on the night of the fatal incident, she had been planning to leave her husband once and for all.

"I should have just left, sneaked away," she explained to Lee and, later, the jury. "But I had been married to the man for ten years. I felt I owed him at least an explanation."

Her explanation earned her a broken collarbone, two broken ribs, and a face that looked like hamburger meat. As always, however, by the time the case got to court her injuries had healed. Luckily, she had sent her fourteen-year-old daughter to a friend's for the night, because Kurtz had not been above beating her up, too. The daughter was from her first marriage, to a man who had died in an industrial accident. The Kurtzes had only one child of their own, a boy of six. He had never been touched by his father, Jane testified, either in love or in anger.

"Jane," Lee had asked in private, "will you tell me exactly what happened on the night you killed your husband?"

"Well, after I told him, and he beat me up, he dragged me by the heels into our bedroom. I was in pretty bad shape, and I kind of just collapsed in a little ball on the floor. He loosened his belt and got on the bed, all stretched out comfortable. He told me he was going to grab some sleep, and I should stay right there, because when he woke up he was going to take up where he left off."

"What then? Did he go to sleep right away?"

"Pretty near. I could hear him breathing regular, and then he began to snore. I would say he went to sleep in five minutes."

"And you remained on the floor by the bed for how long?"

"I couldn't tell you. I was hurting pretty bad, and I was thinking about what he said, back when he was beating on me."

"What had he said?"

"Oh, stuff about finding me wherever I went and killing me. He said he'd kill me and Lisa—that's my daughter. He said he'd kill Lisa first, and then me. So I could watch, he said."

"Has he made these threats before?"

"Not in so many words. When Lisa was young, he used to try to scare me. If she cried he said he'd smother her in her sleep. The first time he socked her—she was about seven—I thought I'd go crazy. . ."

Jane Kurtz related the events, sordid and tragic, of her everyday life in calm, reasonable tones, as if she were giving Lee the details of a bake-off. No, she didn't think Kurtz had ever assaulted Lisa sexually, although there *had* been the time when Lisa wet the bed and he had threatened to sit her on the hotplate. Yes, Jane had intervened, and that was the time he burst her eardrum with a clout to the head.

"What did you do after you were sure he was sound asleep, Mrs. Kurtz?"

"I decided to go for help. I crawled out of the room and down the hall, and in the kitchen I eased myself up, but I had a terrible pain just here." She had touched her abdomen. "I was afraid I had one of those internal injuries you read about, where the broken bones inside float around and cut into your heart or your spleen, you know? I was coughing and showing blood—that turned out to be from the split lip, but I didn't know—and I was sure I'd die out there in the hall, going for help, and then where would my children be, left with him?"

"I was even going to call the police, but they take so long to get there on a domestic call, forget it, and I was afraid he'd wake up. I just saw the knife hanging in the rack, and I thought, why not? That's the best way. It's the only way."

Again, she had turned her doe eyes on Lee with the innocence of a woman discussing recipes. "To tell you the truth, Miss Redwing, he didn't deserve to live."

"I agree with you, Mrs. Kurtz, but you must not say that in court. Juries and judges don't like to hear defendants make value judgments—that's their territory."

Lee thought there was another factor in their favor. Kurtz, unlike Sally Carlson's husband, never drank. He had been a teetotaller. Men on juries tended to get itchy about crimes committed while under the influence; they could all too read-

ily imagine themselves doing the same. But a man who brutally beat his wife and step-daughter when he was in full
command of his faculties? Such a man was either evil or insane.

She had no doubt that she could make the jury detest
Kurtz, but how was she to make them understand the woman
who had stayed with him for ten years? Every woman on the
jury could relate to the maiden who married a prince only to
see him turn into a frog, but most of them would never be able
to take the horror of seeing the prince turn into a cobra.

It was a puzzle which intrigued and tormented her so much
that when a New York publisher called to ask if she would
consider writing a book about women who killed, she said she
would consider the matter.

All through that endless summer, while she was flying
back and forth between Washington and Montana, while she
was feeling guilty for abandoning Dominic and guilty for des-
erting the scene of the trial, she considered the book. Why
shouldn't she write it? She didn't need the collaborator or
ghostwriter the publishers had offered. She could do it on her
own. She would gratefully acknowledge Sally, Jane, and the
others, but no one else. A summation in a courtroom reached
a limited audience, but a book would reach thousands.

While the jury was hung, and just before she was hospital-
ized for anemia, Lee called New York and said yes.

On a perfect day in autumn, when the leaves were beginning
to turn, Rachel happened to see Delaney in the window of the
Oak Bar. She couldn't see if Carlotta was with him or not.
Delaney hadn't seen her. She hesitated for only a moment,
then stepped briskly up the little stairs and into the Plaza
Hotel. She had a most uncharitable desire to catch Carlotta's
husband doing something sneaky. At the door of the Oak
Room, she saw that he was alone. Probably waiting for somebody.

She crossed the room, and midway he looked up and saw
her. He smiled, looking not at all as a guilty man should, and
half rose to his feet. She had to admit that Delaney was im-
pressive. It was early in the afternoon, and there were only
half a dozen women in the Oak room, but she could just bet
every one of them envied her.

"Hello, Brendan," she said breezily, sitting opposite him.

"I was just passing by when I saw you. Waiting for an assignation?"

"What an amazing creature you are, my dear Rachel. I wouldn't have thought a lady of your years was familiar with that expression. It was out of date when *I* was a boy." He smiled again and asked her if she would have a drink.

"I'll have one, yes," said Rachel. "A Black Russian. But you haven't answered my question."

"I am waiting for a man from the mysterious East who wishes to make some investments. In short, I am doing business. He won't arrive for at least twenty minutes."

"Is this where you do business? At the Oak Bar?"

"Occasionally," he said, as if it didn't interest him. He gave her order to the waiter and then turned his full attention back on her. And Delaney's full attention was quite something, Rachel thought. It was one thing to be with him in a room humming with people, or with Carlotta beside him; it was quite another to be alone with him. Well, hardly alone, but if sitting across from him in the Oak Bar felt sexy and dangerous, what must it be like to be really alone?

He was wearing a beautifully cut three-piece suit, and for the first time she noticed what it was Carlotta must mean when she spoke of Delaney's *perfection*. There wasn't a single thing about him that wasn't pleasing. Most men had some flaw. With Cotter it was eyes just a fraction too close-set. There were gorgeous men who, on close inspection, had unattractive hands or thin lips or legs a trifle too short, but Delaney was definitely without physical flaw. She thought the signs of aging only made him more attractive, and wondered if Carlotta hadn't, after all, caught him at his most desirable. As a young man he might have been unbearably pretty; even at forty he wouldn't have attained the aura of absolute masculine power that cloaked him now. The only other man she had ever seen to match him was Carlotta's father. Of course.

Her drink arrived and she forced herself not to gulp it immediately. What had begun as a lighthearted adventure now seemed to her a mission. He was being amusing, in his effortless manner, relating a story about a Greenwich hostess who had served venison full of buckshot at a dinner party, when she plucked up her courage and said, with more intensity than she had planned: "Brendan, you must let Carlotta have a baby.

It's so vital, you have no idea. It is your *duty* to get her pregnant."

"I see," he said, sounding amused. The blue eyes were alert, however, and anything but amused. "Go on, Rachel. I am listening."

"Carlotta is unhappy," she continued. "Not with you—far from it—but in her life. She badly wants to have a baby while you, it seems, do not. I can understand your reasons, I think, but you are being selfish."

"Has my wife told you these things?"

"Not about your being selfish—it would never enter her mind. But she told me the rest months ago, the day we gave the party for that designer in the Hamptons and you joined us from the city."

Delaney reckoned back, a slight smile playing at his lips. "Don't you think," he inquired gently, "that this is a matter entirely between Carlotta and myself?"

"In the polite world it is, but I'm more concerned for her happiness than with being polite."

"I'm glad of that," he said. "We're both concerned for her happiness. But has it ever occurred to you that things might change greatly if Carlotta had a child? She might find the situation you mentioned reversed."

"I don't know what you mean."

"She might find herself happy with her child, but not with me. It's quite a gamble."

Rachel lit a cigarette to give herself time to figure him out. It sounded as if he were issuing a threat, yet his tone of voice was sad, not angry. "Brendan," she said finally, "it's really very simple. You're not going to live forever. You're going to leave Carlotta a widow at some point, and what will she do then? If she had your child, she wouldn't be so totally shattered."

"Thank you for reminding me of my mortality," he said, lifting his glass and toasting her. "I will certainly consider your advice, although I can't help but wonder how much of it is prompted by your dislike of me."

"I don't dislike you," Rachel said truthfully. "I didn't trust you at first, but I never disliked you. As a matter of fact, I like you better all the time. If you weren't married to my best friend, I'd probably try to seduce you."

He laughed. "If I weren't married to your best friend, I would allow you to, with pleasure."

Delaney's client arrived then. His eyes quickened with interest when he saw Rachel, but she finished her drink with haste and left, feeling disturbed. She reflected that trying to persuade Delaney to do something was like making a pact with the devil.

SIXTEEN

THE WINTER SEA WAS GRAY AND HOSTILE. IT BROKE ANGRILY against the strand, and Carlotta thought of the trawler that was still missing. Gloom had settled over the village, because the men were presumed dead. The wind was high, and she felt the cold penetrate the many layers of wool that shielded her body. Tears of cold stung her eyes, but she did not turn back.

Any other woman would have gone to the Caribbean, she thought. When women left their husbands to think things over, they usually chose sultry, sybaritic locales to do their thinking in. Certainly they didn't go to the wild western tip of Ireland in the winter! This was exactly what she had wanted, though. Solitude and no distractions. Her life with Delaney had been one long round of pleasure and comfort, and she didn't need more of the same now. She welcomed every discomfort—the cold, the difficulty of getting the fires going in the farmhouse, the difficulty, in fact, of getting even the simplest things done. The struggles distracted her from the deep unhappiness, the sense of emptiness, which had prompted her to run away.

A sea bird wheeled over her, flying low, and screamed angrily. Carlotta smiled at the bird because it seemed they were in the same mood. During the last three weeks or so, her

unhappiness had escalated to such a pitch that she had wanted
to scream. If she hadn't been brought up to behave in a certain
way, she might have permitted herself to wail and curse at
Delaney, but instead she had run off to examine her unhappiness in private. She had left him a note so he wouldn't worry,
saying that she had gone away for a while to try to make some
sense of things. He wasn't to worry. She would be back,
whatever conclusion she came to. The only thing she didn't
tell him was where she was planning to go.

A wave nearly broke over her foot, and she realized she
had almost wandered into the sea. The trouble was that she
had come to want nothing but a child of her own, and that was
the one thing Brendan was unwilling to give her. Her life was
an empty one by any real standard; surely it wasn't right for
her to spend all of her energy on looking beautiful and enjoying herself.

She walked along the higher cliffs toward the farmhouse.
Normally she enjoyed the view of the sea from the clifftops,
but today she averted her eyes. It seemed too dangerous and
cruel, and she couldn't help but think of the men from the
trawler. She cut across the moorland, and encountered Mrs.
Feeney pedaling by on an ancient bicycle. "Any word?" she
called. Mrs. Feeney shook her head grimly and pedaled on. In
happier times she would have dismounted and engaged Carlotta in conversation. The people were kind here. Once they
had overcome their surprise at finding Carlotta alone, they had
made it a point to speak to her, offer to help her in fetching
supplies to the farmhouse. She had the loan of a bike so that
she didn't have to walk all the way back from the town with
her groceries. The boy who had offered her the bike had been
shocked to hear that she had never learned to drive a car! "Ah,
now surely ye're coddin' me," he had said. That was nearly a
week ago, and now the boy was probably at the bottom of the
ocean.

The farmhouse looked dark and melancholy, and she
wished she had thought to leave a lamp on before setting off
for her walk. She never liked to return to a dark house. She
unlocked the door with stiff, cold fingers and went inside. She
left her coat and scarf in the hall, and went through to the
largest fireplace to warm herself. Even the Aran sweater she
wore over a cashmere couldn't keep the cold out. She would
have to build the fire up.

As she was crossing the room she heard the tiniest sound, but it was enough to make her spine tingle. She was sure someone was inside the house with her, and as she turned in terror there was a sort of rushing noise and something caught at her and held her close from behind. A hand went over her mouth, silencing the scream before it was born. She stood like that, captive, for what seemed a very long time. Her heart was pounding hard, but the quick breathing of her captor seemed to mean that he was frightened, too.

"Don't be scared," came his voice, after what seemed an eternity. "I won't hurt you, not if you don't scream. You won't scream, will you now?" His accent was strange, and not from Donegal. He pronounced *now* as if it were *nigh*. Carlotta shook her head, and after a few more moments the hand was withdrawn. Still, he did not release her. "Are you alone here?" he asked. "Who else lives here?"

"I'm all alone," she told the disembodied voice. "This is my husband's house, but he's three thousand miles away."

"Jesus! A Yank," said the voice. "Okay, you can turn around now."

Now she almost did scream, because the stranger's face was completely covered by a black ski mask. She could not see his eyes, even though there were holes for him to see out of, and it was like confronting a monster. "Yes, I'm a Yank," she said. "Who are you?"

He laughed behind his mask, not unpleasantly, and said, "Anyone else would know." Now she noticed the gun he was holding in his right hand. It was particularly big and ugly-looking. "Don't worry," he said. "I won't hurt you. I'm not going to rob you or rape you or any of that Yank stuff. I just need a place to hide for a couple of days. You understand?"

"Yes," said Carlotta, keeping her voice low and reasonable. "You are a fugitive. Are you from over the border?"

"Now ye're beginning to understand, love. I just dropped in from the occupied counties to Donegal, and I can't very well register in a hotel. I'll be no trouble, and if you'll be reasonable I'll put the gun away."

"The gun doesn't bother me as much as the ski mask. Isn't it hot in there?"

"Hot? Jesus! This is the bloody coldest house in Donegal. You don't know how to make a proper fire."

He put the gun back in his belt, asking only that she stay

where he could see her, and knelt to build the fire up. Very soon he had it blazing, and Carlotta found she wanted a cup of tea and offered him one, too. He followed her to the kitchen, and they waited for the kettle to come to the boil. The farmhouse had no telephone, and no one ever came here except to deliver milk. She didn't think she had much choice whether she would harbor him or not. Oddly enough, after the first few moments of terror, she found she wasn't at all afraid of him.

"Is *that* how you make tea?" the man asked when Carlotta began to damp the leaves. He shook his head and said he'd make the tea, if she didn't mind.

"I'm a terrible cook, terrible in the kitchen," she told him.

"Not too good with fires, either," he replied. "I can see I'm goin' to have to do everything around here."

Suddenly it seemed so crazily funny to her—a fugitive terrorist grumbling at his household duties while they chatted in the kitchen—that she began to laugh helplessly. Once started, she couldn't stop. She slumped over the breadboard, laughing and hiccuping and gasping all at the same time. The man patted her back, handing her a glass of water, and then the tea was ready.

It had become very dark, and he drew all the curtains before he would allow her to light any lamps. "Just the normal amount of light," he said. "What you'd usually have." Carlotta had to convince him that she was extravagant with electricity, and remind him that the house could not be seen from the road in any case.

"You're not a local," he said, settling down. "It doesn't matter if you see my face." He peeled the mask away and she saw he was no more than twenty-five. He had curly red-brown hair and sly blue Irish eyes, like Delaney's, she thought. "You have eyes like my husband's," she told him. "His name is Delaney."

"There's Delaney in my family," he said, gulping at his tea.

"Any Madigans?"

"No, none of them. Would you have any bread about the place?"

She studied him, wanting to laugh hysterically again. He was tall and rather skinny, but nicely made. His curly hair, dragged down by the ski mask, was beginning to fluff up again. Except for the gun at his belt, he might have been a choirboy asking for his supper. She went to the kitchen and assembled cheese and bread and fruit on a tray for him. He was probably starving. She added some slices of cold ham.

As she carried it back to him she reminded herself that it was very important to remember the gun.

Delaney was missing Carlotta as he had never missed anyone in his life. His first reaction had been anger, followed by panic, then both resolving into a kind of aching sadness. He knew she would be back, but he also knew things could never be quite the same between them. He would always remember she had run off and deserted him to make her point. He would give in, because he really could not live without her, but he would resent it.

He thought he knew where she had gone, but he did a little sleuthing to make sure. Unlike most men, he was familiar with every piece of his wife's clothing. He knew exactly how many swimsuits she owned, how many filmy caftans and crisp summer white outfits. If he didn't know the exact number, he could tell if something was missing, some scrap of lifeless cloth which once had had the privilege of being rounded out by her body. None of her strappy, narrow, high-heeled slippers were gone. A regiment of them, row after row, confronted him from the depths of her shoe closet. What *was* missing was a pair of low-heeled, thigh-length leather boots, and, from a sweet-scented cedar chest, the Aran sweater he had bought her in Donegal on their honeymoon. Gone, too, were several cashmeres, a thick tweed coat (she had not taken any furs), and the single pair of jeans she owned. Carlotta was the only girl of her generation who had never worn blue jeans until, quite recently, she had bought a pair to wear while caring for her horse.

By his tally, she was traveling light. She had taken nothing frivolous, nothing glamorous, preparing herself for a cold and rugged place. Her passport was gone. All of it pointed toward the house in Donegal.

He was too proud to follow her, like a puppy, and there was no phone in the farmhouse. He knew, from experience, that it could take days to successfully put a call through to Donegal in any case. Eventually, he would send her a telegram to let her know that she had won.

Crouching in one of her closets, pressing a dress that still contained her scent to his face, he was as heartbroken as a lovesick boy. It was not an attractive position for a man of his years, and he resented it most bitterly. A part of him hated Carlotta and wanted to punish her, but the other part—the one that hurt so badly—longed for her and vowed to do anything she liked in order to keep her close to him forever.

Even asleep, he wore the gun. It was strapped across his chest in what she supposed, from old gangster movies, was called a shoulder holster. He had rejected her offer of one of the bedrooms, and insisted on sleeping in front of the fire on a pile of cushions. He looked even younger in sleep, and the gun strapped to his chest seemed almost obscene. He slept in the clothes he had arrived in—jeans and a black sweater. His leather jacket lay in a corner of the room where he had discarded it.

"But won't they look for you?" she had asked him the night before. "What will I do if they come and search the house?"

"I'll be long gone by then," he had told her.

Carlotta herself was fully dressed, because she had not thought to buy thick, flannel nightgowns. She slept in the Aran sweater, buried beneath mounds of quilts, and dressed immediately upon waking. Delaney had never intended the house to be a retreat in winter.

In the late dawn, she looked at Kevin—that was the name he had given her, though probably not his own—and wondered what would happen if she tried to disarm him. Probably he would spring to life and blast her head off before he was even fully awake. On the other hand, if she were the one to hold the gun, what would she do?

She could not imagine forcing him, at gunpoint, to make the long, cold walk to Dungloe, where she would surrender him to the local constable. She did not know what he had done to place him outside of the law, but she knew he was an IRA man. She had heard of no bombings or particular violence on the radio, so perhaps he had escaped from prison. She was not going to judge him or even tell the authorities after he had gone. It troubled her a little, but she felt a kind of sympathy for him. If she ignored the gun, he had to be one of the most courteous and least troublesome guests she had ever harbored.

She wished he would wake up so she'd have someone to talk to, and the house could use one of his blazing fires. She would never go back to sleep now, and between the sleeping, armed figure and her ceaseless thoughts about Delaney, she felt unbearably anxious. Kevin looked so tired she thought he might sleep for hours more.

"Now," he had said to her, "I can sleep with my body in front of the door, or I can sleep here. Which is it to be?"

"It's awfully drafty in front of the door, Kevin." She had been honestly perplexed at the suggestion. When she saw what he had meant—that she would have to step over him in order to escape—she had laughed. "But there are two doors. You can't sleep in front of both of them."

"I've locked the back door from inside. The key's on me. I can't do that with the front. Ah, Jesus, Mrs. Delaney, give us a wee break. I haven't slept for two days."

Carlotta sat in a wing chair, huddling in her sweater, remembering the look on his face when he'd asked for a break. She curled up, hugging herself for warmth, and continued to watch the sleeping boy. He breathed evenly and deeply, as if he slept with a clear conscience. He fascinated her, and she wondered if he had given her a thought beyond her potential for betrayal.

The world was turning lavender outside the curtained windows. Normally, she would go and watch the spectacular dawn, but today it held no charm for her. Her body missed Delaney even when the rest of her did not. She had become accustomed to his passionate lovemaking, almost taking it for granted in the end, and now—deprived—she realized that sex should never be taken for granted.

She imagined lying on the cushions beside the baby-faced terrorist and caressing him into arousal while he slept, but there was the problem of the gun. And the cold. There would be no going back if she betrayed Brendan with a stranger, in his house. It would be a way of making sure that her marriage was over.

She shut her eyes, trying to think of something that would neither make her long for Delaney nor conspire to be unfaithful to him. She selected the view from her room on the ranch when she was a child. She saw the cottonwood trees and wild rosebushes, the rippling meadow beyond and, far off, the mountains, and she dozed off.

When she awakened with a start, she was alone in the room. She could hear the sounds of the radio in the kitchen and smelled coffee. The fire was going nicely, and Kevin had covered her with his leather jacket. She headed for the smell of coffee, calling out so he would not be surprised. "I'm coming to the kitchen!" she shouted. "Don't shoot!"

He was buttering toast when she arrived. "I don't think you take me very seriously," he complained.

"Oh, I think you're dangerous, all right," she said, pouring herself a cup of coffee. "But somehow, I don't think you're dangerous to *me.*"

"Right." He nodded, approving. "Are there any more of the apples?"

"We ate them last night. There's a little ham, but we're out of eggs. Unless you want to live on bread and cheese, you'll have to trust me. I'll cycle into the village and get more stuff."

"No. That you will not." He spoke curtly, and then, at her look, softened. "It's not that I don't trust you, though I don't know why I should. I can't risk it, Mrs. Delaney."

"Carlotta. Unlike you, I tell you my right name."

"You don't think my name is Kevin?" He looked amused, as if she were a bright schoolgirl drawing conclusions for the teacher. They took their breakfast to the fire in the living room and settled on the cushions.

"Did you hear anything about that missing trawler on the news?" she asked him. He shook his head. "Did you hear anything about yourself, then?"

"What would I hear about myself?"

"Oh, 'Missing terrorist still at large,' that kind of thing?"

He laughed gleefully. "You're a cool one, Carlotta," he said. "Is that how you see me?"

"No, but that's how you're labeled. I'll tell you what I think. I think you're in the IRA, and probably very idealistic. If you've killed anyone, I don't want to know about it."

"I don't want you to know anything about me," he said. "It's better that way. Nobody's goin' to hassle you, Carlotta, bein' a Yank and all." He laughed again, silently. "I'll tell you one thing, though—if I was what they call an international terrorist, you'd be looking at an international terrorist who's never been out of Ireland."

The sound of the milk truck approaching galvanized him. He crouched at the window, the gun in his hand. "It's only the milk truck," she told him. "You can hear the bottles jingling, Kevin. It's probably still a mile away. He'll just leave me two bottles, and go away. He leaves them on the stoop."

When the small drama of the milk delivery was over, he relaxed and asked if she would like to play cards for a while. "It's going to be a long day," he explained. When Carlotta told him she didn't know how to play poker, he brightened. "I'll teach you. It's a good way to pass the time."

They unearthed an ancient pack of cards, and used wooden matches instead of money. The black-tipped matches, Kevin said solemnly, would be five-pound notes, the red-tipped ones tenners. She proved to be a very good pupil, and the luck of the cards was hers. If Kevin thought he had her with three kings, Carlotta would stun him with a full house. If he had a straight, she would apologetically produce a flush.

"Christ, woman—are you sure ye're not a card sharp?" he wailed when she had cleaned him out.

Late in the long day, she asked him if he needed money. Real money. "Doesn't everyone?" he said.

"I don't. I'm rich, or my husband is. It's all I'm good for, really, but I can give you all I have in the house. I have an account in Dungloe."

He colored painfully, and averted his blue eyes. "It's of no use to me," he said gruffly. "It's Irish money. When I go back over the border, I need Brit money." There was a long silence, as if he were angry with her. Then he touched her arm briefly and said, "Thanks, though." It was little more than a whisper.

She wakened with dread, sensing the dark figure in her bedroom even through her sleep. The illuminated hands on the bedside clock told her it was 3:15 A.M. She sat bolt upright. "Kevin?" He was standing over the bed now, dressed in his leather jacket as if for departure. "What is it?"

"Don't be afraid," he whispered. "I just wanted to say goodbye."

"You're leaving *now?*"

"It's time."

She felt disoriented and sad. She sprang from the bed, clad in her usual nightwear—the Aran sweater and a pair of knee-socks. "You can't go now," she said. "Where will you go at this hour?"

"Best time for travelin'," he said. Now that her eyes had adjusted to the dark she saw him clearly. He was staring at her so intently that a great fear closed over her heart. He was going to have to shoot her, after all. The sadness in his eyes was because he didn't want to. "Carlotta," he said. "There's something you should know. Before, when you offered me the money? You said it was all you were good for."

She nodded.

"Well, you must know that's not true. You're good and clever, brave and beautiful. When I first saw you, I thought I'd die. You mustn't have such a low opinion of yourself." He stood there uncertainly. "Well, that's it," he said. "Kiss us goodbye?"

They were the same height, and when she put her arms around him she felt the gun pressing against her breasts. She kissed him full on the lips and felt his skinny body trembling at the contact. His arms came around her and they kissed as lovers, long and desperately. She knew that the passion she felt was not erotic love, but sorrow, and her cheeks were wet with tears.

She watched from the window as the black figure went running into the night. He was no longer the Kevin who had taught her to play poker, but a terrorist in a black ski mask.

Two days later, just before the telegram from Delaney arrived to summon her home, she read of Kevin's death in County Tyrone. He had been shot in a field while trying to elude the security forces. The picture of the wanted terrorist did indeed make him look fierce. His real name had been Timmy John O'Hara.

SEVENTEEN

ANYTHING YOU WANT, NOW AND FOREVER.

Those were the words on Delaney's telegram. The boy on the bike had said "All right, missus?" and she had shaken herself out of the paralysis of indecision and given him some coins. She understood what Delaney meant. He wanted her enough to agree to a baby. Why wasn't she happier about it?

At the time, she had told herself it had to do with Kevin's death. She was uncomfortable in the farmhouse now, and everything around her had become tainted by the cruelty of what was happening over the border. She had planned to leave the house and go to Dublin, but her husband's telegram changed all that.

Now that she had been home for nearly a week, she thought her indecision had been based on something else. Delaney himself—his character, the fatal flaw that allowed him to hold a grudge through wounded pride—was the reason. It was a flaw she had never perceived, and when she asked herself what had made her grasp it, three thousand miles away, by merest instinct, she had no answer.

Tonight they were entertaining people she had never met, business associates of Delaney's, and all much older than she was. She was nervous, even though she had always been at home with people of all ages. She had nothing to do but plan the menu, which had been done two days ago, arrange some flowers, and look lovely and decorous when her guests arrived, so her anxiety had nothing to do with the actual event. She had a tiny little fear that Delaney had planned this evening to show off his obedient, repentant, adoring wife to people who might have heard that she had left him. Where always before he had seemed spontaneous and generous, she now saw something conniving in him. Her homecoming, for example.

When she had stepped out of the customs hall at JKF and looked anxiously around for him, she had seen not Delaney, but Fred, his driver. Her husband, it seemed, was waiting for her at their town flat, in the city.

All the way in to Manhattan, with silent Fred separated from her by the pane of smoked glass, she had squirmed with eagerness and fear in equal measure. Was she being punished after all? And how she wanted him! Now that Delaney was so close, it was as if he was touching her, here in the back seat of his car. Her body was shivering with need for him. There was a painful throbbing in her breasts that made even the pressure of her clothing uncomfortable, and she was so wet between her legs that the mere act of crossing them made her gasp with desire. She was ashamed of the hot, wanton feelings that tortured her through the seemingly endless ride, and she wondered how she could keep from jumping Delaney the moment she saw him. When the lights of Sutton Place came into view she nearly cheered. And when, at last, she actually stood in front of him, alone in their apartment, did he grab her in his arms and take the ache away?

He did not. Here was a new Delaney—one she had never seen before. This new husband welcomed her home with a chaste kiss on the cheek and a bottle of champagne. Where was the man who had sent the desperate telegram? He seemed to have disappeared, and in his place was a big, handsome *acquaintance*, someone who seemed pleased to see her but hardly overwhelmed. He even made her feel a bit like a recalcitrant schoolgirl, joking about the jeans and boots she had traveled in, so that she wondered if her appearance had turned him off.

She sat, sipping champagne she didn't want, a full twenty feet away from him. Behind his head, the beautiful view of the East River and the twinkling, lighted bridges held no charm for her. He talked casually of trifles, inquiring politely as to whether it had been very cold in Donegal, and all the time the surging pulsations in her belly were turning to pain. "All right, you bastard," she had said to herself. "I've had enough." She told him she was going to have a shower and walked off with as much dignity as she could muster.

Somewhere in the middle of that long, mainly sleepless night, he made love to her. On his terms, when she was least expecting it. Half in half out of sleep, she began to feel exquisite sensations plucking at the nerves of her body. She was drawn tight as a bowstring, every inch of her wracked and jumping, and she came to consciousness on the brink of the orgasm she had needed hours ago. He was toying with her, taking his time, using his magical fingertips and skilled tongue like instruments of torture.

Her body arched up, mutely pleading for release, but she bit her lip to keep from begging him. She was no longer herself—only that single, hot center of her existed—and she wanted to tear him to shreds with her teeth and nails until he was forced to give her what she needed so terribly.

He was like a vampire, drinking her in hungrily when she burst and flowed against his lips, sucking her dry, feeding from her sobbing ecstasy. He knew her well, and when she was still quaking and shuddering, he thrust himself inside and searched out every bit of her which hadn't been fully pacified. She had no more control, no will of her own. If only once he had shown that the passion was a mutual affair, she could have accepted its animal nature, but all through the night he withheld himself from her on some level. His pleasure, he seemed to say as he brought her from one shuddering climax to the next, was of secondary importance. It was that essential coldness that made her feel humiliated and uncherished.

The next morning, she had hardly been able to look at him without feeling ashamed. It was not the homecoming she had imagined.

As she arranged the flowers for the table, she wondered if she had exaggerated the incredible tensions of that first night. Ever since, he had been the Brendan she seemed to have loved since time began. He lay in her arms and listened to her tell him about her time in Ireland (although for some reason she omitted the most important part), and seemed in all ways to have reverted once more to the man who was her soulmate.

The doctor had removed her IUD, and now, when they

made love, Carlotta was transported by the knowledge that they might, at any moment, be creating the child she so wanted. Delaney, too, seemed eager for her to get pregnant. But if that was the case, why was he drinking so much more than he used to?

A thorn from one of the hothouse roses nipped into her finger and Carlotta, frowning, sucked the blood away.

The analyst was a thin, neat, colorless woman named Dr. Bishop. Her first name, Rachel knew, was Dorothy, but Dr. Bishop did not encourage intimacy. She was the third doctor Rachel had consulted in her search for a sympathetic shrink. All of the doctors had been recommended by friends, and each was worse than the last. The first had been a fatherly fellow whose idea of analyzing Rachel was to repeat everything she said. *You wonder if you are a good mother, hmmm? So—you are concerned about your relationship with your husband?* It had been like sharing a room with a talking bird.

The second shrink had been, quite simply, crazy. He never said anything, and sometimes the minutes of the shortened hour ticked away in utter silence. She understood that this was his technique, but what made him unacceptable was his twitching. She hadn't discovered it right away, but she *had* heard the noise—a little dry, staccato, ticking that was always in the room, like a time bomb. When she noticed that it came from the doctor himself, was, in fact, the product of finger-nails snapping together in a manic, ceaseless twitching, she decided he was in worse shape than she.

Dr. Bishop leaned her long body toward Rachel and said, "I wonder if you'd care to explain that last remark more fully." Unlike the other two, Dr. Bishop liked to get in on the conversation. She called it "entering into meaningful and therapeutic dialogue."

"Oh, sure. When I said I was afraid I'd fallen in love with my husband, I meant it quite literally. We were so young when we got married, and we both came from the kind of family where a suitable marriage is kind of *required,* and we just kind of recognized that we were a good match. Oh, I pretended I was in love with him, even to myself, but I really wasn't."

"How can you be sure of that?"

"I was unfaithful to him, right from the start. I expected to be. It was my reward for marrying well and getting it out of the way. He was unfaithful to me, too, and I didn't mind much. We were just like kids who happened to be married and enjoyed sex together, and that was about it. Until Chloe."

"Is it she who made the change, then?"

"I suppose so. It's as if he grew up once he had a child. Cotter—that's his name—used to be kind of a jerk in some ways. He was always handsome, and he's rich, of course, and pretty decent, but in the past I always felt I could laugh at him. My trouble is, I've come to respect him, and it's driving me up the wall. *Respect Cotter?*"

"Most women would be very happy to have a husband they respected, Mrs. Vere. Let's try to find out why it alarms you, shall we?"

"I know why, Dr. Bishop. It's because *he* doesn't respect *me*. Well, how could he? That wasn't part of the deal. He's fond of me, and he adores Chloe, but that's all, I'm afraid."

"Perhaps you could make him learn to respect you?" Dr. Bishop inquired, smiling thinly.

"Well, I don't see how. There's nothing to respect about me. I'm not that kind of person."

"You are intelligent, Mrs. Vere. Would you deny that?"

Rachel was about to reply that intelligence was no virtue, since it was simply a matter of good genes, when she remembered the stupidity of her parents. She supposed she was pretty smart for a Windolm. Where had it come from?

"Look, Dr. Bishop—I'm not trying for anything lofty here. I'm just afraid that Cotter will fall in love with someone else. If I could buy a love potion I'd do it, but now that psychotherapy has replaced witchcraft—" She gave her most charming smile and let the sentence hang in midair.

"I would like you to make a list of your faults for me."

"Oh, that's easy. I'm selfish, lazy, spoiled—"

"Next time, Mrs. Vere. Our hour is up. I'd like you to make another list, this one of what you think are your virtues. Bring them with you for our next visit."

Rachel found herself back out on the street with a bewildering swiftness. It was humiliating, and made her feel like a student whose advisor has brushed her off. Nevertheless, she began compiling her list in her head as she walked toward Park Avenue. Her heels clicked determinedly as she reeled off her faults. Selfish, lazy, spoiled, click, click, click. Depraved? No. What did you call someone who was overly fond of sex, drugs, and wanton admiration? Self-indulgent, narcissistic. Clickety click. Jealous, petty, mean . . .

She was so absorbed she failed to nod to the doorman. The list interested her for reasons she could not yet fathom, and once inside her apartment she went straight to her yellow room and sat down with paper and a felt-tipped marker. The written words were more solemn and accusatory than the ones in her head, and she saw she had not been fair to herself. She had included "lazy" because it seemed to go with "spoiled and selfish," but in reality she was not lazy at all. She had abundant energy; how she expended it was another matter.

"Mommy?" Chloe stood at the door, looking as if she had lost her best friend. "Mrs. MacDougall has a headache and wants to take a nap."

"By all means. Does she need anything?"

Chloe shook her head. Rachel saw that she was feeling lonely, but reluctant to intrude. You had to be a diplomat to negotiate deals with Chloe; the child knew when a grown-up's head was elsewhere, and was almost morbidly afraid to call attention to herself on such occasions.

"Tell you what," said Rachel. "Why don't you come in here with me? I'm very busy right now, but if you bring paper and some crayons, you can draw while I work. That way we'll keep each other company."

Chloe's face brightened and she ran off to get her drawing materials. When she returned she was walking with an exaggerated, tiptoe movement to show she was not going to disturb her mother. She settled down on the floor and selected an orange crayon.

Rachel also crossed "jealous" from the list, and, on second thought, "mean." That left selfish, spoiled, petty, self-indulgent, and narcissistic. She added "deceitful," for she was an imaginative and resourceful liar. This business of list-making was harder than she could have dreamed, because when it came to making the list of her virtues, some of them would dovetail with the vices. Could you claim imagination and resourcefulness as virtues, if you only used them to embellish lies?

She looked down to see what Chloe was drawing and beheld a mass of orange in the upper reaches of the paper. Below it, stick figures with enormous heads were being laboriously sketched in. A day at the beach? She returned to the list of her good points and could only give herself high marks for physical courage and generosity. How could a selfish person also be generous?

"Chloe, darling, can you think if some nice things about me?"

"You always smell good," said Chloe without looking up.

Good hygiene? Was that a virtue? Rachel now saw that the rudimentary figures in the drawing were running. Chloe was working on the biggest of the enormous heads, giving it a sad, crying face. The lips were extravagantly turned down; huge tears rolled down its cheeks.

"Why is that man so sad?" she asked.

"It's not a man. It's me."

"Oh, Chloe, are you so sad?"

"In the picture I am."

"And why is that?"

Chloe pointed to the orange blob, as if it were too indelicate to mention. Like the artist responsible for a pornographic masterpiece, she averted her eyes and whispered something Rachel couldn't hear.

"What, lovey?" Rachel leaned down and stroked the flaxen head coaxingly. "What did you say?"

"They're so scared," Chloe said. "That's why I'm crying in the picture." She sidled up close to Rachel's knees and allowed herself to be hoisted into her mother's lap.

"But what is it that scares them?" Rachel inhaled her daughter's delicious fragrance and tightened her arms around the small body. "What's so scary, my pumpkin?"

"You know," said Chloe, again dropping her voice to a whisper. "The bomb."

Much later, after she had fed Chloe supper, bathed her, put her to bed with many reassurances about the bomb, and looked in on the suffering Mrs. MacDougall, she got it all straight. The nanny of a boy called Jason was obsessed by the bomb and sure the end of the world was at hand. It was not a healthy topic for three-year-old ears, and Mrs. MacDougall had severed her friendship with the nanny, but Chloe, bless her, never forgot anything.

When Cotter called to say that he would be late for the Nicolsons' party and she was to meet him there, Rachel tried to tell him about Chloe's fears, but he cut her off, sounding busy and pressed for time. "Later, dear," was what he said.

Rachel dressed for the party feeling thoroughly depressed.

Only her recent list-making kept her from indulging in a few lines of cocaine to revive her flagging spirits.

In the space of one afternoon, she had become the mother of a tiny child who worried about thermonuclear destruction, and the wife of a man who called her *dear*.

There was no doubt about it. Delaney was drinking in an insidious, peculiar sort of way that worried her more than if he had turned into a roaring drunk before her very eyes. Carlotta watched the levels of the Jameson's bottles, and was fascinated to see that they followed a sort of mathematical progression. In the first three months after her return from Ireland, Brendan had begun to drink approximately twice as much as he had before. It didn't seem to affect him much, and she told herself that a big man, such as her father had been, could drink large amounts without any bad results.

Now that she was definitely pregnant, the levels seemed to increase every day. When she missed her period, the bottle went from whole to half in one night, and a new one made its appearance on the bar only one day later. Once the doctor told her that she was indeed with child, giving a seal of official approval, the bottle greeted the morning light three-quarters empty.

She didn't know what to make of it. He seemed never to be without a drink in his hand, but since it didn't much alter his behavior, how could she complain? Above all things, she feared nagging at him. A dim memory haunted her, from a time when she could have been no more than six, of a conversation she had overheard. Her mother had implored her father not to have another drink. Had it been just before a dinner party in Washington, or Montana?

Please, Tom, not another. There'll be the wine at dinner.

Don't nag, Martha. It's not attractive. It's the worst thing a woman can do.

Except for her worries about Delaney, Carlotta felt wonderful. She had experienced no morning sickness, and the doctor had told her she was in perfect shape. She felt strong and glowing and wished that there was some outward sign of her condition so everyone would know. For now, she looked exactly as she had before.

She sat, dressed for the evening, watching Delaney knot his tie. He stood before the dressing table in their bedroom, confronting himself in the mirror. A glass of watered-down Irish was close at hand, as always these days. Was she imagining it, or was he having trouble with his tie? His sure fingers seemed to falter, and she heard him curse softly.

"Shall I tie it for you, darling?" The minute the words were out of her mouth she regretted them. She had not meant to sound patronizing, and the shrewd look he gave her was chilling. He finished knotting the tie with admirable dexterity, as if to prove that he was completely sober. He toasted her with the Jameson's, his smile ironic. "Here's to my beloved wife, who sees to all my needs."

She went to him, embracing him from behind and laying her cheek against his back. "Oh, Brendan, what is it? Please don't be unhappy. Are you angry with me?"

He turned and took her in his arms. Her dress was cut low in the back, and she felt his warm hands on her bare skin as he stroked her. "I love you, Carlotta. It's only because I love you so."

"I don't understand." She looked up at him pleadingly. "I'm so happy, and I need you to be happy, too."

"Of course," he said, kissing her gently. "Of course I am."

They dined at an inn near Greenwich with Delaney's son, who was passing through New England on his way to Baltimore. He was a man of thirty-five, tall like his father, and well-built, but there the resemblance stopped. Patrick Delaney had sandy hair and hazel eyes, and none of his father's sexual magnetism. Carlotta had never met him, and she had dreaded meeting him for reasons that were unclear to her, but the moment she was introduced to him, she relaxed.

Patrick was the soul of politeness, never showing in any way so much as a hint of surprise at his father's choice of a wife younger than himself. He talked mainly about his children, who were, after all, Delaney's grandchildren, and Brendan listened with a studiously interested expression. Carlotta guessed that he didn't much care about them, and to make up for his indifference she asked many questions about Patrick Jr.'s school and Delia's musical ability.

Father and son were mildly affectionate toward each other, but she sensed a small current of hostility flowing through Patrick. Perhaps he had never forgiven his father for leaving his mother. Patrick drank sparingly, while Brendan had two drinks before dinner, most of the wine that came with it, and now, as they sat over coffee, a large snifter of brandy. He was being amusing, as always, and his speech was only imperceptibly slurred. If you didn't know him well, he would have seemed perfectly sober.

Carlotta kept stifling little yawns. One of the few signs of her pregnancy was the tendency to get sleepy much earlier in the evening. It embarrassed her when Patrick caught her, but she didn't know what to say. Delaney had not brought the subject up, and she wasn't going to be the one to do it.

"Ah, my poor little Carlotta is sleepy," said Delaney tenderly. "You must forgive her, Pat. It's her *condition*, you see."

Patrick looked from Carlotta to his father in confusion. Delaney's shoulders were shaking with silent laughter.

"Aren't you well, Carlotta?" Patrick asked with concern.

"She's blooming, as you can see," said Delaney. "My wife is going to have a baby, Patrick. A proverbial bundle of joy."

Poor Patrick could not conceal his astonishment at first, but he struggled valiantly and congratulated them both. "Well, that's wonderful, Dad, I mean, that's terrific, Carlotta—"

Delaney's laughter, long held in, seemed to be getting the better of him. Ignoring Patrick's discomfort and Carlotta's burning face, he said, "Just think of it, Pat. This splendid, young, exquisite creature, this Carlotta of mine—going to all that trouble to give you a little half-brother or -sister. Now isn't that grand?"

The dining room had become very silent, and Carlotta wished she could simply vanish. Patrick covered her hand with his in a gesture of sympathy, then rose to go.

"Good night, son," Delaney said. "Give my best to your wife."

EIGHTEEN

THERE WAS A MIDDLE-AGED WOMAN ON THE CARIBBEAN IS-
land who troubled Carlotta. She thought the woman was in her
mid-forties, but she could have been much older. The women
who could afford to come to the island were skilled in putting
cosmetic surgery to their advantage, and certainly this particular woman was concerned with her image. By day, she wore a
series of chic maillot swimsuits that showed off her slim figure; by night she dripped jewels and slithered by in designer
gowns that made the most of her tanned, bare shoulders.

It was not the woman's narcissism that bothered Carlotta,
but her familiarity. She knew she had seen the woman, known
her quite well at one time, but she couldn't remember how or
where or when. Discreetly, she catalogued the artfully
streaked hair, the delicately aquiline nose, the startling eyes—
green as new grapes—in an effort to remember, but it was no
use. She traveled in a pack of similarly well-cared-for women
of all nationalities, and Carlotta could not imagine what they
were doing on a Caribbean island, seemingly alone and on the
prowl.

She was also not quite sure what *she* was doing here. Delaney had said it would be good for her to relax in the benevo-
lent sun of the West Indies while he indulged in some deep-sea
fishing. It would be her last chance he had told her, to experi-

ence the hedonistic life-style that would end, forever, once the baby was born. His enthusiasm—that almost boyish fervor that could not fail to convert one to his point of view—had won out.

So here she was, sitting with an untouched rum punch before her, wondering how she had been so duped. Didn't he understand that her whole life had been like this? She had seen enough sugary beaches and turquoise oceans to last several lifetimes. She had played and played and played some more, and none of it had satisfied her—why couldn't he understand? It might have been different if he had been with her, but Delaney disappeared for most of the day, abandoning her for his mysterious, masculine pursuits, and reappeared only at night, in time to take her to dinner.

At dinner, he drank too much and became sentimental, and when they retired to their private bungalow, beneath the tropical moon, he fumbled at her clothing, swearing undying love, and fell asleep.

In the mornings, he was always alert and himself. He was always the commanding, powerful Delaney she had married, but he was no longer hers. Morning after morning, she watched the bronzed thighs she loved disappear beneath white jeans. The chest which still bore the marks of her teeth was regularly covered, and Carlotta was left alone on the bed, wondering what had happened to her marriage.

On one such morning, she put on a bathing suit, slipped a beach dress over it, and wandered out of her little pink bungalow, through the lush jungle of the courtyard, and on to the wide terrace where drinks were served. There were clusters of little tables shaded by striped umbrellas, and she sat at one furthest away from the other guests. Far off, she could glimpse the blue-green Caribbean, but she had been told the beaches were not good for swimming, and all the hotels had gigantic pools. The air was so thick with the fragrance of frangipangi it was almost heady, but what was the good of beautiful surroundings if there was no one with whom to share them?

A waiter came and brought her a rum punch, although she had not ordered it. Perhaps he was as dazed as she. Surreptitiously, she placed one hand flat on her belly. It comforted her, although there was nothing to feel yet, and she smiled to herself. Soon, she would never be lonely again.

She heard a familiar cackle of voices behind her and knew the little band of seemingly predatory women had arrived for their morning drink. The one who troubled Carlotta was wearing green, to match her eyes, and her high-heeled sandals clattered against the tiles of the terrace as if she wanted to make sure everyone took note of her arrival. There were only three of them this morning—the woman in green and two raven-haired Latin Americans. They settled near Carlotta and called for drinks, twittering and laughing and admiring their freshly manicured fingernails.

"Good morning," called one of them, noticing Carlotta. "And where is your handsome father today?"

She felt a terrible confusion. Her handsome father was in his grave, and what business was it of theirs? Then she understood and forced a smile. "He is my husband," she said.

"Oh, my dear! What good fortune," said the woman in green. Her accent was French, and even her voice was disturbingly familiar. "But don't you think it's naughty of you, taking one intended for *us?*" All three of them laughed uproariously.

"Ah, but we are being rude," said one of the South American women. "Don't be offended, lovely girl—Danielle didn't mean it."

Danielle. The memory was floating quite close to the surface now. *Dani,* it had been. Danielle was staring frankly at her now as if she, too, was remembering.

"You look so familiar to me," said Danielle, tapping one long, blood-colored nail against her dazzling teeth. "Have we ever met, *chérie?*"

"I think we have, but long ago," said Carlotta. She felt trapped in a stifling dream. She was not at all sure she wished to have the mystery solved, but there was no way out but straight ahead.

"My name is Carlotta," she said.

The long nail froze in its tapping action, and the green eyes widened, then narrowed. She gave a little gasp of recognition and nodded. "Carlotta! Little Carlotta! No more than a child, you were. Eleven, was it? Oh, but I always said you would grow into a beauty, *chérie,* and you have proved me right. Such a tragedy about your dear father—I wept when I heard." She turned to her friends and explained that she had once been a good friend of the ravishing girl's father. Carlotta knew that if she had not been present the name of Tom Madigan would have been rolling around the terrace like a thunderbolt, and also the details of his death. Or perhaps they all knew.

"Yes," said Carlotta calmly, "I remember you. But where was it? Where did we meet?"

"In Sardinia."

There seemed something almost wicked in the innocent words, as if she had invoked a curse. "I take it," Carlotta said, not able to stop herself, "you were not also a friend of my mother?"

Danielle looked slightly wounded at such indelicacy, but she smiled sweetly. "No," she said. "I never met your mother."

Carlotta excused herself and went straight through the hotel to the place where the small fleet of island taxis congregated. She asked a driver to take her to the beach. If she couldn't swim, she could at least look at the sea. If she stared long enough, she might remember what had happened. In Sardinia.

"Aren't you happy here, Carlotta?" Delaney looked genuinely puzzled when Carlotta begged him to let her leave the island.

"I'm lonely," she said.

They were dining at a restaurant perched on the ledge of a steep cliff; it was necessary to walk down a stone staircase cut into the cliff's face to get there and Carlotta, looking down on the moonlit sea below, had felt momentarily dizzy during the descent. The seafood was fresh, and no doubt superbly cooked, but it was wasted on Carlotta.

"Lonely." Delaney put his wineglass down and studied her. He seemed quite sober and his voice was gentle and concerned. None of the irony that so often tinged his words lately was present. "I have been neglecting you," he said, taking her hand. "I'm truly sorry, darling. I'll make it up to you. I've almost completed my business here."

She stared at him, wondering how this man she had married could be such a complete stranger to her. What business could he possibly be conducting on a Caribbean island? For all she knew, he was fomenting a revolution—although this particular island didn't seem very revolutionary—because, she had to admit, he was probably capable of anything. He was a dark, mysterious man, a kind of emotional pirate. Why not a real one?

"I never dreamed you were lonely. I pictured you doing all sorts of things while I was gone."

Every instinct in her told her to shut up. He could always do it to her, confuse her with his mercurial moods, make her believe that it was she who was in the wrong. Just when she was sure that he preferred a bottle of Irish whiskey to her, he popped back resiliently and became her miraculous, dark knight. The man every other woman wanted. Even so, she had to speak up.

"What did you think I could be doing? Delaney, darling, there is nothing for a pregnant, married woman to *do* on this island if she's all alone."

He pushed his plate of crab away and lit a cigarette. "Well," he said uneasily, "there are all these girls your age here. I thought you might make friends with them. At the pool, maybe."

"Excuse me, love, but where are all these women my age?"

"There's one now," he said. "She's staying at our hotel."

Carlotta followed his glance and saw a girl of perhaps fifteen passing by. She was flushed and excited, and wore hibicus in her long brown hair. She sat down at a table with a couple who were clearly her parents.

"Brendan, she's a teenager. Can't you see? She's a child."

Delaney studied the girl covertly from under his black, girlish lashes. She happened to be laughing, and the candlelight revealed the braces on her teeth. He gave an odd little laugh himself and said, "Quite right. From my vantage point, ages become blurred." There was no self-pity in the remark, only a humorous admission of error.

Later, when they returned to the hotel, Danielle and her friends were dancing on the terrace with men Carlotta had never seen. "Who are those women?" she asked Delaney as they strolled through the jungle courtyard to their bungalow.

"Retired whores, I imagine, having a good time."

"Do whores ever retire?"

He laughed and patted her back as if she were too innocent to speak of such things. "Whores isn't the right word. They're playgirls, women who were courtesans when they were young. Some of them have married millionaires, and some have salted away enough to roam around the world until they die. They're a good-natured lot."

Inside the pink bungalow, he did something he had not done since the early days of their courtship. He brushed her hair with infinite care and patience and, when it was exactly to his liking, undressed her and slipped a short white nightgown over her head and placed her between the cool, starched sheets. He stayed beside her, stroking her and murmuring words of love, until she felt she was being hypnotized. She wanted him, and she wanted sleep, and she was afraid sleep would win and struggled against it.

She could dimly hear the music from the terrace. She fought to stay awake, but it was a losing battle. Delaney was a magician who could as easily deaden her senses as he could inflame them.

"Brendan," she heard her own voice whimper, "don't let me go to sleep."

But she was losing. Sleep was sucking her down. Her last thought, before she succumbed to oblivion, was that he would rather be with the gallant whores than with her.

In Sardinia.

Rachel had stopped seeing Dr. Bishop because she really couldn't see the point of it, but she had not stopped worrying. She worried, in addition to Cotter, about Chloe's overly sensitive nature, and when Carlotta returned from the West Indies, she began to worry over her, too.

They had arranged to meet at The Russian Tea Room for lunch, and when Rachel, already seated, saw Carlotta walking toward her, she knew something was wrong. All heads turned to watch Carlotta as she crossed the room, and all eyes reflected admiration, but Rachel saw beneath the radiant shell straight to the unhappiness beneath.

"Hi, Rachel," said Carlotta, smiling and trying to appear very upbeat. She seated herself and began immediately to fidget with a packet of Tea Room matches. She was tanned to a lovely light bronze, and the strapless sundress showed the satiny finished of her skin to wonderful advantage. Around her throat, a delicate gold chain punctuated with sapphires drew attention to the long, patrician neck.

"Nice necklace," observed Rachel.

Carlotta touched her throat briefly. "Yes," she said. "It's a gift from Delaney." She ordered a white wine and Perrier from the waiter and then, because she seemed to think Rachel expected it, launched into an account of what a great time she'd had in the Caribbean. While she talked, her fingers were mangling the matchbook.

Rachel waited until she had devoured most of her blinis with caviar and Carlotta had made a pretense of eating to say what she thought. "Excuse me, honey, but this is your old friend Rachel, right? You don't really think you can put one over on me, do you?"

"I don't know what you mean." Carlotta turned misty blue eyes on her.

"What's wrong? That's what I mean."

"Nothing's wrong, Rachel. What makes you think anything could be wrong?"

"That poor matchbook. You've murdered it."

Carlotta glanced down at the mutilated object and sighed. "I guess I'm just nervous. About the baby, maybe. You should know—don't pregnant women get nervous?"

"You're into your fourth month and you haven't gained a pound. You never have morning sickness, and you wanted the baby in the first place. What's to be nervous about?"

Carlotta shrugged, looking embarrassed.

"It's Delaney, isn't it? The honeymoon is over."

And then, bit by bit, it all came out. Rachel kept her face perfectly neutral as she heard of his on-again, off-again behavior, his protestations of love despite seeming indifference, and his new devotion to whiskey. What she had known would happen was beginning already. She felt vindicated, but took no pleasure in it.

"It's as if he's two people in one," Carlotta said, "like in those dreadful movies. I never know which one I'm going to meet up with. I knew he didn't want me to have a baby at first, but I thought . . ." The sentence trailed off.

"You thought you knew better, because all men want to have children with the woman they love."

Carlotta nodded. "Something like that," she confessed.

"You may be Delaney's wife," Rachel said steadily, "but you're also his little girl. Little girls aren't supposed to have babies."

"No, it's not like that," Carlotta protested.

"Isn't it? He dresses you up, and buys you treats, and all he asks is that you be a good girl. When you ran away from home, you were very bad. Now you've gone and gotten yourself pregnant. That's even worse."

Beneath her tan, Carlotta's face was flushing with indigna-tion. "That's disgusting, Rachel. Just because he's a bit older than I am—"

"Let's see," said Rachel, pretending to count back. "Why, Delaney is just about the senator's age, isn't he? Just about your father's age when he died."

Carlotta got up from the table and walked out of the Rus-sian Tea Room without a backward glance. Rachel ached for her, and hoped that she'd done the right thing. "Somebody had to tell her," she said out loud. She paid the check and wandered out to Fifty-seventh Street, feeling lousy. Every-where she looked, she saw couples strolling in the sunlight, arm in arm or hand in hand. Most of them looked very happy, and Rachel uncharitably hated them all.

She thought of herself and Cotter, of Carlotta and Delaney, and wondered if anyone was ever really happy at all.

Lee made Dominic take a firmer grip on her hand. There were such multitudes of people she felt a real fear that they might be separated. She, the great celebrity of Butte, Montana, had never been in New York before, and she found it both exhila-rating and terrifying.

"I want that," Dominic informed her, pointing to a big silver balloon. It was attached to the hand of a little girl, and Lee explained that he could not have that particular balloon, because it belonged to someone else. She saw the vendor standing near the monkey cages, and they struggled through the crowds toward him.

The Central Park zoo depressed her. For one thing, she hated to see animals caged. For another, animals caged in the middle of an urban park seemed disturbingly surrealistic. She bought a balloon for Dominic, explaining that it was filled with helium and would float away, and tied it around his wrist. They went to watch the seals cavorting in their pool, and Dominic was convulsed with laughter. Every time one of the seals barked, he giggled uncontrollably. He was such a happy child. She had been happy, too, but in a more serene and unexplosive way. She thought her son's jolly nature came from Victor.

"Domi, we have to go," she said when the carillon clock chimed two. "I have an appointment, but Kathy will play with you while I'm talking."

Kathy was a junior editor at the firm of her publishers, Cumberland & More. Cumberland & More was the reason for her being in New York, and she blessed them daily for being the kind of outfit that provided junior editors to play with little boys while their mothers were having an editing conference.

She and Dominic walked down Fifth Avenue, swinging hands. Sam Cumberland, son of the publisher and the organization's president and editor-in-chief, had taken a personal interest in her book. He was her own editor, and although she had been bristly about his criticisms of the first hundred pages, she had come to see that he was right. At his invitation, and with his money, she had come to New York to hammer out the problems. The main fault he found with her style was its lack of emotion. Her book, *Last Resort,* could not afford to sound like a legal brief. Neither could it read like *True Confessions.* Somewhere between the two extremes, they would find the proper tone.

"Are we going to Sam's?" Dominic asked. "Where is it? I'm lost."

"We turn here, and then it's only about five more blocks." Lee maneuvered him across the street at Fifty-seventh, and they headed west. Lee saw a woman come out of something called The Russian Tea Room and was moved to study her because of the look of determination, mixed with anxiety, which marked her lovely features. She was young and exquisitely pretty—a small woman with blonde hair and the kind of offhand, expensive clothing that proclaimed her to be very rich. She passed Lee, nearly brushing by her, and for some reason Lee was reminded of Carlotta.

The petite blonde was physically very different from Carlotta, but she thought they belonged to the same world. They were set apart by their money and privilege, or something indefinable. Lee suddenly felt shabby, definitely Montana, but a glance in the plate glass doors of Carnegie Hall reassured her. She could pass muster, even here in New York. She looked like a young executive, or perhaps a very exalted secretary, and that was enough for her. She had never set out to pass for a senator's daughter or an Eastern socialite. How could she?

"What are you laughing at, Mom?" Dominic had actually felt the silent laughter (a Cheyenne *socialite?*) pass from deep within her to their joined hands. They were very close. She told him she was still laughing at the seals.

Funny, though. On their first day in New York, she had tried to locate Carlotta. There were many Delaneys listed in the Manhattan phone book, but no Brendans. She had rung up a B. L. Delaney only to find herself talking to an obviously elderly woman named Bridget. Then she remembered that Carlotta lived in Connecticut, but it was impossible to track her down without knowing the name of the town. Finally, she told herself that people like Brendan and Carlotta Delaney would be unlisted in any case, and abandoned her attempts to reach her old friend.

Carlotta's brief messages to her over the years were just the result of *noblesse oblige,* and they would have nothing to say to each other. In fact, the very last person Carlotta would wish to talk to, given the senator's lurid demise, was a person signed to write a book like *Last Resort.*

NINETEEN

"I AM A TOLERANT MAN," DELANEY SAID WITH DECEPTIVE softness, entering the library as if he intended to murder her, "but Christ knows there are things that even *I* can not tolerate."

Carlotta, who had been sprawled on the huge couch reading, looked up in astonishment. She could not imagine what had happened. He continued to advance on her, hands on his hips, head lowered like a bull. She sat up and watched with awful fascination.

"One of the things I will not tolerate is having important telephone conversations interrupted on the whim of your moronic friend, Rachel. I was on the phone to bloody *Venezuela*" —he shouted the word and Carlotta fancied that the whole room shook—"when the operator interrupted with an emergency call! And what was the catastrophe, Carlotta? None other than that little twat's desire to speak to you." He was standing directly above her now, his powerful shoulders hunched in fury, his fists knotted.

Carlotta tried to speak calmly, but her voice emerged meek and small. "What did she want, Brendan? I hope nothing has happened to Chloe—"

"I do not give a flying fuck in the seventh circle of hell *what* she wanted," he shouted. "Her whim may have cost me half a million dollars, Carlotta. Tell her if she ever dares do

something like that again, I will personally break her neck."
He turned and wheeled out of the room, only to come back
immediately.

"What she wanted," he said in a calmer voice, "was to
know if you were all right. She seemed to find it a matter of
doubt. What have you been telling her? Does she imagine big,
bad Brendan mistreats his sweet little wife? Does she think I
beat you or something?" He stalked toward the couch again,
his soft voice more frightening than his shouting.

"Maybe I *should* mistreat you," he said, looming over her.
"Is that what you'd like, Carlotta?" He reached down and
hauled her off the couch, holding her so that she was sus-
pended three feet off the ground. He shook her until her head
snapped back and her hair was flying. "Do you want to play
rough? Is that it?"

She could not answer even if she had wanted to. The breath
had been forced from her and she could only gasp in horrified
protest. As suddenly as he had snatched her up, he let her drop
back onto the couch like an unwanted burden.

"What's the matter, Carlotta, little hothouse flower of
mine? Have you nothing to say to your brute of a husband?"
He was grinning hatefully, his hands fisted at his hips. "Or are
you waiting for me to leave the room so you can call your
little friend and give me a bad mark?"

She thought she would be able to speak now, but she did
not know what to say. He was like a dangerous animal poised
for attack. If she screamed that she hated him, which was
what she wanted to do, he might charge at her. That was how
she thought of him, yes, a maddened bull who might charge at
her at the slightest provocation. He wouldn't listen to reason
—there was no room for reason in him now—and she remained frozen and mute, calculating the danger.

"What is it, my love," he said in a soft, venomous voice.
"Cat got your tongue?"

She got to her feet, hoping he couldn't see how unsteady
she was. "You're not yourself, Brendan," she said. "I'm going
to go upstairs now. We'll talk later."

He smiled at this, as if she had said something endearing or
witty. She thought the smile seemed crazed. She looked
beyond him to the door of the library, and thought she would
have to travel fifteen paces to gain her freedom. Then there
was the obstacle of Delaney himself, the problem of getting

around him without showing her fear.

At the first step she took he said, "Is that how we resolve our little lovers' quarrels? By going to our room?" At the second he laughed softly, and she could feel the heat from his body so close to hers. She wanted to run for it and bolt herself in upstairs, but she walked on, head erect. Delaney was moving closer, his eyes dark with fury, dreadful in contrast with the fixed smile.

He was muttering now, his soft voice filling the library with incomprehensible words. Something about how she bolted at any sign of trouble, like a highstrung horse. She ran away from him, ran to Ireland, ran upstairs... always running.

She had nearly gained the door when she felt the charge. His hands bit into her shoulders and he whirled her around, shaking her again as if he meant to destroy her. She raised one hand and tried to strike at him, ward him off, but now he was dragging her back in the direction of the couch. Her heels bounced over the Oriental carpet and her flailing arms were useless. She had no chance against him; her feeble blows glanced off him like tiny hailstones pinging against the side of a glacier.

"I'd kill you if I could," she gasped. "I'd kill you."

He stopped immediately, holding her immobile in his grip. "What was that?" he demanded. "What was that, Carlotta?"

She repeated it, and he hurled her to the floor in a motion so swift and brutal she did not feel herself falling. One moment she had been his prisoner, the next she was sprawling on the floor, dazed and frightened in a new way. She felt a sharp pain in her knee, but it was not that pain that terrified her. She had felt a wrenching deep inside, a tearing, warning sensation in her belly, and for the first time since Delaney had begun his assault she remembered her baby.

"Don't," she cried out, curling herself into a ball, protecting what was most vulnerable. "Don't, Brendan."

Her voice emerged in a whimper and she detested it, but she wasn't pleading for herself. With one arm shielding her face, she looked up. She was lying between his feet. She could see his hands, curled into punishing fists, hovering in the air above her. For one cowardly moment she imagined what those fists could do. No one had ever struck her, but she knew one blow from him could shatter her jaw and leave her disfigured forever. If Delaney was going to beat her now, it was not her face that needed protecting, but her baby.

She resumed her fetal position, guarding the baby, and lay that way in the violent, appalling silence for what seemed a very long time. She could hear nothing but the beating of her heart. There was no ragged breathing from Delaney; it had cost him no great effort to drag her across the room and throw her to the floor.

At last she heard him leave the room, closing the door in a quiet, courteous fashion, and she was able to drag herself to the couch. There were no further protests from the baby, and she lay, gazing with loathing, at the spot where he had stood. She was afraid he might return, and the thought of seeing him again filled her with such hatred she writhed as if poisoned.

He was a madman. She had married a madman, and she would have to pay for it. What was required of her?

Across the room she saw the sharp, jade-handled letter opener beckoning to her. It was a pretty thing, meant chiefly for ornament, but it would do the trick. If he came raving back to the library, she would protect herself and her baby. Her hand ached to curve itself around the jade handle, and she could imagine the surprised look in his crazy blue eyes when she plunged the thing into his chest . . .

She was on her feet, crossing the room, when the enormity of what she was doing froze her where she stood. The hatred ebbed away, and she was shaken. She had never been a violent person, had she? What was happening to her?

Confused and wretched, she returned to the couch and lay down, shielding her stomach with her arms. She wondered if the murderous rage she had felt had communicated itself to her baby, and the thought made her feel ill. "Your father is a good man," she whispered. "Really he is, basically. It's only that he has a temper."

So, it seemed, did she. After a while she began to weep quietly into the cushions of the couch.

Delaney's hands were shaking so badly he might have had palsy. He felt sick with remorse and self-loathing, and too ashamed to go back and try to apologize. Except for those women who enjoyed a few brisk slaps during lovemaking, he had never hit a woman in his life, much less a pregnant one. He could no more beat Carlotta than he could cut his own throat, but she would never believe that now.

The timing of Rachel's call had, indeed, cost him dearly, but that was no excuse. He went back to the desk where he had been sitting and buried his face in his hands. He wanted a drink, but he denied himself. What was needed was not a blunting of his pain, but a sharpening, so he could try to make some sense of his behavior. Where had such fury come from? It was fury against Carlotta, not the silly Rachel creature, and it was merely the reverse side of his consuming love for her. It didn't make sense, not even to him, so how could he explain it to her?

Maybe it was harmful to love a woman so much. Carlotta was his obsession, and he was too old to have an obsession. His feelings were those of a teenage boy. It was grotesque. He felt that he would weep in another moment, and then his shame would be complete. He felt his heart jolt painfully and wondered if *that* would be in store for him soon. A heart attack. What fun for Carlotta—to administer to the needs of a baby and a sick old man.

He got to his feet and walked unsteadily back to the library. She was still in the same position, weeping into the cushions of his oversize couch, looking like a little girl lost at sea on a raft. All he needed to completely break his heart was the sight of her starting in fear at his entrance, and the way she struggled to get to her feet to run away from him.

He reached her before she could stand up and knelt down at the couch. His voice was cracked and shaken as he begged her to forgive him. He told her that he would die before he would harm her, that he would try to do better, be the man she had once loved, and that when their baby was born he would love it and be the best father the world had ever seen. He buried his face in her lap humbly, and after a while he felt her hands on his hair. She touched him tentatively at first, and then with love and forgiveness.

Finally he lay beside her on the couch, holding her in his arms until the world grew dark beyond the windows.

Maybe this was how marriage was supposed to be, Carlotta thought in the weeks that followed. Certainly, it would have been impossible to sustain the manic, unadulterated happiness of their earliest days together. Delaney had kept his promise, mainly, and she was reasonably happy on the whole. She still

loved him physically and felt, when they were with other people, the thrill of knowing she possessed such a man. He was
tender and attentive now, his lovemaking a shade milder only
on account of her pregnancy.

The mocking, ironic attitude he had adopted toward her
had disappeared along with the heavy drinking. Why, then,
did she feel uneasy? Even at her happiest, it nagged at her like
a persistent, low-grade fever. Most of the time she succeeded
in suppressing it, but she knew that something was wrong.

On a night when they were going to a party in New Canaan, though, she felt a particular sense of well being. For the
first time, in her bath, she had seen the definite swelling that
proclaimed her pregnancy. Her belly was slightly more
rounded and it delighted her. She showed it to Brendan, who
kissed it, getting his hair wet in the bathwater, and then they
wanted to make love, but they were late as it was. They
agreed to wait until after the party. She would be wanting him,
pleasantly, all evening long, and when they came back from
New Canaan, she would have him. She smiled, thinking of
how she made Delaney sound like dessert.

Standing at the windows in the drawing room, waiting for
him to come downstairs, she told herself for the hundredth
time that she was a lucky woman. Dressed in a beautiful Ve-
netian robe, standing in a beautiful house, she was awaiting
her beautiful husband, who would whisk her off to enjoy a
nice evening with other fortunate people. Best of all, there
was the new, round belly beneath the brocaded cloth.

It was still warm, but autumn was in the air. Her favorite
season. She had so much to look forward to, and so little to
complain about.

Delaney came downstairs tossing the keys of her little
white MG in his hand. He wanted to drive himself, he said,
and give Fred a rest. He enjoyed driving the MG, which he
had bought for Carlotta when she returned from Ireland. He
had been teaching her to drive before she got pregnant, and
she had her learner's permit, but she stubbornly refused to
continue the lessons once she was with child. It seemed a
foolhardy pursuit.

Before they left the house, she put her arms around him
and told him how happy and lucky she felt. And Brendan,
who never referred to God except to take His name in vain,
said something odd as he embraced her. "God bless you," he
said.

His little benediction stayed with her all through the pretty drive to New Canaan. She sat beside him, her hand on his thigh, in perfect peace.

The party was a large one, with an elaborate buffet dinner and live music. Because of the unusual warmth of the night, it spilled out onto the long lawn behind the house. The couple giving the party were friends of Delaney's, and Carlotta liked them, but there were dozens of younger people, too, among them an artist she had known in London. His name was Ian Wilson, and she naturally sought him out.

"Caroline!" he cried, "what a marvelous surprise!" He threw his arms around her enthusiastically and kissed her on both cheeks. She had forgotten the business of her name, but when she said she was Carlotta Delaney now, Ian said, "Of course, love—why not?" He introduced her to his friends, and soon she was in the center of a laughing group of bright, attractive people her own age. She wanted to introduce them to Brendan, but every time she searched the crowd for him he was not in sight, or deep in conversation with someone else.

She learned that Fiona had married a Harley Street doctor, very much displeasing Lord and Lady Kitson, who had set their sights on an aristocrat for their only daughter.

"And Malcolm?" Carlotta asked, remembering how badly she had treated him and feeling ashamed. "Did he and Belinda marry?"

"Finally," said Ian. "Years after they were supposed to, actually. He was suffering from unrequited love, you know. He never mentioned the girl's name, but Fiona told me who it was." He gave her an amused look. "It was that girl you used to know, Caroline Moore. She broke his heart."

"I'm sorry," said Carlotta. "Oh, I'm sorry now."

"Never mind, love. You were young and heartless then, and now you're young and in love. I assume you're in love with your husband. Where is he?"

Carlotta spotted Delaney in the act of replenishing his drink from a long table in the garden. She pointed him out to Ian, and one of the women said, "Oh, I say! He's like a film star!"

Delaney did, in fact, look amazingly handsome, but the look he sent her was the shrewd, sardonic one she hated. She called him to come over, and he sauntered down the lawn, toasting the group with a tumbler of Irish. Most of the guests were drinking chilled wine, passed out by white-coated servants, but the thoughtful host had provided every sort of alcoholic beverage anyone could possibly want.

Carlotta introduced him to Ian and the others, and he was formally polite. He automatically, from force of habit, dispensed some of his charm to the women present, but then he suddenly shrugged as if it wasn't worth his while, and wandered away again.

"I think your husband is jealous, Carlotta," Ian said. "He isn't going to throw a punch at me, is he?"

She laughed, although in fact she felt anxious and embarrassed, and excused herself. Delaney had gone back into the house and, when she found him, was locked in conversation with a handsome older woman. She joined them, but Delaney barely acknowledged her presence. She drifted back into the garden, but after that, all evening long, the anxiety remained with her. Once, wondering how her appetite could have vanished when she had been so ravenous before, she looked up from her plate, feeling his eyes on her. He was standing alone in the lighted dooorway, staring at her with hypnotic intensity. She put her untouched plate aside and stood up to go to him, but he drank off the rest of his glass and went to the table for more.

She joined him at the table, heart sinking at what she knew she had to say. "Please, Brendan," she whispered. "Please don't drink so much."

"My darling," said Delaney, filling his tumbler, "I was drinking long before you were born. I can handle myself."

"But you have to drive all the way back to Greenwich."

"I was also driving before you were born, Carlotta. Drinking and driving, driving and drinking." He laughed. "Go back and join your friends. I've never had an accident in my life." She turned back unhappily, and he caught her arm and murmured, "Just remember what it says on your ring, Carlotta. Don't ever forget it."

The rest of the evening passed in a kind of blur of misery. Twice she tried to get him to leave, and each time he announced that they would stay a bit longer. Finally, just before midnight, they thanked their host and hostess and walked to the white MG. He didn't lurch or stagger, but Carlotta knew he was profoundly drunk.

"Brendan," she said casually, knowing better than to plead, "why don't I drive us home?"

"With your little learner's permit?" he said. "Ah, Carlotta,

I told you I've never had an accident. You weren't much of a driver, truth to tell, and you haven't been behind the wheel for five monthes."

"I could manage, I know I could. There aren't many other cars on the road at this hour."

He sighed. "Will you get in the bloody car, or do I have to put you there myself?"

"I want to drive,' she said, her voice trembling. ''I insist."

"You insist!" He laughed softly. "You *insist*." He touched her face gently, lovingly. "Get in the car, darling. I really do know best."

She climbed into the car wearily, and Delaney got into the driver's seat. She still hoped he would see the impossibility of it and relent, but he pulled out onto the country lane and headed for the main highway with perfect control. He drove fast, as always, and the road near New Canaan was full of sharp turns, but he really did seem to know what he was doing. Carlotta marveled at how a man who had probably drunk half a bottle of Irish could be so steady, and wondered if she had been naive. "You see?" he said. "Nothing to fear, my love."

"I'm sorry, Brendan. People who don't drive have all these *fears*. I'm sorry I was so silly."

"I love you, silly Carlotta."

Ten minutes later, on the main highway, he swerved sharply to avoid some construction he had seen too late. The MG crossed over the line and he swerved back with too much force, lost control of the wheel, and rammed into a telephone post. It all happened so quickly she had no time to react, or even to cry out. She shrank instinctively away from the on-coming post and at the collision was thrown sideways against the window. There was a great white flash in her head, and then nothing.

Delaney escaped by some miracle without a scratch, but she was unconscious and couldn't know that. Nor could she ever know how, weeping, he loped along the highway seeking help. He was sure she was dead, and wished it had been himself.

Her first impression was of light and movement. Frenetic activity. Her head hurt badly, and someone was talking from miles away. She seemed to be moving, spinning, and then it was much easier to drop back into oblivion.

The second time she woke, she was in a cool, dim place and it seemed there was something terribly important she must do, but the effort was too great, and her task escaped her. At last—she had no way of knowing how much later—she awakened and understood that she was in a hospital. Her head ached dully, and she tried to put her hands up to touch it. One hand was attached to an arm which was itself attached to an IV pole, but the other encountered only her usual mass of hair. There was no bandage, no blood. Slowly, she began to try to remember what had happened, and then a nurse looked in and smiled to see her eyes open. She disappeared, and Carlotta tried to cry out for her to stay, but her voice emerged in a feeble croak.

Moments later, a tall young doctor with a brown beard entered the room. "Welcome back," he said, shining a little pen-shaped flashlight into her eyes.

"Hospital," said Carlotta in her croak. "How long have I been here?"

"For nearly three days now," the doctor said.

"What happened?"

"You were in an automobile accident, Mrs. Delaney. You've had a concussion, but we've X-rayed your skull, and there shouldn't be any lasting damage. Later, when you're feeling better, we'll do a few simple neurological tests to make sure, and then you'll be able to go home."

She nodded, and then, with a flash almost like the one that had exploded in her brain at the moment of impact, she remembered what it was that was so terribly important.

"My baby," she begged. "I'm pregnant, doctor. Is my baby all right?" Nothing would ever again be so important as his answer, but his evasive eyes told her the truth before he spoke.

"I'm sorry, Mrs. Delaney," the young Doctor said gently. "I'm afraid you've lost the baby."

"Oh, no." It was a wail of despair and disbelief. "Oh, no, no, no."

Sighing, the doctor gave her a shot and remained with her until it took effect. Once again she made the journey to oblivion, but this time it was a much briefer journey. The last thing she felt was the tears sliding down her cheeks.

* * *

She was clear-headed now, and numb. She remembered exactly what had happened down to the smallest detail. When the doctor came to her she asked him what had happened to her husband.

"Oh, he's fine, Mrs. Delaney," the doctor replied enthusiastically. "Not a scratch. He's been here the whole time, with you, and out in the hall. I imagine you want to see him now?"

Carlotta shook her head so vigorously the aching began again. "I don't want to see him," she said. "I never want to see him again. Not ever."

"Now, Mrs. Delaney," the doctor chided, "he's been terribly concerned about you. I know you're upset, but surely you'll see him? I don't think he's slept for seventy-two hours."

"If you let that man come in my room, I will rip the IV out of my arm and run out of this hospital, Doctor. I will scream and create such a scene you will wish you had never seen me. I mean it. Tell him. Tell him the only thing that matters to me is never laying eyes on him again."

The doctor rubbed his beard and looked worried. "I can tell him, Mrs. Delaney, but I don't think that will make him go away."

"What will?" She heard her voice rising dangerously. "What in the name of God will make that man go away?"

"Please don't excite yourself," he said. "It's not good for you."

"That's it," Carlotta said. "Tell him his very presence in this hospital is bad for me. Tell him I'll never recover as long as he's anywhere near me. Tell him anything, just please get rid of him, Doctor, *please!*"

"All right, Mrs. Delaney," the Doctor said dubiously. "I'll try."

He was halfway to the door when she realized what would make Delaney believe her. She called to him to wait, and when he came back to her bedside, she twisted off her wedding ring and gave it to him.

"Give this to my husband," she said. "That will convince him."

TWENTY

"La-la, why are you so sad?" Chloe climbed into bed with her, as she had been doing for some time now. Both of them woke up long before anyone else in the Vere establishment, and both because of anxiety. Carlotta considered her own anxiety justifiable, but that a child as young as Chloe should suffer from it seemed tragically unfair.

She moved aside to make room for Chloe, who snuggled up to her with something like content. "I'm getting better," she said, "don't you think?" Everyone had agreed that nothing approximating the truth must be told to Chloe. She was far too sensitive, and would worry about people having accidents in cars and ladies "losing" babies, and how did you *lose* them, anyway? All she knew was that Carlotta had been ill and was coming to live with them for a time until she could find her own apartment.

Carlotta put her arms around the little girl, thinking how heavenly it was to hold the warm, satiny body, how comforting to have her nostrils tickled by Chloe's fine, flaxen hair.

"I'll tell you," she said, "what's worrying me, Chloe. I have to get a job, and there's nothing much I can do."

Wide eyes regarded her with dismay. "Won't Brendan take care of you anymore?" she demanded.

This was problematical. Chloe knew about divorce, as did

any New York child old enough to think, but in her world, the divorced mothers assuredly did not have to go to work. "He would," she said. "But I won't let him. I'm a big girl now, and I have to take care of myself."

Chloe took up a strand of Carlotta's hair and wound it around her wrist. "Why don't you take him for every penny?" she asked. And then: "What does that mean?"

"It means that he is very rich, and I could get lots of money from him, but I don't intend to do that. I know your mother thinks I should—"

"That's where I heard it. She said it to Daddy."

"Well, many people would agree with her, but I'm the only one who has to make the decision, and I'm not going to do it. What I'm going to do is get a job."

"I know a job you could do," said Chloe. "You could be my nanny instead of Mrs. MacDougall. Then we could be together all the time."

Carlotta laughed and hugged her. "Then your mama would have to pay me, and you can't have friends *paying* each other. I'm your pal for free because I love you."

Chloe wriggled happily, and then, as sometimes happened, fell back asleep. Lying with the child in her arms, Carlotta wondered how many people thought her a fool for not taking money from Delaney. Certainly he had tried to be generous, offering, through his lawyer, an amount so staggering she would never have to worry for the rest of her life. She had never known just how rich he was, just as she had never known so much about him. She knew what people thought— that she hated him so much she couldn't bring herself to touch his money or accept anything from him. That Delaney himself was bound to think this pained her a little, but she could not afford to set him right.

She had never set eyes on him again, or returned to the house in Greenwich. When her possessions had been sent to her at the Veres' apartment, there had also been the key to a safety deposit vault containing her jewelry. She had gone directly to the bank and ordered that every piece of jewelry he had ever given her be returned to him. It was so important that no channel of communication be kept open between them. Even the tiniest laxity on her part could bring him into her life again, and that would be fatal. He was far too dangerous, and far too persuasive.

Even now she didn't truly hate him. The real reason she would take nothing from him was that she had already taken so much, not even questioning her right to do so. It was better like this—they were quits.

Chloe stirred in her arms and Carlotta felt a pang so sharp she bit her lip. If things had been different . . . If. Hers, they had told her, would have been a boy.

It was awkward living in Rachel's house, but until the check from her father's estate made its annual appearance, she really had no choice.

What made it awkward was that she knew Cotter was having an affair, and she wasn't sure if Rachel knew. He was especially loving and thoughtful toward his wife, as men often are when they are being unfaithful, and Rachel seemed to bloom under his affection. It wasn't like her to be so unaware; in the old days Rachel Vere would be the first to suspect Cotter's motives, but she had changed.

The way Carlotta knew about Cotter's affair was this: On a crisp day in late October, she had seen him kissing a young girl in a SoHo studio. What had made the whole thing so odd was that she had been in the studio opposite, lunching with her old friend Ian Wilson. On impulse, she had strolled to the window, just in time to see a young woman, her face in profile, lifting a glass of wine to an unseen guest. She was laughing and tossing her long, brown hair back in a spirited gesture, and then a man had come into view, taken the glass of wine from her hand, and kissed her. The man had been Cotter. There was no possibility that she had misinterpreted what she had seen—the kiss was passionate, and Cotter was dressed only in his jockey shorts.

She often thought about her brief glimpse into his secret life. She had ducked quickly out of sight, and Cotter had no idea that she had seen him, but the image haunted her. How incredible that she had been standing in Ian's loft window at precisely that moment! She began to have the odd feeling that at any moment, if she glanced up or around, she would see something she didn't want to see.

The girl had been very ordinary-looking, even plain, but Carlotta knew that he was in love with her. The way he had kissed her made that clear. Besides, if Cotter Vere came to SoHo to see her—Cotter, who knew only Wall Street and the east side of Manhattan—it *had* to be serious.

One evening when they were at dinner, she decided it was only fair to warn him. "I'll be going down to Spring Street quite a lot," she said, taking a sip and hoping Rachel didn't notice that Cotter had nearly dropped his fork.

"Where is that?" Rachel cocked her head to one side. To her, Spring Street was as far away as Hoboken.

Carlotta explained. "Ian Wilson is painting me, and his loft is there. It's really quite nice, and enormous."

Cotter's face was a bright, flaming red. Unlike his wife, he had never been good at deception. She felt sorry for him— Rachel, after all, had hardly been a blameless wife—but she also hated seeing her savvy friend duped.

"Ian Wilson is an abstract painter, isn't he?" Rachel asked. "You won't be at all recognizable, darling. Why bother?"

"He makes an exception for portraits. He only does one or two, at most a year, and they're quite realistic."

"Do you think he'd do me?" Rachel asked, her vanity stirred.

"No!" cried Cotter.

"No? What do you mean?"

"I only meant you have enough to do already without sitting for an artist," Cotter mumbled.

This, at any rate, was true enough. To everyone's mystification, Rachel had suddenly become public-spirited. She had got herself onto a hospital board, and was very active in Save the Whales. Quite recently, she had announced she was thinking of becoming involved with the rape crisis hotline. It wasn't fair, Carlotta thought. The old, wicked Rachel had been often rewarded, and the new, altruistic Rachel was being shafted.

Occasionally she appeared in Carlotta's bedroom dressed in one of her ultra-feminine nightgowns, and plopped down on the bed for a little chat. It reminded Carlotta of school days in Switzerland. On the night after the conversation about SoHo, she said:

"Do you think Cotter's having a serious affair?"

Carlotta continued to brush her hair without missing a stroke. "Why should I think so?" she asked languidly.

"He called me Vivian the other night, when he was half asleep. Of course I woke him up and told him what he'd said. I demanded to know who the hell Vivian was and he got all flustered and told some ridiculous story about dreaming a scene from *Gone with the Wind*. Vivien Leigh, right? Have you ever heard a more transparent lie?"

"It's not necessarily a lie, Rachel. Don't you remember that girl at school who used to dream about Paul Newman all the time? She would even murmur his name, 'Oh, *Pole, Pole,*' in her French accent. What was her name?"

"Anne-Marie Beauville, and don't try to distract me. Anne-Marie was a randy schoolgirl. Grown men do not dream of *Gone with the Wind* and murmur the name of Vivien Leigh."

Carlotta was silent.

"He only makes love to me once a week, as if it were his marital duty, just like old people. He's often dreamy and far-away, in a most annoying way. He's always leaving the house to take *walks,* for Christ's sake, and I'm sure that's when he calls her from pay phones. Add it all up, and don't forget the Vivian thing, and what do you have? An affair. Not just fucking someone, but an affair of the heart."

Carlotta said the usual things about affairs—if it was true—having a tendency to blow over if not too much was said about them, but Rachel could not be comforted by cliches. "Shit!" she said. "Shit, shit, shit!" Tears rolled down her cheeks and she pounded the pillows on Carlotta's bed with her fists. Carlotta was astounded. She had never thought that Rachel was so attached to Cotter. She found herself hugging Rachel just as, in the early mornings, she hugged her daughter.

The next day she set out to do a little sleuthing. Ian was painting her seated in a medieval carved chair. He had draped a Spanish shawl over her shoulders and asked her to place her hands formally on the dark arms of the chair. It was a comfortable enough position, and she enjoyed his silent companionship. Ian admired her, but without sentimentality, and they were simply friends. He had once told her that very beautiful women roused his artistic passion but left him cold sexually, and she felt safe.

"Ian? Is it all right if I talk?"

"Of course. Just don't move your hands, love."

"Are all the people down here artists? All your neighbors? That girl I sometimes see from your window, the brown-haired one, for example—is she a painter?"

"Oh, Vivian. She's an aspiring painter, but she really ought to pack it in." The subject of Vivian didn't seem to interest him much, and Carlotta searched for ways to draw him out.

"There was a time when *I* wanted to be an artist, believe it or not. When I realized I could never be first-rate, I gave the idea up, but it's still the only thing I know a lot about. This Vivian looks awfully young. Maybe she'll come to her senses, as I did."

"She's just out of art school," Ian said. "But she doesn't have your senses to come to, if you see what I mean. She's what you call *dippy* here in America, I believe. She's more in love with the idea of being a painter than the thing itself. Now, if you'll just sit still like a good girl, I promise you a break in twenty minutes. I have some lovely cold pasta for our lunch."

"Maybe this Vivian will meet a man and forget her artistic pretensions," said Carlotta desperately.

"Never fear. She has one already. She tells everyone who'll listen all about him. The gentleman, unfortunately, is married, but our Vivian never tires of telling people that she has a lover *in the social register*. That's the way she puts it, as if the poor bloke were squashed between the pages."

"I wonder how she ever met a man like that? It doesn't sound very likely."

"Oh, she'll tell you all about that, too. She was a waitress in a place he used to frequent. She thought he was just so *soulful*-looking, and he was always so kind and courteous. One day she handed him his check, and with it a little note that said: *Your eyes are beautiful and wounded. Can I help?* Now, don't laugh, Carlotta. Your thumb just moved. The left one. I won't tell you amusing stories if you wiggle your thumbs."

Carlotta was thinking of Cotter's eyes as beautiful and wounded, and imagining how such a description had worked on his imagination. "Does his wife know?" she asked.

"Oh, definitely negative," Ian said. "The wife is a society beauty who doesn't appreciate the gentleman. The wife is a great villainess, feckless and—in Vivian's words—*uncaring*. He journeys down in great secrecy to be cared for, and returns to his princely domain and unattainable wife, who thinks of nothing but herself."

When they broke for lunch, which was mercifully not in a corner of the loft that over looked Vivian's windows, Carlotta asked her final question for the day.

"Is he going to leave his wife for Vivian?"

"Shouldn't think so," said Ian, opening the wine. "It's a cruel old world, Carlotta. Unqualified admiration is a powerful aphrodisiac for a while, but it wears thin. We're poor creatures in a way, but we tend to seek our own level."

"Do we?"

"Well," said Ian, filling her glass and throwing her a strange look, "most of us do. You, my poor lamb, are an exception. You just don't fit, not yet. One day you will."

"I'll drink to that," said Carlotta.

Chloe was taking swimming lessons. A child had drowned on Long Island the summer before, and all the women who summered in the Hamptons had suddenly become aware of how important it was for their children to learn to swim.

Standing in her long white nightgown just before her bedtime, she told Rachel and Carlotta that she could swim quite well now, and would soon learn to dive. Hooking her thumbs together and dipping her head, she showed them the approved stance. The two women, who were dressed to go to the ballet, stood smiling in their fur coats and Chloe, who wanted to delay them, thought of yet another anecdote from swimming class.

"Sometimes, for a special treat, Mr. Tinsley jumps off the diving board with us."

"How do you mean, darling?" Rachel asked.

"He picks us up, like this—" Chloe pantomimed the act of holding a child to her chest—"and then he bounces on the board and jumps in the water still holding us. Only one at a time, though."

Carlotta felt a wave of nausea pass over her and put out her hand as if to deflect something hurtling toward her.

"It's my favorite thing," Chloe called back as Mrs. MacDougall led her off to bed.

"Are you all right, Carlotta? You're deathly pale," Rachel said.

Carlotta's eyes were closed, and she could feel her legs trembling. "I don't feel well suddenly," she whispered. "Maybe it's that new flu." She persuaded Rachel to go to the ballet without her and stumbled to her bedroom, still wearing her coat. She lay down in the darkened room and stared at the ceiling, her heart pounding unpleasantly. How horrid that it should have been innocent Chloe who made her remember what it was that had happened all those years ago in Sardinia.

She remembered everything with a merciless clarity. The sixty-foot yacht was called the *Sophia Maria,* and the man who owned it was Umberto, a friend of her father's. They sailed the *Sophia Maria* to Sicily and Corsica that summer, but on the day she was remembering, it was moored just off Cagliari, in Sardinia . . .

Carlotta is so happy she can barely contain herself. She is always happy when Daddy takes her off on one of "their" special holidays, but this one is the best of all. Not that she doesn't like to travel with her mother, too, but the times she and Daddy go alone seem the most adventurous.

It is a glorious day, and she is eleven years old and proud of herself, because she has learned to be an excellent sailor. She doesn't ever get seasick, not even during that rough weather in the Tyrhenian Sea, and she is sure her father is proud, too. Right now he is relaxing on the deck of the *Sophia Maria,* a drink in his hand, talking to Umberto.

There are lots of other people on board, too. There are several pretty ladies who have been traveling with them, but the prettiest is Danielle, who is called Dani. Dani wears the tiniest bikini Carlotta·has ever seen, and her whole body is caramel-colored from the sun. She is French, and has a funny accent. She calls everyone *chéri,* but once Carlotta has heard her call Daddy "Tommy:" Her accent makes it sound like *Tomee.*

Dani comes into sight now, carrying a tray with glasses and a bottle. Carlotta wishes she could look like that. Dani's scrap of a bikini makes Carlotta's own two-piece red swimsuit look dumb. But of course, she doesn't have bosoms like Dani's, which are so big and round they resemble melons. She doesn't have any bosom at all, as a matter of fact.

Carlotta decides to go for a swim, and as she is approaching the ladder, her father looks up and smiles. "That's the hard way," he says to her. "Just dive on in, honey." The distance suddenly seems very great, and Carlotta hangs back. Daddy laughs and comes over to her. Effortlessly, he picks her up in his arms and says, "All right, we'll go in together." She smells the martini on his breath. She feels no fear whatsoever there in his arms, and when he jumps off the boat, holding her, and they go hurtling down into the sea, it is the most exhilarating feeling in the world.

In fact, it's so much fun she pleads with her father to do it again. He is in a very good mood, and even though Dani protests—laughing and saying that Tomee is an overgrown boy who acts no older than his daughter—they go into the sea that way at least half a dozen times. Finally, Daddy tires of the game and has another drink. It has become sultrier, and the sun has gone behind a cloud. This, Dani remarks, is the time when people with sensitive skin are likely to get burned. She has poured out a little wine for Carlotta and Carlotta drinks it, not liking the taste but feeling very mature. Dani tosses her a tube of gel to block the sun, and tells her to rub it on her arms and legs and shoulders. She can't reach her back, of course, and her father tells her to lie down on her stomach and he'll do the bits she can't reach.

Carlotta is almost purring like a cat as Daddy's big hands rub the oil into her back, moving with a lazy but purposeful motion. It is so relaxing, after all that jumping and swimming and horsing around, Carlotta feels she could fall asleep. Her father's hands seem to be pressing her into the deck, and the *Sophia Maria* is rocking so gently and the wine has begun singing in her veins . . . Now she feels funny and itchy, with Daddy's hands on the backs of her legs, as if she wants him to stop and doesn't, both at the same time. There is a peculiar sensation in her stomach, as if she has to go to the bathroom, and being pressed down on the deck makes it worse. Or better. She wonders why she likes that feeling and shuts her eyes so no one can tell. They will think she's asleep.

But she has miscalculated. Daddy's hands stop their movement and leave her. Pretty soon she hears Dani giggling and protesting. "No, Tom, not here. Stop!" Her father murmurs that Carlotta is asleep and Umberto below deck, but still Dani giggles and objects.

Carlotta can't contain her curiosity any longer, and she squints between lowered lashes to see what is going on. There, not five feet away from her, her father is lying on the deck beside Dani. He is rubbing her, too, but in a different way. His hand is buried between her legs, wiggling away under the bottom part of her bikini, and Dani is beginning to squirm instead of giggle.

Carlotta shuts her eyes and makes a little noise, as if in her

sleep, and they go below deck. When she opens her eyes
again, there isn't a soul in sight. She is utterly alone, a speck
in the vast blue Mediterranean, and desperately ashamed. She
is ashamed, there in Sardinia, because she knows she is jealous of Dani. She also knows what it was she was feeling when
her father's hands were on her flesh.

It is all so momentous, and forbidden. She tells herself she
will really go to sleep now, and when she wakes up, she will
have forgotten. It never really happened . . .

Lying on the bed in the darkness, Carlotta thought of how
artfully she had managed to deceive herself, and for so many
years. How much she had known as a child, and how fiercely
she had forced that knowledge down; what a career she had
made of refusing to acknowledge the truth! Even when the
woman, Dani, had uttered those fatal words—*in Sardinia*—
staring at Carlotta with her knowing green eyes, even then she
had refused to remember.

Over fifteen years had passed from the day on the *Sophia
Maria* until the encounter in the West Indies, but that could
not account for it. Danielle had passed from her prime into an
expensively maintained illusion of preserved beauty and sexual allure, but no one, not even a child of eleven, could see
those eyes, hear that voice, and fail to remember. It was all
part of the elaborate bulwark of defenses she had constructed.
If she was a very, very good girl, if she believed that her
mother really preferred to stay at home on those special holidays, if she ignored the tension hovering in the air between
her father and the scores of pretty ladies they encountered on
those holidays—why, then, everything would be fine. They
would go on and on forever a happy, lucky, blessed family, a
little unit of three upon whom the gods had agreed to smile.
They had been a triangle, but not, Carlotta thought, an equi-
lateral triangle. She and her father had formed the longer
arms, leaving poor Martha a narrow wedge. Martha's base of
power had been very small, and Carlotta felt an aching pity
for the woman she had thought of, unconsciously, as her chief
rival.

She wished her mother were alive again so she could take
her hand and explain to Martha that they had both been dupes.
Carlotta had only *seemed* important, and in Sardinia she had
understood that her importance was as fragile as her mother's.

Chloe's innocence had forced her to remember, because

she had once been innocent, too. She thought her innocence had been tainted long before the incident on the *Sophia Maria*, but that day had been the beginning of her battle against the truth.

The worst part was that she could see her father so clearly, as he had been that day, and the face so close to hers when they jumped into the sea together was Delaney's.

She had fallen in love with the same man twice.

TWENTY-ONE

THE GALLERY HAD HAD A LONG AND COLORFUL HISTORY. IN the 1920s, it had been bought by a gangster as a gift for his mistress, who sold sentimental pictures of flappers cradling poodles in order to prove her respectability. After the war, when everything had been rearranged, it enjoyed three decades of real respectability as one of Manhattan's stuffiest and most society-minded "small" galleries. In the sixties, it had gone radical under the leadership of its new owners, who were rich hippies. The hippies had never understood that radical chic was destined to be a short-term phenomenon, especially on Madison Avenue, and that they could only sell so many paintings with names like "Eldridge Cleaver and LBJ in Harlem" or "Woman as Nigger" before the trend peaked. It had eventually become the headquarters for a group of Scandinavian furniture designers and, finally, at the end of the seventies, been reborn once again as a gallery.

It was now called The Global Village Gallery, in deference to the international flavor of its painters and patrons, and was acknowledged as the best of its kind outside of SoHo. It was owned in equal shares by three men, and managed by Carlotta Madigan.

Ian Wilson had helped to find the job for her, and Carlotta had suspected that she was a bit of a charity case at first, taken

in by the partners as a favor to Ian. Initially her duties had
been slight. Someone had to be in the gallery all day, and the
partners were frequently absent on other business. Carlotta
was decorative, elegant, poised, and—as they soon learned
—surprisingly knowledgeable about art. In the early days she
answered the phone, handled correspondence, catalogued
slides, greeted prospective customers, and helped plan the
parties for openings.

When she made her first sale, it was entirely by accident.
She was not supposed to make sales, since that was not part of
her duties and she was on a fixed salary, but it happened that a
customer came in when she was the only person on the premises. Simon, the English partner, was in Europe acquiring
canvasses. Piet, the South African in exile, was lunching, and
Bobby, who was a New Yorker, had been laid low by the flu.
She sold the man a glowing, small abstract painting—one of
Ian's—for five thousand dollars. She was extremely
apologetic about it when Piet returned from lunch, and Piet
was so amused that he insisted she take the commission. As
an afterthought, he ran out and bought her a spray of exquisite
camellias.

All in all, she had been happy enough in her early days at
the gallery. There were worse things than sitting in pleasant
rooms, surrounded by fine works of art. She could walk to the
gallery from her tiny two-room apartment on East Sixty-
fourth, and even though she had never had to get up at a fixed
time and report to work in her life, she adjusted to it well
enough. The partners were kind, and if the time sometimes
hung heavy, it was not their fault. What she could never have
dreamed, then, was how important the gallery would eventually become to her, and what an important part she would play
in its life.

Now, a year from the time she had first entered The Global
Village, she was mounting an important show, consulting with
artists, and occasionally traveling to other cities to report on
the work of promising newcomers. For the first time in her
life, she felt a sense of purpose, and her days at the gallery
filled her with quiet happiness.

Her personal life was another matter. The one-bedroom
apartment, which might have seemed perfectly adequate to
most young working women, seemed like a cell to Carlotta.
She had lived her life in large, baronial houses—her father's,

then Delaney's—and her quarters in Europe had been almost palatial compared to the tiny flat on Sixty-fourth. She had tried to make it as pretty as possible, but it remained what it was—the sleeping place of a lonely woman.

That she was lonely was not her fault. She kept as busy as possible, was always lunching with Ian or Rachel, and was invited to many parties. She seldom had to spend an evening home alone, but her loneliness was so extremely profound that parties and friendly company could never completely eradicate it.

She needed to be in love again, for she was a woman with a deep capacity for love, but no one came over the horizon who had the power to move her that deeply. She remembered how cruelly she had treated Malcolm Kitson and regretted it, and she remembered her playful, childlike nights with Antonio, and marveled at how much she had changed. She was no longer the same woman.

What she was, she thought ruefully, was a woman whose strong sexual appetite had been awakened, nurtured, and brought to an exquisite pitch—for what? She never missed Delaney himself, but she missed what he had made her feel. Frequently, she could bury her longings through her work, but when they became too strong, she sometimes acted unwisely.

No one who saw her, sitting at her rosewood desk at The Global Village on a snowy afternoon in late January, would imagine that she was secretly counting up the one-night stands she had had the past year. She looked so coolly elegant it was impossible to imagine her rolling around on the floor of a dirty loft, or being fucked standing up in a guest bathroom while a party roared beyond the locked door, but both had happened.

When Simon popped in to give her a message, he must have wondered why she was blushing. All he would have seen was a lovely young woman, her bright hair now cut so that it swung, bell-like, to her shoulders, wearing a high-necked silk blouse and a narrow skirt of nubby wool. She looked nearly angelic, if angels could be permitted to dress so well.

"Thanks, Simon," Carlotta said, trying to control her blush, which was impossible. He disappeared again, and she was left with the image of herself in the bathroom. She and the man had been eyeing one another all evening. He hadn't been particularly attractive to her, but he was obviously mad for her and she—face it—had been in heat. She had finally walked off, looking over her shoulder, and he had followed her.

There in the little guest bathroom, surrounded by the pretty guest towels and scented soaps, she had leaned against the wash bowl, her panties around her ankles, while the man unzipped and presented her with his all-too-ready magic wand. It had been difficult to maneuver in such a small space, and the marble, she recalled, had been cold against her buttocks, but somehow they had managed. He had pulled her up and onto him with rough hands, and after a few violent, grinding movements, it was all over. Not very satisfactory, really, but the measure of her need had been the fact that even such brief and brutal lovemaking as that had brought her pleasure. She had never seen him again, and didn't know his name.

He had been number three. Before him had come the young artist who had taken her on the floor of his loft because his sheets were dirty and paint-spattered, and before *him* there had been a handsome actor who had come into the gallery, bought nothing, and invited her to dinner. Then there were two encounters after the one with the man in the bathroom. That made five in all. It sounded terrible, but when you thought of it, it merely meant that she had had sex five times in one year, which was the most terrible thing of all.

She couldn't help the sordid little grapplings, because it had to be like that. If she had given herself to any of the many men who wanted to become a part of her life, things would have been much worse. She would be put in the position of having to deal with nice, lovesick men whose passions she could never return. She never wanted to hurt a man again as she had hurt Malcolm, and thought it much better to relieve herself with men who were all but faceless. Men who only wanted from her what she wanted from them, and would not turn up on her doorstep with roses and promises of undying love.

The most recent of her little adventures had been humiliating. In San Francisco, traveling on business for the gallery, there had been a man staying in the room next to hers at the St. Francis. They frequently passed one another in the halls of the hotel, and the man's admiration was obvious, although unvoiced. He wasn't very tall, and his clothes fit him badly. He was the sort of man who could pass unnoticed in any crowd, and normally Carlotta would never have given him a thought.

Nevertheless, when she found herself alone with him in the glass elevator, ascending in the glittering San Francisco night sky, she had felt breathless and unbearably aroused. He would be her salvation tonight; he had been placed in the room next to her in order to take her ache away.

"Hello, neighbor," was what he had said. "Beautiful ride."

She knew better than to speak, and simply loosened her coat so that he could feast his eyes on her breasts pressing against the cashmere of her dress, the nipples hardening beneath his excited gaze. No one else got on the elevator, and they rode to their mutual floor in a state of perfect lust.

When she walked before him down the hall, she felt his eyes devouring her, and she was already imagining the moment when his frantic hands would discover their secret—that she was more desperate than any woman he had ever met.

As it turned out, her desperation had frightened him. She could read it in his face, mingling with desire, when she began to undress the moment the door was closed. She stripped herself naked in record time, throwing her cashmere dress and underclothes to the four corners of the room, going to him and placing his hands on her throbbing breasts. How humiliating it had been, the way her urgency made him hesitate. He kept mumbling about how beautiful she was, and when his hands at last began to move over her rock-hard nipples and trail down over her belly, the sensation was so agonizing she fell on the bed, unable to stand.

By the time those reluctant fingers made their way between her legs she was shuddering uncontrollably and crying out, and at the first touch of his tongue she exploded. It had been the first of many orgasms. Once he was sufficiently aroused, he proved to be a good lover, and she couldn't stop coming. He tickled and lapped and rubbed and teased her to ecstatic climaxes, and then, when she thought she couldn't stand any more, he entered the burning core of her from behind, pumping into her with long, smooth strokes while his hands played over her breasts and convulsing belly until she screamed in delirious pleasure and collapsed.

If only he hadn't said what he had, before he got dressed and vanished to his own room. Standing over her, slipping on his badly tailored jacket, he had whispered, "I can't figure it out. A beautiful babe like you, so starved for sex she gets off with strangers? It doesn't make sense, honey, where've you been, anyway—in jail for five years?"

She had made no reply, and the next day she checked out of the hotel and flew back to New York.

That little encounter had been almost two months ago, and the ache was back. She tried never to involve herself with anyone who had anything to do with the gallery, but when the artist who was waiting to show her his slides walked into her office, she contemplated breaking her rule. He was very handsome.

He was also, she soon discovered, very gay.

Rachel, too, had been suffering for the past year. A part of her support system had slipped away when Carlotta had gone off to her own apartment. With Carlotta in the house, she had felt she had an ally. Now she was alone in a hostile camp. Mrs. MacDougall seemed to despise her, the cook thought her superfluous, and Cotter treated her like a family heirloom—something to be polished tenderly, at intervals, and placed on a shelf.

Only Chloe seemed to need her, but Chloe's needs were so peculiarly strange and intense that Rachel was not sure she knew how to meet them. If Chloe got wind of an earthquake in Turkey, for example, a calamity which had buried hundreds of men, women, and children beneath the cracked and suffocating earth, she was likely to sob and refuse her supper. If she happened to become acquainted with film clips depicting starving children in places like Bangladesh or Biafra or Ethiopia, she became distraught.

Rachel had banned any television news, telling Mrs. Mac-Dougall to watch the horrors of the world in strictest solitude. No acts of God—no earthquakes, volcanoes, hurricanes, tornadoes, monsoons, floods, tidal waves—were to collide with Chloe's wide eyes. In addition, Chloe was to be protected from any knowledge of the following things: nuclear testing, coal-mining disasters, drug addiction, crime, child abuse, random muggings, police brutality, rape, hijacking, revolution, torture, vivisection, famine, and genocide.

In short, Chloe was to be insulated from the broader world in which she lived, and gradually drawn into the world her parents so gracefully inhabited. For her own good, of course. The head teacher of the fashionable private kindergarten Chloe attended was forever summoning Rachel in for worried talks about Chloe's emotional fragility.

"I don't mean to worry you, Mrs. Vere, but I think that it might be helpful if Chloe were to receive professional care."

"You mean a *psychiatrist?* She's barely five years old!"

"Just my point, Mrs. Vere. She is the only five-year-old I have ever come across who cries because she is worried about the children in Cambodia."

"Maybe she's just more civilized than the rest of us."

"That's entirely possible, Mrs. Vere. But it's not appropriate to be so civilized at her age. I recommend therapy."

Rachel, who had a low opinion of shrinks, dutifully sent Chloe to the best child psychiatrist she could find. She took her to the doctor's office herself, and waited while Chloe and the shrink did whatever they did behind the closed door. It always broke her heart when the door opened and such a tiny person came out.

It seemed the one fine thing she had created was dangerously flawed. What good was Chloe's beauty and intelligence and sweet nature if she was unhappy? Rachel might have felt guilty, thinking that her own unhappiness and Cotter's had somehow infected Chloe, but the little girl's sensitivity had manifested itself long before the current crisis.

The name of the current crisis was Vivian, as she had suspected. Six months ago, Cotter had put down his nightcap and burst into tears. He had looked like a heartbroken little boy, standing in his bathrobe and pajamas, his nose red and eyes streaming. Cotter, however, was not crying for the children in Cambodia or the newsdealer with the humped back on Lexington; Cotter was crying because he loved a girl maned Vivian and couldn't bear to go on deceiving Rachel, whom he also loved.

"It's *killing* me," was what he said.

They had had approximately fifty conversations on the subject since then. Usually, Rachel was too proud to show much interest in her rival, and listened to Cotter's ravings with a superior little smile on her lips, but inwardly she felt sick. One night, when she was quite drunk after a charity ball, she had grilled him.

"Is she prettier than I am?"

"No, not nearly as pretty, Rachel. She's quite ordinary, actually."

"Is she better in bed?"

"No. She's not very, ah, innovative."

"She's younger, of course."

"Well, yes, but that doesn't mean anything to me. You look as young as she does."

"Well, what the hell is it about her, then?"

"She makes me feel important, Rachel."

"For Christ's sake, Cotter, you ought to be ashamed of yourself. Grown men shouldn't have to have their egos stroked."

"I am. Ashamed."

Ashamed or not, his affair with the hateful Vivian (whom Rachel pictured as a cartoonish bohemian with unshaved legs and hair that smelled of turpentine) limped on. Rachel gritted her teeth and acted civilized, which was what all the women's magazines said a wronged wife should do. She told no one, except for Carlotta, and when it turned out that Carlotta had known all along, she stopped speaking to her. After a week, though, she reflected that Carlotta had behaved exactly as *she* would have done if their positions had been reversed, and she went over to the gallery and cried on Carlotta's shoulder.

Just before Christmas, Vivian had taken to calling the apartment and hanging up if Rachel answered. It had been the proverbial straw, and Rachel had girded her loins for battle. She put on a teal blue Halston and spent an hour applying her makeup. She was ruthless about her face, regarding it as a blank canvas capable of transmitting a variety of messages. One was: *Age has no meaning when you're as impossibly pretty as I am.* The trouble with that one was that Rachel, carried away with the heady business of highlighting her clean-cut jaw and marvelous cheekbones, came off as a colorful death mask. She scrubbed that face away with mineral oil and embarked on another. This time she aimed for a youthful, bare effect; she would beat Vivian at her own game. She worked skillfully with silver eyeliner to achieve the desired look, but it was no good. Her eyes were too dramatic. Any attempt at innocence only made her resemble a high priestess from a horror movie.

She grimaced into her mirror, looking for lines around her eyes. There were none, but she fancied she could see the beginnings of two long troughs, leading from her nose and ending at her chin, which were the legacy of her mother. Shuddering, she smoothed Oil of Olay into the troubled area and began again.

It was no use trying to beat Vivian at her own game. Cotter, when first smitten by Rachel, had not been in love with a barefaced girl, nor even with a girl who skillfully applied foundation, blusher, and mascara in an effort to appear to be natural and untainted by artifice. He had fallen for a frankly seductive and well-turned-out woman, a creature whose glamour was her stock in trade.

Good then. It was business as usual. Humming cheerfully, Rachel stroked creams and powders over the pleasing contours of her face. She used a teal eyeshadow and rejected scarlet lipstick as too harsh and mature. Very uptown. One made these small decisions.

Her image in the mirror was gratifying, but something was missing. Some small, understated but overwhelming touch was needed. The cut of her dress was too perfect to ruin with a necklace or chains; Rachel instinctively understood such things and did not wish to appear vulgar or gaudy.

She pulled lightly at the tips of her hair, admiring the new, electrified-look do which was just becoming fashionable, and when the lobe of one small ear poked through the tawny mass she grinned and leaped up in triumph. Of course—earrings! And not any earrings, but the water sapphires surrounded by diamonds Cotter had given her on their tenth anniversary.

For a moment she was afraid the water sapphires might be over in Newport, but no, there they were, winking up at her when she opened the little safe concealed behind a wall of shoebags in her closet. She sped back to the dressing table and artfully arranged her new curls so that each ear was bared, and then she put the earrings on and studied the effect. Perfect! They provided that touch of wicked glamour she wanted to toss in Vivian's face. The lovely stones bracketed her made-up-to-seem-artless face, calling attention to its beauty.

She hoped the Rachel she saw in the mirror would be the Rachel Vivian would see—you couldn't always be sure of things like that. She knew she looked smashing, but there was always room for improvement. She atomized her face with Evian water to achieve that glowing, youthful look and made some minor adjustments to her hair.

When she was sure she was as gorgeous as she could possibly be, she slipped into her Blackglama and took a taxi down to Spring Street. Cotter had actually once had the nerve to suggest that Rachel might want to meet Vivian—now she was going to, but not on the terms he had imagined.

She rang a bell that summoned a creaking freight elevator in Vivian's building, and rode up to the fourth floor. She knew exactly where Vivian's loft would be, since Carlotta had told her it faced Ian Wilson's. The girl who answered the door was a few inches taller than Rachel, and she had abundant, long dark hair. Aside from the hair, Cotter's assessment had been correct. Vivian was ordinary-looking. She wore jeans and a navy blue sweater, and her expression on seeing Rachel at her door was one of polite surprise. "Can I help you?" she asked. At least Cotter hadn't shown her his wife's picture, and obviously she didn't read *W*.

"I'm looking for Vivian Hayes," Rachel said.

"That's me," said the girl.

"I am the wife of the man you've been fucking," said Rachel. "May I come in?"

Vivian's face became the shade of one of her paintings, which Rachel could see through the half-open door, but she beckoned to Rachel and opened the door wider. The loft was large and not very tidy. Rachel strolled about, looking at the girl's paintings without comment. She didn't think they were very good, and she was not amused to see an enormous portrait of Cotter in what was probably the place of honor. Vivian simply stood against one wall, taking her in. Rachel opened her coat to show her how nice she looked in her Halston; then she did a slow turn, like a high-fashion model, and smiled dazzlingly.

"I just thought you should know what I look like," she said sweetly. "You must see that you can't compete with *me*."

That was it. She had just walked back out, leaving Vivian gaping, and taken a taxi back uptown. She never knew if the girl had told Cotter or not, but several weeks later, on Christmas Eve, in fact, he announced glumly that he had ended his affair. The news should have cheered her, but he was so clearly broken-hearted, and so determined to show it, that there was very little cheer at the Veres' that Christmas.

Only Chloe, riding her new two-wheeler with training wheels, seemed happy. She rode through the dining room and down the halls, humming softly to herself, but Chloe's happiness could be so easily shattered that it was, at best, an illusion.

Tomorrow would be Valentine's Day, and Rachel wondered if Cotter would send her flowers. The little things she had once taken for granted meant so much to her now. He didn't seem to be pining for Vivian anymore, but he was still glum.

She thought she had won, but she wasn't sure.

TWENTY-TWO

LEE HADN'T RECEIVED ANY HATE MAIL FOR A LONG TIME. THE letters and calls had come after the trials and in the wake of the article in *People*. They had peaked at the time of Jane Kurtz's acquittal, when the hung jury had unpredictably gone back for one more try and emerged with a verdict of not guilty.

She wasn't on guard, as she would have been then, and opened the envelope with no misgivings.

Dear Miss Redwing,
    God will punish you for defending murder and en-curidging wicked women to kill their lawful husbands. You are a murdering halfbreed whore and if God doesnt punish you soon maybe I will.

She crumpled the letter in a reflexive motion of distaste, but then she smoothed it out again. It contained an actual threat, and although she had been threatened before, this particular letter disturbed her. She always threw her hate mail away, and now she wished she had saved it, because it seemed to her she had heard from this person before. There had been a letter referring to "lawful" husbands after the Kurtz verdict. She hadn't bothered to look at the postmark, but this one had been mailed from Utah.

It was written in big, childish capitals, but that meant nothing, because half of them were done that way. Some of the anonymous correspondents might have been semiliterate, but most of them were simply disguising their handwriting. The misspellings might be genuine, or they could be red herrings. If it was disturbing to think of a God-fearing farmer sitting down in his overalls to pen a venomous note, it was downright chilling to imagine a corporate executive doing the same thing. That was the trouble—you never knew who your enemies were. If it had been postmarked from Butte, she would have thought about going to the police, but Utah seemed a comfortable distance away.

It struck her as odd that he would call her a half-breed, and she puzzled over that for a while, but in the end she put the note away and mentioned it to no one.

Generally, this was a happy time in her life. She had finished her book, and it was going to be published in a month. She was proud of the book because, with the help of Sam Cumberland, she had written something she considered valuable. As far as she knew, she was the first person to get inside the minds and hearts of the women who married in good faith, discovered that they were expected to endure endless punishment, were torn between the residual love they still felt for their husbands and the hatred those husbands instilled in them, and finally rebelled. If her notoriety helped to sell the book, that was fine with her. She hoped that those who bought it for a cheap thrill would come away feeling pity, both for the hapless women and the tortured men.

She was going to New York in a month to publicize the book, and the idea of the TV cameras and bookstore autograph parties intimidated her. She was used to performing in public, but it was one thing to be the center of attention in a courtroom—her home ground—and quite another to duel with the media in front of all of America.

It didn't help to know that somewhere someone who planned on helping God punish her would be watching.

The Global Village was more like someone's house than a gallery, which was one of the things Carlotta loved about it.

There were deep armchairs scattered about the three main display rooms, and soft carpets. With the commission of the Ian Wilson she had sold, Carlotta decorated her own tiny office. She papered the walls in a shade of bottle green, and painted the woodwork shiny white. She bought a bronze pitcher which she kept filled with fresh flowers.

When she had first transformed her room, she had fetched the T'ang horse from its safe deposit vault and placed it on her desk.

Piet, the South African partner had stared at it in disbelief. "Jesus, Carlotta," he had murmured in his soft Afrikaaner burr, "where did you get this?"

When she told him it had belonged to her father, who had willed it to her, Piet said it was far too valuable to leave lying around. Reluctantly, she had returned it, since all three of the men insisted it was priceless—"Well, seven figures, anyway," was how Bobby put it—and ever since they had teased her about wanting to have a museum piece on her desk.

The partners were fun to be around, and in a sense Carlotta now thought of them as her family. Scrappy, shrewd Bobby was the brother closest to her in age, and sweet Piet was the protective, older brother. Simon was more like an elegant cousin, or a youngish uncle.

Together, they comprised a trio of concerned relations who seemed to want the best for her. The trouble was that they went about the "help Carlotta" venture in wildly differing ways. Bobby was a firm believer in physical activity. He regularly played squash, and three times a week he swam an impossible number of laps in the pool at his health club. Once, when Carlotta had spent the weekend at his summer place in Bridgehampton, Bobby had tried to persuade her to swim in the cold, unwelcoming ocean and jog along the beach with his athletic and cheery wife. Bobby thought she needed a *regimen*.

Piet, on the other hand, occasionally took her to the opera, or showed up with tickets to mournful plays about apartheid, seeking to raise her political consciousness and improve her mind. He was, Carlotta thought, like a gentle tutor. Piet undoubtedly had a life of his own, a secretive one, but he cared enough for her to take time out to make the effort to educate her.

Simon was much more conventional. He played the role of matchmaker, thinking that she needed to form an attachment. At several small and glittering parties in Simon's Greenwich Village flat she had met unsuitable partners: a member of the English aristocracy, who reminded her a bit of Malcolm Kitson but without his grace, and who was (although Simon didn't understand it) not basically interested in women; a polo player who stank of garlic; a deposed Baltic prince; and an opportunistic photographer from San Francisco who was making a name for himself. None of them pleased her. None of them would do, and she wished Simon would give up.

In spite of their failures at making her life more worthwhile, she loved them for trying. She could accept their favors and attentions without guilt, because she was indispensable to them at the gallery, a valued member of the quartet, and they wanted nothing of her but her capability and friendship. Once, when she had been down with a bad cold and couldn't come to work, they had taken turns visiting her every day, bringing flowers and hot liquids and gossip.

On her birthday this year, Bobby announced they were closing the gallery at noon in honor of the occasion. Laughing like children playing hooky, they piled into Simon's red Lancia and drove out to a restaurant on Long Island renowned for its Bretan cuisine.

"Thirty-one years old," Carlotta told them, her voice incredulous. It didn't seem possible to her that time could have passed so quickly.

"Poor old darling," said Simon, tasting the wine. "You could pass for nineteen."

"Well, twenty-two, let's say," said Bobby.

"You have decades more in which to be beautiful, a woman like you," said Piet, sounding mournful.

They toasted her and introduced her to the owner, a man from Brittany who insisted, in honor of her birthday, on gifting them with a very fine bottle of wine from his private cellar. She ate delicate veal and drank the wine and began to feel very happy to have such a loving family. It was a beautiful, fragrant day in May, and she had friends and her new family, a career and a place in the world. She had *possibilities*.

"By the way, Carlotta," Bobby said when they had nearly

finished the second bottle, "would you like to run down to Washington next week? There's a one-man show I'd like you to check out."

Washington. She put her glass down carefully, selecting the right words. "I will go anywhere in the world for the gallery," she said. "Anywhere but Washington."

Three pair of eyes regarded her with perplexity, but no one spoke. At last Piet made a polite little gesture that seemed to say he would like to know why she avoided Washington, but would not press her. She had always assumed, without dwelling on it, that Ian knew her background, either from Rachel or because he seemed to know everything, and that he had passed the information on to the partners.

"The lady doesn't like Washington," said Bobby. "Okay, Carlotta. It's not important."

Piet's sad exile's eyes were still questioning, and suddenly Carlotta found that she could speak of her father quite easily. It astounded her that what once could not have been dragged out of her by torture, she was now prepared to divulge to these three men, in a restaurant on the North Fork of Long Island.

"My father was murdered in Washington," she said evenly. "There are too many unpleasant reminders, and people gossip about me there."

Piet had not been in America at the time of her father's death, but both Simon and Bobby registered shock. "Your father was Senator Madigan?" Bobby asked.

Carlotta nodded, still speaking mainly to Piet. "My father was famous," she told him. "He was murdered by his mistress, whose very existence was a surprise to me. There was a long trial, and a lot of ugly publicity. So you see."

"Poor child," said Piet. "How very sorry I am."

Carlotta laughed, shocking them and surprising herself. It was a genuine laugh, and it had to be explained. "I'm laughing because I'm so surprised at myself! Except for a very kind woman in Italy, I've never told a soul. I knocked around Europe for three years using a pseudonym." She laughed again. "Caroline Moore, I was. Ian remembers, of course. Wasn't it just ridiculous of me to think I was so important?"

"I take it you still don't want to go to Washington?" Bobby suggested.

Carlotta grew pensive again. "Yes," she said, "I don't want to. I'm not completely cured, even now."

Piet picked up his glass. "To Carlotta's complete cure," he said softly.

Lonely without Dominic, and dreading the first of her interviews, Lee wandered down Madison Avenue looking in the shop windows. She was particularly entranced by some silver buckles in one elegant window and went in to ask the price. She came out repressing a laugh and continued to wander. Her book was not yet in the stores, but she had received her advance copies, and she was well pleased. The photograph on the dust jacket was one her father had taken just a year ago. It showed Lee and Domi standing at the edge of the ranchland in Bozeman, where her father now worked. Cumberland & More had wanted her to be photographed by someone apparently famous in New York, but she had insisted and Sam, who understood about such things, had backed her up. Her father had really been set up to see his name in print. *Author photo credit: Charles Redwing.*

She looked at some shoes in a fancy place with an Italian name. There were no prices listed, but she was sure you could feed a moderately small Third World nation for what they cost.

More appealing was the window of a gallery called The Global Village, which featured two paintings by an artist from the East Indies. They were primitive abstracts, and the wild use of color she found arresting and beautiful. She knew she was not going to buy any paintings, but something seemed to be propelling her inside. She resisted it, walking on, but then she sighed and retraced her steps, entering the gallery. If something was telling her to go in, it was best to obey her instinct.

"Good afternoon," said a fortyish man with an English accent.

"May I just walk around?" Lee asked. Something about New York always made her feel uncharacteristically timid, and the English accent increased her feeling.

"But of course," said the man. He had a nice smile.

She walked through into a comfortable room where more of the East Indian paintings had been hung. In an adjacent room, a man and a woman were mounting some pictures together, probably for a new exhibition. The woman's back was turned to Lee, but something in the bright auburn hair and the fluid grace of her familiar movements caught her attention. She wished the woman would turn around because, although the odds were a hundred to one that she wasn't Carlotta, Lee had to be sure. The man noticed her and called out, asking if he could help her. His companion turned, too, to see who he was talking to, and Lee found herself looking at Carlotta for the first time in fifteen years.

Carlotta stood perfectly still for a moment, her eyes wide with astonishment. "Lee?" she whispered. "Is it really you?"

They embraced as grown woman, something they had never done as children because there had been no need. Lee felt a sort of desperation in Carlotta's embrace, and she hugged her fiercely. Carlotta was crying now, her tears dripping down Lee's neck, and when the two men came over, looking worried, Carlotta rubbed her eyes and said, "This is my best friend, my sister, really."

Lee smiled. By calling her "sister," Carlotta had managed to whisk her from New York and place her squarely back on the Madigan ranch. More precisely, in the cottonwood break where, later, they had once experimented with marijuana. Instead of the expensive furniture polish and delicate scent of fresh flowers which permeated the gallery, Lee smelled the raw wet earth of a Montana spring. She saw again the bright blood oozing from the fleshy cushion of her thumb.

They had been very young, not yet nine, and the business of becoming blood sisters had seemed an occasion of high solemnity. Curiously, it was Lee's brother Ray who had set the process in motion. There had been a fight—Lee could no longer remember what it had been about—and she had kicked Ray as hard as she could, aiming to hurt, straight in his scrawny behind. Ray had not taken kindly to this humiliation, and Lee had found herself face down in the mud, her arms twisted behind her back.

Enter Carlotta, dressed for her trip back to Washington, coming down to say goodbye at the end of the Easter break. Although Lee had forgotten the source of the fight, she would always remember what Carlotta was wearing. She had looked up from the mud, her face streaked and contorted with rage, to behold an apparition from another world. Carlotta was clad in a gray suede coat with a collar of some dark, furry material. There were no buttons, zippers, or hooks and eyes to keep this garment secure around Carlotta's slight frame, and even in her pain and indignity Lee wondered how the black Chinese-ey brocade things worked.

"Frogs," Carlotta would tell her later. "They're called frogs. I don't know why."

But in that moment, it was not the frogs that made Carlotta's presence freeze for all eternity in Lee's memory; it was the look of absolute horror on her face—a terrified and uncomprehending silent scream—that made Lee go limp with surrender and call for quarter from her brother. Ray must have seen it, too, because he went slinking into the house without a backward glance.

"It's okay," Lee said, bounding to her feet and wiping at her mud-darkened face. "We were just having a fight."

"But he's your *brother!* How can you fight with your brother?"

"Happens all the time. It's natural. No big deal, Carlotta."

But Carlotta thought otherwise. Pale and impassioned, stammering a little, she told Lee that if *she* were lucky enough to have brothers and sisters she would never fight with them. They would all live together in perfect harmony, and settle their differences in civilized ways.

"You can say that because you don't have any," said Lee, stung by the criticism.

"And I never will, either. My mother told me I never will."

Her unexpected humility, together with the bleak tone of voice, had touched Lee. Carlotta, who had so much, had become underprivileged.

Among the cottonwoods, unseen by anyone, Lee had explained how they could become sisters. With a straight pin filched from her mother's sewing kit, Lee pierced her own thumb and that of her friend's. They rubbed their thumbs together and felt the precious commingling of the blood.

"Are we sisters now?" Carlotta asked.

"Absolutely."

"Forever?"

"Forever."

When Carlotta returned in the summer, she confided that the ritual hadn't worked. "You're not getting any lighter and I'm not getting any darker," she whispered urgently. "I thought we were mixing."

Lee didn't know if Carlotta's words were meant to be a joke or not. With her you couldn't tell.

"I didn't know Carlotta had a sister," said the younger of the two men hovering in the gallery.

"Oh, yes," said Lee. "We've been sisters for years now."

Carlotta gave a happy little sniffling laugh and nodded her head in mute agreement. At that moment she seemed very like the little girl who had invented elaborate excuses to explain away the mud on the hem of her gray suede coat.

Because she did not own a television, Carlotta went over to Rachel's to watch Lee do a live interview on a program called "Live with Lionel."

"This is definitely not stuff Chloe should hear," said Carlotta.

Rachel fetched a little portable set and plugged it in in her yellow room. "It really bowled you over, seeing her after all these years, didn't it?" Rachel said.

Carlotta confessed that it was true. She could not explain to Rachel, who had been her only close female friend since the age of sixteen, how powerful her feelings for Lee Redwing were. Lee had been the friend of her childhood, her heart's sister, and the sight of her, standing like some emissary from another, vanished, world in the Madison Avenue gallery, had been overwhelming.

"I remember how you used to talk about her at first in Switzerland. After the first year, when you went back home in the summer, you kind of lost track of her. In our second year at school you never mentioned her at all."

Carlotta tried to remember back, to figure out how it was she had not picked up the threads of their friendship on returning to the ranch. It had been a matter of coincidence that first summer, when she had already turned sixteen. Lee was over in White Sulphur Springs, where she had a job as a chambermaid in a hotel. When she returned for a visit, Carlotta had been whisked back East by her mother, and then sent back to Switzerland. The next summer, when she and Lee were both seventeen, Lee was in summer school at Berkeley, where she had a scholarship. Every time she tried to contact Lee, her mother would smile sadly and say things like: "You're grown up now, darling. Lee was a nice playmate for you when you were a child, but you wouldn't have much in common now."

She remembered going to the two-story frame house the

Redwings inhabited on her father's ranch and asking Lee's mother how Lee was doing in college in distant California. Mrs. Redwing had been kind, as always, but a distance had opened up between them. "She's just fine, Miss Carlotta. Her letters home are happy ones."

Miss Carlotta! This from a woman who had brewed her a special tea when she had her first menstrual cramps! Even little Dominic, who had been about eleven then, had seemed to be in awe of her, forgetting the many hours she and Lee had amused him in his infancy.

Only Mr. Redwing, Charlie, had seemed to appreciate how bereft and isolated Carlotta felt. He had followed her down the path from the house, looking sad. "Here's what you have to understand," Charlie Redwing had said. "You and Leana, you have different destinies. Don't feel bad about it."

The face of Lionel Beezely appeared on the screen and Rachel turned the volume up. "What's he like?" Carlotta asked. He had a broad, rather supercilious-looking face and, when he smiled, as he did when his signature tune faded, the smile looked deadly.

"Oh, he's a real bastard," said Rachel. "If he scents weakness, he goes right for the jugular."

"Oh, dear—and Lee was so nervous."

"I hope someone warned her about him."

Lionel Beezely held the name of Lee Redwing up tantalizingly, promising an interview with her later in the show. She was to be the star turn, and for the titillating privilege of seeing her, they would have to endure two extremely boring interviews first. Of course, he didn't say any of that, but it was obvious as he plunged into a chat with a grim-looking sociologist. The sociologist told everyone watching that the city's schools lacked "enrichment programs."

"Seems to me what they lack is a little law and order," said Lionel. "You hear all the time about teachers being *physically assaulted,* right in their classrooms . . ." The idea seemed to enrage him. The guest said that if there were more enrichment programs, the students wouldn't be so angry.

"No wonder I don't watch television," Carlotta said.

"I couldn't live without it," Rachel said in a small voice. "Not this stuff, though. Old movies. What I love is to sit in front of the TV at three in the morning, smoking grass and watching Barbara Stanwyck movies. I wonder what we'd be

like if we'd been born back then? Everything seems so much
simpler in those movies."

Carlotta looked at her with sympathy. If Rachel was
watching old movies in the middle of the night, it meant
things still weren't good with Cotter.

"When we return, we'll be talking to author-attorney Lee
Redwing about her sensational book, *Last Resort,*" promised
Lionel Beezely.

"Don't be taken in by that," Rachel warned. "There'll be
another boring one first. Lee's the carrot."

Carlotta pictured Lee waiting nervously in the Green
Room. She would have seen how the host had polished off the
sociologist on the monitors, and her anxiety would increase.

"Is she pretty?" Rachel asked as a designer of children's
playwear was introduced.

"*I* think she's beautiful."

"Then she might be in trouble. He likes pretty, vapid
women, but he gets threatened enormously if they're too attractive." Rachel frowned, touched her hair, which she had
lightened again and was wearing in ringlets, a style she had
assured Carlotta was about to become big. "Am I still beautiful, Carlotta?" she asked earnestly. "Tell me the truth, don't
lie to me. Am I?"

Carlotta nodded. "I swear," she said.

"Oh, fuck," said Rachel. "Sometimes I can't tell anymore.
It's that shit, Cotter. Going and falling in love with someone
else—it made me lose my confidence. I know I'd get it back
if I had an affair, but I'm trying to be good. I mean, I can't
reward Cotter for giving up she-whose-name-will-not-be-
spoken by running out and getting laid, can I?"

"Ian Wilson thinks you're one of the most beautiful women
he's ever met," Carlotta said. It wasn't true—what Ian had
said was that Rachel's prettiness verged on being spectacular
but missed the boat—but she knew it would make her happy.

"Did he?" Rachel brightened, and was about to investigate
the compliment more fully when the commercial faded out
and Lee Redwing was seen sitting in the studio, live with
Lionel, just as promised. "Oh," sighed Rachel, "cheekbones
to die for!"

Lionel introduced Lee, predictably using the words "controversial" and "sensational." The camera came in on a close-
up of Lee, who looked perfectly composed. They had put a lot

of makeup on her, but it was subtly done, and Lee looked exotic and very lovely. You had to know her as well as Carlotta did to notice the slight dilation of her nostrils, which signified that she was struggling to look calm.

"Oh, boy, he's going to hate her," said Rachel. "Intimidation City, darling."

"Miss Redwing," Lionel said with deceptively friendly tones, "there are those who would say you have written a how-to book here." The camera came in close on the book. "Of course, how-tos are very popular at the moment, but I don't think any of us realized that we'd be getting a book on how to kill your husband."

Lee smiled pleasantly. "I'm glad you didn't realize it, because then you won't be disappointed when you find out I haven't written it."

Lionel Beezely picked the book up and found the passage he'd had marked out for him. It concerned the Jane Kurtz case in Seattle, and he read with lip-smacking gusto of Mrs. Kurtz's private admission to Lee Redwing that her husband didn't deserve to live. Then he put the book back down with dramatic care and said, "Which of us has the moral right to decide who will live and who will die?"

"Only those of us who are being killed, Mr. Beezely. If a total stranger broke into a woman's house and attacked her with the intent to kill, nobody would blame her if she saved her life by taking his. The men who provoke these attacks become total strangers to their wives when they are violent, only twice as deadly because of the psychological factors I've discussed in the book."

"Go for him, sweetie!" yelled Rachel.

Lionel Beezely asked all of the questions that Lee had been asked so many times before, and she had her answers ready. She had told Carlotta that none of the interviewers were to touch on her earlier personal life, as an oblique way of reassuring Carlotta that her father would not be mentioned. Apparently her later personal life was fair game, because Beezely had the incredible bad taste to say: "Miss Redwing, you are raising a son alone. Could one venture to suggest that you, yourself, have been the victim of wife abuse?"

"One would be wrong," Lee said, giving him her biggest smile.

"Oh, she's too divine," said Rachel. "I want to go to her

pub party, Carlotta. Can you arrange it?"

"Shhhh, yes. I want to hear." Lee's eyes were sparkling dangerously. She recognized that look, and knew that Lee was so angered by smarmy Lionel Beezely she was no longer at all nervous. Whenever she tried to speak rationally, he cut her off and smiled his mirthless smile and said something dumb. Just before the end of the program he said, "We've been talking to Lee Redwing, who has come to New York from the wild West to preach her brand of frontier justice." Then he turned to Lee and shook his head and pursed his lips. "Sorry," he said, tapping the book's cover, "I still don't buy it."

"Of course you don't," said Lee. "You get a free review copy, just like all the other talk-show hosts."

Rachel screamed with delight.

Later, Lee told Carlotta that Lionel Beezely had called her a ball-buster and predicted that she would make many enemies.

TWENTY-THREE

CARLOTTA FIRST SAW SAM CUMBERLAND AT LEE'S PUBLICA-
tion party. Lee had mentioned Sam frequently, and she was
intrigued at Lee's descriptions of the man who had sought her
out to write the book, and then helped her through the difficult
parts as if he were an ordinary editor, rather than the president
of the company. Lee spoke so warmly of Sam that Carlotta
suspected she might have more than an author's relationship
with him, and that was what so fascinated her.

In their exhaustive talks since Lee had first turned up at the
gallery, Carlotta had discovered that her friend enjoyed discreet affairs and felt no need to find a soulmate and marry
him. Unlike Carlotta, who required consuming and overwhelming passion, Lee claimed to want only affection and
sexual release. Her real passion was her work and her son,
whose photograph she showed Carlotta with shy pride. Of
Dominic's father she spoke with the same warmth she might
have used to describe one of her brothers. Only Sam Cumberland seemed to command her respect and affection both.

Because of the seriousness of Lee's book, the party wasn't
held at Tavern on the Green or in some socialite's apartment
or townhouse. It was at Cumberland & More, on the top floor,
where they kept a suite for entertaining.

Carlotta was in high spirits as she stepped off the elevator and entered the crowded, smoky room. Ian Wilson was by her side, as so often these days, and she was wearing a slate-gray silky dress with little slits up the sides that made it seem Chinese. Neither Ian nor her dress caused the feeling of happiness; it was all to do with Lee's success, and Lee herself. She had been watching her for a week now slugging it out on TV and felt very proud of her old friend.

"I've always wanted to meet a red Indian," said Ian. "There she is, isn't that your friend? Of course, it must be. Hair like the proverbial crow's wing, blue-black. I wouldn't mind painting her, actually."

Carlotta was looking at the man standing with Lee, because she was convinced he must be Sam Cumberland. He was tall and slender, and he had wonderfully floppy, pale hair. It was neither blond nor brown, but something in between. She decided it was the exact shade of the lighter streaks in oak wood.

"Isn't this like an art opening?" Ian was saying. "Instead of canvasses, there are stacks of books, and everyone is pretending to be interested in them, but really they're all checking out the crowd." He pointed out a famous literary agent, who was scanning the room with cold eyes even as he carried on a conversation with a woman so swathed in gold chains she might have been a walking advertisement for precious metals.

Carlotta, who had done battle with Bobby, Simon, and Piet to upgrade the quality of wine they served at openings, took a glass from a passing tray, sipped, and approved. She was still watching the man she believed to be Sam Cumberland, and as she watched he bent, placed his hand on Lee's back, and whispered something to her. Lee nodded and moved away in the direction of a group of people who were dipping crudités hungrily, as if they hadn't eaten for years. The man watched Lee's progress with a look of pride, then turned away and meandered down the room, greeting people with a lazy good cheer, as if he had done it a hundred times before.

Which, if he were Sam Cumberland, he had. His manner to most of the guests was courteous and offhand, in contrast to the intense intimacy he had displayed with Lee. *You're the window dressing essential to this business,* he might have been saying, *but she's the blood and bone of it. That's what I care about.*

Rachel made a triumphant entrance, dressed all in white, and when Carlotta introduced her to Lee, Rachel said,

"Sweetie, you were *fabulous* on the Beezely show. You got him by the short and curlies and *twisted*."

Cotter said, "How do you do. So nice to see you."

It was relatively late in the evening when Lee dragged Carlotta across the room, saying that she must meet her wonderful Sam, and Carlotta was presented to the man with the oak-colored hair.

"Carlotta, meet Sam," was what Lee Redwing said, flushed with her victory. "This is my sister Carlotta."

Sam Cumberland had gray eyes, she saw, and a warm, mobile mouth. He reminded her of a painting she had once seen in Florence—a painting of a young, northern Italian nobleman. She thought he was in his late thirties. He took her hand, holding it with none of the over-intimate pressure many men exerted on first meeting her, and smiled. She introduced him to Ian, and Sam Cumberland seemed to make a connection.

"Of course," he said to Carlotta. "Now I know where I've seen you before. Some time ago, Mr. Wilson had a show, and a portrait of you was included. It was not for sale, as I recall."

"That's right," said Ian. "I got too fond of it."

"With good reason, Mr. Wilson." His eyes lingered on Carlotta for a moment, and then they returned to Lee again, leaving her feeling oddly bereft. They all discussed Lee's victories on the television interview circuit, laughing especially over the Live with Lionel show, but Carlotta found herself feeling shy and peculiarly awkward. She thought inanely that Sam Cumberland's eyes matched the color of her dress, and that he must imagine that she and Ian were lovers.

The real reason for not putting her portrait up for sale was not as Ian had said. It had been photographed and included in an article about Ian in the New York *Times* magazine, and the very next day a man named James Hanigan had called and offered Ian a very large sum for the portrait. Hanigan was Delaney's lawyer, and it had made Carlotta's flesh crawl to think of Delaney owning that image of her. It would be a primitive form of repossessing her, and she had begged Ian not to sell it to him.

"You're lucky I'm rich," Ian had said, laughing. "That would be a hell of a thing to do to a starving artist."

And so Carlotta's portrait had hung at the exhibition with a little *not for sale* sticker, and Sam Cumberland had seen it, and undoubtedly thought that Ian would not part with it for sentimental reasons. But what did it matter? Cumberland was Lee's man, and it was of no consequence what he did, or didn't, think about Lee's friend.

A small group of them were going out for dinner at Le Cirque, and Cumberland invited Carlotta and Ian to join them. For Lee's sake she accepted, and when the pub party was over and they had all regrouped at the restaurant, she recovered some of her poise. They were all toasting Lee: first Sam, then several other editors. They predicted that her book would be a great success and said they were proud to have worked with her. Lee's black eyes glowed, but she pretended to be embarrassed by so much attention.

"I would like to make a toast," Carlotta said. "May the power granted to Lee by Maheo on Bear Butte give her strength and protect her for always."

Lee's eyes became very gentle, and she drank and the others followed suit.

"Translation, please," said Ian.

"Bear Butte is a monolith in Montana, sacred to the Cheyenne people," Lee told the table. "It is one of the few places a woman can go to get power. You must bring an offering of tobacco. My father drove halfway across the state to take us there once."

"You and Carlotta both?" Sam Cumberland asked.

"Yes."

"And did you find power, too?" he asked Carlotta, smiling softly.

"Lee's father told me I did, but I think he was just being kind," Carlotta replied, trying not to look into his gray eyes. She thought there had been something mocking in his question.

Cumberland & More had been run by three generations of Cumberlands. Under Sam's father it had gone very commercial for a time. Bennett Cumberland was a man of erratic character, and he had made many bad choices. By the time his son, who had been a journalist and war correspondent, took the company over, it was a legendary shambles. The trouble was that Bennett had been neither one thing nor another, and no one knew in what light Cumberland & More could be regarded. In spite of some of the huge commercial successes they had managed, Bennett—who involved himself intimately with decisions—managed to acquire a great deal of dead wood that never went anywhere and was, furthermore, of no literary merit. When he retired and his son Sam took over, Sam was only thirty. It took Sam three years to turn the place around and get it running smoothly. By the time he was thirty-eight, Cumberland & More was one of the most highly regarded publishing houses in New York.

Like his father before him, Sam involved himself on every level, but unlike Bennett, he had unerring taste and a good eye. He was completely fearless, trusting himself, and could lavish time and money on a book no one else would gamble on and come up a winner. If Sam bought a novel, it almost always became what people in the trade called a "crossover" —a novel that would both win literary prizes and find its way onto the best-seller list.

As a correspondent in Vietnam he had traveled with the Marines into the combat zone, and he was not about to be frightened by the risk-taking required of him in publishing. There was something determined and daring about him, beneath the easygoing surface, and it was precisely that quality which had ruined his marriage. His wife, a lovely and docile woman named Helen, had been frightened by that quality. Often, during the years of their marriage, Helen had accused him of not caring for her. What she said was, "Sam, why aren't I enough for you?" What she meant was, "Sam, why don't you play it straight? Life is supposed to be easy for people like us. Why do you complicate things by taking it so seriously? If you cared for me, the world wouldn't matter."

He had been divorced for five years now. Helen was remarried, to an orthopedic surgeon, and had children of her own. She sent him a Christmas card every year, and each time he looked at her smiling, placid face, and the faces of the surgeon and the two babies, he laughed softly, wishing her well, and thanked whatever powers that be that he was no longer responsible for Helen's happiness.

He loved women, and indulged his love for them frequently. The bodies of women seemed to him to be connected to their minds. A smart woman, for him, was generally, though not always, desirable as well. He thought Lee Redwing very desirable, but he did not like to mix business with pleasure. He was entirely content to be her friend and mentor, and on the night of her pub party he had acted as her escort because she knew no one in New York, aside from Carlotta.

He had heard about Carlotta. In the time that he had known Lee, she had told him about her childhood on the senator's ranch and about the senator's daughter, who had been her friend. Lee said Carlotta had been married, unhappily, and was now divorced. She seemed, quite clearly, to be the mistress of the talented painter Ian Wilson. Ironically, Sam had wanted to buy the painting, which had simply been called "Carlotta, Seated," without making any connection between the hauntingly beautiful face on the canvas and his author's childhood friend.

Carlotta in the flesh had been ten times lovelier, so lovely it hurt him to look at her, and still he had not made the connection until Lee introduced her. All evening long, at the pub party and in the restaurant, he had been so intensely aware of her that he could barely function normally.

When Lee asked him if Carlotta could be included in the guest list of a small dinner he was giving for her, he agreed with extreme, secret reluctance. He really did not want to see her again. How wrong she had been when she said she hadn't received power. The attraction he felt for her was so powerful that, if she belonged to another man, he preferred never to set eyes on her.

"Sam?" Lee had sounded incredulous. "Of course he's not my boyfriend, Carlotta. I don't think he's ever given me a thought that way. I adore him, and we're very good friends, but that's all."

That was what Lee said when she telephoned to invite Carlotta to the party. "This will be a small dinner, his real friends. The other was for people important in publishing." Carlotta was not, in fact, listening. At the news that Sam Cumberland was not her friend's lover she had felt a relief so exquisite it made her unsteady. She was in her office at the gallery, and she gripped the edge of her desk and felt herself smiling foolishly at the lilacs in her bronze pitcher.

"Carlotta? Are you there? I have to go sign books at a store on Fifth Avenue. See you later."

Now there would be the problem of how she would live through the next three days, until the time when she would see him again. She sat through a conference with an artist who was having a show at The Global in June without hearing much of what he said, and later she misplaced his slides.

Late in the afternoon, she told Piet she didn't think she was of much use to anyone on this particular day, and left the gallery, walking west to Fifth Avenue. She peered into Rizzoli's, but Lee wasn't there, and she continued downtown to Doubleday, determined to find her. Indeed, the entire window of the Doubleday bookstore was full of copies of *Last Resort*, and Lee was seated behind a table, dutifully signing copies of her book. Carlotta already had hers, but she took another and joined the long line. She noticed an armed policeman nearby, thinking it odd.

Lee laughed aloud when she saw Carlotta in the line, and when it was Carlotta's turn she said she'd be free in an hour, and why didn't they meet at the Plaza? It wasn't until she had wandered into the park to kill time that the significance of the policeman came clear to her. She had been so preoccupied with thoughts of Sam Cumberland she had forgotten about the threatening letters Lee said she sometimes received. The cop was there to make sure some crackpot didn't try to kill her.

She walked on in the sunlight, but some of the day's warmth had disappeared with the thought of any harm coming to Lee.

Sam's apartment was in a big building on Central Park West. Carlotta rode up in the elevator, a lovely old elevator with an interior of carved dark wood, the kind you hardly ever saw now, feeling something she could only name if she put quotes around it, because it was such a cliche: "Breathless with anticipation."

She, who never agonized over what to wear, had tried on and discarded so many dresses that her tiny bedroom looked like a whirlwind had hit it. Ultimately, she had settled on a plain black dress made of linen, which was so simple as to seem severe. It was without sleeves, but otherwise she was well covered, since it was high at back and throat. For some reason, she had worn no jewelry, and as the elevator sighed its way up to the twelfth floor, she began to fear that she looked very plain, or worse, in mourning.

There were about a dozen people assembled when she arrived, and Lee, looking fierce and splendid in a gown of bright scarlet, introduced them to her. Her host was not in sight.

She heard a swell in the conversation level and turned

to see a tiny little man approaching. He was dressed in an oatmeal-colored cloak and was protesting, in a soft, baby voice, that he had to run. He had only come by for a drink, he was expected elsewhere. "That's Truman Capote," Lee's voice said in her ear.

Carlotta felt the little jolt of recognition that was so rare for her. She was used to seeing famous people and had been all her life, but Mr. Capote was something special. Statesmen and movie stars were familiar ground to her, but she had never met a famous writer whose work had influenced her. She had read *Breakfast at Tiffany's* and seen the film, and she wished she had the courage to tell this puckish and notorious man how much she liked Holly Golightly. How much she wished she, Carlotta, could have been more like her.

She was too shy, and she imagined that writers grew bored with such accolades. He took Lee's hand and wished her well. Before he swept out, like the Little King of cartoon fame so long ago, he caught Carlotta's eye and did something unexpected. He winked at her. It was almost imperceptible, but she saw it.

Before she had a chance to reflect on the meaning of Mr. Capote's wink, she was caught up in the conversational tide of the party. She found herself talking to a very well-known novelist who insisted that she, a newcomer to the place, step out on the terrace with him and experience the setting of the sun over Central Park. She saw that there were other people beyond the tall windows, sipping drinks and talking happily, leaning on the railings of the terrace like passengers on a trans-Atlantic sailing, and followed him.

The sky was spectacular—a flaming sheet of crimson stippled with deep cerise—and she admired it dutifully, aware that Sam was somewhere to her left, down the long, curving terrace.

"It's probably a pretty evil sunset, to be that gorgeous," the novelist said. "All the chemicals in the atmosphere change the colors, I think. We've entered the age of the Toxic Sunset."

"I prefer to think it's being done by Gauguin," said Carlotta, at last turning to see Sam more clearly. He was leaning against the balcony, his back to the sunset and panoramic view of Central Park, and talking to two women. He saw her and nodded pleasantly. Soon he brought the two women over and introduced them. "Where's Mr. Wilson?" he asked. "Couldn't he come at such short notice?"

Once more she felt stupid and tongue-tied. What could she say? That she hadn't known he had been invited? That if he *had* been invited he might very well be inside now, although it didn't seem probable? That *she* had not invited him? She wanted to say that she and Ian were not inseparable, but that sounded rude, and in the end she mumbled that Ian couldn't come.

When the sky became a less violent mauve and all the guests moved into the dining room, Carlotta found that she had been seated as far from him as possible. Her dinner partners were the novelist who worried about chemicals and an actor she had always admired; Sam's were Lee and a very pretty Finnish woman with perfectly straight white-blonde hair.

A part of her could see, and admire, how very nice all the arrangements were. Sam's friends were charming, and very good at what they did. The long dining table was a beautiful piece, and the room itself Spanish in flavor. The windows were open so everyone could see the pale new moon rising in the sky over the park—it hovered above them as if a part of the decor of Sam's dining room. The food was probably excellent, but Carlotta knew she would not remember what she had eaten. For the first time in her life, she thought she knew what it was to feel totally undesirable to someone.

Sam seemed to take no notice of her at all. He seemed on affectionate terms with all the other women, and on possibly intimate terms with the Finnish girl, Anja. Carlotta tried to laugh when the nice actor told her funny stories, or the nice novelist made jokes, but what she wanted was to go home now, before her dashed hopes overpowered her. Since she could not simply leave, ruining Lee's party, she forced herself to behave normally. She made quite a hit at her end of the table, dipping into her bag of memory and withdrawing Mrs. Hooks, her charwoman in long-ago London, for them to laugh about. Mrs. Hooks reminded the novelist of a character he had created once, and Carlotta drank another glass of wine and became even wittier. There was so much laughter in the little group around them that Lee called down and asked what was so funny. "Gloom and doom," they all shouted back. Sam was forced to look her way then, but he merely smiled at all of them, a good host, glad his guests were enjoying themselves.

Later, she asked Lee if the glamorous Anja were Sam's girlfriend, or fiancee. "One of his girlfriends, I think," was

Lee's reply. "He's supposed to be quite a ladies' man."

"Shame on you, Lee," said the novelist in passing, having heard only the last two words. "A feminist like yourself ought to know it's *women's man* now, and I hope you were referring to me."

Carlotta took her brandy and went back out on the terrace. It was quite dark now, and the fragile moon had climbed higher. The air was dense with the fragrance of spring and here, so far up, were none of the smells of the street. She smelled the blossomy air and felt numb. Would she have settled for being one of his girls? She thought, bitterly, of what a fool she had been to think Sam had wanted her. She had assumed, with no right, that she would mean much more to Sam, but it seemed she was invisible to him.

Lee was leaving early the next morning on a ten-city tour for her book, and Carlotta hugged her goodbye and begged her to be careful. "Where's Sam?" Lee asked, searching the room. "Maybe he's paying off the caterers or something. I'll go get him."

"Oh, no, don't bother," Carlotta said hastily. "Thank Mr. Cumberland for me. It was a lovely party."

TWENTY-FOUR

THE WEATHER TURNED FROM THE BALMY, PLEASINGLY PRO-
longed spring and plunged New Yorkers into the sultry torments of summer in the space of one week. Carlotta was a
veteran of only one other such summer, and she remembered
being astounded by it. All of her life, she had been able to
escape the heat of city summers, going to the Hamptons or
Nantucket, fleeing back to England from Rome, going wherever she liked. Now these pleasures were available to her on
weekends only.

The first summer she had stayed in the city, the first she
had found herself a working woman, she had been bewildered
and exhausted. The gallery was air-conditioned, and after the
first week of torrid heat, she had done something she vaguely
imagined was what you did. She had gone to Macy's and
bought an air conditioner. It didn't seem to work right, and
Bobby had come over to her apartment, taken one look at it,
and explained that she had bought the wrong voltage.

"I'll return it for you, baby," he had said pityingly.

"No, no. I have to learn about these things."

Back she had gone to Macy's, returned the air conditioner,
and got the right kind to be delivered, and by the time she got
home felt as if she had taken a five-mile trek in Sumatra. She
was able to walk to work, and she could afford the occasional

taxi, but she wondered how the people who had to ride the subways could possibly endure it. It seemed to her that they were in a life-and-death situation when the thermometer reached the mid-nineties, and for a while, Chloe Vere-like, she agonized over their plight.

This was her second summer, and she was not quite so horrified. She had learned to wear only light-colored clothing, to go bare-legged (although Martha would spin in her grave, believing a lady *never* appeared that way in the city), to avoid those crossings where the tar melted and trapped your shoes, to shun wine at lunch, and to keep her lipstick in the refrigerator. She accepted that it was necessary to wash her hair every day in the New York summer, whereas it remained silky and clean in normal climates for at least three or four days, and mourned the ten inches she had cut off to celebrate her new status as a working woman. Very long hair had been so easy to put up.

Lee was off on her tour, Rachel had decamped to Newport with Chloe, and Ian Wilson was in England visiting his family. She knew dozens of people, but her three best friends were gone and, of her adopted family at the gallery, only Piet seemed to be around at present. The humiliation she felt at so badly misjudging her possible importance to Sam Cumberland still burned brightly, but it was more than humiliation. She thought of him at the oddest times, vividly, and her thoughts were not of the vindictive kind at all. She would be talking to an art rep on the phone and an image of his gray eyes would appear, or she might be walking along East Sixty-Fourth, headed for home, when she would think of that soft, floppy quality his pale hair had. *Now I'll never have a chance to touch it and find out if it feels the way I imagined it would,* she thought. There was a quality of real mourning to these aborted little longings, and she wondered why she had worn black to his dinner party when she should be wearing it now.

If it weren't so hot.

Patriotically, Rachel's mother died on the Fourth of July. Mrs. Windolm had been a formidably healthy woman all her life, and her death had been a freak accident. She had been playing mixed doubles at tennis, and in the moment while she crouched expectantly, waiting for Cotter to serve, a bee alit on her upper arm and stung her.

She had given an outraged squeak of pain, dropped her racquet, and died ten minutes later, there on the courts at the Windolm place in Newport. The doctor later explained that there were people allergic to bee bites, but no one had ever expected that Rachel's mother was one of them. Cotter and the other participants in the game—Rachel and her older brother Anthony, who lived in Singapore and had come home for a visit—had watched with horror while poor Mrs. Windolm expired. It seemed that she swelled internally from the bite of the bee, and died of suffocation.

Rachel's father was asleep in an alcoholic stupor at the time of the incident, and Chloe was packed straight back to New York in the company of Mrs. MacDougall before she could discover that all her worst fears about life had been confirmed. Mrs. Windolm was buried in the garden, as she had desired, facing the sea. The family feeling, voiced by a sobered-up Mr. Windolm and Anthony, was that the incident had been too grotesque to make publicity desirable. Poor Elizabeth, poor Mum, would have been embarrassed by the peculiar nature of her passing. She would not wish to have it be a matter of public record, say in the "Milestones" section of *Time* magazine, that Elizabeth Mary Bradford Windolm had perished, at the age of fifty-five, at her residence in Newport, "of a bee bite." No matter how many mentions there might have been of her charitable nature and tireless efforts *on behalf of;* no matter how glowingly her aristocratic lineage might be called into prominence, nothing could counterbalance the ignominy of her death.

No one could have imagined that Rachel, who had always considered her mother a fool, would be the person most devastated. Rachel herself could not understand it. Mrs. Windolm's last remark to her was in relation to her backhand. "Practice makes perfect!" her mother had advised, prancing in place. And now the old cliche-monger was dead, and both Rachel and Anthony, neither of whom needed the money, were richer than ever, because their mother had had money of her own. It all seemed so senseless. A part of Rachel's devastation came from seeing how randomly, easily, life could end. The other, deeper, part had to do with the fact that she had always felt superior to her mother, and now, by dying, Mrs. Windolm had surprised her.

The day after the funeral, Rachel called Carlotta at the

gallery. "Hello, my mother died," was what she said when Carlotta answered, and then she burst into tears. While Carlotta made surprised and soothing noises, Rachel described the fatal bee sting. "That's why it wasn't in the papers," she said. "When you say a woman my mother's age died 'at home' people assume it was a suicide."

"How awful, Rachel. I'm so sorry. Is your father all right?"

"It's pretty much passed him by, I'd say. He's practically to the point where they should just rig him up with an IV drip of bourbon. He took me aside for a fatherly chat and ended up forgetting what he was going to say. Finally he mumbled something about ashes to ashes and dusht to dusht. That's how he said it, *dusht*."

Carlotta asked if she should come to Newport, but Rachel explained she would be coming back to New York day after tomorrow. "There *is* one thing, though," she asked shyly. "Would you mind tossing a few cliches at me? I kind of miss them."

"Now? Let's see—a stitch in time saves nine."

"More, more."

"A watched pot never boils. Don't put all your eggs in one basket. It's always darkest before the dawn. Every cloud has a silver lining. Pride goeth before a fall—"

"I think maybe that last one is from the Bible or something," Rachel said. "Your voice sounded funny on that one. Have you had a fall?"

Carlotta made a very small sound that might or might not have meant yes. "Never mind, darling," Rachel told her, "I'll be back to help you out, whatever it is."

"Don't cross bridges until you come to them," said Carlotta.

"Sometimes I just don't believe you. Christ, Carlotta, you are just too dumb. For a person who is intelligent, I mean."

"Thank you," said Carlotta. "Why am I dumb this time?"

They were having a picnic in Rachel's yellow room because, as Rachel said, it was too hot to have one outside. They were sitting on a large blanket, eating cold chicken and cucumber sandwiches from Rachel's Fortnum & Mason wicker basket. Carlotta watched Rachel opening a bottle of champagne, leaving her question dangling in the air. Rachel's eyes were red-rimmed from crying, but in all other respects she looked particularly splendid. She was wearing a straw hat tied round with a chiffon ribbon, as if she really were at some splendid picnic from a bygone age.

Rachel poured the champagne, sipped, and selected a deviled egg from the hamper. "If a man who is polite, charming, hospitable, and civilized, a man who is said to *particularly* like women, if this man is sweet to every woman in a room but one, don't you see what that means?"

"That that one woman isn't sufficiently interesting to merit his attention," said Carlotta primly. "And anyway, he wasn't rude to me. He just didn't notice me."

Rachel sighed. "Okay, turn it around. If you were the only woman in the room he looked at, all night long, you would assume he was interested. The reverse is true, believe me. Your problem is that men have always fallen over themselves to get to you, and you've never had to maneuver them. You've never played the game, darling."

"I don't think he plays games. He's not superficial."

"Sweetie, if the man can get you in this condition by pretending not to notice you, he plays games, believe me. Unless there's some other reason."

"I think he believes Ian and I are a couple, but that wouldn't account for it. And there's no way I can reasonably tell him that Ian and I are just friends. Not if he won't even *talk* to me."

"Wait a minute!" Rachel held her hand up dramatically. "Something's coming through here. Maybe you're right, maybe he's not manipulating you. Maybe he just, well—forget it, you wouldn't understand. You have to let him know Ian's not your lover. I don't care how, just make sure he finds out. If it were me, I'd just send him a note saying, "By the way, I am not fucking Ian Wilson,' but that's not your style."

Preposterous as it seemed, Carlotta felt a gleam of hope at Rachel's encouragement. She couldn't imagine how she was going to manage it, but manage it she would. If he still chose to ignore her, it would be shattering, but if it brought him to her, it was worth a try.

When she walked back the short distance to her apartment, her mind selecting and rejecting various schemes, she was followed by a man. He was about forty and rather handsome, and so well-dressed she couldn't imagine he planned to mug her. He was probably, she thought, just heading in the same direction as she. Just before she reached her apartment, he caught up to her and murmured something innocuous about what a lovely evening it was.

His words were innocent enough, but the hot-eyed way he looked at her was frightening and a little exciting. She had never yet picked up a man from the street for one of her sordid little one-nighters. It was far too dangerous even to contemplate. His eyes could be saying "Come, and I will make shattering love to you in perfect silence, and then withdraw from your life. *Use* me," or they could telegraph something more sinister: "Please don't be whorish enough to let me have you, because then I shall be obliged to kill you." She shuddered and walked on, but her eyes had been held by his long enough to make him feel he had a chance. When she turned in at her apartment, he caught her arm desperately. "Anything you want," he said, pleading. The words echoed those of Delaney's telegram summoning her home from Ireland, and seemed doubly horrible.

She shook her head, keeping her face mask-like, and his hand dropped away from her arm. Some neighbors passed by then, and he furtively hurried on when she called hello to them. It had been a very small incident, but she found herself shaking when she let herself into her own apartment. Last year, in her greatest desperation, she might have said yes. The future, if she could not find her love, she did not even wish to think about.

"Who shall I say is calling?" asked the clipped voice of the Cumberland & More secretary the next morning.

"I'm calling for Ian Wilson," Carlotta said, pulling the petals off one of the roses on her desk.

"In reference to—?"

"A personal matter involving the painter Ian Wilson," said Carlotta, denuding the rose in her nervousness.

There was a brief pause during which she was afraid the phone had gone dead, and then another female voice, insufferably bright and perky and also, she thought, foreign. Oh, dear God—Finnish? "This is Mr. Cumberland's personal assistant," said the voice. "May I help you?"

"I would like to speak to Mr. Cumberland," said Carlotta, starting in on another rose. "I have a personal message for him from Mr. Wilson."

"Mr. Cumberland is in conference," said the voice. "If you could leave a number?"

But just as she was giving the gallery's number, the assistant gave a joyous little cry and told Carlotta to wait. She pictured the doors of the conference room opening, Sam walking innocently out into the hall, the assistant—Anja?—signaling to him that a call of no very great importance awaited him, if he liked.

"Sam Cumberland," he said, rather abruptly. Now or never.

"Mr. Cumberland, this is Carlotta Madigan. I'm Lee Redwing's friend, and you were good enough to invite me to your apartment for a dinner in her honor?"

"Yes, Carlotta," said the soft, seductive voice in surprised tones.

"I'm really calling to invite you to a party for my old friend, Ian Wilson. He's over in England at the moment, but he'll be back in two weeks. He's bringing his fiancee with him, and the party is to celebrate their engagement. All his friends are so happy for him—you can't imagine!"

She felt she was babbling hysterically, and there was a silence at the other end. She began on another rose to subdue herself.

"At any rate," she said coolly, "he was awfully glad to meet you, and I thought to include you in the festivities." She tried to get her voice into the bright, impersonal register of a Cumberland & More functionary, and gave him the time and place of the manufactured party.

"Thank you," said Sam Cumberland, "I'll try to make it." There was a gentler edge to his voice, and then a long pause during which she wondered if she was supposed to hang up. "Carlotta," he said. "Carlotta, where are you now?"

"I'm at the gallery, where I work," she told him, surprised that she could speak at all. "It's The Global Village, on Madison Avenue."

"Yes," he said, sounding rather dazed. "Yes, I know it. Of course. Your gallery handles Ian Wilson." There was another long pause. "I have to go to Los Angeles for a week. I wonder if you would have time to see me for a few moments today? I could come to the gallery."

"Of course," said Carlotta.

She put down the phone and laid her head on the desk,

smiling. All around her the shredded rose petals, evidence of her passion, released their sweet odor. She swept them up in her hands and placed them in her wastepaper basket. She would have to tell Ian how outrageously she had lied about him. Some day, she hoped she would tell Sam.

Twenty minutes later, Simon showed him into her office. He stood in her door, dressed casually in light summer pants and a pale blue shirt. Carlotta sat behind her desk, trying not to shake visibly, and welcomed him.

Today she seemed to be anything but invisible to him. His eyes never left hers as he sat in the chair across from her. "This is where I first saw you, actually," he said. "I wanted to buy that picture, something you couldn't possibly have known."

"No," said Carlotta, thinking irrelevantly that Sam was sitting in the position of Rodin's "Thinker," only with his head up. His physical presence was overwhelming in her little office.

"Normally," said Sam, "I would go about this very differently. I would ask you to dinner and be easy and charming and court you, but I'm going away on business, and I don't think I could stand to wait a week. You will have to consider these few moments in your office my courtship, Carlotta. May I see you a week from tonight?"

"Yes," she said immediately.

He sighed in relief and smiled for the first time. "I had to see you," he said. "I couldn't have said that on the phone. This is serious, for me."

"I'm glad."

When he rose to go she felt she couldn't bear it. She got up to see him to the door, and when she was within two feet of him she felt dragged by a magnet. He shook his head slowly, as if in pain, and then caught her to him, kissing her so hungrily there could be no mistaking his need. His trembling hands caressed her hair, and he was murmuring her name over and over, his voice first soft with wonder, then breaking with passion.

There were voices outside, in the next room, and they were coming closer. "Until next week," Sam murmured. Then he groaned. "Christ, a week. Goodbye, my love." He kissed the palms of her hands, and then he vanished as quickly as he had arrived.

TWENTY-FIVE

THE PHRASE "MADE FOR EACH OTHER," WHICH HAD ALWAYS
seemed a harmless but silly notion, like the lyric of a cheap
song, took on a new meaning for Carlotta. Whoever had
coined it had probably known the consuming and totally satisfying feeling she shared with Sam, and he—or she—had understood that the quality of that love could be experienced
with only one person in all the world. If you were unlucky
enough never to meet that person, you would never know, and
she felt sorrow for all those people who had never found the
person for whom they had been created.

She even, at times, imagined a creator who painstakingly
drew up the plans. The creator was a sort of pagan god of
love. While other gods determined that no two snowflakes
should be alike, just as no human fingerprints were, the creator lavished time and energy on making sure that for every
living man there existed a perfect woman, or vice versa depending on who was being considered, and then left it up to
cruel fate to see if they ever discovered one another. What did
it matter to the god if the man was born in Egypt, the woman
in Pennsylvania? It was up to them to make the connection.

This theory amused Sam, who said he thanked the creator
for at least planting them both in America, where they had had
a better chance of meeting. Even with that extra edge, it

chilled him to realize how narrowly he had missed her. If he had not been excited by the implications of a Cheyenne woman lawyer's victories and offered her a book contract, and if Lee Redwing had not happened to have lived her early life on the ranch of a Democratic U.S. senator from Montana, and if Carlotta had not been the daughter of that senator, their paths would never have crossed. Carlotta Madigan was not a woman he would have met in the normal course of time.

He shivered, standing in his kitchen and opening a fresh bottle of tonic water, at the thought of having lived his life without Carlotta. He, a man in his late thirties who had not shown fear in Da Nang or Long Binh, felt an actual cold tremble pass over the length of his body. She was, at that moment, outside on his terrace, lying in a chaise longue under the starlit sky. They had now been together for six weeks and the long, sultry summer was coming to an end.

He remembered the night he had come back from Los Angeles, so eager to see her he had called from the airport, and then gone straight to her cramped little apartment on East Sixty-fourth. Her passion had stunned him, for he had imagined that she, like many very beautiful women, might be slow to arousal. The moment he stepped through the door, he sensed how wrong he had been. Her eyes had closed, her lips had parted as if they were already making love, and when he took her in his arms she cried his name and clung to him as if he alone kept her from falling. He felt the heat radiating from her body, felt the throbbing of her breasts crushed to his chest. Without breaking their kiss, they had somehow managed to reach her bed, their hands frantic as they discovered each other. How had their clothes come off? He had gasped at the sight of her naked body, had wanted to adore it, but they were both too excited to wait. There would be all the time in the world to make leisurely love, but that first time was immediate and cataclysmic, Sam deep in her, held by her as she arched to him violently and seemed to burst in wave after wave of ecstasy.

He had marveled at it, at her need, and found himself more excited by her than by any woman he had ever had. And then, she was so achingly sweet. Lying in his arms afterwards, trembling uncontrollably, she had whispered, "Oh, Sam, I waited for you for so *long*." And now, six weeks later, none of their ardor had ebbed away.

He went through the dining room and out to the entrance to the terrace. He could see her, the long, graceful shape of her wonderful legs, the spill of her silky hair against the pillow of the chaise. He wanted to look at her forever, but he wanted to touch her, too, and as he stepped out onto the terrace she turned and smiled at him, and he thought he was the most fortunate man on earth.

"What were you thinking about?" he asked her, coming to sit next to her. "I could tell you were thinking instead of just lying there because you were wiggling your left foot a little."

"Do I always wiggle my left foot when I think?"

"Sometimes the right, but yes, you always do."

"Well, at first I was just looking for Orion's Belt in the stars, because it's always the easiest to see. That made me remember the sky in Montana, and then I was thinking of Lee, and then I got afraid for her."

Sam took her hand and stroked it. "She came through her book tour fine, baby. Oh, there was some crazy group that picketed her in Kansas City, but there were no personal threats."

"But she gets hate letters. She tries to make out they don't bother her, but I know they do. There's one person who has written several times. She always knows it's him, because he calls her a half-breed and says he's going to punish her." Carlotta turned to him with stricken eyes. "I'm more afraid for her in Butte than when she travels. Lee called and said she'd got another one, and this time it was posted from Wyoming. It's as if he's getting closer, state by state."

"What makes you so sure it's a he?"

Carlotta sat bolt upright. "Oh, Sam, surely it is. It's got to be a man."

Sam thought of the bales of hate letters that had arrived at Cumberland & More over the years, and more particularly of the recent spate to do with Lee. Many of them were signed by women, or, if they were anonymous, revealed the sex of the writer. *I am a good Christian mother,* some of them began, or *As the wife of a man who has sometimes had to discipline me . . .*

"Odds are it is," he told her, not wanting to alarm her. "Look, darling, the people who write poison pen letters are generally harmless enough, except in their own minds. Lee has had good security. I don't want her to come to any harm any more than you do." He touched the tender hollow of her throat with his fingers. She was wearing one of his old T-shirts and very little else. He felt choked with tenderness. His poor Carlotta had lost so much, it was quite natural for her to worry that she would lose her surrogate sister, too.

"I want to tell you about something that happened to me once in Ireland," she said, shutting her eyes. "I've never told anyone."

Automatically, he felt his throat constrict. Carlotta often told him things she had kept secret, not from any furtive instinct, but because there had been no one else to tell. Foxy little Rachel Vere was her confidante, but there were things Rachel would not receive and assimilate with the seriousness Carlotta needed. As for her ex-husband, he could hardly bear to think of him. He knew only that Brendan Delaney, a man he had twice seen around town, had smashed her into a lamp-post while he was dead drunk, causing her to lose her baby. He could not think of Delaney without anger and contempt, and the fact that the man's reputation as a stud was a matter of record made him horribly jealous. His throat had constricted because he feared that she would tell him something which would torment him. None of this was her fault, though, so he continued to stroke her, his hand now sifting through her hair while she made her little confession.

There had been a lost trawler in Donegal, and she had been in flight from her husband. Bastard. He pictured Carlotta walking on the deserted beach, approaching the farmhouse. Then the story took a different turn, and when she came to the part where the masked figure grabbed her, he sat bolt upright.

He listened as intently as an editor whose author is "talking out" the plot, and with the same respect and interest. Deftly, she sketched in the character of the IRA man, and he saw he didn't have to fear that she would become, retrospectively, the victim of a rape. Now he only feared she would reveal that she had fallen in love with him, but it was a small fear. Carlotta was delicate by instinct and nature. She was telling him the story for quite a different reason. He continued to listen.

"He was shot in a field in Tyrone," she concluded. "I read about it in the paper." Her eyes were still closed. He knelt beside her, kissing the closed lids. "Oh, Carlotta," he whispered. "You're not a jinx, my love. The world is a dangerous place, and you are very good. You are a good, sweet woman, and none of it is your fault."

"That's what *he* said," Carlotta murmured. "Words to that effect." She seemed sleepy now, and drained from her confession.

Shortly after, they went to the bedroom and Sam removed the cotton T-shirt and made love to her so gently she passed from pleasure to oblivion before his very eyes, as if she had fainted. He remained, propped up on an elbow, watching the face of his sleeping love for some time.

"Marry me, Carlotta," he whispered. "I will be everything to you that you've never had. Marry me." Knowing her deep distrust of marriage, based on whatever horrors she had undergone with Brendan Delaney, he had refrained from uttering those words when she was conscious.

He was waiting.

Everyone came back to town in the autumn. Rachel came back from a prolonged time in Norway, where Cotter had whisked her to help her recover from the unexpected grief over her mother's death, and Ian Wilson returned from England. The partners at The Global, who had scattered themselves far and wide during the summer, reappeared with serious expressions, ready to do business with a vengeance.

Everyone who had known Carlotta understood one thing: They were, for the first time, seeing a happy woman. Carlotta knew it, too. She had thought she had been happy with Delaney at the beginning, but she could see now the futility of trying to live a life with him. They had deluded themselves, and each other. There were still areas of her marriage to Delaney she did not wish to think about, and if she felt her thoughts slipping in that dark direction she purposely turned her thoughts to more pleasant things. Like Sam.

Sam's love was like a miraculous balm that cured all her hurts; the old scars and the newer ones alike became healed by his presence in her life.

"I feel so lucky," she told Rachel one day when they were lunching at The Stanhope. "It isn't fair for one person to have so much luck."

"I wouldn't beat myself up over it if I were you," Rachel said. "You were overdue for some luck."

But there were, it seemed, people who weren't so thrilled by her happiness. The Finnish woman, Anja, who was not Sam's assistant after all, made a point of snubbing Carlotta when they passed each other on Fifth Avenue one day. And one woman actually came to the gallery on a drizzly day in November and demanded to see Carlotta.

Confused, thinking she was about to meet an artist, Carlotta found herself confronting a beautiful woman who introduced herself as Marietta. She found it odd that Marietta offered no last name, until a second glance at the impossibly high cheekbones and slanting eyes made her recall where she had seen that face before. A decade earlier, Marietta's face had graced the cover of every fashion magazine from *Vogue* to *Glamour* to *Elle*. She had been one of the most-photographed models of the era, and now, though she couldn't be more than forty, she was completely unknown. The demand was for youth; some of the models were only in their mid-teens, and Marietta's exquisite but mature beauty was no longer a valuable commodity in the fashion world.

"What a pleasure to meet you," Carlotta said warmly. "Is there anything I can do for you?"

Marietta strolled to the window, looked down at Madison Avenue, and came to sit opposite the desk, crossing her long legs with insolent precision. "I have been out of the country for a year," she said firmly. "One of the things I looked forward to on my return was seeing my dear friend, Sam Cumberland. And what do I discover? That he is off the market, so to speak. No longer available. A few discreet inquiries turned up your name." She lit a cigarette, squinting her long, plum-colored eyes briefly, and then snapping her lighter shut with a smart click. "I came to have a look at you."

"I see," said Carlotta. She felt almost breathless with indignation, but she was not going to show it. "And what do you think?"

"Sam always had good taste in women—I never doubted that you would be less than attractive. What I wanted to see was what kind of a woman would be foolish enough to believe Sam Cumberland belonged to her alone?"

"Is that what your discreet inquiries turned up?" Carlotta laughed. "I'm sorry, I don't mean to be rude, but how can you possibly know what I believe? You speak of Sam's being 'off the market' as if he were a pesticide!"

Marietta smiled dangerously. "You knew quite well what I meant," she said. "I don't know if you're aware of it—possibly you're too young to have discovered it—but there aren't very many good men out there. There are a lot of unattractive men, and men without any money, and married men, and fags, but men like Sam are quite rare. Almost extinct. There is an unspoken rule among women like myself. We constitute a sort of sorority, my dear, and one day you'll belong to it. We share men like Sam among ourselves, rather than trying to *get* him. You didn't know that, did you?"

"Goodness, how unselfish you make it seem. Doesn't he have anything to say about it?"

"Ahhhhh. How amusing." Marietta curved her lips, forcing the fabled cheekbones to fly into high relief. "I see what you're thinking. Well, my dear, if a whiff of marriage is in the air, the sorority relents. We don't begrudge a member who manages to carry *that* number off. But I'm sure he hasn't asked you to marry him, has he? Let's play 'Truth', Carlotta Madigan-Delaney-Madigan-again—has he?"

"I'm not fond of truth games, Marietta. I don't play."

"I thought not. Poor little misguided darling, let Marietta give you some advice. Sam will never marry you, not in a million years. He was married once before—marriage bores him. You're a novelty, but your newness will wear off. You won't even know what hit you, not if you continue to regard him as your exclusive property. I don't know what you've done to him, but it won't last."

"Thanks for your friendly advice," said Carlotta, rising to show that the interview was at an end. "I have to be in SoHo in half an hour. Is there anything else you wanted to say?"

"Only," said Marietta, languidly propelling herself from her chair, "that if he belongs to anyone, it's me. We've had an understanding for three years. I am a sort of unofficial fiancee. In other words, honey, if any woman gets him, it will be me. Look at it as a sort of lottery. For sure, you'll be the loser, and all I'm trying to do is make you lose gracefully. I don't want you to be embarrassed."

"How nice and noble of you."

"Well," said Marietta, "we're sisters, aren't we? We're the same kind of woman."

This, Carlotta thought, was far from true. She declined to answer, but when Marietta was out of sight she acknowledged that she was shaken. She didn't believe for a minute that the ex-model was Sam's "unofficial fiancee" or that Sam functioned as a sort of prize in a sexual and romantic lottery, but Marietta's assertion that marriage bored him chilled her. What if he wasn't capable of staying in love with one woman? Carlotta pictured a time in the future when Sam would tell her he was sorry, it wasn't her fault, but he had lost interest in her. She didn't think she could bear it.

She felt sorry for Marietta, even while she disliked her. Marietta had known what it was to be the chief love interest in Sam's life, and now she had lost him. For that reason alone, she was not going to tell Sam about her encounter, even though she longed to be reassured. In that one small way, she belonged to Marietta's sorority.

It was odd that it should be Sam himself who later gave her a chance to mention Marietta obliquely. Watching her walk the length of his living room, he said, "It's so like you that you never thought of getting a job modeling. Any other woman who had to find work and looked like you would have gone straight to the agencies, but you were right. You belong with the fine art, not the commercial."

She stopped inches away from him, wondering what to do with her heaven-sent opportunity. At last she said, "I wouldn't have liked modeling. It's a career with a short life span. What ever happened to the greats, like Marietta? Do you remember her?"

Sam laughed, drawing her down to sit beside him. "Indeed I do. She and I used to be friendly, actually. Never fear, she's alive and well. Just returned to New York after a year away."

"What was she like?"

Sam thought for a moment. "Amusing," he said. "Slightly poisonous."

"Do you still see her?"

He drew her close, kissing the lobe of her ear. "No, my lovely. You're all I want."

But for how long? That was the question that haunted her all evening, through the long formal dinner with one of his more distinguished authors, and up to the time when they were alone together and she lay beside him, weak with passion, kissing the hands that caressed her.

How long?

TWENTY-SIX

IN THE MONTHS FOLLOWING HER RETURN FROM NORWAY, Rachel began to feel that she was now as content as she would ever be. Cotter had admitted to her that, like it or not, her grief at her mother's death had made him fall back in love with her. "I never stopped loving you, not even when I had that thing with Vivian," was the way he had put it to her, "but I never felt you *needed* me for anything."

Nothing like the midnight sun over a deep fjord as a backdrop for lovemaking, Rachel thought. Chloe, too, had seemed content on that long holiday and now, deep in winter of the following year, Chloe's therapist had informed Rachel that the child's progress was so great she was very nearly normal. Chloe would always be sensitive, but she would not be driven to despair by it.

It was a peculiar thing but Chloe, for whose sake Rachel had elected not to have another child, was now pestering her mother for a sister or brother. Rachel had long ago decided that her daughter was a full-time affair and could not tolerate the insult of having her mother's attention divided, but she had misjudged her. At seven, Chloe was able to state her case very well.

"You always said it was sad for La-la not to have any

sisters or brothers," Chloe said, "because then she was all alone after her parents died."

Rachel, who had not said these things *to* Chloe, but no doubt in her hearing when she had been so young no one could imagine she would comprehend, was stunned. "But darling," she pointed out, "Daddy and I are young. We're not going to die and leave you alone." She had been about to say "not ever," but logic restrained her, and Chloe was too polite to point out the obvious.

"La-la isn't sad now," Rachel continued, evading the issue. "She and Sam will probably get married, and then she can have a baby of her own."

"That's good," said Chloe sternly, "but her baby won't be my brother or sister. Yours would."

Rachel understood the severity of Chloe's longing, because normally any mention of Carlotta brought forth a flood of questions. Her daughter's beauty moved her, as always. She had lost the roundness of babyhood and was a miniature of what she would become, a small, fine-boned girl with pure features framed by the extraordinary flaxen hair. Rachel felt some of her daughter's desire for a baby catch hold of her. She was still young and in excellent health, and the truth was that she needed very little persuading. She was sick of IUDs that hurt and had to be removed, and of hearing about the side effects of the pill, and she wanted to experience again that triumphant, invulnerable physical power she had known at Chloe's birth.

"You know, don't you, that if it's a boy, Daddy will want to name him Walter?"

Chloe giggled. "I don't believe you," she said. "Nobody wants a baby named Walter."

"I will give it some very serious thought," she told her beloved child. "Daddy and I will talk about it. Having a baby is a very important thing, Chloe, and takes lots of planning and consideration."

Chloe nodded solemnly. Rachel preserved her pondering attitude, but she had already made up her mind.

"I had a letter from Lee," Carlotta told Sam. "There's going to be a big conference on wife abuse in Washington, D.C., and she's been asked to be one of the main speakers."

"When?" ask Sam, frowning at some galleys which had

been delivered to his desk. They were sitting companionably in his office, because he was working late.

"Oh, not until the fall, not for months."

Sam looked up from the offending galleys. "You must be starving," he said gently. "I'll be a little longer. Do you want me to order up some food?"

Carlotta shook her head and pretended to go back to the book she had been reading while he worked. From between its pages, she withdrew the new photograph of Dominic that Lee had included in her letter. He was sitting astride a pony, laughing, and he was as beautiful in his dark-skinned, black-eyed way as Chloe Vere was in her porcelain fragility. She did not show the picture to Sam for fear he might think she was hinting at something.

Now she studied Sam. The light from the desk lamp formed a nimbus around his soft, pale hair, and his eyebrows were drawn together just a little in concentration. She knew him so intimately now that she realized, just by a slight movement of the hand that held the pencil, that he was about to speak in irritation.

"This," he said disgustedly, "is an author who expects to do his rewriting on the galleys. Goddamn nuisance."

She didn't ask him why he hadn't given the galleys to some junior editor to deal with, as most men of his position would do. Sam was a perfectionist. Just as he had personally helped Lee to edit her book, he would sweat out these galleys himself.

There were other things she knew about him of a more personal nature, and she could not help but think of them now. They were the only people left in the building, and his office seemed as companionable by night as his bedroom. His eyes were cast down, but she knew the way they darkened when he was aroused. She also knew the terrain of his body, which was as familiar to her as her own—the precise manner in which the muscles in his back rippled when pleasure came to him were recorded on her fingertips, and the shape of his lips was imprinted on every inch of her flesh. He liked to sleep on his back, holding her in such a way that her head was pillowed on his chest, and one of her legs thrown over his. His lower lip was especially sensitive, and if she stroked it with her thumb, as lightly as possible, he became quite frantic.

The snap of the pencil between Sam's fingers interrupted

her reverie. *"Jesus,"* he said plaintively, "the guy can't do this!"

Carlotta rose and went to him, standing at the back of his chair. She laid her hands on his hair and stroked it comfortingly. "Couldn't you take them home?" she asked. "At least there I could make you something to eat, and you'd be more comfortable. And you could have a drink."

He swiveled around in the chair to face her, staring up at her with a strange expression. He took her hands in his and pulled her down, almost roughly, into his lap. "I love you so," he whispered fiercely, holding her so tightly it hurt. "Oh, God, Carlotta, I love you so much."

She kissed him, biting lightly at his sexy lower lip. She was straddling him, and she felt him hardening against her, pushing at her where she ached to be joined to him. "Oh, Sam," she moaned, "on the floor, anywhere, please."

Somehow he rose from the chair, carrying her, and they collapsed to the floor. Feverish fingers ripped away at clothes, and both of them were laughing softly, knowing what they must look like, grappling on the floor of the executive office at Cumberland & More, but soon the laughter stopped, and there were only the noises of two people lost in mindless pleasure. Her orgasm was a floating one. She seemed to leave her body and float in waves of bliss somewhere near the ceiling, but at the same time Sam anchored her to the carpet, sighing her name.

When she opened her eyes, she was staring straight at the grim face of what she took to be Sam's grandfather, framed on the wall. He looked disapprovingly at her from his place in eternity.

"Oh, dear," she said. "Is that your grandpa, darling?"

Sam struggled up to follow her train of vision. Then he collapsed again, his face on her breast. "No," he said. "That's More. Cofounder. Neville More."

A little while later he said, "Carlotta, marry me. I know your first marriage was a bad one, but I've given you all this time to see how good things could be with us. We don't have to set a date just now; if you'll only agree to be my wife—just *think* about it—that's enough for me. I'll make you so happy, I promise, and it's almost as if we were married now and—"

She laid her fingers over his mouth. "Of course I will," she said.

* * *

She saw Delaney, quite by chance, at a party for the Museum of Modern Art. Sam was in Atlanta, and she had accompanied Ian Wilson to the party, knowing that every luminary important to the gallery would be in attendance.

He was standing at the far end of the room talking to a group of people, and she didn't recognize him at first. When she realized that the older gentleman she had been looking at was, in fact, the man she had been married to, she nearly gasped out loud with shock. For a long time she had wondered how she would react if she ran into Delaney and, of all the possible reactions she had imagined, this was the strangest. To look at the man whose body she had known as intimately as Sam's, whose child she had carried and lost, without recognizing him—it passed all understanding.

She wanted to leave the party immediately, but she could not allow herself to be so cowardly. Delaney no longer had any power over her. She was in no danger. In fact, she felt a little pool of residual tenderness for him. He looked older, less glowing than the man she remembered. He was, she could see when she studied him more objectively, a handsome man, but he was well over sixty now and the Carlotta she had become thought of him as elderly. She wondered if he had been ill.

She crossed the room to him, knowing he had seen her and was refraining from making eye contact or acknowledging her in any way, probably because he believed she still hated him.

"Hello, Brendan," she said. "How are you?"

"Well, thank you, Carlotta. Yourself?" He spoke with his old raffish charm, but the blue eyes seemed dimmer, and sad. She told him she was fine, feeling trapped in a nightmare of banalities. "And are you happy now?" he asked gently.

"Yes, yes I am, Brendan."

"I wish you the best. All the best."

It was what they said in the pubs in Ireland at the evening's close—*all the best*. She raised her glass to him and repeated it. Delaney smiled, then lifted a hand as if to touch her shoulder. Apparently he thought better of it because he turned away abruptly, and within five minutes he had left the party.

Last Resort was flirting with the best-seller list, and doing much better than anyone could have expected. Five common market countries had bought it, and at the upcoming paperback auction, Lee had been told, sums of money—vast, to her—would be offered.

She had her eye on a frame farmhouse a few miles out of Butte, close to where she boarded Dominic's pony. The flat in town was not an ideal place for a little boy to spend his childhood, and she wanted her son to have a roomy backyard where he could run free, as he did when he visited his grandfather.

Recently, Charlie Redwing had expressed concern for Lee. Shyly, he told her that she ought to have a husband. "I'm proud of you, honeybunch," he said. "Your mother would have been proud, too, but it's not natural for a woman to live her life alone. I mean without a man." And then, astounding her, he had put his hand on her shoulder, stopping her as they walked over the high pasture at the ranch in Bozeman, and said, "You be honest with me, Leana. I'm not going to judge you. You're not one of *them,* are you?"

Her first impulse had been to laugh, but her father was so clearly suffering agonies of embarrassment she restrained herself and said, "One of who, Daddy?"

"Well," Mr. Redwing looked over her shoulder at a clump of cottonwoods, avoiding her eyes, "nowadays they call them gay, I believe. We used to say queer, but seems like you can't say that anymore."

"No, Daddy, I'm not gay. I like men, I have boyfriends, you know. It's just that I don't feel I have to get married. If I met a man I loved, I would certainly marry him, for Dominic's sake, but I haven't. I'm not unhappy, and I wish you wouldn't worry."

"It's only natural for me to worry, being as you're my only daughter. Well, I'm glad you're not, *you know,* because I think it would make life harder for you."

Walking up the steps of the courthouse, Lee recalled this conversation and smiled to herself. She wished she could make her father understand how happy she was. She was so very fortunate she was sometimes stunned by her own good luck. She had a career she loved, a child she adored, a book that had received admiring reviews and was, apparently, going to bring her a lot of money. She also—although she could not tell him this in so many words—had a regular and satisfying sex life and never suffered from loneliness. Her lovers did not stay all night, and Dominic was never greeted with strange, half-naked men in the morning. On the other hand, she had plenty of male friends who *did* play with Domi, including his natural father, Victor Rainwater. Why did she need a husband? Most of the marriages she saw were unhappy ones, some brutally so.

She was, even now, going to appear on behalf of a woman in the preliminary hearing of a bitter custody case. That would never happen to *her*. It was something her father was unable to understand, Lee decided. It was a generational thing.

"What's so funny, Counselor?" A young attorney named Green had caught her smile as they passed on the steps.

"Something my father said," she told him.

"I didn't know you had a father," he said. "I always assumed you emerged full-blown from the forehead of a goddess." The jokes about her supposed radical feminism were tiresome, but Green had spoken teasingly and with a hint of flirtation. He was a good-looking man, with the kind of long back Lee preferred. She gave him an encouraging smile and said, "Just for that, you'll have to take me to dinner some night and pay the bill for both of us."

His long back made her think of Sam Cumberland, who, it seemed, was going to marry Carlotta. Carlotta was so happy now, telling Lee in her letters and on the phone of her happiness, of how she and Sam would probably marry sometime around next Christmas, or better yet, New Year's Eve, so they could start married life in 1980, a fresh new decade.

Lee thought the combination of Sam and Carlotta came as close to perfection as any she was likely to come across on this earth, and was pleased she had inadvertently brought them together.

Sometimes, her love seemed an embarrassment to her, like a large, unwieldy carry-all that poked at other people's legs on a crowded bus. It spilled into every part of her life, and she wondered if she deserved such happiness. She was divided on so many things. She wanted to be with Sam every minute, yet she knew it was unwise for a woman to cling too closely. She suffered torments of jealousy, but knew better than to question him. He had women friends, just as she had male ones, and if she smelled a perfume not her own lingering near him, or he was seen having a drink with a brunette, she had to assume it was something harmless, or perhaps even business.

They had agreed that she would keep her apartment, even though she spent so much time at his place. It was near the gallery, and it was a sensible thing to do, but she wondered if Sam was relieved that she had not, as he had sometimes asked her to, moved in with him.

The times when he was out of town were hardest for her, because her imagination ran wild. She pictured him in the arms of a legion of women; once, when he had called her from Palm Beach, she had actually thought she could hear a female voice in the room with him.

She tried never to be alone in the evenings when he was away. Tonight, Ian Wilson was the instrument of her distraction, because Sam had gone for three days to Chicago. Ian had taken her to dinner at the trendiest of the new SoHo restaurants, a clangingly noisy place called Lucifer's, and they sat shouting at each other. People came to Lucifer's to see and be seen; Ian was famous enough to belong to the latter category, and not to care.

It was a relief to be back in the quiet of his loft, sipping brandy and seeing his new paintings. Ian had never stopped teasing her about his imaginary fiancée; he was, he said, much too selfish to marry, ever.

"But you were married once," Carlotta pointed out. "For a year. You told me so."

"A terrible mistake. She was a lovely girl, too." He glanced over at her, seeming amused. She was sitting in the same carved chair in which he had painted her, cupping her brandy in her hands. "Are you having second thoughts about marrying Cumberland? I hope not, because I was planning on giving you 'Carlotta, Seated' for a wedding present."

"No. I was wondering if he was having second thoughts about me. Is it normal for a woman to be jealous all the time?"

"Bloody hell, Carlotta, you're the woman, not me." He laughed and went to get more brandy. "My wife had every reason to be jealous of me," he shouted back from the kitchen section. "I was stuffing everything that moved. That's why we parted company." He reappeared, grinning sheepishly. "It's my fatal flaw—I can't be faithful to one woman. It bores me. I loved her, too, but that didn't make any difference."

He gave her a little more brandy, sinking to his haunches beside her chair and patting her hand comfortingly. "Do you suspect Cumberland is like that?"

"I don't know. In some ways I'm so naive, Ian. Sam is wonderful to me, but I keep thinking awful things." She leaned back against the hard wood and shut her eyes. "Lots of women say they can accept a marriage where the husband runs around, as long as he comes back to them at the end of the day. I guess I'm just not like that. I love Sam too much—if I knew he was with other women, that I wasn't *enough* for him, it would kill me." Warm, balmy air blew through the open windows. She took another sip of brandy and kept her eyes closed. It was easier to confess her fears to Ian that way. She had thought to talk to Rachel, but marital infidelity was hardly the appropriate topic to pursue with Rachel. "It's a funny thing, but I don't think Delaney was ever unfaithful to me. For all his faults, he found me enough. I don't want to smother Sam the way Brendan smothered me. Aren't there people anywhere who just love each other without getting all obsessive about it?"

"Sure there are, love," Ian said, but he didn't sound very convincing. Later, when he took her down on the elevator, he said, "My theory is that you're scared to death because you're so happy, and so you're creating something to be unhappy about."

"Why would I do that?"

"Well, Carlotta, you haven't had a very happy life so far, if you'll excuse me for saying so. Unhappiness is your natural state, and part of you wants to return to it. You're like a fish out of water."

She kissed his cheek, laughing ruefully. "I do love you, Ian. Maybe you should have been a shrink."

"I make more as a painter," he said.

As the taxi made its way down Spring Street, Carlotta reflected that this was the place to which Cotter Vere had come in order to have his love affair. Rachel had not been enough for him, but then he had not been enough for her right from the beginning. Martha Carshaw Madigan had been far from enough for her father. Ian's marriage had lasted a year. Both Delaney and Sam had divorced earlier wives. Malcolm Kitson had fallen in love with *her* when he was engaged to be married to a girl he adored. Anything could happen, but it seemed it was almost always the man who tired first.

When she got back to her apartment it was eleven, the hour he usually called if he was going to. Although she didn't go to bed until two, the phone remained silent.

Against her will, the images began to form. Sam was in Palm Beach, in a fabled pink house by the sea. He was there because a Kuwaiti sheik was about to take possession of the house. Its owner, an American heiress whose name was a household word, was retiring to Morocco, and the whole transaction—so dry and dull on the face of it—was, in reality, an *event*.

Every major figure of the latter twentieth century had, at one time or another, been a guest in the pink mansion. Poets and financiers, courtesans and prime ministers had frolicked there—it was not an overstatement to say that the heiress had had a role in shaping the world simply by entertaining the people who made world policy. A little war here, a mighty painting there; the cultural and literal boundaries of the planet could often trace their origins to a languid week in Palm Beach.

So far so good, Carlotta thought. Sam had every reason to be present at the demise of such an important institution. At some point, an important book would emerge as a result of his diligence. Perhaps it would be called *Last Days in the Pink House,* or *Palm Beach—The Vanished Colony.* It would appear under the imprimatur of Cumberland & More, and lay yet another laurel on the brow she adored. Why did she persist in imagining him at the heart of an orgy?

For the assembled press, the heiress would be sure to assemble a bevy of young, photogenic beauties. There would be swarms of vacuous debs and what Ian called "Eurotrash." The debs and Eurotrash didn't worry Carlotta. What tormented her beyond all reason was the image of a woman very like herself. Sam could meet, in Palm Beach, a superior version of Carlotta.

What would this woman be? She would be Carlotta stripped free of all the doubts and indecisions. The perfect, impossible woman who would capture Sam would have no past.

She fell into an uneasy sleep and dreamed not of her rival in Palm Beach, but of her mother.

* * *

On the day Sam was due to return, Bobby told her he had phoned while she was out, but he had not been calling from the office and said he would try her later in the afternoon.

She sat at her desk, happy again now that he was back, and dialed the number of the Central Park West apartment. On the third ring, a woman answered. This seemed so comically in keeping with her worst fears that she wanted to laugh. It could be one of his staff, or an author, or the sister she had never met. The one thing it could not be was his cleaning woman.

"Sam's not here right now," the voice told her. "I think he'll be back in an hour. Do you want to leave a message?"

It was a voice she had heard in this very room, light and distinctive, a trifle clipped. She had to make sure. "Marietta?" she asked.

There was a low laugh. "My, my," she said, "I think I'm talking to Carlotta. Am I right?"

Carlotta said nothing, but she could not hang up. "You remember that lottery we discussed a year ago? My number just came up again, dear. I'm sorry, but you seem to be out of the running. Now, do you still want to leave a message?"

Carlotta replaced the phone and sat, for a very long time, looking at nothing. At last she got up and walked out of her office and into the clients' room. There was a small teak rack containing magazines next to a deep leather chair, and Carlotta sorted through them in search of *W*, a publication Simon found addictive and never failed to buy. It seemed odd to her that she had never thought to ransack the pages of *W* for pictures of the man she loved.

There was a four-page spread on the Palm Beach affair. The tiny, aging heiress was photographed, with her Burmese cat, deep in conversation with Picasso's daughter. Glittering couples and the very rich, who could afford not to glitter, swam before her eyes. On the third page she saw the face she had been searching for. He was talking to a novelist who played polo, his face immortalized in a half-smile. She thought it was his ironic look, but couldn't be sure. Anyway, it didn't matter. Sam could be bored or amused or even enlightened, and she would never know. There would be no time when she would lie in his arms, after love, and say: "By the way, darling—what were you and what's-his-name talking about when the *W* photographer snapped your picture?" Marietta had removed this possibility from her life, and here was the proof.

Just behind Sam's left shoulder, caught in the act of lighting a cigarette, Marietta lurked with a possessive air. The hollows beneath her magnificent cheekbones were thrown into spectacular relief as she inhaled the smoke, and Carlotta imagined the moment in which Sam would turn away from the novelist and touch her arm.

Carefully, she replaced the copy of *W* and went in search of Bobby. He was alarmed when she said she had to get out of New York, but he listened to her argument, which was stated quite rationally, and in the end he agreed to her request.

Four hours later she was on a plane, flying to Paris.

TWENTY-SEVEN

WHEN SHE HAD COME TO PARIS WITH HER PARENTS, THEY HAD always stayed at the Georges V. Now that she was here on behalf of The Global Village Gallery, she had to make do with a small hotel on the rue de Longchamps. It was raining in the City of Light when she arrived and it continued to rain, off and on, for the first four days of her stay. She was glad, because it made the city seem less romantic, and she had certainly not come to Paris to savor its romantic atmosphere.

She had come to place distance between herself and the man she no longer wished to think about, and to work. If she kept to a routine, she would be able to exhaust herself and sleep at night. She had a printed list Bobby had given her, and she rose each day, dressed quickly, and breakfasted on coffee and a croissant at the patisserie on the rue de Longchamps, checking the small galleries and private showings on the list against her street map. She decided where she would go, charting her course as carefully as an explorer over her morning coffee. That way she didn't have to think about anything but business.

Whenever possible she walked, because it was a good way of tiring herself. She lunched with gallery functionaries and art reps, and occasionally with artists themselves. Her French

was excellent, but the slight strain of always expressing herself in a language not her own was useful—it prevented her
mind from wandering.

In the early evening, she returned to her hotel, stopping
first at the charcuterie to pick up her supper and take it to her
room. She ate listlessly, and then wrote long reports of what
she had seen, and how she felt about it, which would later be
typed up and placed in the The Global's files. It was the first
time she had traveled for the gallery with the power to acquire
a work of art, and she wanted to be scrupulously careful.

If she was lucky, a great exhaustion seized her after her
nightly bath, and she fell on her narrow bed and slept until
morning. If she was not, she woke in the small hours, aching
with misery, and with nothing but the misery to keep her company.

On her fifth night, she wakened at 3:17 in the morning, and
found that her face was wet with tears. She sat up in bed,
trying to recollect the dream that had made her cry, and found
she could not. There was an unpleasant smell lingering in the
room. Good. She would find its source; something concrete to
do. She turned on the overhead light and prowled the room,
determined to eradicate the cause of the odor.

It turned out to emanate from a paper umbrella she had
bought during a cloud-burst from an Algerian street vendor.
She went to the window and scanned the darkened streets. All
was silence. The post office, patisserie, and charcuterie were
wrapped in darkness. The street musicians, sidewalk artists,
dancers, and mimes that drifted over from the nearby Centre
Georges Pompidou had all folded their tents. Fastidiously,
holding the offending umbrella between two fingers, she
dropped it from her window to the paving stones below.

Sam's fault, she told herself, was not that he could not find
one woman involving enough, but that he had not read her the
rules. If she had known the rules of the game she was playing,
she might have declined to play at all. It wasn't fair. She had
been pitted against world-class players, like Marietta, when
she was only an amateur. Carlotta's sole consolation was the
maintenance of her dignity.

She had instructed Bobby, and told him to be sure to pass it
along to Piet and Simon, that if Sam Cumberland called, he
was to be told that she was on assignment for the gallery,
somewhere in Europe, and not to be reached.

* * *

It was impossible to walk in any other way than single-file on the rue Saint-Marie and as Carlotta was pacing down the narrow street, searching for the Gallerie Sevignac, a man came out of a door a little distance away. He walked away from her, so all she could see was his back, but he had the same kind of hair as Sam. How could she forget about him if she had to be continually reminded of him? Watching the stranger move on, she entertained herself with a fantasy. He *was* Sam, who had wrung Carlotta's whereabouts from gentle Piet, say, and, armed with the list of galleries, he prowled Paris searching for her. There had been some fabulous mistake, it had all been a misunderstanding. But of course, there had been no mistake, and the man with the floppy, soft pale hair was at least six inches shorter than Sam.

She had gone beyond the gallery and had to retrace her steps past a cloister whose bells were ringing. She passed through a small inner courtyard and pressed a bell marked Gallerie Sevignac, and twenty minutes later she had made her first acquisition—a group of heavily textured scenes of urban life in the artist's hometown of Marseilles.

The gallery owner was a slender, impeccable Frenchman with dark eyes and an elegant, sensual manner. He insisted that Carlotta drink a glass of wine with him to celebrate his client's first major success, and as they toasted each other Carlotta could see that he was about to ask her to dinner, and already envisioning taking her to bed. When he did ask, she declined pleasantly, pleading her work. She could no more enjoy another man now than she could have when she had thought she and Sam were a permanent item.

When she was back on the rue Saint-Marie, she had an unpleasant thought. How long would it be before she was eyeing strangers in elevators again?

In her entire stay in Paris she spoke to almost no one but the people who showed her the paintings. Once, on the Left Bank, almost in the shadow of Notre Dame, she thought she saw a woman she had known as a schoolgirl in Switzerland. Of course, it was hard to tell—the passage of time had changed the woman, naturally—but she felt sure it was Laure. She sat swiftly in a chair of a cafe, holding a menu before her face to avoid being seen. The woman had two small children clinging to each hand, and Carlotta thought she could not bear to confront Laure, a radiant mother, with the evidence of her own failure.

At the end of two weeks she had completed her survey, and she felt sufficiently hardened to return to New York without looking visibly wounded. She had needed the time alone, like an animal who creeps off and licks its wounds in solitude.

She said goodbye to the man at the charcuterie, who she had talked to more than any other soul in Paris, packed her clothes, and flew back to New York.

There was a curious little note from Sam waiting for her at The Global. He had penned it on the gallery's stationery, and Simon explained how that had come about. Sam had, indeed, come looking for Carlotta, and Simon, acting on her instructions, had been very vague.

"It was most unprofessional," he told her reproachfully. "I told the man you were traveling on business for us, and when he asked where you'd be, where you would be staying, I said 'Somewhere in France, I should think.' Was that vague enough for you, Carlotta?"

"Perfect, Simon. I'm sorry if you felt unprofessional."

He bent and kissed her cheek. "Welcome back," he said. "It was quite dismal without you. By the way, he left a note. Sat at your desk to write it. You *are* heartless, darling."

She went to her office and opened the note with shaking fingers. It was cool in tone, asking her why she hadn't let him know she was going away. *What's going on here?* Sam had written. *Since no one at the gallery seems to know when you're coming back, I will assume that you'll call me when you return.*

"What was going on, my darling," said Carlotta in her empty office, "was that you were screwing Marietta, and I'm afraid you've assumed wrongly."

Her apartment was stiflingly hot from being closed up for two weeks, and even though the air conditioner helped the temperature, it could do nothing about the smallness of the rooms. The peonies that had stood in a vase by her bed were dried and dead, and the place looked like a mausoleum. Each time the phone rang she jumped with residual hope, but of course she was the one who was to call him, and the voice at the other end would be Rachel, or Ian, or one of the partners.

Rachel was pregnant again, in her second month, and suffering from morning sickness, but she was quite cheerful about it. She gave a huge party to celebrate her pregnancy, and then decamped to the Hamptons. Carlotta had gone to the party alone. In her efforts to appear normal, she had overdone herself, and was so flagrantly beautiful—although she didn't know it—that several men later asked Rachel if Carlotta was a courtesan. She declined all invitations from men, and to those people who had known her and Sam as a couple and inquired about him, she smiled and said, "Oh, that's all off," as if it were a matter of no consequence.

She restricted herself from parts of the city where she would be likely to run into him. Central Park West, the blocks near Cumberland & More, and all his favorite restaurants were off limits. She didn't have to worry about bumping into him if she visited Rachel, because he had once told her he hated the Hamptons party circuit. Still, unpleasant little surprises often awaited her.

Once, glancing through a magazine, she encountered Marietta's face smugly regarding her from her glory days. She appeared as one of the ten models a famous fashion photographer had enjoyed shooting most throughout his long career. Another time—and much worse—the sedate Sunday New York *Times* betrayed her. In the book section, a number of well-known editors had been invited to talk about the role instinct played in buying a manuscript. Before she had even grasped what she was reading, Sam's face came into view, and she had actually dropped the *Times* with a little hurt cry as if it had stung her.

"A clean break is the best break is what my mother would have said," Rachel told her on the telephone, "but I don't know."

"I heard you ditched my pal, Sam Cumberland," Lee told her, also on the telephone. "He called me about my auction, and when I asked how you were he laughed, *mirthlessly,* as they say, and said he hadn't the slightest idea, because you hadn't *seen fit* to let him know. He sounded *mad.*"

"I guess I'll have to give 'Carlotta, Seated' to the Met," Ian told her at Sardi's, where he had taken her to celebrate the sale of a painting.

And then one day, she read in the "Couples" section of a magazine she normally didn't read that Gina Rafaello, the new Italian film goddess, was being escorted here and there by

Sam Cumberland. There was no picture of Sam, but the one of Gina was spectacular. Carlotta dropped the magazine in her wastebasket.

"I guess it really is over," she said.

There was a young artist attached to the gallery who was exceptionally handsome. With his blond curls and noble profile, he was what would have been called in another time a golden youth. He was prodigiously talented, and The Global was planning a one-man show for him. Carlotta had assumed that he would be confident, even cocky, but it turned out that Stephen Quinn was so shy he could hardly look at her without blushing.

Although he was twenty-eight, he had the sort of ingenuous good manners Carlotta associated with a well-brought-up schoolboy. He came from a blue-collar family who had initially disapproved of his wanting to paint, but they had come round and were now very proud of him. In the interim, he had lived in great poverty in a Hoboken tenement with good light, where he had often skipped meals in order to buy materials for his paintings. Bobby had told Carlotta these facts—Stephen would never have done so—and she wanted, on this business lunch, to take him somewhere very nice.

"Oh, anywhere would be fine," Stephen said, indicating a coffee shop off Madison.

"Oh, no, Stephen, this is a celebration." She glanced at him quickly. He was not wearing his usual jeans and work-shirt, but a lightweight summer suit with shirt and tie. He could be taken anywhere. Because of his unusually well-proportioned body, the cheap suit looked dashing. He was standing in the middle of Madison Avenue, oblivious to the streams of people eddying around him, looking anguished. "Well, I don't know," he said. "I don't go to restaurants, you know, and I can't think of any names."

"Haven't you ever passed a place and thought it looked nice?" It was like talking to Chloe, except that Chloe would have a dozen answers. "Try to think of a place like that."

"The place with the horses," he said almost inaudibly. "It's a hotel, and all those poor carriage horses hang out there."

"The Plaza."

"I guess."

Once she settled him with a menu in the Oak Room, he blanched at the complexities of choice, but after his first glass of wine he loosened up considerably. "Do you eat at places like this every day?" he asked her.

"No—far from it. Half the time I eat at my desk. I told you, Stephen, this is a celebration."

After his second glass of wine, he began to talk freely about his work, and when it was time to order, he chose potted prawns and prime ribs gleefully. She convinced him that he must also be sure to have dessert with his coffee. At the end of an hour of listening to him talk, and covertly watching him eat as if this one meal had to last him all his life, Carlotta decided that Stephen Quinn was the rarest of things—a man who lived only for his art. She was quite sure that he had no interest in women, but she didn't think he was a homosexual, either. Food and sex and comfort and pleasure were not important to him—only painting. She was signing the check, marveling at Stephen's dedication, when she looked up and saw Sam entering the Oak Room with his Italian starlet. Her hand began to shake so badly that she had to put the pen down.

She had known it would have to happen sometime, but she had thought she'd be better prepared. Sam had not seen her, and she allowed herself to study Gina Rafaello. In the photograph, she had appeared to have dark hair, but it was really auburn, like her own. She was extremely beautiful, and moved with effortless grace.

Carlotta turned back to Stephen Quinn. "Stephen," she said in an undertone, "don't ask questions, just hold my hand for a moment and pretend you're talking very seriously to me. I'll explain later."

"What am I supposed to be pretending to be saying?"

"Anything, but give the impression that we're, well, *intimate*."

He took her hand in his rather awkwardly, as if he intended to give her a manicure, bent toward her and said, "I could do something like blow you a kiss across the table."

"No, I don't think that would seem quite—" Carlotta felt too terrified to attempt the long walk through the Oak Room that would take her past Sam's table. She was afraid she would tremble visibly under Sam's contemptuous glance, under his new love's sympathetic one. She thought Gina *would* be sympathetic; one look at her had made Carlotta think she was probably extremely nice, as well as beautiful. That made it worse, of course.

"Well, are we leaving now?" Stephen asked, having run out of things to say.

"Could you sort of hold my arm when we walk through the room? I'm feeling a little unsteady."

He was very strong, and the manner in which he gripped her arm made it seem as if she were leaving the Oak Room under police custody, but he did make the trembling stop. Anyone as good-looking as Stephen never had to fear looking ridiculous, and as they passed by close to Sam's table she had her revenge. Sam seemed to lose his composure when she nodded at him distantly. He had almost certainly caught sight of her moments after Stephen had taken her hand, and the expression in his eyes was one of wonder and hurt.

Then, too, she thought, Stephen had an advantage over Sam, being young. Sam would soon be forty, and she thought men of his age were particularly sensitive about such things.

When she had been safely landed on the pavement, she turned to Stephen and thanked him. "I know you'll think me very childish, but there was a man in there I once thought I was going to marry. He was with his new conquest, and I couldn't bear for him to think I was all alone."

"But you were with me," said Stephen. And then: "Oh, I get it. I could have been just what I am—someone attached to the gallery."

They walked west on Central Park South, since Carlotta did not want to pass by the windows of the Oak Room. They arranged a date for mounting his show, and just before he left her to get a bus at Seventh Avenue, he said, flame-faced, "I pretty much retired from the regular world to get on with my work, but I'm basically a normal guy. And as a normal male I'll tell you this—that guy was crazy to let you slip through his net."

For weeks afterwards, she had a vision of Sam with a huge net, casting, casting, and coming up with dozens of desirable women, wriggling and gleaming like fish. The wounded look in his gray eyes was because one of them had escaped, and he wanted them all.

In the first week of September, The Global presented a

one-man show by Stephen Quinn, who became the art world's instant darling. *New York* magazine featured him on its cover, looking like the answer to every woman's dream, and it was impossible to live in New York without seeing his face everywhere.

TWENTY-EIGHT

"YOU'LL NEVER GUESS WHERE THEY'VE GOT ME STAYING," said Lee into the telephone. "Go on, just guess. It's so bizarre."

Lee had just arrived in Washington for her conference, and seemed positively gleeful. "In Jimmy Carter's bedroom," Carlotta said, "so he can lust after you in his heart?"

"The *Watergate*," crowed Lee.

Suddenly, Carlotta had a positive desire to go to the city she had shunned since her father's death. She wanted to see Lee at the Watergate, and to hear her speak in front of hundreds of people, but it was a particularly busy time for the gallery, and they couldn't spare her. Lee promised to run up to New York for a visit when the conference was over, and then rang off.

Carlotta walked out to the hallway and was surprised to see a lovely young woman standing there, as silent as she was, in surprise. Her shiny, thick, bright hair was up in an Edwardian pouf, with little tendrils escaping at the neck, and her feline blue eyes were wide. She was wearing the same cream-colored suit, the same blue silk blouse, as Carlotta; she *was*, of course, Carlotta—reflected in a nineteenth-century Italian mirror someone had put up experimentally.

"Like it?" said Piet, coming down the hall. "I thought it looked nice there."

Carlotta assured him that she liked it very much, and then went back to work. She had been astounded by her own image, caught unawares. The woman in the mirror looked as young and smooth and innocent as if life hadn't even started for her yet. How could she look that way, Carlotta wondered, when she felt cold and dull and unloved?

She was tempted to call Ian and ask him if the face of "Carlotta, Seated," had grown hideous and twisted, like that of Dorian Gray, but she restrained herself.

Lee had never been in Washington, D.C., before, and for some reason it thrilled her to turn corners and bump right into the Supreme Court, say, or the White House. New York was merely an exciting but alien place to her, but Washington was an icon, something from schoolbooks made real. She who was the original *native* American, who had lost a brother in Vietnam, nonetheless believed in the power of law and democracy, and loved her country in all its imperfections.

She never knew quite where she was, but the congresswoman from Rhode Island who acted as her guide and shepherded her around in the days before the conference began told her it didn't matter. "You only need to know your way around if you live here," she had said. "Just think of it as one big *idea* rather than a town."

Lee thought, instead, of how odd it must have been for Carlotta, as a child, to spend half of her time in Washington and half on the ranch in Montana. Once she found herself being driven through Georgetown, to a cocktail party for Women Against Violence Toward Women, and remembered that it was in Georgetown that Carlotta had lived, and that it was here that the senator had been murdered.

The conference itself was to be held in one of the convention rooms at the Hilton, and on the first day Lee was given a little name tag which she was supposed to stick on her chest as a means of identification. She disliked tags, but seeing that the other participants wore theirs with a good will, she cheerfully stuck *Lee Redwing/Montana/Keynote Speaker* to her chest, and mingled with the throngs.

She had a very interesting conversation with an English woman whose tag read *Belinda Kitson/London/Battered Wives*

Shelter, and by the time she had to give her opening speech, she felt calm, powerful, and invincible.

She spoke of historical roots of the practice of wife beating, and of the various societies which condemned, condoned, or ignored it. She told them how she herself had never given it much thought until one day she met, and agreed to defend, a tormented woman who had killed her husband. There was a great wave of applause, acknowledging Lee's successful defense of Sally Carlson. Lee bowed her head and continued when the clamor had died away. "Before you applaud so victoriously, you might wish to ponder the following statistics." She read them a list she had compiled, showing how many women were in prison on manslaughter charges in the United States, and of these how many had murdered a husband, or common-law husband. From this letter pool she told them how many had never had a previous conviction, or ever been in trouble with the law. The figures spoke for themselves.

It would be a great mistake to consider men as the enemy, she went on, because declaring enemies gave strength to the illusion that men and women are at war. The war was against the aberrant practice of wife abuse, and the best weapon was making all sections of society aware of it.

She concluded with a stirring passage from her book, which she had memorized so as not to seem to be publicizing it, and sat down to tumultuous acclaim.

At the end of the keynote speakers' speeches, everyone was free to attend various workshops. Lee headed for a workshop called "The Legality of Self-Defense," obligingly smiling for the photographers. Several times women waylaid her, flourishing copies of *Last Resort* and asking if she would autograph them.

A woman with salt and pepper hair who wore a button that said *Castrate Rapists* said, "I'd like to shake your hand," and did, grimly.

At last she was free to make her way to the bank of elevators. A tall, rangy man was approaching her, trying to get her attention. "Miss Redwing," he called, "Oh, Miss Redwing— could you spare me a moment?" He had a western accent, not unlike her own, and she drew away from the elevator, prepared to see what he wanted of her.

He seemed oddly excited, like a junior newspaper reporter about to get his first story, but he was in his late forties, and far too old to be a cub. He had bright, blue eyes and thinning, sandy hair. He was wearing a business suit, but like men from her part of the country he wore with it a bolo tie.

"I have something here," he said, fumbling at a canvas bag of the sort you might carry on a plane. "Something I think will interest you. I think you'll want to see this."

His hands seemed to be shaking a little as he unzipped the bag and fumbled inside. Lee looked longingly at the elevator carrying people to the self-defense workshop. "Here we are," he said, "here we are."

Lee turned back and saw he had a gun, and, too late, she knew exactly who he was.

"Hello, half-breed," the man whispered.

There were three shots, and then a great deal of screaming and shouting, and finally the sirens.

Carlotta had been shopping, replenishing all the dreary little items it took to keep her apartment clean. She was walking up the narrow stairs in her building, and she could hear her phone ringing. She grasped the bag of scouring powder, sponges, liquid detergent, and Windex, and hurried upward. It was probably nothing important, but she hated to have the phone stop ringing just as her key was in the lock.

She got to it before the caller had given up, and, as she had suspected, the voice on the other end was Rachel's.

"Carlotta," said Rachel, "have you heard?"

"Heard what?"

"Oh, Carlotta, oh, honey, it's bad. They've shot your friend, some crackpot, down in Washington. He shot Lee Redwing."

Now that the words she had dreaded to hear were being spoken, she couldn't believe them. "When?" she asked, her voice harsh with pain. "How—?"

"It happened about three hours ago. He shot her right in the Hilton, in front of dozens of people. Oh, Carlotta, I'm so sorry."

"Is she dead?"

"She's still alive, but . . ." Rachel's voice faltered, then became calmer. "They don't expect her to live," she said gently.

Carlotta replaced the phone, took her handbag and charge cards, and went to find a taxi. Dressed in the jeans and white cotton blouse she had worn in anticipation of performing household tasks, she waited at LaGuardia for a place on the next shuttle to Washington.

She bought a newspaper, a late edition, which informed her, under the headline FEMINIST LAWYER GUNNED DOWN IN D.C., that Lee had just finished delivering her keynote speech when an unknown assailant had approached her. According to eyewitnesses, Lee had been conversing with the man when he opened a canvas bag, produced a .22 caliber pistol, and shot her three times at close range. He had been taken into police custody, and his identity had not been revealed. Miss Redwing was in critical condition at Georgetown University Hospital.

Carlotta took her seat in the shuttle and folded her hands so tightly her wrists ached. "Let Lee be all right, let her live," she chanted silently, over and over, all the way to Washington. She continued her chant in the taxi that took her to the hospital. There were a knot of reporters at Georgetown University Hospital, but no one recognized her in her jeans, and she passed unnoticed. They told her at the desk that Lee was in an IC unit after three hours of surgery, and her condition was still critical. The surgeon who had seen to her was due to give a press conference shortly, but it was out of the question for anyone but immediate family to see her.

"Has anyone notified her father?" Carlotta asked.

"Her father is en route from Montana," said the woman at the desk rather curtly, as if Carlotta were accusing the hospital of inefficiency. "He was notified immediately, when she was admitted."

The wait for the surgeon to make his report seemed endless, but when the press sprang to attention and the minicams appeared, she knew he was on his way. She also knew his expression would be grave, and resolved not to be frightened by it and jump to conclusions. Surgeons who had been fighting to save lives always looked grave.

When Dr. Arthur Belasco appeared, he looked not merely grave, but grim. Everyone grew silent as the TV lights bathed the lobby with artificial incandescence. "Miss Redwing is in extremely critical condition," he told the assembled reporters. "She was shot three times with a .22 caliber pistol. One bullet lodged in the left shoulder, and two in her left chest." He went on to tell them that the surgical team had reinflated her collapsed left lung, but that her body had undergone massive trauma. He avoided mentioning her heart. When he had concluded his report a man from one of the newspapers asked, "What are her odds?"

Dr. Belasco gave him a withering look, said, "I am not a bookie," and then walked wearily back in the direction from which he had come.

"Where are the intensive care units?" Carlotta asked a passing nurse. "What floor is Miss Redwing on?"

"No press up there," the nurse said.

"I'm not press," Carlotta said, "I'm family."

The nurse gave a little laugh. "If you're a reporter, you sure haven't done your homework," she said. "You can't be family, honey. Miss Redwing is a native American."

"I know that. I grew up with her, on the same ranch. Someone should be close to her until her father arrives. Isn't there at least some sort of waiting room for the IC units?"

The nurse looked as if she were about to relent, but she had had long experience with the wiles of reporters, and a crafty glint replaced her sympathetic look. "Who are you, that you grew up on the same ranch? Are you aware of whose ranch that was?"

"Perfectly aware," said Carlotta. "It belonged to my father, Senator Madigan, who was dead on arrival at this very hospital over ten years ago."

Something in her voice must have had authority, because the nurse didn't ask for any identification. She told Carlotta where to go, giving her a little pass. "I hope she makes it, honey," she said.

Carlotta made her way to the room the nurse had indicated. There was one old man sitting, hands on his knees, staring down at the floor. Normally, Carlotta would have wondered what sorrow held him captive, whose life connected to his was in question beyond the doors of intensive care, but now she could not think of anything but Lee. Doctors and nurses came through occasionally, always hurrying, and when Carlotta asked one doctor if there was any change in Lee's condition, he merely pursed his lips and shook his head.

When Charlie Redwing was brought to the room, about an hour after she'd arrived, he was too enclosed by fear and grief to notice her. He had aged since Carlotta had seen him at her father's funeral. There was much gray in his black hair now and he stooped slightly, as if he might have developed rheumatism, but his face was carefully composed and his eyes were dry. Apparently he had been briefed on his daughter's condition on the way up, because he went immediately into the IC unit with Dr. Belasco.

When he came back out he reeled a little, and his first instinct was to grope for a place to sit. He landed heavily on the leatherette couch where Carlotta was sitting and stared, unseeing, into space. She could see his lips moving. She placed a hand on Charlie Redwing's arm, and he turned toward her.

The dark eyes came into focus. "Why, Carlotta," he said. "Why, Carlotta." It was not a question, but a stunned recognition of her presence.

"They wouldn't let me go in to see her," she said. "How is she?"

He moistened his lips. "It's not Leana in there at all," he said. "You wouldn't know her, honey." He began to cry softly, his once powerful shoulders shaking helplessly, his hands hanging down as if he had no further use for them. "They got all these tubes in her, tubes everywhere, and machines attached to my girl. She's lost her color, and she's shrunk some. Looks like Leana is already dead, honey. Only the machines say she's alive."

Carlotta took Charlie in her arms and held him while he sobbed quietly. When he had finished, he took out a large pocket handkerchief, blew his nose, and resumed his vigilant position. He held Carlotta's hand in his, sometimes squeezing it so tightly she nearly cried out in pain. They sat this way for hours, ignoring the cups of coffee that were brought to them and seldom speaking.

Occasionally Charlie would say something like: "Lee's a good fighter, don't you think, Carlotta?"

"The best," Carlotta would agree. And so they sat on through the night, hoping that Lee's warrior spirit would be great enough to fend off death.

It was 4:30 in the morning when Sam Cumberland finally arrived at the hospital. He had not heard the news until just before midnight, and rather than wait for room on a shuttle that possibly didn't operate past midnight, he had simply gotten into his car and driven straight to Washington.

He knew immediately who that stricken man sitting on the

leatherette couch must be, and felt a sort of awesome sense of guilt. If he had not encouraged Lee to write her book, she might not be lying near death at this very moment. Mr. Redwing, absorbed in private thought, looked at Sam without interest. He was sitting motionless, one arm cradling what Sam now saw was a sleeping girl, clad in jeans. He wondered if the girl might be another of his daughters, but from what he could recall, Lee had had only brothers.

The girl's face was obscured, hidden in the crook of Mr. Redwing's arm and laid against his breast, but Sam saw that the hair could not possibly be that of a Cheyenne. Lee's father sheltered the girl tenderly, and with great protection.

"Mr. Redwing," said Sam, taking a seat opposite them, "I'm Sam Cumberland, Lee's publisher."

The dark eyes flickered, recalled from some other time and place. "Her book," he said. "Yes, she always spoke good things about you."

Sam noticed that he was already mentioning Lee in the past tense, and then, as if he had been dealt a massive blow, his entire body was jolted with the realization of who the sleeping girl must be. Who else was close enough to Lee's father to sleep in his embrace? Who else with red-gold hair would be prepared to wait, hour after hour, in this grim room? That she had finally surrendered to an exhausted sleep, pillowed against Mr. Redwing's chest, was entirely natural. It must have happened often when she and Lee were children.

Charlie Redwing seemed to intuit his thoughts, and nodded at the sleeping form. "This here is Lee's white sister. They grew up together, out in Montana on the Madigan ranch. When I say sister, it's just a way of speaking, but they were as close as that." Two of the fingers of the hand not holding Carlotta crossed tightly.

"Yes," said Sam, "I know." Even as Lee's father confirmed what he had known, his eyes were registering what had once been so familiar to him. The legs were Carlotta's—they could belong to no one else. The long, slender fingers, the tender crescent of her half-concealed cheek, even the endearing way in which her feet, clad in sneakers, were pigeon-toed in sleep, all were Carlotta's. It was terrible to realize that the anguish he felt at beholding his lost Carlotta was even greater than his sorrow for Lee.

"Poor little Carlotta," said Charlie Redwing suddenly. "Her

daddy died in this very same hospital."

Then his eyes lowered quickly as if he had said too much, and there was only silence.

Just before dawn, Dr. Belasco came to tell them that Lee was conscious, and much improved. Sam watched while Lee's father gently wakened Carlotta, and led her into the intensive care unit. When they emerged, Carlotta said, as if it were the most natural thing on earth to be addressing him, "She winked at us! She can't talk yet, but she *winked!* They're moving her to a private room now."

Sam got to his feet, stumbling up to meet the glad news, and Carlotta paused, hand to her throat, as if suddenly stunned at seeing him.

"Oh, Sam," she said. "When did *you* get here?"

TWENTY-NINE

CARLOTTA WAKENED, NOT KNOWING WHERE SHE WAS, IN A darkened room. When knowledge returned, she stumbled from the bed and found the telephone. At Georgetown University Hospital, they told her that Lee was in serious but stable condition.

She was at a little hotel up in back of DuPont Circle. The Tabard Inn. Charlie was at the Watergate, in Lee's room. She could barely remember coming here, only that Sam had somehow arranged it. She didn't know where he was, and she almost wondered if his appearance there in the waiting room was something she had dreamed.

She showered quickly, put on her jeans and sneakers and white shirt, and brushed her hair. It was colder outside than it had been the night before, and she shivered as she waited to flag a cab on Wisconsin. People in fall coats and jackets looked at her curiously.

"You can go on up," the woman at the desk told her, giving her Lee's room number. "Her father says you're a family member."

Outside Lee's room, she saw Dr. Belasco conversing with Sam. Sam smiled at her oddly, and Dr. Belasco told her she was not to stay with Lee more than five minutes. Carlotta thanked him and went in.

Charlie was sitting by the bed, and a nurse was doing something to Lee's arm where the IV joined it. Lee lay flat, her hair fanned over the pillow. Carlotta remembered what Charlie had said about her loss of color, and it was true— Lee's beautiful bronze skin was several shades paler, and yellowish. She looked heartbreakingly fragile, but when Carlotta bent over her recumbent form, she could see that Lee's eyes were very much alive.

"Hi," Lee whispered.

"Hi," said Carlotta, feeling the withheld tears beginning. She willed them back, but one escaped and fell directly on Lee's bruised arm.

"Hey," whispered Lee, "no crying."

"Now don't you go talking," said Charlie. "Just you save your strength, Leana honey." To Carlotta he said, "She's been worrying about Dominic, about what he might hear, and I've already told her—I've got it under control. All she has to worry about is getting strong again."

"Blood sister," Lee tried to say.

"She has a fever," the nurse explained. "She's a little muddled."

Dr. Belasco appeared to tell them it was time to leave. In the corridor, he assured them that Lee was making phenomenal progress, and said they could come back in the evening. "Not until then?" Carlotta protested, but Charlie reminded her it was already mid-afternoon. She had lost track of time.

The strange little trio, Sam, Charlie, and Carlotta, made their way out of the hospital and stood awkwardly together in the cold autumn wind.

"You must be cold, Carlotta," Sam said. "Won't you take my jacket?" He started to remove it, but Charlie said he had a better idea. Carlotta was to come with him to the Watergate, where she could borrow any clothes she needed from among Lee's things. Sam said he'd drive them, and they headed for the parking lot.

From nowhere, a man with a camera leaped out and took Carlotta's picture. She fell back, startled, and Charlie held her protectively. "Miss Madigan," said the man, putting his camera down, "how does it feel to be visiting the same hospital where your father died?"

"You bastard," said Sam, advancing on him. "How the fuck do you think it makes her feel?"

Charlie hurried her on, and the man withdrew.

"I was afraid of something like that," Sam said, getting behind the wheel of his car.

"Why?" asked Carlotta. "Why should they suddenly remember *me?*"

Charlie sighed. "You haven't seen the papers," he said. "They've gone and resurrected all that old stuff about your pa, on account of what happened to Lee. They know you're here in town, and they want to write trash."

Sam hovered in Lee's suite while Carlotta put Lee's coat on and selected a white sweater and one nightgown. He had mumbled something about driving her back to the Tabard, and although she knew she ought to refuse, she couldn't bring herself to say no. She told herself that she needed some protection from the carnivorous reporters.

It was getting close to the rush hour, and Sam maneuvered through the traffic uttering a few soft, picturesque curses. Carlotta sat beside him, feeling she was in a dangerous position. She was emotional over Lee, and felt she might lose control. It would be so easy to weep with relief, and then Sam would have to comfort her. If once she felt his arms around her, it would be all over. She had neither the strength, nor the desire, to turn him away, even if he only wanted her as an occasional object of his desire.

"Carlotta," he said, when they were approaching DuPont Circle, "do you recall that I once asked you to marry me?"

"Very well," she said. The words, like Lee's, emerged in a whisper.

"I recall it well myself. I also recall that you replied in the affirmative, and shortly thereafter vanished without a trace. No explanation, nothing. Once, when I thought you were still in Europe, I ran into your friend Rachel's husband in the city. I asked Carter, or Potter, or whatever the hell his name is, when you were expected back. He told me you'd been back for weeks. What kind of thing is that to do to a man?"

Carlotta looked at him for the first time. His eyes were on the traffic, but his voice had been unsteady.

"I'm sorry. I had my reasons. It was for my own protection, Sam."

"Protection from *what?*" He nearly shouted the last word.

She saw that he was about to take a parking space two blocks from the hotel, and told him not to bother, just to drop her off.

"Oh, but you see I'm staying at the Tabard, too," he said,

smiling for the first time. It was a hard grin.

They walked along, not touching, toward the hotel. A group of Hare Krishna devotees, shivering in their saffron robes, came running down the street, singing ecstatically.

"You didn't answer my question, Carlotta. Protection from what?"

"Oh, Sam, it was a long time ago. What difference can it make to you now?"

"Christ, you are unfathomable. What if Lee had died, and in a few months I asked you what difference it made to you?"

"It's hardly the same thing, Sam. You're not lonely."

"How the hell do you know that? How do you presume to come into my life, become all-important to me, walk out, and then tell me I'm not lonely?"

They walked up the steps to the Tabard and passed inside. In the lounge, scattered with deep, comfortable couches and armchairs, someone had lit a fire. Carlotta dropped, exhausted, into a wing chair facing the fire. Sam was still waiting for an answer to his question. He wasn't going to let her evade him. It was too early for the cocktail crowd, and they were alone in the warm, darkened lounge. The flames of the fire were hypnotic, and Carlotta stared into them for comfort.

"You have Gina," she said at last. "That's why I presume to tell you that you're not lonely. She's lovely, Sam."

"Yes, she is," he said. "Very nice, too. She's also back in Italy. It was casual, for both of us." He sat in a chair near her, his face hard with anger. "I didn't meet Gina until well after you'd ditched me, Carlotta. Did you expect me to be celibate for the rest of my miserable life?"

"Never that, Sam," she said, trying to sound ironic. "Oh, never celibate."

"I'm still waiting," he said.

"For what?"

"An explanation."

She felt anger, hard and pure, spurt up in her. "Why are you torturing me like this? Why do I have to suffer just to put some balm on your wounded ego? I came to Washington to be with Lee, not to answer a third-degree from a man who can have nearly any woman he wants." She remembered Stephen Quinn's allusion to nets. "You're just angry because I slipped through your *net*."

"My net," said Sam dully, as if he were addressing a madwoman. "Ah, yes, my famous net. I think I need a drink, but I'm afraid if I step through to the bar there, you'll vanish."

A smiling young hotel employee came bouncing into the lounge with the evening papers. "Would you like to see the papers?" she asked.

"No," said Sam.

"Yes, please," said Carlotta.

The name of Lee's would-be assassin was revealed in the *Post*, and Carlotta read the article out loud to Sam. " 'Hubert Prior, 48, originally from Tulsa City, Oklahoma, told police that he had been corresponding with Miss Redwing for some time. Prior maintained that his victim was expecting to meet him at the convention, and had agreed to accept 'divine punishment' for her sins. A sometime ranch hand, his last known address was in Laramie, Wyoming. He is currently under psychiatric observation. An eyewitness to the shooting, Leonora Silver, 42, of New Hope, Connecticut, says that Mr. Prior's hands were shaking so badly it was surprising his shots did not go astray. Ironically, the gunman's shaking hands may well be the reason that Miss Redwing, who was shot at a distance of only a few feet, is still alive today. The 34-year-old attorney and author is in serious but stable condition at Georgetown University Hospital.' "

"It was the one who called her half-breed, Sam," said Carlotta, putting the paper down. And then, because she remembered how his hands had stroked her when she confessed —lying on his terrace—her fears for Lee, she asked briskly for the other papers. He seemed to have taken them from her, and was holding them protectively. She asked again.

"Carlotta, I'd rather you didn't look at this one," he said.

"The *Star?*"

"No. The rag. The best thing with papers like that is to throw them away."

"If you don't give it to me, I'll just go out and buy it," she said.

Sighing, Sam handed it over to her. A quartet of women's faces, cropped to cameos, surrounded a photograph of her father. Around Tom Madigan, like tendrils issuing from a bud, were her mother, herself, Joly Nesbit, and Lee. The caption read MADIGAN RANCH WOMEN—DOES TRAGEDY STALK THEM?

"They're really stretching it a bit," said Carlotta unsteadily.

"Joly Nesbit was hardly a feature at the Madigan ranch."

"Where did they get that picture of you?" Sam asked.

Carlotta studied her cameo. "I think it's an old AP," she said. "It was taken at a very grand party, when I was married to Delaney."

"That would account for your rapturous expression," said Sam.

By the time she had read the article, striving to find what tragedy was stalking her, it was time to go back to the hospital.

Slowly, Lee began to gain strength. Her color returned, and she was able to eat Jell-O and speak in a nearly normal voice. Her doctor predicted that, aside from the scars she would always have, Lee would be herself again by the beginning of the new year.

At the end of the first week, Dominic was brought to Washington and Carlotta was allowed to hold him on her lap while he told his still-supine mother "knock-knock" jokes, bellowing with laughter at his own punch lines.

"Where's Sam?" Lee asked Carlotta one day, when Dominic had been taken off by his grandfather.

"In New York, but he's coming back."

"Why should he come back?" Lee furrowed her brow. "I'm out of danger. What do you suppose keeps drawing him back?"

"I haven't the slightest idea," said Carlotta.

There was a soft hiss of laughter from the hospital bed. "Oh, Carlotta," said Lee, "it's now or never, you know. I'm not going to almost die a second time to bring you together. This is a once-in-a-lifetime opportunity."

"Is that how you see it?"

"Sure," said Lee. "Life's too short. Believe me, I know."

Carefully, in the neat hand in which she had once written school papers in Switzerland, Carlotta wrote Sam a long note. In it she tried to explain the kind of woman she was, and wasn't, and how she had felt that sharing him with others would be her ruination. She told him about Marietta's visit to the gallery, and what Marietta had said a year later on the telephone, speaking from his apartment. *My number just came up.* She said she had been happier with him than ever in her life, and had fled to Paris to save her sanity when that happiness was shattered. *You have your explanation,* she concluded.

She sealed the letter in an envelope and asked the desk clerk to put it in his box when he returned. She felt giddy with daring, but when the third day arrived and he had not returned, she contemplated asking the clerk to give the letter back so she could destroy it. She resisted. They were being very understanding at the gallery, but she had promised to return by the end of next week.

On the fourth day she came back from the hospital and found a note in her own box. Her letter to Sam, she saw, had disappeared. She stared at the little scrap of paper, not understanding at first. The writing was familiar to her, but it was not Sam's. *Sold, to S.J. Cumberland—Carlotta, Seated, oil on canvas, 6 ft x 4 ft 3 in. Price: $1.00.* The signature, even more illegible than the rest, was Ian Wilson's.

No more thinking, Carlotta decided. No more pondering the possible pitfalls, imagining the worst. Action was what was needed. She ran up the narrow, carpeted stairs and then forced herself to walk more sedately up the hall. At his door, she stopped, took a deep breath, and knocked.

"It's open," he called. He was sitting on the bed, looking through some bound galleys. He tossed them aside and said, without preamble, "Marietta? *Marietta? She's* the reason I had to go through hell? Because some poor, cross-wired woman the whole *world* knows has been crazy for years drips some of her poison in your ears? Why didn't you just ask *me?*"

"Well, she *was* in your apartment, Sam. It didn't seem to me to be an unreasonable assumption." She leaned against a fine old wardrobe to prop herself up. She was breathing shallowly, and didn't want to alarm him. Being around hospitals so much gave you unhealthy ideas, and she thought her heart was acting peculiarly.

Sam got to his feet and walked toward her. "She certainly was," he said ominously. "She was practically camped on my doorstep when I got back from Chicago. It's an old trick of hers, and I'm not the only one she haunts, either. I'm one of many. Poor Marietta—right now I'd love to kill her—has been unstable for years."

He paused, searching her face. "I'm going to tell you the truth, Carlotta, and you can believe me or not. I let Marietta in for two reasons—to tell her I was getting married, so she'd leave me alone, and because I felt sorry for her. We'd been lovers once, and I couldn't just give her the news and tell her to bug off in the hallway. I thought I'd invite her in, give her a drink—maintain an illusion that she was a normal person. A friend."

"And she wouldn't go," said Carlotta.

"That's right. She's one of those people who just don't listen to what you're saying. I was longing to see you, and I had to get to the office, and finally I told her I was leaving. I also told her if she wasn't out in ten minutes, I was sending the security guard up to evict her by force. It wasn't very pleasant, but it was better than manhandling her myself." He laughed softly. "It's funny, because during those ten minutes I had visions of Marietta doing crazy things—setting my curtains on fire, pouring coffee grounds on my bed, ripping up my books—but in my wildest imaginings I never thought she'd do the most dangerous thing of all. Oh, darling—your timing."

He was very close now, and his gray eyes were darkening.

"I would rather," Sam said in a husky voice, "have lost everything I owned than lose you for four months."

She edged away from the wardrobe and walked the few short feet to cover the distance that separated them. She reached up and touched the beloved, floppy hair and raised her lips to his. At the first contact, she felt life flow back into her veins. It was as if she had been a barren, winter tree in all the time she had been without him, and he had the magical power to restore her to a sapling. She felt herself grow pliant and liquid in his arms, full of the juice and heat of spring.

THIRTY

"Once upon a time," said Chloe Vere to her baby brother, who had been christened William Cotter, "there was a beautiful princess from the west. She was called the Princess Lalania."

Billy Vere, who was five months old, lay in his crib, chewing his fist with cheerful unconcern.

"The princess had long red hair, and she was the nicest person in all the realm, but she wasn't happy. Her mother and father were dead, and she didn't have any brothers or sisters. She was all alone in the world, and she decided to explore her kingdom, hoping to find a prince who would keep her company. None of the princes were good enough for her, but an evil old magician cast a spell on her, and she married him."

The baby belched and smiled.

"She married the magician," Chloe continued austerely, "and for a long time she was under his spell, and did his bidding. The golden-haired Lady Rachel knew that it was wrong, and worried, but it was not until the sorcerer killed her first-born son that Princess Lalania went into flight.

"She suffered greatly in exile, but she was ever courageous and noble. She went out among the people of her realm, and earned her daily bread. One day, a new prince rode over the horizon, and Lalania fell in love with him. All her unhappiness was at an end, she thought, but alas!—a great war happened, and they were separated. Lalania did not see her love for many years, but when he came back, victorious, she placed the golden crown upon his head, and he became her husband."

Chloe leaned forward to make sure that Billy was still awake for the end of her narrative. He gave a gurgling laugh and kicked his pudgy legs with a manic vigor.

"The princess dwelt with her loved one in a miraculous castle on Central Park West," Chloe said with dignity. "I have been there, and over the bed of the prince and princess there hangs a miraculous picture. It shows Lalania as she was in exile, lost and lonely."

William Cotter Vere had gone to sleep, and Chloe left the room, aware of her mother's voice summoning her from another part of the house. Her story had been cut off just at the finishing point. She darted back, and whispered into her brother's tiny ear.

"She's a completely different woman," Chloe said. "She's not lonely anymore."

Billy Vere slept on, oblivious.

More Bestselling Books From Jove!

Bestselling Books
from Berkley